My Happy Ending
Part 1

Time Stands Still Book 3

A novel by Carlie Yates

Cover photography Sebastian Mark
Cover art Kayla Ries

ISBN: 978-1-7332649-7-6

My Happy Ending
Part 1

For my Visions (et al) tribe. May we always remember.

CHAPTER 1

TALIA

I hate packing.

Hate isn't even a strong enough word.

I loathe packing, with everything in me.

I would rather work a double at the hospital, drink Diet Coke instead of Diet Pepsi, have my eyes gauged out, listen to Starship's 'We Built This City' on a loop, and eat an eggroll with shrimp.

That's how much I loathe packing.

I could always have it done for me. It would probably have been easier—less hassle, less mess. But no, I had to do it myself, and I had to do it my way. I couldn't risk coming across something that shouldn't be there, something that I intended to get left behind.

The way I had been.

"Talli?" Sondra's voice broke into my thoughts as I was rummaging through the cabinets in the kitchen, separating dishes, taking what I would need, what the children would need.

"Yeah?"

"The movies… the music…"

"Leave it."

I didn't mean for the two words to sound so cold, so biting. I didn't want anything from the room he'd made for me.

"Some of the pictures on the wall,"

"Sondra, right now… I couldn't fucking stand to look at it, okay? I really have no desire to be reminded of this… prison."

"A prison," I heard the prick say as he entered the kitchen. "You could have said something if that was how you felt."

I refrained from throwing the butcher knife in my hand directly at him, wrapping it carefully and placing it in a box instead.

"The children's movies, Talli," Sondra continued.

"They can be replaced," I said.

"Don't do that to them, Talli," the prick said. "This isn't about them; this is about us."

What us, you asshole? The us that hasn't had a civil word to say to each other in weeks? The us that hasn't slept in the same bed in months? The us that you threw away? WHAT US?

"Damn it, Talli, look at me!"

"Jase," Sondra spoke up, completely in my defense, "now is not the time."

"Stay out of this, Sondra," he snapped.

"If you hadn't been a fucking idiot, you wouldn't have to worry about me being in this, now would you?" she snapped back. "Go ahead, fucking fire me! You think I care about that now?"

"Sondra, don't," I said softly, as I passed her.

"What, are you defending him?" she asked quietly as she followed me to the great room.

Oh…fuck.

There were pictures everywhere.

Our perfect fucking happy family.

I wanted to take that butcher knife and carve him out of every single one of them.

But I didn't let it show. I was never going to let it show.

He'd said he was so proud of me when I went back to school, finishing near the top of my class in spite of my high-risk pregnancy. I received my master's degree less than two weeks before Michael had been born, a scant two and a half years after Elizabeth. He'd been planned, too. Both of them had.

Emily had not been planned.

Emily was a big surprise that neither of us was expecting, and that quite honest I wasn't ready for. I had received my Nurse Practitioner's license and was working in the OB/GYN area, showing one of the new techs how to use the doppler to hear the baby's heartbeat. Jokingly, I had told her to practice on me.

Emily was born six months later.

So here our kids were five, almost three, and eleven months.

Elizabeth was Daddy's girl, Michael was an easygoing child, and Emily clung to me like glue.

She didn't know Jase.

Jase never took the time to get to know her.

Jase was too busy getting to know someone else.

"The kids' clothes are packed," Sondra was saying as I took the dreaded trip up the stairs.

"Great."

"I took out their favorite toys," she continued.

"Fantastic."

"Did you need me to get your things?"

I paused outside the bedroom door, my hand on the doorknob. This room held so many memories, so many long sleepless nights. This room had seen love, and loss, joy and pain...

I faltered for a moment.

"Talia, I can..."

"No, Sondra, I've got this," I said, regaining composure as I opened the door to the room.

I hadn't slept up here in months. Hell, I hadn't even slept upstairs in Em's room in weeks—not since I came back from Ohio a bit early. Emily had been on one arm, and Elizabeth and Michael had been directly behind me when I had opened that door to the room I'd once shared with their father, unprepared for what I saw.

Candles.

Roses.

Jase.

And... Bree.

Breeann Hamilton, tiny blonde actress/singer extraordinaire.

Their clothing discarded haphazardly around the room.

Jase on top of her, even in the tangled sheets I know he was inside of her by the way they were both moving, the way she was moaning, her hands buried in my husband's hair, and he… he was kissing her, too.

Fucking her and kissing her.

In our bed.

Elizabeth's voice had trailed from behind me asking what was wrong with Daddy, and his head snapped up.

And my world stopped.

I remembered briefly taking the children downstairs and putting in some video while I went to the kitchen to gather my thoughts. I couldn't yell, I couldn't scream—that was not something I wanted my children to witness.

None of it was something I wanted them to witness. Ever.

God, was this really happening? Had the man who had sworn before… before God, before everyone that he would forsake all others… was he really in bed with someone else?

Well, the answer to that one was a literal no as I heard his footsteps come into the kitchen. I stood there, my back up against that island, my arms folded, waiting.

But I could see it in his eyes.

It was really over.

We… we were really over.

His hands were shoved into the pockets of the jeans that he had just thrown on, he hadn't even bothered with a shirt. His hair was still disheveled, probably from her hands running through it. I could see where a bead of sweat was still hanging to his bangs, and it made me absolutely nauseous.

But I held my ground.

I kept my head high, somehow, I kept the tears away. I knew… I *knew* something had been going on, but I had trusted him blindly, every time he told me that he wasn't that type of person. Fuck, of course he was! How quickly I had forgotten.

I wonder what he had told her about me.

I wonder what he had told her about us, or the lack thereof.

I wonder if he had told her that we hadn't even made love since shortly after Emily was born. Hell, he obviously didn't need me.

Not when he had her.

I had glared at him, screaming in my head for him to talk to me, tell me that somehow I was mistaken, tell me he was drunk even though I could tell by his eyes that he was stone cold sober...

Just tell me that he loved me.

He swallowed heavily and looked away, a faint blush marring his cheeks.

You. Bastard.

When he looked back at me, his eyes were nearly blank, as if they were devoid of all feeling. Then he had the nerve... the nerve to say two little words.

"I'm sorry."

"Bullshit," I spit back at him, low enough so the children couldn't hear.

"Ah, you're angry. Nice to know you have some emotion left in you."

Where the hell did THAT come from? He was going to attack ME? Put this on ME?

And then Bree sauntered lazily into the kitchen, having the nerve to wear my robe.

"Listen... um... Talli,"

"Put your clothes back on," I said, my tone angry but even, "get back in your car, and get the hell away from this house."

"You know," she tried to continue, but I cut her off again.

"You may not respect me but respect the fact that my children are here now, and they don't need to see or hear any of this."

"They're his kids, too," she said, placing one hand on her tiny hip.

"Bree," he said, in a soft tone he used to reserve for me, "not now, okay? She's right... not now."

She. I'm a *she* now. Not his wife, not the mother of his children, not the person he dragged across the country to share his life with. I'm just a *she*.

I could see it all like it was yesterday as I walked silently across the carpet to my dresser. I pulled out my duffel bag like I had so many times before, for one trip or another, and emptied my drawers one by one.

Every love letter I found I threw on the bed, leaving them behind for him.

I hope he choked on every fucking word.

When I was through with the closets and the bathroom, I picked up the suitcase and the duffel bag, which were now quite heavy, and made my way down the hall to the stairs.

"Let me help you with that."

Jackie was suddenly beside me, taking both items from my hands, motioning for me to go on down the stairs. I kissed him on the cheek before I silently walked down, not knowing if I could say goodbye to him in front of everyone. I could almost swear I heard a sniffle from him, but I couldn't turn around to look.

It seemed that everyone was upset by my leaving.

Everyone except Jase.

The U-Haul had been packed, one of the maintenance workers from the hospital behind the wheel. The car was also packed, except for the kids and me.

Linda handed Emily to me, who went straight into her car seat without so much as a whimper.

Michael waved goodbye to Jase before running up and taking his booster seat, still smiling as I strapped him in.

Elizabeth was sobbing in Jase's arms.

I had long suspected that perhaps she was the only reason he had held on to this lack-of-us for as long as he did.

"It's time to go," I said softly to her, holding out my hand.

"Don't make me go, Daddy," she whined into his shirt.

"Baby girl, you need to go with Mommy," he was whispering to her.

"I'll be good, I promise, don't make us go."

Oh... god.

I can't cry. Not now, not in front of him.

"Elizabeth,"

Jase motioned to me that he'd put her in the car, and I stepped aside, part of me wanting to scream at him, demand to know.

Was Bree worth it?

Was she?

I moved quickly to get into the driver's seat, knowing I had to get the hell out of there as soon as Jase had Elizabeth strapped in. Her screams and sobs set the other two off, but did he say anything? To any of us?

No.

He shut the door.

And he walked away.

He walked past everyone into that fucking house closing that door behind him, shutting me out for the very last time.

And he would never... never know how much it hurt me. I would make sure of that.

JASE

"Don't make me go, Daddy."

Elizabeth was clinging to me as if her very existence depended on holding on. I kept my eyes shut tight, calling on every bit of strength I could to keep from crying. This was hard enough on her without me breaking down, too.

And Talli... she wouldn't give a damn if I cried.

"Baby girl," I managed to whisper, "you need to go with Mommy."

This was so hard.

It hurt so... so much.

"I'll be good, I promise, don't make us go."

I choked back a sob, cradling her to me, wanting to scream at the top of my lungs.

I don't want you to go, Baby Girl. I don't want any of you to go. Please don't cry... this isn't your fault, I swear, and I'm so... so sorry.

I couldn't say it out loud.

Saying it out loud would be a sign of weakness, and I couldn't be weak, not now. Not in front of Talia, not when she had been so very clear for so long that her feelings for me had changed.

I know she didn't love me anymore.

I had resigned myself to it.

But now... now with this happening—now that she was really leaving, walking away from me, taking our children across the city with her... God, it was over.

It was really, really over.

Knowing Talli couldn't pry Elizabeth from me, not wanting to put either one of them through that, I motioned that I would strap her in.

I had to be quick with this.

She screamed as I placed her in her booster seat, securing the straps as quick as I could. I couldn't look up. I couldn't risk a glance at Talli, see how cold those eyes had become.

I knew I would break.

Who the hell was I kidding?

I was already broken.

My heart had ached every time that Talia had pushed me away, every time she had told me she was too tired or too busy. I died a little inside every time she had canceled our plans for her to come out and see me at whatever city I was in. I shut myself off even further when I came home to find her sleeping in the single bed in Emily's nursery, with her claiming it was easier to get up with her in the middle of the night if she was right there. I gave up when she refused to move her crib to our room.

I just gave up.

I know I was wrong.

Fuck, I *know* I was, but what the hell was I supposed to do?

I couldn't remember the last time Talia had told me she loved me.

Then there was Bree…

Bree who had actively pursued me from day one.

Bree, who went out of her way to touch me, brush up against me.

Bree, who was there, reaching out to hold my hand when Talia had called and canceled for the third weekend in a row because she just couldn't get away.

Bree, who kissed me when I was feeling low.

Bree, who held me at night without a promise of anything more because she said she longed to be close to me.

Bree, who told me she loved me and understood that I couldn't say the same.

I couldn't love anyone else.

Not when I was still so in love with Talia.

I changed my plans around to be home early, surprise Talia who couldn't find the time to fly out to Texas to spend time with me, only to find that she had packed up the kids and flown out to Ohio.

Ohio. Further away than Texas. Gone longer than she would have been to come and see me.

I couldn't pretend, I couldn't fool myself anymore. Even with everything we had gone through, even with our family, our children, it wasn't enough for her.

And then, Talia couldn't even find it in herself to give a shit when she found me with Bree. She didn't question, she didn't ask for an explanation, not that she would have listened or even believed. Her only concern was that it not happen in front of the children. She didn't raise her voice; she didn't ask why. As soon as Bree had gone, Talia quietly informed me that she and the children would be leaving as soon as possible. She didn't see any more reason to stand in my way.

I just wanted her to care.

I wanted her to fight.

I wanted to believe that I was worth it, that we were worth it, that our family was worth it.

But here we were.

"Daddy, please!" Elizabeth was screaming.

And there went my little man, his tears starting.

Oh God, not Em, too... Please not Em, too. I know she barely knows me, I know she's probably crying because they are, but it still...

"Talli," I choked, my voice barely audible as she started the car. She didn't turn, she didn't even look in the rearview mirror.

Stay, damn it. Fucking stay. We can fix this, I swear, I know we can.

But I know better. Even if I had the chance to explain, even if she would listen, even if she would believe me... I know better.

I shut that door as quickly as I could and walked the hell away, hiding my face, pushing my way through everyone. I felt the sobs building, the tears threatening, the anger... the anguish so overwhelming...

I slammed the door to the house behind me.

She couldn't see this. Fuck, she wouldn't care.

I grabbed our wedding photo off the wall as I passed on my way up the stairs, the tears already falling freely as I walked by my babies' rooms.

There wouldn't be any laughter in the house today.

No little handprints all over the walls.

No resolving disputes between Elizabeth and Michael.

No Talia softly consoling Emily in the middle of the night.

My family was gone.

I threw the door to my bedroom open, seeing through my eyes how it looked when Bree had surprised me, the candles and roses everywhere.

It should have been Talia.

I closed the door, sinking to the ground, the sobs racking my body as I cradled that photo to me, letting the grief consume me, asking myself over and over... what have I done?

What have I done?

CHAPTER 2

TALLI

I have come to the conclusion that someone out there really fucking hates me. More than Chris Webber hate, more than Keith Anderson hate. Those I can handle.

I mean… every single radio station was playing some sort of heart-wrenching break-up song. No happy, poppy little tunes; no I'm-so-happy-you-left tunes, not even any love songs.

Break-up songs.

From rock to country to pop to…

"Can you turn on something else, Mommy?" Elizabeth asked between sobs in the back seat. She hates it when someone incessantly changes the channels.

"Like what?" I asked, forcing a smile.

"Daddy's cd!" Michael yelled, and Elizabeth quickly agreed.

"Please, please, please, please Mommy?"

I think all of the break-up songs in the world would have been better than this.

It was a mixed cd of the kids' favorite songs off of all of Jase's albums. Song one, of all songs in this world, was *Hard to Believe*.

I felt the first tear fall as I remembered our trip to Steamboat Springs, our time in the lodge. That was the first time he had played that song in front of me, in such an intimate setting. Even though it was someone else who had requested it, I felt he was singing it for me. Things were so different then. I can't say they were uncomplicated, because we were going through our fair share of problems then, too.

Oh, and there's the end of the song.

A fucking BREAK-UP.

But back then, in Colorado, when he had sung that, poured his heart into it, he had loved me. He had put me above all others. He had put up a fight when he thought I was leaving.

Today, he couldn't have cared less.

"Don't skip it, Mommy!" Elizabeth called out to me as my hand reached for the button.

'Okay,' I thought. 'For them, I'll endure it.'

For them, I'll let my heart break just a little more.

Jackie, bless his heart, showed up less than an hour after I drove away. I think I would have been lost trying to put together half of the kids' beds and things. Sondra came with him and was helping me wash and dry dishes, putting them in their place in the cabinets.

This three-bedroom condo was tiny compared to that spacious house the kids were used to. It was still bigger than my apartment back in Ohio, but back then it had been just me. I told myself it was smart to get a smaller place, though; smart on my limited budget, smart that I didn't have too much space to lose these children in.

Although when Elizabeth and Michael started their fighting, I wondered if it was such a good thing.

I couldn't exactly ask them to cool it with their sibling… whatever it was between them to spare me today; they were far too young to understand, and I wouldn't want to burden them anyhow.

I stared at my cell phone, wishing I could call my mom. Even after all of this time, I missed her beyond the telling of it. And it was times like these… not just that day, but the entire three weeks prior, that I could have really used her sound advice.

She'd know what to do.

I had Emily's highchair assembled and in the dining area about the time there was a knock at the door. Linda arrived with dinner already cooked and in disposable foil containers; she'd made the kids' favorite,

Pepperoni Macaroni.

"How are you?" she asked, taking my hand in hers.

I'm hurting, I'm wounded, my heart and dreams are shattered, my husband threw me aside for some tiny little waif of a girl... how do you think I feel?

"I'm fine, Linda," I replied, smiling. "I've been through worse. Would you like to stay for dinner?"

"Thank you, but I can't," she said, grabbing her keys. "If you need anything, you call me."

Where? At his house? I couldn't afford a maid, even part time, anyhow.

"Thank you," I said, hugging her before she left. The kids, smelling dinner, began to wander out. I told Jackie and Sondra that dinner was there also, and I wouldn't take no for an answer from them, they were going to eat.

I had to remind myself that I wouldn't always feel this way, as if I were merely going through the motions without any emotion behind them. Hell, I'd already been accused of doing that for months. Sometime, someday, some way I'd feel something other than this ache in my chest.

"Where's Daddy?" Michael asked as soon as I placed his plate in front of him.

I faltered.

"His house, dummy," Elizabeth said for me, although a bit meaner than I would have.

"Elizabeth Christine," I said in a warning tone, still handing out plates.

"That's *our* house, Mommy," Michael said to me, ignoring his sister as always. I looked at his face, so serious, the carbon copy of Jase's, even more so than Elizabeth as her eyes were the color of mine. I bit the inside of my lip, remembering the day he was born, how Jase had proclaimed that was his Little Man.

"Not anymore," I had to finally say since for once Elizabeth was listening to me and not making some smart remark.

Jackie reached over and kissed Elizabeth's cheek, and only then did I notice that she wasn't eating but was crying silently at the table. I put Emily's food on her tray, leaving just myself to eat but that could happen any time. I held my hand out to Elizabeth, who took it tentatively, walking with me to her bedroom to sit on her bed. Her feet were dangling over the edge and she was kicking them absentmindedly, the same way Jase always did.

"Hey," I said softly, breaking the silence as I put my arm around her.

"I want Daddy," she sobbed, her tiny shoulders shaking. "Mommy, didn't you hear him cry? Didn't you hear him say your name? Why did we have to go?"

What?

No... no, she's imagining things, because if he had cried... no, if he cried it was over them, not me.

"Why doesn't he love us, Mommy?"

"No... no, baby, don't think that," I said, choking back a sob. "He loves you, and Michael, and Emily... all of you, very much."

"And you, too?"

No... there's no way in hell that man loves me. He would never do those things if he loved me, never in a million years.

"Baby... it's... complicated," I finally said.

"Do you love Daddy?"

"Yes," I answered without hesitation.

Of course, I love him.

If I didn't love him, this wouldn't hurt, it wouldn't be tearing me up inside. If I didn't love him, it wouldn't matter to me that he had thrown our wedding vows in the trash when he cheated on me. If I didn't love him, it wouldn't matter to me that he didn't find me attractive anymore, that he didn't give a damn that I was leaving.

I glanced down at my left hand, tears hanging to my lashes as I tried to help our oldest child.

If I didn't love him, I wouldn't still be wearing my wedding rings.

I did my best to hide them from him today.

I don't think I could bear it if he asked me to take them off.

"I think... I'm better now, Mommy," Elizabeth said, wiping her tears away with her hands, smoothing her hair back away from her face. "You can go eat."

"You need to eat, too, baby girl," I reminded her.

"I need to," she paused, glancing a little sideways at me, "go wash

14

my face."

"Okay," I agreed, "then you come back and eat."

She followed me out to the kitchen, then seemed to remember she wanted to go wash her face. Jackie was doing his best to entertain Emily, who was distraught as always that I had left the room.

"Are you okay?" Sondra asked, and I turned to where she sat, getting a small spoonful of the dinner for Michael's plate.

Holy cow that kid can eat.

"I'm fine," I replied, pasting on a fake smile. "Why?"

"You've been crying," she said.

"No, I haven't," I lied.

"Your nose is red, Mommy," Michael said before taking a bite of his food.

"Is it?" I touched it absentmindedly.

"Like a reindeer," Jackie said, shrugging. "I speak the truth."

"It's Mommy the red-nosed reindeer!" Michael spoke up, raising his spoon in the air, and I couldn't help but laugh. Oh, it felt so good to laugh, even if it was only for a second. I reached down and kissed him on top of his head before turning to walk to the washroom to get Elizabeth.

"Hi, Mommy," Elizabeth made me jump as she walked around the corner. "Daddy loves you."

"Excuse me?" I asked, taken aback.

She proceeded to give Emily, and then Michael, a hug and a kiss before sitting down at her place at the table.

"I wanna talk to Daddy!" Michael whined.

"Young lady,"

"I called him." She looked right up at me, her blue eyes defiant. "Just like you showed me how to before. Aren't you proud of me, Mommy?"

I bit the inside of my lip and rubbed my temple where the tell-tale pounding had begun. There's no way he would have said that he loved me, we had made a promise to not bold face lie to our children, Christmas and the Easter Bunny in the exempt category of said declaration.

"T, you need to eat," Jackie said, pointing his fork in my direction.

I looked down at my size-6 body clad in sweats and a large t-shirt, remembering Bree's absolutely flawless size 0 being swallowed whole by my robe.

"Later, Jackie," I replied. "I'm not very hungry right now."

JASE

How pathetic am I?

I was sitting on the floor of our room leaned up against the wall, said thought going through my head, staring at our picture. My fingertips ran over it, tracing the side of her beautiful face, remembering when it was taken.

It was at our reception, during our first dance as husband and wife. I can still remember the feel of her small hand tucked in mine as I started to lead her, but had stopped—yes, there. There it was, the lily I had picked from one of the bouquets, breaking the stem before I tucked it behind her ear. I remember thinking how its beauty paled in comparison to her, and how my heart soared knowing that she was mine, all mine. I had pulled her close to me, losing myself in those beautiful blue eyes... oh, I remembered all of it. Our smiles were soft as we danced, never losing eye contact, knowing this was our forever.

Forever.

'What a joke,' I thought with a laugh.

I felt my phone vibrating in my pocket, and my chest constricted. I found myself wishing, hoping, praying—

It was as if my heart jumped into my throat.

Talia.

Please, please tell me this was a mistake... you've found a way to forgive me, you're coming home...

You still love me...

"Hi, Daddy."

Elizabeth was crying.

"Baby girl, please don't cry," I said, wiping tears of my own away.

"You are."

Damn.

"I'm okay," I lied. Anything to help her. "And you're going to be fine, too."

"I want to see you," her tiny voice wavered through the phone line.

"You'll see me Friday," I reminded her, per the only agreement that Talia and I had no trouble reaching—I got at least every other weekend with the kids. I wanted to believe it was for the right reasons. Still, it was three days away—three long days, three sleepless nights, and then I could see them again.

It wasn't soon enough.

"Is that when you move here?"

Elizabeth, you have no idea how much you're ripping my heart out right now.

"Daddy?"

"No, baby," I answered finally. "I'll be staying here."

"Alone?"

Yes... alone. In this big fuckoff house that isn't even close to being a home without all of you.

"Baby girl, I'm fine," I said, forcing the lie, forcing my voice to be stronger. "And I need you to be my happy girl—my sunshine, okay?"

"Okay, Daddy," I heard through her sniffles.

"And don't fight with Michael," I added, knowing she was probably already giving her little brother grief.

"Daddy..."

"Don't 'Daddy' me, Elizabeth," I said, smiling through my tears. "Be good." I swallowed hard, now realizing how difficult it was to say the next two words over the lump in my throat. "Help Mommy."

"Like you used to."

Used to.

That hurt.

But it was true.

I used to help all of the time. I used to be right by Talia's side, tag-teaming all aspects of everything around our home. From the dishes, to baths, to clean up, to bedtime...

Why had I stopped?

Oh, right. I had stopped out of spite. If she was going to push me away, then she could do it all—every last bit of it—by herself.

"Don't quit like Daddy did, baby girl," I said, my hands trembling, my heart breaking in two. "That was wrong, and I shouldn't have done it."

Would it have made a difference if I had continued trying?

"I won't quit."

"Promise?"

"I promise, Daddy." She sniffled again, and I could almost see her using her hands to smooth her hair back from her face. "Mommy says I have to eat now. Do you want to talk to Mommy?"

Oh God, yes, I want to. I wish I could tell her what I was feeling, how much it hurt to have her gone.

I heard Talia's laughter in the background, and my heart stopped.

Her life was going just the way she wanted it to.

Mine was falling apart.

"Not right now," I said softly, knowing I had to hang up before Elizabeth heard me break down. I knew it was coming, I could feel it coming... "Listen, you tell Little Man and Princess that I love them, okay?"

"And Mommy? You love Mommy too?"

I covered my eyes, hating how much they burned.

"Yes, I do," I said, refusing to lie to her... refusing to lie to myself.

"Mommy said she loves you, too."

I knew better.

"Sure, sweetheart," I said, my voice even softer than before.

After I assured her that I would absolutely be there on Friday and we had hung up, I was still sitting on that damn floor.

I had to pull myself together.

First step was getting out of this room, dealing with this house and all of its memories taunting me. I stood and flipped on the light, squinting and blinking at my surroundings.

Seeing them as they really were this time.

A couple of drawers on Talia's dresser were still open, empty. I pushed them shut, turning and looking at the bed that was littered with small pieces of paper. I picked up a random one, unfolding it, recognizing my handwriting.

These were little notes I had left for her throughout the years, in various places, at various times.

Of course she didn't want them.

I tossed the note back on the bed, turning towards the door. I would deal with this room later.

As I walked down that long silent hall, my phone began buzzing in my pocket again. This time I was unwilling to delude myself into thinking it was Talia.

I still wasn't prepared for it to be my Nan.

I took a deep, shuddering breath, reminding myself that my mother adamantly refused to peruse the tabloids or listen to rumors before I answered the phone.

"Hi sweetheart," her voice floated through the line. "I'm sorry it's been so long."

"That's okay, Nan," I said, my voice sounding odd. I suppose that's what happens when you spend so much time crying, and I cursed myself and my weakness.

"Are you okay?" she asked. "Are you coming down with something?"

"I think so," I lied.

"Be careful not to give it to those babies. You know Em and her croup and ear infections."

"Yeah, I know."

This was one of those nights that I was happy that she didn't follow the gossip magazines or Celebrity Gossip. I'm sure there were plenty pictures of Talia and the kids leaving—hell, Nan didn't even know we were having any problems, or at least hadn't had it confirmed by me.

"I just wanted to tell you," she was saying, "like I said, I'm sorry it took so long, but we will definitely be out there for Emily's birthday party. I know Jaden and Pete are going to be there."

Emily's birthday party.

In three weeks.

At this house.

In the middle of all of this mess, we had obviously forgotten.

Everyone was going to be coming in for this, from both sides of our families. Our friends were coming in, too... all to celebrate our Princess's birthday.

What were we going to do?

We couldn't be in the same room, hold a civil conversation. What would be different three weeks from now?

"Jase—are you sure you're okay?" Nan's voice broke into my thoughts.

"I'm fine, Nan. Seriously."

"Do you need me to bring anything for the party?" she asked.

"No, we've got everything covered," I said softly.

We as in Talia, who had this entire party planned while I was still on the road.

"Right," Nan drew that word out as only she can. "Let me speak with Talli."

I felt that knife twist in my heart.

"She's not here."

It wasn't a lie. I knew Nan would find out—she was bound to.

I just couldn't bring myself to talk about it at that moment, not when it hurt so much.

I promised her I would have Talia call, but I had the distinct feeling that when she didn't, Nan would be calling her cell.

And I'm sure I was bound to catch hell over it.

I was rummaging through the refrigerator for something to eat, but nothing caught my eye. I just didn't feel like eating at the time.

I walked back through the great room, surrounded by pictures of our family—smiling, happy, mocking me. Down the hall, I paused just outside of her room... Talli's room, the room I had put together for her. Taking a deep breath, I stepped in and flipped the light on, bracing myself for it to be completely gutted.

It was still the same.

Nothing had been touched.

I stood, frozen to the spot, looking around at the books, the movies, the music. I remembered the first time Talia had seen this room, and how she's stared at that picture of her parents. And then, she had turned to me...

I glanced back at that Italian leather sofa, knowing I'd never be able to count the number of times we had made love there.

I spotted a knitted blue blanket on the floor beside one of the overstuffed chairs. I picked it up to fold it and place it on the end of the couch when the faintest hint of jasmine invaded my senses.

Talia's blanket.

This must have been where she had slept the past three weeks. Here. Not in Em's bedroom. Here.

I sunk down into the chair, holding that blanket close, its scent enveloping me, equal parts painful and comforting.

I had forgotten how to pray. Hell, I don't think prayers work. And wishes, did they really come true?

Did it matter anymore?

I knew I needed to talk to her about that damn birthday party, but not right then.

'Tomorrow,' I thought. 'Tomorrow would be another day.'

CHAPTER 3

TALLI

I had one more day off to get the condo together. It was not going to be enough.

Especially when I couldn't sleep.

It's not as if I wasn't used to sleeping alone; Jase and I hadn't shared a bed since Emily was about three months old. Still, it didn't make it any less lonely.

I gave up sleeping around 4 a.m., wandering into the kitchen to make a pot of coffee. I glanced at my cell phone, which had been plugged in to charge next to the coffee pot and saw that I had seventeen missed calls. I wasn't surprised that Jase wasn't one of them. Hell, he was probably busy with his little blonde Barbie doll in her size zero clothes with her perfect, tiny body and her uncomplicated, wild, child-free Hollywood lifestyle.

It took me a minute before it registered that Nan had called. Twice.

There was one call from Tish, and one from Cass as well.

Three calls from Pete—those really surprised me. Maybe he felt guilty over how much he had gushed over Bree and all of her talent before.

The rest of the calls were from Jaden.

Jaden, my best friend whom I hadn't spoken with since I had left Ohio. By now, she knew about the split. The whole world that followed Hollywood gossip, tabloids, or TMZ probably knew. Hell, they had all been speculating about Jase and the Barbie for weeks—they must have been awfully proud of themselves.

'Well, look,' I thought as I flipped open my laptop and the browser began to load. 'We even made the front page.'

Rock star and wife of five years split—Rumors of infidelity run rampant.

They would have to have a picture of Jase and me... together, smiling, happy... wouldn't they? Oh, and look—there's Hooker Barbie, in her tight, tiny skirt, her blonde hair styled impeccably, promoting her new album that *my husband* wrote over half the songs for.

I can't believe I actually contemplated clicking on that story, but lucky for me Jaden couldn't sleep either.

"What the hell is going on, Talli?" she said when I answered the phone.

"Don't stress, Jaden," I said softly, "it's not good for the baby."

"Don't lecture me, lady. What the hell happened?"

I opened my mouth to tell her, tried to repeat the words as I had said to Sondra, to Jackie, to Chris who had the fucking nerve to hug me and tell me he was sorry... but I couldn't say anything. The room was starting to blur, and that stupid picture of the two of us smiling for the whole world seemed to melt as hot tears began to pour down my face.

"Oh... God, Talli, it's true?" Her voice was softer, her pitch slightly higher. She couldn't see me nod my head, but she must have heard the sniffles and sobs coming from me. "Where are you, are you at the house?"

"N...no," I stammered. I heard commotion in the background on the other line before Pete was there.

"Where are you, T?"

"I moved out," I managed to say, wiping my tears hastily, uncomfortable talking to Jase's brother.

"Talli—whatever happened, is it really bad enough to..."

"Pete, I walked in on him in our home, in *our* bedroom screwing his precious Bree in *our* bed," I hissed, trying to keep my voice down. "Now if you don't mind, I don't feel like talking about it, okay?"

I almost felt guilty about talking to him that way, but a part of me had wondered ever since that night exactly who had known.

"T, I'm so fucking sorry." His voice broke as he said the words. "I haven't talked to him in forever. I swear I didn't know."

"It doesn't matter," I muttered, sighing as I closed my laptop.

"I'm going to put Jaden back on here, okay? I have to go... we'll talk later, I promise. Do you need anything, T?"

I need my husband back, my family back together, my heart to stop aching so badly...

"I'm fine; don't worry about me."

"What about the kids?"

"They're with me," I said quickly. "And they're..."

They're heartbroken, they're confused, they don't understand...

"They're fine," I finished, nearly choking on the last word.

"I'll be seeing you soon, okay?" he said to me, but I was unable to respond. By the time Jaden got back on the phone, I was sobbing uncontrollably once more.

I had to get myself together...

"Talli, I need your new address."

"Why?"

"Because I am online booking my flight for today out to see you, that's why."

"Jaden, don't."

"Talli, bite me." I couldn't stop the short laugh that came from me when she said that. "Now, either you give me your address, or I go to Jase's and pry it out of him using every single torture device that I can get my hands on and believe me he doesn't want to see me right now. What? Don't look at me like that, Pete."

"Jaden, stop, please. I... I don't want the two of you in the middle, and here you are six months pregnant, and..."

"Okay, then, what about Em's birthday?" she asked, interrupting me. Oh... hell.

Three weeks until Emily's birthday, and I had completely forgotten. What was wrong with me? I prided myself on doing everything I could to prove that I could handle this mommy-and-a-career thing, curb the absentmindedness... I didn't need anyone's help, and now what?

Now I have dozens of people coming in for Emily's birthday, expecting the perfect, happy family in the big, sprawling house.

Even if we did two separate parties, I still didn't have the room for everyone here, and I couldn't afford to rent some hall, or get another cake, or…

"Jaden… I … I don't know what to do."

"Okay, I've got this."

"Jaden…"

"I have to pack, Talli. I'll see you this afternoon."

Emily's piercing cry kept me from saying anything more and I rushed to her side, as I always did. Any time she would turn and not see me in the room with her, this is how she woke. I knew if I didn't act quickly, the rest of the children would wake up as well.

Even in the short stretch between the kitchen and the crib, her sherry curls were already damp with sweat and large tears were rolling down from her bright blue eyes. She lifted her arms, her chubby hands opened, beckoning me to pick her up.

"Sshh, Princess," I whispered to her, smoothing her curls as I held her to me. She laid her head on my shoulder, twirling my hair in her fingers… just like she always did. She was a tiny me, like Michael was a mini-Jase and Elizabeth a female Jase with my colored eyes. Our family pictures were always perfect, no one could ever doubt our happiness.

I had been happy, once upon a time.

It had spiraled downward, slowly at first. Between the hospital and the new baby when I already had two small ones, I was exhausted. Three kids under the age of five—who wouldn't be? I couldn't focus, I didn't have time for myself let alone time for me and Jase. When Jase went on the road, I started sleeping in the twin bed that was in the nursery, just so Emily would sleep a little better, a little later. Anything to help.

Then Em started getting sick, coming down with croup on a regular basis. I couldn't leave her with anyone, not with her being sick. I couldn't put her on an airplane either, not with ear infection after ear infection. I thought Jase understood.

I was wrong.

He was so different when he came home… distant, snappy, grouchy. I figured he was exhausted and needed all the sleep he could get, so I refused to move Emily's crib into our bedroom. After that argument—

however short it was or seemed to be—we were wedged even further apart.

It didn't occur to me that he would turn to someone else, especially not to someone I knew, someone I naively trusted, at least in the beginning. I never in a million years dreamed he was screwing that little Barbie right under my nose the entire time. God, no wonder he didn't bother with me, never touched me. Why bother with the frumpy, fat, baby-making machine when you can have the epitome of Hollywood perfection?

Emily sighed and snuggled into me, and the tears that touched my eyes matched the guilt in my heart.

I didn't regret having her. I never regretted having any of my children.

Just as I could never regret loving their father.

JASE

My phone had buzzed nearly every half hour all night long. Various people had called at various times... some leaving messages, some not. There was Nan, Pete, my dad, Damien…

Bree.

I didn't answer any of them, listen to any of their messages. I wish I could say I wasn't wallowing in self-pity, but I would be lying. At that point I'd done enough lying, and it was time for the truth.

I fucked up.

It was only going on five in the morning, but my phone was once again buzzing. This time it was signaling a text from Pete.

Talked to T. Call me. NOW.

I sighed heavily, deciding it was time, but my cell battery was running low. I walked to the kitchen to grab the receiver to the home phone and start a pot of coffee when my cell was buzzing once more.

Bree. Again.

I hit the ignore button but decided against turning it off when I remembered that this was how Elizabeth contacted me. Apparently, though, pushing the ignore button was a big mistake because the home phone began ringing. I knew exactly who it was.

"I've been waiting for you to call me," Bree whined.

"I'm not in the mood to talk to anyone right now," I said, my voice strained.

"But... it's me, Jase. You can talk to me."

"I don't want to talk," I repeated.

"I thought you would have wanted me over there," she purred. "You know... so we could celebrate."

"Are you fucking kidding me?" I couldn't stop myself from saying. "What the hell do I have to celebrate?"

"We're free and clear," she went on. "No one is standing in our way anymore."

"We aren't... a we... and fuck! Damn it, I just..." I took a deep breath before continuing, thinking that maybe she would listen like she had for all of those months. "I just lost my family, Bree. They are...were... *fuck*, they're my world, and you know that."

"I want us to finish what we started, Jase. She knows; she's gone. And just a reminder, I happen to know how much you want me. I knew before our night together..."

"Bree, stop!" I ran a shaking hand through my hair, my nerves even more on edge while I was speaking with her. "I never made you any promises, you know that every bit as well as I do, and don't... don't drag Talli into this."

"I promise you," she cut me off, "you will be a very happy man very soon."

I remained silent, questioning my judgment or lack thereof, now feeling the brunt of the consequences of my actions.

"So, what time?" she asked.

"What time, what?"

"What time do you want me over there today?"

"Today's not a good day, Bree," I said with a sigh, not in the mood to fight any more with someone so unwilling to listen. I had spent months doing that already.

"Well, I'm out of town for the next two days. When this weekend, then?"

"I have the kids this weekend," I tried to explain.

"Good. They need to get used to me."

"Just… stop!" I knew she couldn't see me have my hand spread open wide, the same way I did when I would tell the kids to stop or slow down. I clenched my hand into a fist, the reminder of them one more painful blow. "They are going through enough, I am not going to do anything that would confuse them any more than they already are, don't you get that?"

"You're… kidding me, right?" she said, her voice raising slightly. "You let her talk you into this, didn't you? She's just trying to keep us apart."

"She's not…"

"She didn't want you, Jase. And now she doesn't want me to have you either."

Ouch.

"Now's not a good time," I said through clenched teeth, rubbing my temple that was beginning to throb.

"I'm not going to let you push me away," she said after I heard her light a cigarette. "I love you."

I felt empty when she said the words; I always did. I wondered many times if I had simply closed myself off over all of the hurt I had been through with Talia.

Could I ever love Bree?

Did I want to?

"Go ahead," I sighed into the phone when I finally called Pete.

"Are you really giving me license, Jase? Because I could say a hell of a lot right now that you may not want to hear."

"Maybe I need to." I sipped at my coffee and stared blankly at the empty chair across from me.

"Fuck, Jase, you didn't even…" His voice trailed off and I could tell he was trying to find a little privacy. "You didn't say anything the last time I talked to you. You haven't even called in, how long?"

"I'm sorry."

"And Bree? Jase, really? That's just," he sighed before continuing. "Jase, it's not you. You... the Jase I know, the Jase I grew up with, the brother who had me stand up and be his best man at his wedding would have never done that." When I was silent, he added, "Did you not think about your wife, Jase? With as much as you and Talli love each other... this is just killing her."

My heart constricted in my chest at his words, but I didn't bother to fill my brother in on all of the facts.

I couldn't stand the thought of her hurting, being in any kind of pain. What hurt even worse than that was knowing that what Pete said wasn't true. No matter how much I wished it were, I knew better. When Talli's hurt, she lets the world know. She couldn't even pretend, couldn't even raise her voice. Seeing that lack of reaction, after every time she had pushed me away, confirmed my worst fear, my living nightmare.

"Talli doesn't," I almost choked on the rest of the words, "She doesn't... love me, Pete. Things are just... different, they're just different. And don't, okay? I know I was wrong; I know I should have waited..."

"Waited?" Pete nearly shouted the word, again not giving me a chance to tell my side, what really happened. "Jase, your wife... your *wife* was crying so hard she couldn't even speak this morning."

"Huh uh," I said quickly, shaking my head, trying to keep the vision from invading my mind. "No, she wouldn't."

"You think I'm lying? Ask Jaden. My wife is packing right now to catch a flight to go be with her best friend who is falling apart."

"She doesn't *care*, Pete. She *doesn't love me*."

"Did she say that to you?"

"She didn't have to."

"So, suddenly you're a mind reader."

Part of me wanted to reach through that phone and knock his teeth in, but the other part of me—the stupid, idiotic, romantic part of me that believed that happily ever after had to exist—was clinging to that glimmer of hope that had long since faded from my mind.

"You..." I stood, pacing, running my free hand through my hair.

"You haven't been here, Pete. You don't know how long I have tried, how many times I have tried to talk to her, how many times I heard, 'Not now, Jase,' or 'I'm tired,' or 'Just leave me alone' or one of the… dozens of others I've heard. No, she'd rather be at the… at the hospital, or she was busy with the kids, or some other excuse that she came up with to not be anywhere near me. Did she bother to tell you through those tears that you're so sure you could see through the phone that she had been sleeping in Em's room? That she started that before I got back, and…" I stopped talking, my breathing labored as I tried to control my emotions.

"And you just accepted it," Pete said, his words clipped.

"What the hell was I supposed to do?"

"Talk to her, you asshole!" he yelled at me. "And if she didn't want to talk, then you make her listen."

"Right."

"Jase, you fought so hard for her, from nearly day one."

"Nearly," I said with a laugh, remembering how hurt I was in Cleveland.

"You should have fought to make her hear you."

"How the hell was I supposed to do that?" I asked, my voice faltering.

"What happened to you, Jase? What happened to make you stop fighting for her? Was it Bree?"

"That wasn't…"

Was it?

"Did you fall in love with Bree?"

"No," I answered honestly.

"What, did you just… stop loving Talli?"

"No, damn it… no."

"I remember someone whose opinion I value with everything in me… he said once that I should have never slept with someone else, not when I knew in my heart that I was in love with Jaden."

"That's not what…" I started to tell him yet again, then stopped. What was the use?

"No, it's not different, because you also told me that it had to be resolved, whether or not she loved me."

"I don't have to ask the question, Pete. I *know*."

30

"Sounds real familiar," he commented, and I remembered how he had said nearly the same thing to me about Jaden all those years ago. "Jase, you and T... you two have been through hell and back. You have loved and fought and made up and refused to give up, and... what happened? Because the Jase I know would have fought for T with every last breath in him, even if he thought she didn't love him anymore. And you should have. You shouldn't have stopped until you heard it from her."

"It hurts enough this way."

"Good! Good, I'm glad it hurts because now you know."

"Now I know what?" I asked, annoyed.

"Just a little bit of what she's going through," he replied. "She got that added bonus, though. What you did... what you and Bree did... it broke her."

No, Pete... no, it didn't.

"And if you don't believe me... just do it. Do it anyway."

"Do what?" I asked, pissed off that I apparently still had tears left to cry.

"Call her."

I was staring at the receiver in my hands, chewing incessantly on my non-existent fingernails. What was I supposed to say? 'Hi, I heard you laughing last night when I was on the phone with Baby Girl; hell of a show you put on for my brother this morning.'

Or was it?

How could I not know what to say? After countless hours on the phone, after years together, and this is what it has come to?

I glanced up at a small picture on my desk, the kids' faces smiling up at me, Em's covered in chocolate chip cookies...

Em.

Her birthday.

I dialed Talia's cell number quickly, going over in my mind how to convince her that we should just have the party here. I mean, why not? It was perfectly logical, everything was planned, everyone was coming here anyhow, why not just...

"Jase."

No hellos, no hi, just my name.

Why did it sound so hard for her to say?

"Dase," I heard Emily's tiny voice parrot.

"Em," I breathed, covering my face.

She never called me Dad, or Daddy. Ever.

"Is there something you needed?" Talia asked, a tell-tale sniffle giving her away. Pete wasn't lying to me... she had been crying. And it was all my fault.

"Em's birthday," I said quickly, knowing I had to lay this on the table before I lost my nerve. "Her party, it's um..." I licked my lips, the words suddenly failing me.

"I know, it's scheduled during your weekend."

My...oh, right. That whole visitation thing.

"No, that's okay, because I forgot all about it, and I... we, um... could still do it. You know, here."

Why did I tell her I forgot? What kind of father am I? Oh, great, she's going to think it's because...

"Good, no giving me hell over forgetting, too."

I could almost see the pout in her lips as my heart skipped a beat. One tiny glimpse, I could almost see my Talia buried in there.

"Me? Never."

I miss you... I miss this. Why did you give up? What the hell did I do to make you stop loving me?

"Whatever," she said. It wasn't snarky, it wasn't mean, it wasn't hateful. She almost... almost laughed. She didn't add the 'Warner' the way she used to, but then again since we had married I'd always come back by telling her she was a 'Warner' herself. I bit the inside of my lip, picturing her sitting there playing with Em's curls while she talked to me. "So," her voice disturbed the perfect image that I had in my mind, my stomach in knots as she spoke to me, "this... um, this Friday."

Friday? Oh... Friday, when I was going to pick up the kids... When I would be standing outside her door, and maybe she'd let me in, and...

"Good morning, baby." Bree's voice filled my office as she waltzed in unannounced, and she was completely unfazed at the glare that I shot

32

her.

"I see you're busy," Talia said quickly.

"Mmmm, sleep well?" Bree purred as she curled up to me, her eyebrow raising when I pushed her off.

"Talli, wait."

The line was dead.

"What did *she* want?" Bree asked while she settled into my chair that I had just stood from.

"What the hell are you doing here?" I asked.

"I'm here to see you."

"How did you get in?" She didn't answer my question, only smiled slyly and crossed her bare legs. "Damn it, Bree, how did you get in? It's Linda's day off, no one is out there…"

"I found this," she replied, dangling the spare key that I kept for Pete for when he was in town, pulling her hand back when I went to snatch it from her.

"And the code?" I asked, my breathing labored, my temper about to spiral out of control.

"I've watched you put it in… how many times?" she asked, wiggling her hips slightly as she settled further into my chair.

"Bree," I said slowly, carefully. "Put the key on my desk and get the hell out."

"Oh, you don't mean that." She stood and walked towards me, snaking her arms around my waist. I stepped away from her and left the room before I did or said something I would regret more than I regretted that night with her to begin with.

"Jase," her voice echoed in the hall, "there's no sense in walking away from me."

"Is that how you got in here that night?" I asked, turning to her.

"That night… you mean our night together?" I didn't answer her, so she continued. "No, Linda was here. She let me in. She seemed rather… pleased."

Linda's a kind and caring person and had no idea what was going on… that's why she was pleased.

"You look exhausted," Bree commented, running her fingers through my hair before I pulled away and walked down the stairs. "You are wasting your time, walking away from me. We're still going to be working together very closely for at least the next month."

"Why?" I asked, turning back to her. "The album is done, it is out, congratulations on the success…"

"Congratulations are in order for you as well," she cut me off as she caught up to me again. "And I thought you were coming out on the mini promo tour that we're getting ready to do."

"I don't think that's such a good idea," I replied. "Chris, Sondra, Alison…"

"Are all so enamored with your soon-to-be-ex-wife that they'll say anything to get you to not live up to your obligations."

"Not even close," I muttered, thinking of the long-time tension between Chris and Talia, refusing to comment on the pain in my chest at the words 'ex-wife'. "But with everything going on, they think its best that I not go."

"We have a duet,"

"We don't have a duet, Bree," I disagreed. "I sing back up on a couple of songs. There are no duets, and there's no reason you can't have another member of your band do it."

"We will put out a statement that says,"

"The only statement," Chris interrupted her as he walked in, briefcase in hand, "that will be released on Jase's behalf will come from his publicist and his legal team. There will be no, and I repeat no joint statements, and *no* mention of the two of you in anything other than a strictly professional capacity."

"Coffee's in the kitchen," I said to him, motioning for him to follow me.

"You may have pulled Talia's strings," Bree spoke up.

"You don't know Talia very well, do you?" Chris asked. "Now, we have business, and you, until further notice, should not be at this private residence alone, or in a less than *professional capacity.* Do you understand?"

I kept my eyes downward, although in my peripheral vision I could see her cringe, cowering slightly like a child. I scoffed silently as I thought to myself how Talia would have been cursing him out. I definitely wasn't one to cower from Chris, either, but he was merely doing his job, and since Bree wouldn't listen to me…

"Jase, aren't you going to say goodbye?" I heard her say. I looked up from my spot by the kitchen island and waved silently before I glanced back down at the countertop I could remember with absolute clarity the last time I had to get after the children for chasing each other around it

I just... I missed them.

Even if I couldn't fix this... our family... there was still something I needed to do.

"So, Jase," Chris was saying as we walked back in the office after showing Bree out, "I was hoping that maybe me reaming you a new asshole the other day would bring you to your senses, but... now, we have work to do."

"I need the locks and alarm code changed," I said quickly, looking him square in the eye, remembering our last conversation that had turned into a shouting match.

Chris is a family man through and through.

That is one of the things about him I truly admire.

"Are you sure?" he asked slowly, his brows furrowed together.

I thought of Bree waltzing in unannounced, and my jaw twitched slightly.

"Yeah," I replied, "I'm sure."

CHAPTER 4

TALLI

TV Land held no comfort for me as I sat curled up on that little couch, Emily on my lap. I was running my fingers through her curls, trying to keep the both of us calm.

I just didn't want to cry anymore.

I knew Jaden was on her way, and although I felt guilty for her involvement, I had to admit I needed her there. It was almost like a weakness, admitting I couldn't handle this on my own. I wondered for a brief moment if things would have been different if...

No. No they wouldn't.

Because Bree was a part of the picture, and Jase had obviously left our commitment to make one with her.

It hurt... no, hurt is such a small word compared to the pain coursing through me, overwhelming me, confusing me. I kept going over every morsel of information, trying to figure out what I had done wrong.

My cell phone began to ring, and I knew by the ring immediately who it was.

Why is he calling? Is he sorry for what he had done? Or was he just sorry for getting caught?

If I didn't answer it, it would go to voicemail... would he leave a voicemail? Would he just hang up?

What if something is wrong?

Swallowing hard, trying to calm my nerves, I answered it just in time. "Jase...

I love you, I miss you. Whatever I did to make you stop loving me, I am so, so sorry...

"Dase," Emily said, turning towards me with a smile.

"Em," I heard Jase say, my heart splintering at the tone of his voice.

Don't give in, Talli... he slept with someone else...don't tell him how you feel, it will only hurt that much more when he reminds you who he's with now.

"Is there something you needed?" I asked, trying to keep the conversation light, attempting to cover up a sniffle. He couldn't know I had been crying... no weakness.

"Em's birthday," he said. "Her party, it's um..."

Of course. Of course he would call about Emily's birthday. How very presumptuous of me to mistakenly think he would call to actually speak with me.

"I know, it's scheduled during your weekend." I held my breath, waiting for him to yell at me, give me ten kinds of hell over forgetting about her birthday, expect me to change our plans so it didn't interfere with his visitation, berate me once again over my absentmindedness.

I was not expecting, "No, that's okay, because I forgot all about it, and I... we, um... could still do it. You know, here."

Seriously?

Oh, fuck...

Her birthday. There. With him. And... and...

And did he just admit he forgot too?

"Good," I managed to say, "no giving me hell over forgetting, too."

I buried my face in my hands, praying he would accept my wave of the white flag.

"Me? Never."

"Whatever," I began, stopping short of adding 'Warner' like I always did. I couldn't do it right then, I couldn't handle him saying I was a 'Warner', too... was I still a 'Warner'? Did he still see me as his wife?

How could he?

"So," I continued, my voice a little stronger, "this... um, this Friday..."

"Good morning, baby," I heard Bree's voice filter through the line.

Oh.

OH.

That... that asshole!

He didn't waste any time, did he? Hell, what did I expect? He probably took every opportunity he could to sneak around with her before I left. Why bother sneaking around now?

"I see you're busy," I snapped.

I heard the skank ask him if he slept well as I hung up the phone.

Fuck.

Emily squeaked her disapproval as I held her a little too tight. "Sorry, Princess," I mumbled through my tears before I set her down.

I knew exactly what I had to do.

What I should have done three weeks ago.

"Wow... hi there, little one," I said as I rubbed Jaden's baby bump. "He's definitely grown since I saw you..."

I couldn't get out the word 'last' before Jaden had her arms around me, holding me as close as she could. "It's okay, T... go ahead. Cry."

"I... can't," I stammered, even though I felt the tears surfacing once again. I pushed back slightly and gave her a shaky smile. "I'm happy you're here."

That was the absolute, honest truth; for the first time in weeks I didn't feel alone.

"Okay, let's get these kids... hey, sweetie!" she was interrupted as Michael ran out and threw his arms around her. "Where was I? Oh, let's get these kids occupied so that we can focus on you."

"There's not much here," I admitted "They have their favorite toys and such, but I left all the movies."

"Do you want me to go get them?"

"No," I said a little too quickly with a shake of my head.

"Talli..."

"They need things there, too," I rationalized.

"Well, it's a good thing that... I brought presents!" she called out, knowing Elizabeth would come running.

"Presents? Hi, Aunt Jaden!" She gave Jaden a brief hug, then turned and looked in the bag that Jaden had brought with her.

"Elizabeth Christine," I scolded her manners, but Jaden waved it off.

"You guys go enjoy," she said after Elizabeth pulled out the latest Disney release and ran towards her room with it.

"My room!" Michael protested.

"Just go with your sister," I called after them.

"Where's Emily?" Jaden asked as she sat down on my couch.

"Taking a nap."

"Don't you want them in Michael's room then?"

"Emily's crib is in my room," I explained, grabbing my diet cola and sitting beside her.

"Hope you don't mind my asking, but... why?"

"So she doesn't wake the whole house when she starts screaming," I replied. "Hey... listen, I really hate to do this. I can call Sondra or someone."

"What's up?"

"I have an appointment this afternoon that I need to keep." I bit the inside of my bottom lip, expecting the questions to come firing at me.

"Nah, just leave them with me," she said, grinning. "Is everything okay?"

I paused before answering, not wanting to pull her any more into the middle than she already was.

"It will be," I finally said.

Sherise Adler was a hard-nosed, in your face, ball-crushing divorce lawyer. Under normal circumstances, I wouldn't have been compelled to go straight for the big guns, but these were no normal circumstances.

This was Hollywood, California.

This was the entertainment industry, where I was a mere pee-on and my husband held all the clout.

I couldn't risk losing my children.

And the fact that she'd publicly denounced Bree and Jase's actions made her all the more appealing to me.

"Tell me what you want," she said, crossing her long legs and smiling demurely. "I can hand you his balls in a sling if you so desire."

"I want full custody of the children," I said quickly. "He's... he's on the road so much, Emily doesn't even know him."

"Supervised visitation as well?" she asked as she jotted down her notes.

"No... no, he wouldn't harm them."

"Limited visitation, then."

"No, I don't want to keep him from them either."

"Talia, let me be frank," she said, looking over her glasses at me. "It's very wise that you've taken this step to protect yourself and your rights; I commend you on it. You need to think long and hard, though, whether or not you want your children exposed to the lifestyle that I'm sure they would be subjected to if they spend extended periods of time with a father that is more absent than not."

I opened my mouth to come to Jase's defense, but her next words stopped me.

"Do you see Breeann Hamilton as a role model for your children? Because if you don't mind them being around her on a regular basis, then by all means—unlimited visitation."

"No... no, I don't want her around them."

"Okay, well without her having actually threatened them, the only course of action we have is limited visitation." She pushed her glasses back in place and sat back in her chair slightly. "Now... child support and alimony."

"I've... made sure I can afford my condo," I said, biting the inside of my lip. My retainer to her was most definitely going to dip into that.

"Are you and your children accustomed to living in such a small apartment?" she asked.

"It's a condo, and it's fine."

"Whatever; the whole point is... this man owes you. He owes his children."

"The prenup doesn't leave much room,"

"This prenup can be ripped to shreds in a courtroom given his adulterous affair and the fact that you have three children," she interrupted me. "We subpoena everyone involved and…"

"No, please." I took in a shaky breath, trying to keep my resolve. "Please, I don't want to put my children through this."

"As you wish," she said with a wave of her hand. "Here." She scribbled a number down and showed it to me. "Child support for three children of a very successful musician."

My eyes widened as I looked at the number, my face turning red at the sight of it. That was more than I brought home in a month.

"That's an awfully large number," I said softly.

"Believe me, he can afford it."

"Cut it in half," I demanded. "Please; I've never been after his money, I'm not about to start now."

"All right, I will," she said with a sigh. "I'm telling you, though; when he comes after you—and he will—you'll change your mind."

Would he really come after me? Seriously? Wasn't he getting everything he wanted—his freedom, the blonde bimbette… why would he come after me?

"I'll get the papers drawn up and have him served within the week."

"The week? Really?" I asked.

"Tell me you're not having second thoughts."

I remembered the two of them wrapped in that embrace, moving, moaning, kissing…

"No." I held my head high, tears nowhere near the surface. "No second thoughts at all."

JASE

"I'm really not feeling up to doing any promotional work," I was saying to Chris later that afternoon via phone conference. "It's not my album, it's hers."

"I understand, and I completely agree," he replied. "Right now, though, her legal team is claiming that you entered an agreement."

"I did no such thing," I interrupted him. "She's just pissed off over what happened here, and she's trying to force me to do something that I want no part of."

"For the sake of avoiding negative press, for right now, you will agree,"

"No."

"To appear and perform on Monday,"

"Damn it, Chris, I said no!"

"On Stella Black's show," he finished.

"If we're trying to avoid negative publicity, then that's the last place you want me," I stated.

"You think I don't know that?" he asked with a sigh. "For right now, though, your flight is booked, hotel is booked, and our legal team is working to get you out of the rest of it."

"God, Chris," I said, sinking back into that Italian leather sofa in Talli's room, "promise me you'll do whatever it takes..."

My voice trailed off as I remembered a past conversation with Talia, when we'd lost our first baby, when I'd been an absolute asshole to her. What was it I'd told her? Oh, right... I would do whatever necessary, whatever it took, to make things right between us.

And now it was too late.

"Are you paying attention?"

"Yeah, sure," I lied as Chris's voice broke through my thoughts. I heard a beep signaling an incoming call and glanced at the receiver, the caller i.d. showing Jaden's cell number. Wasn't she at Talli's? "Chris, I need to take this call."

"Is everything okay?" he asked, genuine concern in his voice.

No... no, everything is not okay. It isn't going to be okay.

"I'll call you back," was all I said before switching to the other line. "Talk to me."

"How very cordial of you," Jaden said, no humor in her voice.

"I'm not in a cordial mood." I was quiet for a moment as I listened to the kids in the background, my heart splintering with regret. "Are they... okay?"

"Physically? Yes." I suppose that should have been some kind of load off my mind, but it wasn't. "Talli isn't here, so I took this opportunity to warn you that I will be over there some time before I head back to Groves Point."

"Good," I said softly.

"Are you so sure that's good, Jase? You sure you don't want to arrange to be gone, avoid me the way you've been avoiding your family for the past... wow, how long has it been?"

"I haven't avoided any of you."

"Oh, bullshit, Jase," she snapped. "Every time Pete has wanted to come out, you've been too busy."

"Since when has Pete wanted to come out?" I asked, confused. "I haven't talked to him in... well, I talked to him this morning."

"Anyhow, I know everything that Talli was planning for Emily's birthday, where she kept all of her notes on the presents and decorations," she continued, ignoring my question. "And I promised her that I would help this go as smooth as possible."

"There's no reason that she and I,"

"The other reason, besides yourself, better not be there when I arrive," Jaden cut me off, her tone biting. "You may be my brother in law, but that doesn't make me any less inclined to beat the hell out of you, or her, pregnant or not."

"It's nothing I don't deserve."

"So, for Talli's sake, I'm going to help make sure this party goes off without a hitch, got it?"

"Yeah," I sighed. "Got it."

I was honestly hoping that Talia would speak with me about it, give me a chance to explain that Bree had just walked in unannounced, uninvited. I know she wouldn't believe that I wouldn't hurt her that way, because I already had.

How could I possibly get her to talk to me now?

"Have you talked to Nan?" Jaden asked.

"Yeah... yeah I talked to her," I replied.

"No, I mean since she found out that Talli and the kids left."

"Fuck... who told her?" I asked.

"Well, *you* should have. Instead she was asked the question on the phone by some local deejay."

"That's just... perfect." I sat back, rubbing my temple that was pounding incessantly.

"I never realized until today how much Talli has rubbed off on you," Jaden commented.

"What are you talking about?"

"I mean... when something's wrong, really wrong with her, she shuts everyone out. You know something's wrong, but not what. She isolates herself completely. You, though... you always wore your heart on your sleeve, talked to people when things were bugging you." She paused for a moment before continuing. "I guess that's one of the reasons that I was blindsided by this. You know, unless..."

"Unless what?"

"Unless it doesn't really bother you," she finished.

"What the hell do you mean, doesn't bother me?" I asked, my voice breaking slightly. "How would you feel if Pete didn't love you anymore, Jaden? How would you feel?"

"So you don't love Talli."

"Are you insa... damn it, Jaden, you know better. You *know* I love her."

"Then why?"

"Just... just leave it alone," I said sullenly. "It doesn't matter anymore."

"Jase..."

"Call before you come over," I cut her off. "I had the locks and stuff changed."

"Okay." I heard commotion in the background and Michael yelling for Talli, so apparently she had just gotten home.

"I'll talk to you later," I said, clicking the off button on the phone before I gave into the urge to ask to speak with Talli.

What was the point?

She wouldn't believe what I had to say anyway.

"I don't suppose you're going to tell me your side of what happened, are you?" I had finally answered the phone when Nan called, knowing I needed to talk to her.

"Not all the nasty details, no," I replied. "You don't need to be involved in this."

"You're my grandson," she stated the obvious. "I love you, and those children... and Talli, too."

"We love you, too," I said softly. "I just didn't want to burden you with this, that's all."

"But the last time I talked to you... she had just left, hadn't she?"

"Yeah." Damn it, what was up with the tears? When the hell were they going to stop? I wiped my eyes hastily, angry that I'd allowed myself to get so emotional all over again.

"Jase, why didn't you tell me then?"

"Because." My voice was small, as if I was a child again. "I don't want to talk about it."

"I know it hurts. I've been there, remember?"

I choked back a sob, damning myself for being so weak and wishing I was back at my nan's house, confessing all I had done wrong, hearing of her unconditional love and how it would all be okay.

"I can't do this right now," I managed to say.

"You don't have to talk to me, Jase. Just listen, okay?" I know she couldn't see me nodding, but when I was silent, she continued. "I never in a million years imagined that you would have pulled a stunt like this, never thought you had so much of your father in you."

"Nan..."

"No, right now... listen. I did my best to make sure you didn't have to see how hard it was for your mother, how much she hurt every day when your father left."

"Talli left me."

"Jase, don't... okay? You are old enough now to connect the dots and know what happened when you were younger, know that your father cheated. And even though I tried to shelter you from the brunt of it, you know how much it hurt you to have your family split up like that. How... how could you put your children through the same thing?"

I wiped my eyes hastily, knowing I deserved every bit of hell that my mother was giving me. "It's not the same. I'm not abandoning them the way my parents practically did to me. You don't know the whole story, Nan... I didn't..."

"Are you telling me you weren't in bed with someone else?" she asked. "That Talli didn't see you... that your children didn't see you?"

They saw me? They... Oh... Oh, fuck.

I knew Elizabeth had heard something, but...

I hung my head in shame, unable to bring myself to tell Nan my side of the story.

"Whatever happened, whatever went wrong," she continued, her voice full of emotion, "I want you to be sure... absolutely sure... that you've done everything in your power to make things right. Are you listening to me? Because I know you, and I know how much you love her, how much you love those babies. Do *not*... do *not* give up without a fight, do *not* let it end unless you know there's no way it can be fixed. Got it?"

"Nan, I..."

"Got it?" she repeated more sternly.

How was I supposed to do this?

How was I supposed to fight for someone who didn't want to be with me?

How could I possibly make her listen?

CHAPTER 5

TALLI

I feel so, so guilty. This feeling of guilt is almost overwhelming, keeping me in a stranglehold, second-guessing my actions.

The one thing that he and I could agree upon—the fact that our children needed the both of us—was going down in flames. Sherise Adler was going to see to it that Jase had only one overnight a month, no visitation during the week when school was in session, only five hours when it was 'his weekend' that there was no overnight.

How could I have agreed to this?

The children will be absolutely heartbroken, even more so than they are now. And Jase will be livid…

'Oh, who gives a fuck how he feels?' I scolded myself. 'He wants to be free, he will be. Completely.'

I know it's a hateful, spiteful attitude to have, and I wasn't questioning where it came from. I knew… I knew when I heard that Barbie's voice in the background that I was bound to do something drastic. The divorce? I knew that was coming; I couldn't stay married to a man who didn't love me, and I certainly couldn't force him to.

And the worst part?

I miss him.

I miss him so much it hurts.

I miss his eyes… those beautiful, stormy, dark kaleidoscope eyes, the way they slightly changed color with his moods. I miss his smile, his laugh… it's been so long since he smiled at me, close to forever since we'd shared any kind of laughter. I miss the way we would talk for hours, about everything or nothing. His hands… oh, I miss his hands, the way he held me, the way he'd reach for my hand whenever he could tell something was wrong I miss the way he would touch me… just a little, soft touch… whenever he walked past me. It was such a simple show of affection, one that had been missing for… well, for months. I miss his voice, just the sound of it was equal parts soothing and an aphrodisiac.

An aphrodisiac.

I shook my head to clear it, knowing it was useless to think of it now, no matter how much—how very much—I missed making love with him.

And just the very thought brought back the memory of Jase in bed with that fucking Barbie doll.

Oh, right… *that's* why I was doing this.

But now… now I had my best friend, my sister-in-law, sitting in my condo watching my kids, and it was time to put on the brave face. Jaden didn't need to get pulled into this any further.

As I began walking down the hall towards the entrance to the condo, my phone started to buzz.

Nan.

I sighed and shoved the phone back in my pocket, not wanting to hear how her precious grandson never meant to hurt me.

The moment that thought crossed my mind I cringed, not believing for one second that Nan would actually say anything of that nature. I just didn't know what I could possibly say to her at that moment; I didn't know if I was capable of speaking about it at all without breaking down.

I don't want to cry anymore.

I hesitated as I placed my key in the lock, pasting that smile back on my face, not wanting Jaden, or especially Elizabeth, to catch on to my mood. Michael came running towards me as I walked in the door and I wrapped my arms around him, lifting him effortlessly.

"Have you behaved yourself?" I asked, to which he smiled and nodded.

"They've all been good, even Emily," Jaden commented. "Maybe there is just much less tension here."

"You're on your fishing expedition now, aren't you?" I asked as I looked around. "Jaden... you didn't have to do all of this." She had unpacked several boxes and had put their contents away, stacking the now broken-down boxes by the door.

"I didn't do it by myself," she replied with a smile.

"Moving is hard work," Elizabeth said, sighing heavily as she pushed her hair back from her face. She sat down on the couch beside Jaden and leaned back into the cushions.

"Is that so?" I asked, raising an eyebrow.

"And I played," Michael announced proudly from his perch on my hip, a little half smile on his face that looked so much like his father. "And Em pooped."

"Oh, that's nice to know," I laughed.

"Yeah, it was a joy," Jaden smirked.

"Hey, you have to get used to it," I reminded her. "Of course with all of the practice you've had between Tish's kids and mine..."

"I'll still completely panic when they hand him to me," she finished for me. I sat down beside Elizabeth, moving Michael to my lap.

"I think you'll be okay," Elizabeth said reassuringly, patting Jaden's baby bump.

"Thank you, Stinkerbell," Jaden replied with a giggle, tousling Elizabeth's hair and kissing her cheek.

"How am I Stinkerbell when Emily pooped in her pants?" Elizabeth protested.

"Where is Em?" I asked, looking around.

"She's sleeping," Jaden answered.

"Her poops weared her out," Michael said matter-of-factly with a nod.

"Not everything is about poops," Elizabeth said, rolling her eyes as she started strolling back towards her room. "You're such a boy."

"Duh," Michael called after her, scooting off my lap to follow and torment his older sister. "Better than being a girl."

I smiled wistfully as I stared after them, their sibling squabbles reminding me so much of my childhood. As if on cue, Jaden spoke up.

"Have you talked to Lisa?"

"A couple of times," I replied with a sigh. "I know she and Jack were divorced, but she's still taking his death pretty hard."

"Wouldn't you?"

I shuddered at the thought of anything happening to Jase. "Yeah," I said softly. "I know I would."

"Elizabeth said that Bree was there when you got back home after the funeral," Jaden commented nonchalantly. "In your bedroom, and she thought she was crying."

"Jaden," I said sharply, but she cut me off.

"Talli, Elizabeth was confused," she clarified. "I wasn't prying for information." When I was silent, staring down at my folded hands, she continued. "Is that when you found them?" I nodded, still unable to meet her eyes.

"I really don't want to talk about this now, Jaden."

"Don't shut me out," she said, reaching over and squeezing my hands. "Okay?"

I shrugged, still not looking up. "I'm not shutting anyone out."

"Bullshit."

My head snapped up, my eyes flashing a bit of anger, which immediately dissipated. I really needed to remember who I was speaking with; Jaden could smell bullshit from a mile away.

"Jaden, you're my best friend," I said softly, my smile trembling slightly. "And you're also married to Jase's brother. The situation is difficult enough, and I don't want to make it any more awkward for you. God... I don't even know what to say to Nan; I've lost count of how many times she's called."

"She knows the scoop," Jaden said. "I told her, and I held back absolutely zero of my opinion of her darling grandson. Just between you and me... I think she agrees."

"I can't put her in the middle either."

"No, but she's still their great-grandmother," Jaden said, motioning towards the hall. "And she'll be there for Emily's birthday party."

"Yay me."

"Speaking of Emily's party," she continued, "I promised you I was going to take care of this."

"There's really nothing to take care of," I said. "Other than picking up the cake and stuff. Her presents are there and wrapped, the snacks are in the pantry, the decorations are..." I sighed, sinking back into the cushions. "I really don't want to have to get everything together over there; it's going to be hard enough to just... be there, you know?"

"I told you, I've got this," she tried to reassure me. "Just let me know where everything is, and I'll take care of it. I've already warned the asshole I'd be coming over before I went back."

"Jaden," I hissed, motioning back towards the hall where the kids' rooms were, "I know he's an asshole, I personally think he's much worse," I said in a hushed whisper. "But they're going through enough. Please... please don't let them hear it."

"Ah, Talli," she breathed, her expression sad, "I wish..."

"Let's not... dwell, okay?" I asked, pushing a couple tears back, knowing the worst was yet to come. "No sense in wishing for what will never be."

Jaden stayed until Friday morning, looking after the children when she could. My shift was starting in about an hour and I had to take the kids with me that morning to the daycare on the third floor. Emily was being her normal difficult self, whining because I had the nerve to get her out of bed before she was done getting her beauty rest. Elizabeth was back to playing the boss, giving Michael a hard time when he didn't brush his teeth just the way she wanted him to. Michael, on the other hand, was rather proud of himself for getting dressed without any help... which of course meant that his pants were backwards and his shirt inside out.

"I'm so going to be late," I muttered.

"Here," Jaden said, holding her hand out to Michael, "let me help you, okay?"

"But I got it," he argued. "See?"

"You didn't get it right," Elizabeth said with a bit of added snark. "Cause you're a baby."

"I'm not a baby!" he screamed back at her, which set Emily back off with the big tears.

"They so need to save this for tonight," Jaden commented, winking at me.

"Tonight? What's to…"

My voice trailed off as I remembered exactly what tonight was.

Tonight Jase would be coming to get the kids. I wouldn't see them again until Sunday. Hell, he probably had Linda staying the weekend to take care of them for him. Or… or…

No.

No he wouldn't dare have Bree over, not with our kids there. Not…

"I'm going to stop over there on my way to the airport," Jaden was saying. "He's already assured me he was there alone."

"That's…"

Wonderful. Relieving.

"…no longer my concern."

"The hell it isn't," she disagreed.

I had to smile. The joys of best friends.

She helped me pack the kids and their bags in the car, giving each of them a kiss and a promise to see them in two weeks. When she turned to me, she held me as close as her baby bump would allow, squeezing just a little tighter than normal before letting go.

"Are you sure there's no hope?" she asked, her eyes brimming with tears.

I knew there wasn't, I'd known that for quite some time. No matter how much I wished, hoped, prayed, cried… I knew all hope was gone.

As I drove towards the hospital, my phone began to ring. I checked the caller i.d. out of the corner of my eye, noting it was Sherise Adler's number. I answered it, adjusting my headset slightly, ignoring Elizabeth's protests when I turned down the radio.

"Hello?" I said, trying to sound as if everything was normal.

"Hello, Mrs. Warner." It was Sherise Adler herself. Wow, I must rate… or the money she was sure to get from Jase did.

"Hi."

"The papers are ready to be served, we should have them in his hand this afternoon."

"No!" I said a little too quickly. "No… wait."

"Have you changed your mind?"

"No, no… not at all. It's just… can it wait?" I asked, glancing back at the children. They were so looking forward to their weekend with

Jase; I couldn't take it away from them, or risk him being in a crappy mood with them there.

"Pardon me?"

"Just… just until Monday," I said softly. "Please. Just… for the children."

"Are you absolutely positive?"

"Yes," I replied. "Just one weekend of peace."

"Ah, the paparazzi. Good call."

I didn't bother to correct her and tell her the paparazzi had nothing to do with it; instead I thanked her for her help and understanding.

"Are you okay, Mommy?" Elizabeth asked, catching a glimpse of me in the review mirror.

I paused, biting my bottom lip before I pasted that smile back on my face. "I'm fine, baby girl," I lied. "Just fine."

I kept that smile pasted on my face as I dropped them off for their first day at the daycare, apologizing profusely when Emily began screaming the moment I set her down. I continued smiling as they informed me that I needed to leave a check with them for the rest of the month to cover my portion of their daycare that my work didn't cover, even knowing that between this and my retainer for the lawyer I'd never make my next month's rent on the condo. I smiled all the way through my morning's appointments, through lunch where I avoided all questions, through my apologies in the middle of the day to Emily's 'teacher' when she proceeded to call my office about how she had done nothing but cry since I dropped her off.

I could only hope and pray I could keep that smile on my face when Jase showed up at my modest home to pick up our children and take them away from me, leaving me childless for the first time since Emily was three months old.

JASE

"I'll have another key for you as soon as I can," I was saying to Jaden as she pushed past me, making her stop before she headed to the airport to go home.

"Save it for your brother," she said, her words short and clipped. "I'm going to show you where the decorations and such are for Emily's birthday party are, then I'm headed back out."

"Jaden..."

"Don't," she snapped, her eyes holding more anger than Talia had bothered to muster up. "Don't think my marriage to your brother is going to make me come to your defense."

"Damn it, Jaden, it isn't like I planned this!"

"Is that so?" she asked, swinging the door of the pantry open. "See? Decorations. Oh, look... her notebook that has the name and address of the bakery for the cake... and see this? The guest list."

"You don't need to speak to me as if I were a child, Jaden," I snapped back at her.

"Why the hell not? Judging by the way you spoke to Talli, she couldn't hold this shit together, couldn't handle planning anything without screwing something up."

"I never said anything like that!" I protested, my voice rising. "What the hell is she going around saying about me now?"

"No, asshole, this is from observation," she replied, slamming the notebook with the guest list on the counter. "I can let it all fly now, since the kids aren't here to witness it."

"What the fuck are you talking about?"

"What about 'Jeez, Talli... you forgot something as simple as napkins?' or 'Damn, Talli... you couldn't pick up the bread and milk on your way?' Would you like me to continue? Because newsflash for you—she didn't have assistants doing all of this shit for her, she did all of it herself. You couldn't even bring yourself to help her, let alone appreciate that she could handle this house, those children, and her career without having her hand held."

"You think I didn't help her? You think I didn't try?" I yelled back, guilt driving my anger.

"Did you have to belittle her every chance you got?"

"Did you live here, Jaden? Did you know what it was like living with her? What if Pete pushed you away every goddamn time you turned around? What if you tried to help and he wouldn't let you? What if all you wanted was your family back and Pete didn't give a damn?" I bit my lip and turned around, my admission bringing tears stinging my eyelids. I had to keep them away… no more tears. I walked away quickly, wiping my eyes before I heard her footsteps stomping up behind me.

"If you wanted your family so goddamn bad…"

"You know what?" I said suddenly, a fresh wave of anger flooding through me as I turned towards her. "I am sick and fucking tired of everyone turning on me, okay? I'm tired of hearing the 'poor little Talli' from everyone, because believe me she had her hand in the end of this, too."

"Oh, what? Did she not stroke your ego enough?" Jaden asked, shifting her weight to one leg, her arms draped around her baby bump. "Do yourself a favor and make sure your girlfriend," she said the word with such disdain, "isn't here for Emily's party."

"She's not my girlfriend!"

"No, she's just someone your wife and kids walked in on you fucking!" Jaden spat out, throwing the notebook at me before turning around to storm out.

"Damn it, I wasn't…" I yelled after her, then stopped. She didn't need drug any further into this, and besides… she wouldn't believe me.

No one would believe me.

I knew exactly what it looked like, what it had to look like to Talia, but there was nothing I could do or say to explain it to her. Hell, I had a hard time believing it myself.

I can admit that my relationship, if that's what it could be called with Bree, had stepped over the boundaries, become personal rather than professional. I take full responsibility for the fact that I had opened up to her when I shouldn't, when I knew what she wanted. And I had let her kiss me, on more than one occasion, and I had kissed her back. It was nice to feel needed, to feel wanted.

But she wasn't Talli.

She would never be Talli.

So when she would say that she loved me, I would tell her what she already knew—I love Talli, and I couldn't, I wouldn't do that to her. As time wore on, though, and I waited in vain for Talli to make the time for us, my resolve was wearing thin. It was no excuse for my behavior, though… not when Bree and I were in Texas and she told me Talli called to cancel, again…

That was the first time that I initiated it.

The first and only time that I kissed her.

She wanted more, and I knew it, but I told her once again that I couldn't. I had to go home; I had to find out what was going on, I had to know if Talia still wanted to be with me. If the answer was 'no', I was going to have to deal with that in my own way, but I had to know before anything more happened. So, Bree had left and I held on to my resolve, telling myself that my answers would be waiting for me at home.

I sank down along the hallway, sitting on the floor, remembering that ache in my chest when I had walked in to that empty house. No children running around, no Talia chasing them… just a note to Linda that they were going to Ohio, and would be back on Tuesday.

In two days.

Further away than Texas, for longer than they would have been in Texas with me.

God, it hurt. It hurt so much to know. Hell, I almost chided myself for telling Bree 'no' all of those times. At least I could have been getting laid this whole time, right? Instead of waiting for the woman that I loved to give a damn about me again. No, I knew better. I couldn't do that to her, to us.

I was actually crying there at that kitchen table, my heart lying in shards at my feet, my pride and spirit broken. I felt a hand touch my shoulder and I startled, looking up quickly. "Talli?"

"I think you know better."

Bree was there, right in front of me, as she had been for months. I could smell the lingering scent of cigarette smoke as she ran her hand through my hair. I hesitated as she pulled me close, wiping my eyes and pushing her back. "What are you doing here?" I remember asking her.

"I'm here for you, of course," she'd replied. She sat in the chair beside me, and that was when I noticed that she was barely dressed at all. She was in a camisole, no bra, and thong panties.

"Where the hell…"

"The rest of my clothes are in the bedroom," she purred into my ear, her hand snaking down between my legs. I swore silently, damning my body for having the nerve to respond. "Hey, even if you… say you don't want this now..." She smirked as she stroked my erection. "The least you could do is walk up there with me while I go get them."

"Bree..."

"Hey, you don't have to say that you don't want to anymore. I know better." She pulled back and walked away, and knowing that she was making her way up to my and Talli's bedroom made my stomach take a dive.

"Bree, wait."

I was going to offer to get her clothes for her, but as I rounded the corner, I saw her on the stairs, removing her camisole as she continued up them. Her small breasts were in my full view, and I felt my body twitch slightly. 'No... no, don't do this,' that little voice in my head was saying, and I was going to listen to it.

I really was.

I walked into my bedroom, my eyes adjusting to the dim candlelight—candles, everywhere. Roses scattered about, rose petals on the bed... my and Talli's bed... the bed that Talia hadn't shared with me in months. My jaw clenched as I looked around at the carefully laid out scene. "How..."

"I have my ways." Bree sauntered up to me, her hands moving to unbutton my shirt. "Welcome home, Jase," she said as she peered up at me before she began leaving wet kisses on my chest as she removed my shirt.

Oh... fuck, it had been too long. My entire body was screaming for release that alone time in a hot shower just wasn't taking care of anymore. I couldn't suppress the groan that tore from my throat as she pulled me into a kiss, and I admit it—I kissed her back. More than one kiss even, as my hands trailed up her back holding her against me, stopping just short of pushing her back.

To hell with it.

I couldn't pretend that Talia wanted me, or us. My own wife slept down the hall in our youngest daughter's room, and yet here was Bree right in front of me, completely willing.

Completely...without a doubt... willing.

Before I knew it, I was down to my boxer briefs, tangled in the sheets with Bree, who still had her thong panties on. I hadn't made the slightest move to remove them, I was far too busy having a mental wrestling match with myself.

"Fuck," I muttered through gritted teeth as she began sucking on my neck. I moaned, grabbing her wrists and pinning them above her head as I rolled us over together. I was nipping at her neck as she moved underneath me, her small frame so, so different...

This should be Talli... oh... God, this should be Talli...

"Jase, don't be so rough."

I stopped suddenly, her whine piercing straight through me.

What the hell was I doing?

I let go of her wrists and slid over where I was propped on my side. I knew my eyes were wide as I stared down at Bree, my body finally admitting what my heart knew all along.

I didn't want her.

I wanted my wife back.

"I mean," she continued, turning towards me, "I realize it's been a long time for you, but..."

"I can't do this, Bree," I cut her off, my breathing still just a bit ragged.

"Of course..."

"Any of it," I continued. "This... this is wrong, this shouldn't be happening."

"Who are you going to do this with? Your *wife*?"

"Look, I know... I know that I've done things that... that she may never forgive me for, but if I don't..." I placed a hand on her shoulder to stop her from pressing up against me again. "Bree, you told me once that you understand how much she means to me, how much my family means to me."

"Whatever, Jase," she said, rolling her eyes. "Look, if it's that important to you, I suppose you can be rough."

"Fuck, Bree, you don't get it!" I don't know why I was talking in such hushed tones, but it was as if I wasn't ready to admit to myself what had almost happened.

There was something about the way her eyes were darting to whatever was going on behind me, and before I knew it she had grabbed my shoulder, catching me by surprise, rolling us over as she pulled my face to hers. My hands were braced on the pillow on either side of her head as she forcefully kissed me, moaning as she did so, moving suggestively up against me. There was just no way in hell... no way I was going to change my mind. Not when...

"What's wrong with Daddy?" I heard Baby Girl's voice.

Oh.

Fuck.

Damn it, damn it, DAMN IT! What the hell?

I pushed the covers back quickly as I stood up, my heart hammering in my chest. I started to go after her, then realized that she probably would be pissed if I walked out there in only my boxer briefs. I felt myself breaking out into a cold sweat as I grabbed my jeans and pulled them on.

"You know, it's probably no use to,"

"Don't," I snapped at Bree. "Just... don't, okay?"

A million thoughts raced through my mind as I bounded down those stairs. I heard the television on in Talli's room and I hurried down the hall. My hands were shaking, my stomach in knots... she had to listen. She had to hear me out.

Would she even care?

I stopped short as I saw our children in there, slightly glassy-eyed, probably from the plane ride. Elizabeth ran over to give me a quick hug and kiss. "Are you okay, Daddy?"

"I'm fine," I lied to her, feeling my face turn a deep shade of red. God, this was never something they should have seen either...

"Mommy's rolyl in the kitchen," Elizabeth announced as she walked back over to sit by Emily, who as per usual didn't acknowledge my presence. Michael smiled and waved at me before I walked out of the room, begging the tears to stay away.

Maybe... maybe she would listen now. Maybe her eyes would be open, maybe she would care enough to fight.

But I was wrong.

And now here I sat alone in this huge fucking house looking over all the plans for Emily's birthday party, wondering what the hell would I say to Talia when I picked up our kids for the first time tonight. Should I just smile and say, "Hey! Guess what! I never fucked her. Gee, wanna come home now?"

Yeah, that would go over like a lead balloon.

I had long decided, though, that it really didn't matter whether or not she knew. The fact was I had crossed that line, whether I went through with it or not... and I would have to live with that for the rest of my life.

CHAPTER 6

TALLI

"How many times do I have to tell you?" I asked Elizabeth as I hurried around trying to straighten up. "It's not time yet."

"Are you sure he's coming, Mommy?" she asked for about the millionth time.

'For your sake, baby, I hope so,' I thought to myself before answering, "Yes."

"Is he staying?" Michael asked, and I sighed.

"No, he's not staying," I tried to patiently explain. "He's coming to pick you kids up, to spend time with you."

"Are we going back home?" Elizabeth asked, and I bit my bottom lip to keep from snapping that I was not welcome there. I didn't want to answer and listen to the two of them whine; instead, I busied myself by making sure Emily's diaper bag was fully packed.

"Why are you cleaning?" Michael asked as he followed behind me after I'd finished with Emily's bag. "Is it for Daddy?"

Oh... fuck, was it? No... no, emphatically not.

"It's because you kids won't pick up after yourselves, Mr. Twenty Questions."

"And to express Daddy," Elizabeth piped up.

"It's impress," I corrected her, "and I am not, young lady."

"Sure you are," she said as she flopped on the couch, stretching her feet out, the same way Jase always did. "Or you wouldn't have called me 'young lady'."

"Elizabeth," I began, but was interrupted by the buzzer.

"It's Daddy!" Michael exclaimed, running over to the buzzer and jumping up and down. Elizabeth had joined him before I'd even made my way across the room, and I motioned for them to settle down so I could answer.

I hesitated with my finger a millimeter from that button. How could I be so unsure of what to say?

The buzzer rang again, and Elizabeth immediately pushed her way in front of me and placed her finger on the talk button. "Daddy?" she asked, ignoring the look I was giving her.

"Hi, Baby Girl."

Oh... the chills that passed through me with the sound of his voice.

I rubbed my arms absentmindedly just before I pushed the button allowing him access to the building, trying in vain to calm my nerves. 'You can do this... you can face him, showing no sign of weakness,' I was saying to myself. I looked down at my clothes, tugging at my shirt slightly, knowing there was no way I'd look half as little or glamorous as that fucking Barbie doll, when I noticed the glitter from my left hand.

My wedding rings.

I still couldn't take them off, something in my mind kept telling me to wait. It was as if I knew the moment they were off, in any kind of permanent fashion, that there was no going back.

Who the hell was I kidding? There was already no going back.

I grabbed my sweat jacket off the back of the couch, making sure the sleeves covered my hand and looked over the apartment once more, swearing silently at the lifetime that it was seeming to take him to get up to the tenth floor. Seriously, were the elevators that slow?

My pulse had increased significantly, remembering the last time we had been face to face. I don't think I'll ever forget the glare he'd shot me as he walked into the kitchen the day I left, when I'd referred to that house as a prison. It had been, ever since I'd walked in to see him in our bed fucking that tramp. It was all I saw at every turn, as I would remember all the times she'd been at our house over the past year, putting up the façade of being my friend. I'd felt uneasy from day one, and I had even brought it up with Jase. I have no idea why he'd bothered to tell me that nothing was going on. Why not just admit it? Why not tell me that she was the reason he'd lost all interest in me? Why drag it out, hurt me even more?

I had my suspicions of why he'd hung on, though... two of them nearly knocked him over when he stepped through the door that I held open for him. I turned away from them as the door clicked shut, stifling a sob that had been building up. I wiped my eyes hastily, walking past them towards Elizabeth's room, where Emily was quietly playing with her favorite stuffed toy.

"Hey," Jase called out, his voice soft, and I turned instinctively towards him as I had thousands of times before. As our eyes met, my whole world seemed to stop for just one brief moment. He looked so tired, a bit haggard, dark circles prominently displayed. His eyes were shining with unshed tears as he held our two oldest children close to him. A small smile—so quick that if I hadn't been studying every minute detail of him I would have missed it—crossed his face, and I felt my heart constrict. There was no stopping the slight flutter of a smile that tugged at the corners of my mouth, or the butterflies in my stomach as he looked down quickly, then back at me, peering upwards from his kneeling position, his features relaxing.

Don't fall for it... don't fall for it

He had this way, though, of putting me right under that spell of his... that spell that had me mesmerized before I'd ever gotten to know him. I knew I had to stay guarded, I knew he'd worm his way back in to hurt me even more, all it would take was...

"Where's Bree?" Michael asked, looking around. "She's always with you, Daddy."

I felt my face flush and I spun around quickly to go get Emily as Jase said softly, "She's not here, Little Man."

"She's not coming over, is she?" Elizabeth whined. I cringed as I waited for his answer, trying to seem inconspicuous as I slowed my pace.

"Nope, Baby Girl, it's just me."

Did he sound cheerful when he said that? No... no, it was a figment of my imagination, just as it was merely a fluke that he'd spoken a little louder. No, maybe that wasn't a fluke. Maybe he was just avoiding a fight, to make it easier for the children.

That *had* to be it.

"Hi, Princess," I said as I entered the room where Emily sat, studying her stuffed puppy as if she'd never seen anything more interesting in her life. She glanced up at me, her way of acknowledging my presence, before returning her attention back to her treasure. "Come on... it's time." I picked her up, placing her on my hip, bracing myself before I walked back into the living room where I could hear Jase talking with Elizabeth and Michael.

"Is this really your old couch, Mommy?" Elizabeth asked excitedly. I stole a quick glance at Jase, whose gaze had dropped to the floor, a slight blush touching his cheeks. My heart caught in my throat as I remembered all of the times Jase and I had laid intimately on that couch.

I remembered our wrestling match over the bowl of popcorn, ending in a kiss that curled my toes just before he told me he was at my house because he wanted to be there.

Then there was the night he'd brought me home from Lisa's house, where we'd brought each other to complete ecstasy.

I remembered vividly the night he came back to Ohio, the night I'd agreed to move in with him, the way I yanked him in the door by his shirt and we'd made love with absolute abandon without so much as saying hello to each other...

"You taking Em?" Michael asked, bringing me back to the present. I stepped closer to Jase, keeping Emily on my hip, where she eyed Jase curiously. I studied his face, the hope etched in his features as he reached for our youngest child, the barely masked disappointment when she turned her head away, clutching to me.

"I'll help take her to the car," I said softly, and he nodded.

"Yeah... yeah, thanks," he muttered as he looked around. "Do you um... their stuff..."

"Oh, I have it all together," I said quickly. "Here... Elizabeth, get your bag. And show Daddy where..."

"Wanna see my room, Daddy?" Elizabeth piped up before I could finish asking her to show Jase where Michael's bag was.

"Maybe some other time; I'm sure he's busy," I said.

"It's right this way," Elizabeth continued, dragging Jase by the hand.

"Me, too! See mine, too!" Michael added, running behind them.

Jase looked back at me with a slight shrug, as if to say he was sorry, and I almost laughed.

Just... almost.

I stood there in the hallway, leaning against the wall, my heart aching as I observed them. Emily pushed against my chest, so I set her down to chase after her brother and sister, still eyeing Jase warily.

"It's not as big," Elizabeth was saying. "But... see? Aunt Jaden helped me."

"Did she, now?" I always loved the tone he used with them—so patient, so loving.

"Mommy did Michael's room, after Jackie put up our beds," Elizabeth continued.

"We have no beds at home," Michael spoke up, sounding a bit worried.

"Don't have," Elizabeth corrected him sharply.

"Baby girl, what have you been told?" Jase said to her before I had the chance to. "And you do have beds there."

I blinked in surprise, wondering to myself which one of his assistants he'd sent out for that chore.

"That's not our home no more," Elizabeth said with a pout, stomping past them and shooting me a hateful glare as she made her way to the living room. Emily, not understanding her sister was upset, merely giggled and tried to mimic her, her diaper crinkling as she chased after Elizabeth.

"Elizabeth Christine..."

"Daddy, see my room?" Michael asked, his voice small, stopping Jase from chasing after her.

"I'll get her," I said, the spell broken. Jase nodded at me, then pasted the smile back on his face for Michael's benefit as I walked out to the living room.

"Is he ready to go?" she asked, still glaring at me.

"Elizabeth," I began sitting beside her, "you need to straighten it up. I know you're upset, but you know better than to act like that. Don't start this weekend off on the wrong foot and have it ruin your time with Daddy, okay?"

"I'm not talking to you right now."

"You don't have to, but you will listen to me. Your bag is together, and if all you're going to do is pout then you can wait right there in that spot for your dad." I turned before I caught her rolling her eyes at me, which I was sure she was doing. I didn't need to lose my temper, not with him there. I was already a bundle of nerves as it was.

"Is that neat?" Michael asked, dragging Jase by his fingers.

"Yeah, it is, Little Man," Jase replied.

"You need to see Em's room!" Michael exclaimed, dragging him towards the room that Emily shared with me.

"No, he…" I started, but it was too late. The light was on, revealing Emily's crib in the corner, and my bed—the same bed that Jase and I had shared many nights in before I'd moved to L.A.—adorned the same comforter set that had been on the night we'd broken the old headboard.

I saw the slight twitch in Jase's jaw as he looked over the room before he abruptly turned away, rubbing the back of his neck. I could tell my cheeks were red just from the heat as I recalled the night we'd shared in that bed when he'd professed his love for me while we danced in the rain.

But love is fleeting.

"So… she's in your room, huh?"

Of course he wouldn't be thinking about anything but that. And his mood had most definitely changed, darkened. His words were biting and cold, his eyes hard as he glared at me.

"Yes, Jase, just as always I'm trying to be considerate of everyone else who might like some sleep."

"Damn, Talli, she's not our first! The other two cried during the night, too, remember? You soothe them, quiet them, put them back in their bed, in their own damn room."

"You're seriously going to speak to me this way?" I asked incredulously. "And you know Emily so well, don't you? Guess what, Jase, it's your turn now. Go on. Have at it. Have a wonderful weekend."

"I've obviously done this before, or did that slip your mind, too?" His voice was rising, along with my anger.

"You've been far too preoccupied to 'do this'," I said, adding air quotes around those last two words, "for quite some time."

"You have so much room to preach about being preoccupied."

"You haven't even bothered to get to know Emily!" I yelled at him. "You have never... never been close with her."

"And now it's selective memory. Nice."

"Stop!" Elizabeth's scream interrupted the argument leaving only Michael's sobs to fill the silence.

"Fuck," Jase muttered under his breath, pinching the bridge of his nose.

"Yeah, make another snarky comment about how I don't want this done in front of the children," I said in a harsh whisper as I moved closer to him. The glare he shot me should have brought me to my knees but I was far too angry to care.

"Cut the fucking umbilical cord so we can talk about this."

"Fuck you," I hissed between clenched teeth, then I smirked before adding, "Oh, wait, that's Bree's job, isn't it?"

"Damn it, Talia, I didn't..."

"Please," Elizabeth cried, latching herself to Jase's leg, interrupting whatever he was going to say. My heart was hammering in my ears as we stood there glaring at each other, so close all I would have to do was reach out and..

"I'm sorry, Baby Girl," he said softly as he stepped back from me and looked down at her tear-streaked face. "We're both... sorry." It was only then that he looked into my eyes, almost as if he was daring me to say I wasn't with our children standing right there.

Gah, sometimes he was such an asshole!

"Of course," I said, turning my smile to our children.

"Let's go," Jase said to her. "You and Michael help with the bags, okay?"

"Come here, Em," I said, holding my hands out.

"I've got this, Talia," Jase said sharply. Emily protested, her bottom lip sticking out and quivering as he picked her up.

"Jase..."

"She's my daughter too, Talia."

His gaze was unwavering, unfaltering even as Emily's cry pierced through the air. He turned around, announcing, "Round em up! Do we have everything?"

"Emily's puppy," Elizabeth said under her breath as she ran back to her room, returning with Emily's stuffed dog and running towards Jase. He stood there holding Emily in one arm, my door with the other. "Bye, Mommy!" she called out as she ran into the hallway.

I jumped as Michael threw his arms around my leg. "Love you, Mommy!"

"I love you, too," was all I was able to say as my throat felt as if it would close at any moment. I bit my bottom lip as Emily cried out once more for me before Jase walked out, the door shutting with a bang behind him.

I curled up on the couch, my knees drawn up to my chest, tears falling freely. It hurt so badly... between the children leaving, Emily's screams, my fight with Jase... I don't know what hurt the worst. I wasn't fearful or worried any more than normal; Jase is a good father. I knew they were in good hands. He's always been so wonderful, kind, loving, and patient with them, or at least he had been. Towards the end he would snap when Emily threw one of her fits or the older children would fight, and I sat there thinking selfishly he was going to have his hands full this weekend.

But... they were gone. Family time with Daddy no longer included me.

That's what hurt.

I wiped my eyes, the silence of that condo enveloping me. I should enjoy this, shouldn't I? I mean... wouldn't this call for a girls night of some sort? Oh, right... Jaden had already gone back to Groves Point. Tish and Cass lived all the way back in Ohio. Sondra worked with my soon to be ex-husband, so that would have been awkward at best. The girls from work were exactly that: girls from work. I wasn't friends with any of them. I'd been forced into a rather sheltered life, learning the hard way that there were people out there that couldn't be trusted.

With a resigned sigh, I pushed myself off the couch, taking my first uninterrupted bath in months only to lie in bed and cry myself to sleep.

JASE

Twenty-two minutes. It was exactly twenty-two minutes from my garage to the parking lot of the building full of condos that my wife and kids now called home. I know this because that's how long it took me during my dry run earlier after Jaden had left. I knew it was safe to drive by then, that Talia had been at work. I also knew from Jackie that the kids had gone with her to the daycare center. I wondered briefly how Emily had reacted to that, smiling to myself as I thought about how I never dreamed I would miss hearing her cry.

I do, though. I miss her cry, I miss Elizabeth's snark and bullying of Michael, I miss Michael's quick retaliations that would send Elizabeth away with screams of her own. I miss them running around, spilling their drinks, drawing where they shouldn't, leaving their toys all over. I miss Emily calling me 'Dase', and I miss Talia correcting her, even though it's completely in vain.

I miss Talia.

I miss her smile—that beautiful, sparkling smile, the way her entire face lights up with it. I miss those beautiful blue eyes, how they show every emotion. I miss her curls framing her gorgeous face... hell, I even miss her straightening her hair, how soft and silky it was. I miss her laugh, the way her eyes squint when she laughs really hard. I miss her voice, how soothing it is to me, how she can change my mood by simply hearing her. I miss how she would tell me to not worry about her, even though she knew I would. I miss talking to her, I miss my confidante, I miss knowing every detail, and sharing every part of my life with her. I miss the smell of her—that sweet, intoxicating scent of jasmine. I miss the feel of her, those curves underneath my hands, underneath my body, those lips...

I shook my head, glancing at the clock again. I'd been sitting in this parking lot for nearly ten minutes and I still had a little over ten minutes before it was time to pick up the kids. Even though I knew it was only twenty-two minutes from my house to hers, I still left forty five minutes early, in case of traffic of any other unforeseen problem, such as my nerves.

One glance in the rearview mirror showed what I already knew; I looked as bad as I felt. I'd spent every night since they'd left on that Italian leather sofa in the room I'd put together for Talia. It was the only room left untouched, left the same. It was the only room where I felt any peace.

I rubbed my face roughly, deciding now was as good a time as ever. If Talia was going to refuse to let them go just because I was early, then it was her cross to bear. I felt as if my feet were made of lead, it was so difficult to walk up to that front entryway. I was comforted just a little by knowing it was a secure building, especially with them being exactly twenty-two minutes away from me.

My hands were shaking slightly as I reached for that button. Why did this have to be so hard? And what would I say anyway? Would she bring them down? Would she want me to come up? What if she did want me up there… would she let me in?

Fuck, could I handle seeing her again?

I hit the buzzer, waiting for her to acknowledge and let me in, biting my nonexistent nails as I did so. What was taking so long? Maybe she didn't hear the buzzer. Or… or maybe she was angry because I was early. My impatience won over and I hit the buzzer again, wondering if maybe the system was malfunctioning.

"Daddy?"

I felt tears spring up in my eyes as Elizabeth's voice filtered through that tiny speaker.

"Hi, Baby Girl," I said, my heart filling with love. I heard the tell-tale buzz of the secure door being unlocked, and I pushed my way into the building, wiping my eyes as I did so. I felt like my heart would come straight out of my chest as I remembered the last time I'd seen Talia. Did she really think our home had been a prison? That hurt so fucking badly, hearing how unhappy she'd been. The selfish side of me kept saying she knew what she was signing up for before she ever left Ohio. The other side of me, the side that still admits how desperately in love with her I am, ached for her, longed to give her and our children some semblance of normalcy. I should have done anything to make her happy… if that was really what she had wanted.

But no. No… what she wanted was out, and there was nothing I could do or say to make her stay. I couldn't force her to, I couldn't even bring myself to ask her if she could ever love me again.

I was tapping my foot nervously as the elevator made its way to the tenth floor. The crumpled piece of paper in my hand showed the number 1004, which I'd memorized but kept rechecking. I just wanted to see them again... all of them. I just wanted to hold them close to me, never let them go.

The elevator came to a stop on floor ten, the doors opening slowly. I stepped out into the quiet hallway, standing there momentarily while I gathered my nerve. So close... they're so, so very close...

I was glancing at the doorways, the numbers on them showing that Talia's condo would be on the left towards the end of the hallway. When I finally reached it, my hands were visibly shaking, my palms sweating, my heart hammering fast and hard. I traced my fingers over the gold numbers on the white door, telling myself it was now or never before knocking, chewing on my thumbnail as I waited for the door to open.

I saw a flash of Talia's sherry curls as she swung the door open, standing behind it mostly out of my view. I shyly stepped in, my heart jumping into my throat as Elizabeth and Michael ran forward, throwing their arms around me.

Oh... god... it felt so good to kneel down and cradle the both of them in my arms. Elizabeth had her face tucked in the crook of my neck and I could smell that baby shampoo that Talia had used for her ever since we brought her home. Michael was clinging to me, his ear resting up against my heart—his favorite spot ever since he was a baby. My eyes burned with unshed tears as I held them, reminiscent of when I'd finally come home from my last tour.

Talia was walking away from us, her hips swaying softly just as they always did. I felt that familiar dip in the pit of my stomach... she was there... right there... I just wanted to see her face...

"Hey," I said softly, hoping it was loud enough for her to hear but not so loud that she'd think I was yelling at her. She turned around and my heart stopped...

She was so beautiful.

Her cheeks had a touch of pink in them, setting off her eyes all the more. If I had been close enough, I would have tucked that stray curl behind her ear just like I used to. She looked tired, and just a little anxious as if she'd been hurrying to get the kids ready. I tried to suppress the smile that crept up on me as I remembered her running around the house, chasing after the kids while trying to get ready... what I wouldn't give to see it again.

She...smiled at me! It was small, so very quick, but... just a glimpse of the girl I used to know, the girl I fell in love with...

I looked down quickly to compose myself, then glanced back up at her, completely mesmerized.

My Talli...

"Where's Bree?" Michael asked, letting go slightly to look around.

Fuck.

"She's always with you, Daddy," he continued as he squirmed away from me.

Fuck, had she been? I mean, we'd been so busy with the writing, then the recording, then beginning to promote her album. Nearly every time I'd been home, she was there. Had there been so much as one day without her presence, or a call of some sort?

Had I really told Talia she was no threat to us?

Talia's face turned to stone as she spun and walked away. With a sigh, I turned to Michael as I still held Elizabeth to me. "She's not here, Little Man," I said to him.

Elizabeth looked into my eyes... oh her eyes are so similar to Talia's... and stuck her lip out as she asked, "She's not coming over, is she?"

How could I have been so blind to how much my time had been monopolized by Bree? I know I'd seen a lot of it as work, but some of it I can now admit was out of spite. Why...why had I been so blind to the damage I was doing?

I took a deep breath and smiled, answering her question. "Nope, Baby Girl, it's just me."

You hear that, Talia? It's just me.

Elizabeth plopped herself on the couch with her shoes as she rambled on about how happy she was that we wouldn't be interrupted, and as much as I tried to listen, my attention had been drawn elsewhere. This living room... this whole living room... everything in it had come from Ohio.

There was the coffee table that I used to prop my feet up on all the time. The papasan chair had seen its better days, but I could still see

Talia curled up in it, reading a book. The floor lamp leaned just a little to the left, just as it had ever since we accidentally knocked it over.

And the couch...

I inhaled sharply as I remembered Talia lying there breathless, begging me to not make her wait...

"Daddy, what's wrong?" Michael asked. He always did catch on to everyone's moods.

"Oh, nothing, nothing," I reassured him. "That's... um, Mommy had this couch when she lived in Ohio."

"The same couch?" Michael asked, his eyes wide. "Wow, that's old."

"Easy, Little Man... it's not that old."

"Did you know Mommy then?" Elizabeth asked, and my heart ached. I knew her... or I thought I did...

"Yeah," I replied softly. I saw Talia approaching, holding Emily on her hip, entranced by how much they looked alike, how beautiful they were.

"Is this really your old couch, Mommy?" I heard Elizabeth ask. I dropped my gaze to the floor, blushing as the thoughts of what I wished I could do with Talia on that couch right now. She loved it when I would grab that arm rest with one hand, using it for leverage as I would push harder, deeper inside of her...

"You taking Em?" Michael asked. I brought my eyes back up, resting them on that little girl, repressing a smile at the look on her face. At the same time, though, it was almost sad how she stared at me as if I didn't belong. Had I really damaged our relationship that badly? I couldn't help the tour, that was part of the package, but I cursed myself and that stubborn streak of mine. I should have tried harder. I mean, Emily used to be happy to see me. I was the first person she'd smiled at, the first one she'd cried for when I'd left the room. 'Maybe she would remember ,' I thought as I reached for her. Instead, she turned away, holding on to Talia.

How could I have let this happen? It was so plain to see, so obvious that my relationships with my children had suffered every bit as much as my relationship with Talia had. There had to be some way to make this right, with all of them.

"I'll help you take her to the car," Talia said, and I nodded without looked at her. I just couldn't, not right at that moment.

"Yeah...yeah, thanks," I said. I was looking around, anything to keep from getting lost in her eyes again, and began stammering like an idiot. "Do you... um..." *Do you want to talk about this now? Now that the tempers are in check, now that we've both had time to think?*

No...no, I couldn't.

"Their...stuff?" I asked.

Jeez, Warner! Get it together! This is your wife for fuck's sake!

"Oh, I have it all together," she said. Of course she would. She was asking Elizabeth to get her bag as Elizabeth walked over to me, her big blue eyes sparkling.

"Wanna see my room, Daddy?"

Did I really want to see how Talia had helped them all move on with their new lives away from me?

"Maybe some other time," Talia told her. "I'm sure he's busy."

I bit my lip to keep from snapping at her that I wasn't too busy for our children, but what difference would it have made? Elizabeth was already dragging me by the hand, and Michael was hot on our heels demanding that I see his room, too. I looked back at Talia, shrugging slightly as our oldest drug me into her pink and white room, her bed and bookshelves set up neatly, that bedspread that had so many nights been on the floor of our bedroom when she'd had a nightmare was pulled up over her mattress, her pillows all aligned just so. Elizabeth was all about the neat and orderly... a place for everything and everything in its place. That was not a trait she'd gotten from me.

"I have it set up... I tried to... like my room at home," she said, proudly showing where all of her books were lined up on their shelves. "It's not as big... but see? Aunt Jaden helped me."

Of course Jaden did. Jaden always flew to Talia's side whenever anything was wrong, or right for that matter. And I know she had confided all about me, all about what she'd seen, and...

"Did she, now?" I asked, using the same voice I always did with her, with all of them. Just because I was falling to pieces didn't mean they had to suffer any more than they already were.

"Mommy did Michael's room," Elizabeth continued, "after Jackie put up our beds."

I didn't know whether to laugh or get pissed off at him... no, no, I couldn't get pissed off. They were like family to Jackie, too. I knew that he'd come over to help; he'd probably told me he was going to, and it probably slipped right past me just like everything else had.

"We have no beds at home," Michael whined.

"Don't have," Elizabeth snapped.

Without even blinking an eye, I said, "Baby Girl, what have you been told?" I winced inwardly but wanted to continue before Talia could say anything about me correcting them in her house. "And you do have beds there." I'd seen to that myself, not that Talia would ever believe me if I bothered to tell her.

Elizabeth, in true drama queen fashion, began to pout. "That's not our home no more." She stomped out of her room, past Talia who I hadn't realized was standing in the hallway, and Emily—who had at some point wandered into the room quietly—was running after her sister.

"Elizabeth Christine," I called out.

"Daddy, see my room?" Michael asked me, stopping me from chasing after his older sister. I took a deep breath to steady myself.

"I'll get her," Talia said, and I nodded at her before pasting a smile on my face for our son's benefit. He was as proud as could be to take me to his little room, his race car bed set up in the far corner away from the door, just like he always wanted it at home although I never knew why. His toys were haphazardly thrown into his toy box, a few of his shirts were hanging out of his drawers. Yeah, she may have quickly thrown his stuff together knowing I was coming over, but this was definitely my boy's room.

"I'm getting a night light soon, since I brokeded mine."

"Broke," I corrected him softly, smiling at him.

"I know," he replied, shrugging as if it were no big deal. He led me back out in the hall. "But is that neat?"

"Yeah, it is Little Man," I said, grinning at him. I had absolutely no clue what he was asking about, but it didn't matter. He could ramble on for hours about nothing so long as he was there and I'd be happy.

"You need to see Em's room!" he exclaimed, grabbing my hand and dragging me to the other end of the hall. Em's... room... she had her own room? Talia was going to try, just like I'd argued with her? My heart was full of hope as Michael flung that door open and turned the light switch on.

Oh... God.

No, this... this was Talia's room. There was our....her bed. It was her bed, even if we had shared it all those weeks in Ohio. And tucked in the corner was Emily's crib, right where Talia could reach her in a moment's notice.

Damn it. Damn it... fuck... why...

Why did it have to hurt so bad, seeing where Talia slept at night? Why did my chest ache at the thought of her here, curled up underneath covers that we had once been entangled in? Why... No... no, I couldn't let her see how much she'd gotten to me, how much this hurt...

And Emily's crib. Right there in the corner. She couldn't stand to be anywhere near me, and she'd used Emily as an excuse back at our home. But here? Seriously? Who was she trying to avoid here?

My jaw was set tight and I began rubbing the back of my neck telling myself over and over... don't do it. Don't do it. Things have settled down, don't start an argument. But did I listen?

"So...she's in your room, huh?"

Of course I didn't listen. And I couldn't stop the cold, hard stare that I shot at her, the wounds reopening as I remembered how much it hurt for her to use our own daughter as an excuse to stay away from me.

She snapped back quickly, "Yes, Jase, just as always I'm trying to be considerate of everyone else who might like some sleep."

What the fuck ever, sweetheart. I couldn't stop myself, couldn't control my words as the anger came spewing forth. "Fuck, Talli, she's not our first! The other two cried during the night, too, remember? You soothe them, quiet them, put them back in their bed, in their own damn room."

"You're seriously going to speak to me this way?" she asked, and I felt my blood pressure rise. "And you know Emily so well, don't you? Guess what, Jase, it's your turn now. Go on. Have at it. Have a wonderful weekend."

Something inside of me just… snapped at those words. Who the fuck was she to say I didn't know my own fucking daughter? Emily's first three months were spent mostly in my arms before I had to go back on the road. "I've obviously done this before, or did that slip your mind, too?" I asked, my voice much louder than it had been before.

"You've been far too preoccupied to 'do this'", she said, emphasizing the last two words with those fucking little air quotes, "for quite some time."

My eyes narrowed as I glared at her hissing, "You have so much room to preach about being preoccupied."

"You haven't even bothered to get to know Emily!" she yelled. "You have never… never been close with her."

Who the fuck did she think took care of Emily while she slept her days away? Who took Emily in to her when she was hungry? Who bathed her, who dressed her, who rocked her and sang her to sleep? It was me. Emily had been even more of a Daddy's girl than Elizabeth had been, damn it! I felt a muscle in my jaw twitch and I yelled back, "And now it's selective memory… nice."

"Stop!" Elizabeth's piercing scream halted Talia, who had her mouth open ready for a retort, but we stood there glaring at each other, our chests rising and falling quickly in our war of wills. I could hear Michael crying softly, and the guilt once again began to set in.

"Fuck," I muttered, pinching the bridge of my nose. Fuck, fuck, fuck… Talia was right, they shouldn't see this.

"Yeah, make another snarky comment about how I don't want this done in front of the children," Talia whispered harshly as she moved closer to me. And I knew that… I knew she was right, now that I was seeing it for myself, but for the first time… the first time in I couldn't remember how long we were talking about what was wrong, and I didn't mean to be so fucking hateful, but I couldn't stop myself.

"Cut the fucking umbilical cord so we can talk about this." I didn't mean to say it like that, I swear I didn't. I just meant to tell her that we should drop the kids off somewhere and just… talk. Just talk, even if it involved yelling and screaming and crying because we needed it.

"Fuck you," she muttered between clenched teeth, then she smirked hatefully. I knew what was coming. "Oh, wait… that's Bree's job, isn't it?"

"Damn it, Talia, I didn't…"

"Please!" Elizabeth was clinging to my leg, stopping me from spilling everything to Talia. Now wasn't the time or the place, but it had to be done. I had to be honest with her. Let her call me a liar, at least my conscious would be clear. At least I could say I'd done everything I could. But not now… not now…

I stepped away from Talia and looked down at our daughter, whose tears broke my heart just a little more. "I'm sorry, Baby Girl. We're both… sorry." I looked back up at Talia, silently letting her know this wasn't finished.

"Of course," she said, doing her complete about-face and smiling at our children. Leave it to Talia to pretend like nothing was wrong.

"Let's go," I said to Elizabeth. "You and Michael help with the bags, okay?"

"Come here, Em," I heard Talia say, but I stopped her abruptly.

"I've got this, Talia." I picked up Emily, who looked back at her mother with her bottom lip quivering.

"Jase,"

"She's my daughter too, Talia," I snapped, and immediately felt guilty as Emily began to cry. Who the hell was Talia to say I couldn't do this, though? Just watch me… just fucking watch me.

I turned around announcing to the kids it was time to go, and Elizabeth was the dutiful sister who ran to get Emily's favorite stuffed animal. I stood there, holding the door open, avoiding looking at Talia, trying my best to not let Emily's screams get to me as I held her with my other arm. Elizabeth and Michael were quick with their goodbyes, and Emily screamed just a little louder as we walked out into the hallway. I couldn't look back; if I had seen her face as I walked away with our children, I would have crumbled. I know I would have, because I knew how it felt. And while part of me felt vindicated that now she knew what it was like to watch her children leave, the other part of me wanted to go right back to that door, beg her to come with us.

Just one last weekend.

One last shot at being a family.

Please.

But I didn't do it; I don't know if it was anger or my stubborn streak that kept me going, but I had those children secured in their seats and was on the road back to my house.

Twenty-two minutes. It was exactly twenty-two minutes from that parking lot to the garage of the house that no longer felt like a home to me.

And I cried the whole way.

CHAPTER 7

TALLI

I never dreamed in a million years I would consider it too quiet to sleep. Apparently my body entered panic mode some time close to midnight when there were no diaper crinkles, no one else's breathing.

And when I woke up to an empty condo, my heart hurt. It wasn't entirely for the reasons I'd figured, either... it was painful to be by myself for the first time in years, sure. But right at that moment, of all the things I could have been thinking or feeling, instead I was wondering... was this what it felt like for Jase?

Was it this empty, this hollow in that house without our children running around?

I heard my cell phone ringing from its perch on the kitchen counter and I ran out to answer it, fearful that something had happened. I was short of breath when I picked up my phone, sighing as I saw Lisa's name on the display. For one brief moment, I considered not answering... but I knew if the shoe was on the other foot, if it was my ex-husband that had passed away...

I shook my head to clear it as I answered the phone. "Hello?"

"Oh... um... I was figuring this was going to voicemail," she said, and I had to laugh.

"Is that why you call at these ungodly hours?" I asked. "To get voicemail instead of talking to me?"

"No, I just... I couldn't sleep."

"Same here," I muttered.

"And I was worried about you," she added.

"Oh, I'm fine," I said with a wave of my hand that she couldn't see. "Don't worry about me."

"Talia, don't shut me out."

"No...no, Leesee, I just meant... I know you're having a hard time right now, dealing with Jack's death. You need to focus on you right now."

"I wanted to thank you for coming out here," she said softly. "I know you weren't close with him, or overly fond of him."

"Well, he was... no, no," I stopped myself. "I'm not going to say it. But regardless of your divorce, he still was... well, you were hurting when he died. And you're my sister, I'd do anything for you."

"I wasn't that distracted when you were here," she commented. "I noticed a lot of what was going on, like how disappointed you were when Jase didn't show."

The memory hit me like a sucker punch. Of course he didn't show. He'd taken the opportunity to play house—in my house... in OUR house—with that bleached blonde whore.

"And I feel so guilty," Lisa continued. "I know you had plans with Jase, that you and the kids were flying to Texas. Elizabeth sure pouted enough about that."

"Yeah... yeah she did," I said with a short laugh.

"Oh, she acts so much like you, Talli."

"I was never that dramatic," I disagreed.

"Right, and I was a virgin when I got married."

"I have enough of that visual burned into my brain by walking in on the two of you," I muttered, covering my eyes as if I could still see it. She laughed at my comment, apparently finding it much more humorous than I did.

"Hey, Talli?" she said suddenly.

"Hmm?"

"If you don't mind my prying... did he tell you why he didn't show?"

My face burned as I remembered that bitch's hands on my husband's face as they played tonsil hockey, and...

"No. No, he didn't," I replied.

"It just... I mean, I was talking about this with Eric,"

"Ah, Jase's biggest fan," I mumbled.

"...and he was saying that it... it just didn't seem like him. I mean, he said he'd be there, right?"

"No, I didn't speak with him," I answered as I absentmindedly played with a lighter on the counter. I really need to put this away.

"Did you check to see if he got his voicemail?"

"I didn't leave a voicemail."

"Well, if you didn't..."

"I spoke with Hooker Barbie," I cut her off.

"Who?"

"With... with Bree." I couldn't keep the disdain out of my voice when I said her name. "And once they knew I was gone, they took advantage of the situation."

"That's just... that's awful. Talli, I am so sorry."

"Why? You didn't do it." I was still messing with the lighter, flipping it over in my hand as I spoke.

"Talli... are you okay?"

"I'm fine," I repeated. "Don't worry about me."

"You just... you sound like..."

"Like what?" I demanded, perhaps a bit too forcefully.

"Like you're dead inside."

"Well you've been through a divorce. Were you Miss Mary Sunshine then?"

"Talia, I'm just trying to help," she said. "Have you talked to anyone?"

"About what?" I asked, my eyebrows furrowing together.

"Talia, I saw all of the unfilled prescriptions in your purse."

I grumbled to myself as I made a mental note to clean my purse out. "I don't need any of them."

"Anti-anxiety, anti-depressants, sleep aids..."

"Lisa, it really isn't any of your concern."

"...and the pamphlets on postpartum depression," she finished as I began to rub my temple.

"I'm a Nurse Practitioner," I reminded her. "Besides, Emily's almost a year old. I'm fine."

"Talia, postpartum depression is real... it's a real problem... a real... a real disease, if you will."

"Yeah, well, so is addiction," I snapped, my mouth firmly shutting into a thin line afterwards. Fuck... now Lisa would think...

"Talia... are you..." Her voice trailed off, and then she stated, "I'm coming to see you."

"Right," I agreed. "In two weeks, for Emily's party."

"No..."

"Lisa, I live in a small condo, and I work nearly every day between now and then," I cut her off. "I will see you in two weeks."

"I am worried about you, you know," she said softly. "You know that I love you, right?"

"Yeah... I know," I replied. "I love you, too. Listen... I have rounds tomorrow, so I need to try and sleep."

"Just promise me one thing."

"What's that?"

"That I can kick him in the balls at the party." As I threw my head back in laughter, she added, "Okay, you're laughing. That eases my mind a bit. Go get some sleep."

"What about you?" I asked. "Are you okay?"

"Oh, I'm fine," she sing-songed. "Don't worry about me."

"Fuck you, Lisa," I muttered.

I wish I could say I slept decently afterwards, but my mind wouldn't shut off. Really... I was so bothered being reminded how Jase never showed up for Jack's funeral. I mean, how could I have been any clearer? It was bad enough that Bree had answered his phone, which should have been my first clue that something was up. But he'd gotten every message I'd ever sent through her, and I was in such a hurry to pack and catch that plane, so I didn't think twice about it.

I was unnerved that at the mention of Jack's name, Bree knew it was Lisa's ex-husband and that neither Jase nor I thought very fondly of him. Seriously, how the hell was that any of her business? I just pushed all of it aside, choosing to believe that my husband would never hurt me in that way. So, when I told her that I needed Jase there, by my side, and she said "Of course, I understand," I took that to mean she'd let him know immediately. I have no reason to think she didn't tell him, especially with what I walked in on.

The more I dwelled on it, when I allowed myself to dwell on it, it wasn't just the fact that he was with someone else. It was... it was planned. It was set up to be romantic, not a... booty call, or whatever it is called these days. Not some fling. Not... not something spur of the moment. And it wasn't some elaborate set up for my benefit, either; if it was meant for me, it would have happened two days later.

She... she meant something to him. Being with her meant something.

And that's what hurt most of all.

JASE

"Princess, please... please sleep," I murmured in Emily's ear as she continued to cry. "You're so tired." *And so am I...* I glanced at my watch, shaking my head.

Midnight.

She had been crying for over an hour. I was bound and determined to do this my way; I knew I was right. I'd gone in to soothe her twice, but the last time I'd tried letting her cry just a little bit longer.

"You don't want to do that, Daddy," Elizabeth had said as she sleepily wandered out into the hall.

"It's okay, Baby Girl. I've got this," I'd replied to her. "Just go back to bed."

That was at eleven.

At fifteen after, Michael had whined that he couldn't sleep, so I promised him I'd go upstairs to get his baby sister.

Forty-five minutes later, and Emily was still inconsolable. At least she was letting me hold her by then. The first fifteen minutes she was throwing herself backwards, keeping her body stiff as she screamed as loudly as she could. When she finally willingly went into my arms, I figured it was a matter of time.

Apparently I was wrong.

By twelve thirty, after walking the floors with her, I began humming softly to her, no rhyme or reason really to it. She stilled, as if she was listening between her tiny sobs and gasps from crying for so long, as I felt one of her tiny hands start playing with the back of my hair. I placed a soft kiss on her damp forehead continuing to hum softly.

"Da's da song Mommy sings to her," Michael's voice behind me made me jump slightly.

"Little Man, what are you doing up?" I asked, trying to keep my voice low. Without saying a word, he pointed at Emily in my arms, who whined slightly until I started swaying from side to side. "Get back up to bed, Michael." He stuck out his bottom lip and shook his head 'no', his breathing picking up as the tears filled his eyes. "Come on... Little Man... don't cry, please..."

Michael turned slightly, burying his head in his arm that was resting on the table beside him as he began to cry.

Fuck me running.

That was enough to set Emily off again—where in the world she found the energy or tears left to cry, I have no idea. But I couldn't console one and not the other, so I found myself with Emily on one arm and Michael on the other.

"Sing, Daddy," Michael whined as she snuggled into my neck.

"What do you want me to sing?" I asked.

"*Time Stands Still*, duh," Elizabeth said, incorrectly of course, as she walked into the room.

"*Time Stands Still* Duh, huh?" I teased, resigning myself that the kids were all up no matter what. "Never heard of it."

"Daddy," Elizabeth said in her exasperated tone, and I laughed softly. "We didn't get to see you this tour," she continued as she climbed into the papasan chair. "Cause Em was sick all the time."

"Dey wanna take her ears out!" Michael exclaimed, lifting his head, his eyes wide.

"Nuh uh, dummy, they wanna give her new ears," Elizabeth said.

"Baby Girl," I said in my warning tone, "be nice to your little brother."

"But he gets things wrong," she mumbled, pouting in her chair.

"Really?" I asked her. "They can't give her new ears, you know," I added, assuming that Talia had said something passing that gave the kids the impression that Emily's ears were really bad. I knew of a whole two ear infections that she'd had, and that hardly constituted needing tubes in her ears. I'd also had yet to hear her have problems breathing. Hell, I almost couldn't wait to see what excuses she'd come up with now that I was back home.

"Daddy, you're not singing," Michael said, and I smiled at him.

It was after three before we all finally fell asleep.

The sun was peering through the curtains in Talli's room, hitting right in my face where I slept on that large couch. I groaned, turning on my side and pulling that blue knitted blanket up over my eyes. I felt a tug as the blanket was pulled down and opened one eye to see what the hell was going on. I jumped slightly, not expecting to see Michael's face less than an inch from mine.

"Dude, don't do that," I said with a slight laugh. He still stood there, staring up at me with wide eyes. "You're up awfully early."

"Cereal." He looked completely serious, not even blinking as he said that one word.

"All right, all right. Give me a minute." I stood and stretched, turning my neck side to side. I have no clue how he was up so early... nine. It was nine. Okay, so maybe it wasn't early for him.

"Cereal," he repeated, his little feet shuffling as he made his way to the kitchen. Who was I to say no? Besides, I could definitely sympathize; I was most definitely not a morning person either.

Michael was glassy eyed as he stared at the bowl of cereal, but at least he was eating, which is more than I could say for his baby sister the night before.

Wait... wait a minute...

She wasn't crying. She'd slept for... for six hours without crying! Okay, so it was from three to nine, but progress is progress, so I decided to let her rest. Besides, I had an irate member of my management team demanding my attention.

"What's up, Chris?" I asked as I answered my phone.

"You said you'd call last night."

"You know you sound very girl-like when you pull that shit," I teased.

"Damn it, Jase…"

"Hi, Daddy," Elizabeth said as she walked into the kitchen. "Can I have some cereal too?"

"Of course, Baby Girl, just a minute," I replied. "Sorry, Chris, my kids are here."

"Ah… sorry for interrupting you, then," he said, his tone sincere. "So, um…"

"Just the kids, nosy," I cut him off. "But if it's something I need to know, lay it on me."

"Jase, I think you may want to sit in on the interview portion of Stella's show."

"Are you smoking crack?" I asked suddenly, my volume rising.

"Wha's crack?" Michael piped up, and I held up a finger in an attempt to silence him as I walked out of the kitchen.

"Jase, she films the music first. You know that," he continued.

"Right, and then I'm getting the hell out of there."

"And leaving Bree to answer Stella's questions?" he asked. I sighed, pinching the bridge of my nose.

"Chris, she… there's nothing to say."

"That's bullshit, and you and I both know it," he snapped at me.

"Fine… fine, but with all the negative press right now, she's not going to fan the flames."

"Do you know that for certain?" he asked, sounding so much like that damned Victor Newman character that my heart ached. When I couldn't answer, he added, "Jase, I think… I think if you don't want to be there for the interview, then you should at least talk with Bree."

"Chris…"

"In New York," he added. "With other people around. As much as you may not want to… as much as I don't want you to… I think you're the one person who may be able to talk her out of making any derogatory statements or comments."

I sighed as his words sunk in. He was probably right… fuck, would this ever end?

"Fine," I agreed. "Okay, fine. I'll talk with her."

The kids were all in the kitchen enjoying lunch (brunch for Emily) when I went out to get the mail. That was when I heard the infamous two words.

"Um... Daddy..."

There was something in Elizabeth's tone that I really didn't like.

"What's up, Baby Girl?"

"You might wanna come in the kitchen."

Oh... yay. Elizabeth and Michael were probably in one of their many squabbles.

"Just a minute," I replied, thumbing through the mail as I walked towards the kitchen. I was expecting to hear screaming, or crying following my statement.

Not giggling.

Lots... and lots... of giggling.

Oh, this can't be good.

All... three of them...

"All right, what's going..."

My voice trailed off as Elizabeth and Michael both began laughing in earnest. And Em...

"Oh, Em," I said softly, covering my mouth so she didn't see my smile.

Emily crinkled up her nose as she smiled at me, and that would have been enough to melt my heart, but...

"Oh, Em," I repeated just a little louder, taking in the sight of my youngest daughter, who had dumped her entire bowl of spaghetti over her head. The bowl was still perched up there, noodles dripping down her face and gathering between her bib and the tray, where she reached in to grab a hand full and eat. Of course, Michael and Elizabeth found that hilarious, which made Emily giggle as well.

"Well... she's eating," I heard myself say, which prompted Michael to bury his face in his arm, his laughter muffled.

"Daddy!" Elizabeth exclaimed. "Camera!"

"Oh... definitely," I agreed, fishing my phone out of my pocket.

"Daddy, send it..." Elizabeth stood up, excitedly waving her arms.

"Send it to Mommy!"

"You think I should?" I asked, laughing as I looked down at the photographic evidence, mentally filing it away under pictures to humiliate your children with once they're grown.

"Send it! Send it!" Michael chimed in.

"Mommy needs to laugh, too!" Elizabeth added.

Oh… oh, wow.

She was right.

We all needed a laugh. And it felt so… so very good.

Without a message—none was needed—I sent the picture to Talia, wishing I could see the look on her face when she received it. There was no question the laughter in our kitchen was music to my ears, music to my soul.

"Hey… you two," I said to the older children, "eat up, okay? I've got to…" My phone vibrating in my pocket interrupted me telling them I needed to give Emily a bath.

Talia.

What. The. Hell.

I threw my head back in laughter, almost able to imagine her actually saying it. I quickly sent a text back.

Oh, come on. You know you laughed.

And fifteen minutes later, with Emily splashing water and bubbles all over the washroom from her trusty bath seat, when I still hadn't heard from Talia, I couldn't resist. I sent her another text.

Yep. That's what I thought.

CHAPTER 8

TALLI

Rounds on Saturday weren't always the busiest, but it freed up my time to work on my paperwork, catching up on charts and messages. After I'd finished with my patients as well as a couple of discharges, I sat in my office in the nearly deserted clinic to gather my thoughts. My eyes wandered up to the bulletin board in front of me, my heart constricting when an older picture caught my eye.

It was us—Jase and me—taken in his mother's back yard sometime between Michael and Emily. We weren't looking at the camera, but more over to the side. If I'm not mistaken, we were listening to whatever story Pete was telling. But our arms were around each other, his fingers entwined in my curls as if it were the most natural thing in the world. We looked relaxed. Comfortable.

Happy.

I pulled the pin out that kept the picture in place, sticking it back in the board as I held the picture in my free hand. I sighed as I stared at the picture, drinking in every detail.

The leaves on the tree behind us were a brilliant green, a few of them flipped over in the breeze that I remembered had just started to pick up. I was tucked up against his side, his left arm draped across my shoulder. His fingers—those long fingers—were tangled in my hair, and if I closed my eyes, I could almost feel it. Is it insane to miss him messing with my hair? Hell, I don't know.

His hair was lightly tousled, the wind just slightly picking up a few strands. It was a little longer, almost the length it had been in Vegas, and the sun was catching the highlights just so. The picture was taken from a tad bit too far back to tell what color his eyes were but judging by the smile on his face, I'd guess they were green, which was rare with him but beautiful.

Oh…oh, that's right. They were green.

I remembered that day now…

That was the day he'd lured me down to the basement, into the utility room. The game was playing on the big screen downstairs, the entire basement full of the sounds of cheering as Jase closed that door, plunging us in to darkness.

"Jase, what are…"

He'd cut off my question with a kiss—long, lingering, passionate kiss—leaving me whimpering. His actions were frantic, feverish as he tugged at the button and zipper of my jeans.

"Jase," I'd said in a hushed whisper as he latched on to the side of my neck, his fingertips reaching in between my legs.

"Are you telling me no?" he teased, his fingers expertly stroking, evoking the exact response he was looking for. I was wet nearly instantly, wanting more than just his thumb teasing as he pushed two fingers inside of me.

Oh, fuck no… of course I wasn't…

He pulled his hand away as he helped me with his jeans, our mouths never losing contact, the moans and labored breathing only adding fuel to my desire. The material of his jeans rustled as they fell to his feet just as I wrapped my legs around him, grinding against his erection.

"Oh…fuck, Talli," he moaned into my ear as I moved against him, teasing him without taking him in. "You're… so… so, wet… "

"Please," I begged, shifting slightly. He inhaled sharply as he slowly began to enter me.

"Can you keep quiet?" he asked, his voice a raspy whisper in my ear.

"They'll… they'll never hear me… just a little more…"

It was slow… so agonizingly slow as he entered me. "Mmmm, fuck, baby, that feels so good... "

"Jase... "

"Ssssh, so tight. So... wet... "

"Talia?" Dr. Paul Coffman's voice interrupted my memory, bringing me sharply back to the present.

"Hmm?" I asked, dropping the picture face down on to the desk and shifting uncomfortably in my chair.

"They said you were working rounds today," he continued. "I just wanted to see how you were doing."

"I'm fine," I replied with a tight smile.

"Any more thought to my suggestion?" he asked, taking a seat beside my desk.

"Oh, the support group?" I asked, then attempted to suppress a short laugh. "Paul, you are a kind soul, but I would get ripped to shreds if I went there."

"That's not necessarily true," he replied, his kind brown eyes completely locked with mine.

"Are you serious, Paul?" I asked. "A support group for divorced parents?"

"Right."

"And how many of them would go running to the tabloids?" I leaned back in my chair, closing my eyes briefly.

"I see where you're coming from," he admitted. "But... if you want to talk, I've been there."

I sighed, flipping the picture over a few times as he continued on, talking about his divorce from his wife, how she'd cheated on him—running around the bars, sleeping with various men. I bit the inside of my lip, stopping myself short from telling him my situation was different. Se, Jase... he didn't screw around.

He... he had a... a 'relationship'.

"You know what you need?" Paul asked, tousling my hair playfully, ignoring the look I shot him.

"What's that?" I asked, attempting to keep the annoyance out of my voice. Hell, this was almost as bad as being pregnant. EVERYONE had an opinion or some form of advice for me and had to force feed it to me with a spoon.

"You need to laugh."

"Excuse me?" I asked a bit impatiently.

"Just... laugh." He didn't seem to take offense and merely smiled at me as he continued. "Just let go..."

I pulled my arm back abruptly as he placed his hand on it, then mumbled my apologies. I just don't want that contact... I can't handle it.

"It's all right, Talia. I don't bite."

Why... oh, why did that remind me of Jase? Why did that have to take me back to Ohio, my little apartment there, when he had come to visit me?

"Dr. Coffman, I apologize, I'm just... I'm not great company right now," I said softly.

"I wasn't for a while either," he replied.

And I felt bad. I really did. Paul really is a nice guy—sweet, attentive, caring—and fairly easy on the eyes, too. But at that point I just wanted... well I wanted to decompress. I want time to think, to process, even though I feel I couldn't no matter how hard I tried.

My office phone rang during that awkward portion of the conversation—the point where I wished I could crawl into a hole and disappear.

"Saved by the bell," he said with a wink. Apparently he'd asked me some question and was waiting for my answer. I laughed nervously as I reached for my phone.

"Talia War... Emerson speaking."

"Oh, don't you dare," Jaden scolded me through the line. "You are Talia Warner, and you shouldn't change that."

"Ah... Dr., um... Stewart, hello," I said, shrugging with my best faux smile at Paul.

"What? Have you lost your mind?" Jaden asked, unaware of her role.

"Oh, no... no, sure I have time to look that up."

"What?!"

"Just a sec." I pushed the hold button as Jaden was asking what the hell I was up to and turned back to Paul. "I'm so sorry, Dr. Coffman, I really do need to take care of this." I stood and walked over to the door, hoping he'd take the hint, which luckily he did.

"It's quite all right, Talia. Like I said... my door's always open."

"Oh, okay. Thank you."

"And Talia?"

"Yes," I asked, that smile still firmly in place. Paul gestured over towards the phone.

"Tell Jaden I said hello."

Well, fuck. At least he was still smiling. "Will do," I said, my smile still there until I closed the door. He's lucky I'm not a confrontational person, otherwise I probably would have kicked his ass after hearing him laugh his way down the hallway.

And what the hell was that beeping?

Oh, right. Phone. Jaden.

"I'm so sorry," I said in a rush as I picked the receiver back up.

"Just tell me who you were trying to get rid of and I'll forgive you," she replied.

"Just Dr. Coffman."

"Who, Paul?" she asked.

"Yeah, and he says hello."

"So you were busted, huh?"

"Shut up," I muttered. "What's up?"

"No, see, that's my question for you," she corrected me. "Like... why are you at work on your first weekend with no kids?"

"What else was I supposed to do?" I asked, reaching down and picking up the picture that had fallen on the floor.

"Go out and have some fun!"

"With who and do what?" I asked, a slight scowl on my face as I pinned the picture back up.

"Fine... fine. But next time, come out and see me," she suggested.

What next time? Oh, right... she didn't know. She had no idea how limited my childless time was going to be.

And I missed them so terribly...

My cell phone was buzzing in my pocket as Jaden told me how sorry she was that she hadn't phoned the night before. I hesitated when I saw the call had come from Jase's phone, but only for a moment. I mean, it was just picture mail. How bad could it be, right?

"Seriously, you know we have the room!" Jaden was saying. "And... you could always come when you do have the kids, and..."

Oh, holy hell! I threw my head back in laughter as the picture finished downloading. Emily... a bowl on top of her head, and orange face, and spaghetti noodles dripping down.

"What's so funny about that?" Jaden asked.

"No," I gasped, still giggling slightly as I fired a text back to Jase. *What. The. Hell.*

"No, it's this... oh, I just need to send it to you," I said, still giggling. "It will be on your cell."

"Whatever it is, I could kiss the person who sent it to you," she commented, and my laughter stilled. "Talli?"

"I'm fine," came my automatic response, but before I could add the next line, my phone buzzed again.

Oh come on. You know you laughed.

Yes... yes, Jase I did, and it has left such a bittersweet ache in my chest.

I closed my phone, stuffing it back in my pocket, refusing to answer him and focusing on Jaden instead. "Did you get it?"

"Yeah... hold on, let me download... oh!" Her laughter told me she'd most definitely received the picture. "Damn, I guess this means I owe Jase a kiss, doesn't it?"

"Suppose so," I replied.

"Talli..."

"Look, it's no big. It's something I have to get used to."

"He looked like shit when I saw him," she said.

"Yeah, he looked pretty rough when he picked the kids up, too," I replied.

"He seems to be taking this really hard."

"I suppose his guilt is catching up with him."

"Talli... is... were you two having problems?" she asked. "You know, before?"

"Are you trying to say it's..."

"I'm not trying to say anything, Talli. I'm just trying to understand. Was Bree the *cause* of the split, or just one piece in the puzzle?"

"Does it matter?" I snapped.

"No... no, in the end I suppose it doesn't," she said slowly. "I pulled all of the party plans and stuff out for him."

"He'll probably give it to Sondra," I said bitterly, but Jaden ignored me and continued on.

"I'll help decorate and such, so all you'll have to do is show up dressed to kill. Although, not... you know, literally."

I didn't answer, not wanting to drag her into anything, not wanting her to know Jase wouldn't have the children until I brought them over, and as she was asking me another question, my beeper went off.

"Ah... apparently someone doesn't know I'm here," I said with a nervous laugh.

"Talli?"

"We'll talk later, okay?" I asked.

"As long as you promise."

"Of course I do," I said, knowing even with the best of intentions it would probably slip my mind.

The page was actually my call that one of my patients was ready to deliver, so I bee-lined it back to labor and delivery. It wasn't until a good hour later when I was taking a short break that I noticed I'd received another text from Jase.

Yep. That's what I thought.

I sat my phone down, biting the inside of my lip as I contemplated the myriad of emotions washing over me. Part of me was relieved that we weren't sending hateful messages back and forth. The other part of me, the spiteful part that I couldn't seem to control, wanted to scream at the top of my lungs... Why are you being so fucking nice to me?

"Are you okay?"

I glanced up to see Dr. Coffman once again standing in my doorway. I shrugged slightly without saying a word.

"Do you want to talk about it?" he asked, this time not stepping in without an invitation.

"Not right now, no," I answered honestly, and he smiled.

"Some other time, then," he said before continuing down the hall.

"Sure," I muttered to the empty office. "Some other time."

JASE

How hard could it possibly be to get three children together, ready, packed, and across town on time?

Anyone who really knows the answer, by all means give me a call. Maybe I'll be able to answer the call in between juggling the phone, telling Elizabeth to drop her attitude, trying to convince Michael that the tags go on the inside of clothing, and searching high and low for Emily's stuffed puppy.

I gave up on the puppy and rushed to get them into the car and on the road back home, cursing when Talli didn't pick up her cell. I was already fifteen minutes late from my scheduled drop off time, which was about an hour after I'd actually planned on dropping them off, which had been fine with Talli when I'd asked her before.

She must think I'm some kind of...

Well, I already know what she thinks of me, don't I?

The cell rang just as I was reaching her building, and I answered as quickly as I could. "Jase, where are you?" Chris's voice boomed through the line.

"Pulling in to the parking lot,"

"Oh thank God," he interrupted me, but I had to continue.

"...of Talia's condo."

"Damn it, why didn't you have Linda, or... or Sondra drop them off for you?" he demanded.

"Because I'd be just as late if I'd had to wait for one of them," I replied. While that was true, it was also because I wanted to see Talia myself. I wanted to hold on to that tiny sliver of hope, see if I could gauge by her reaction to me if she felt the same way.

One glance at my watch told me I had about, oh... one minute to accomplish this. That was providing she buzzed us in right away and the elevator had magically picked up speed.

Wasn't it just my luck that neither happened?

First, Talia wasn't answering the buzzer at all, but luckily one of her neighbors recognized us, or at least the children, and let me take them in. Then, as said neighbor proceeded to talk my ear off, the elevator moved excruciatingly slow only to stop on floor six, where it took its sweet time grinding to a halt. The chatterbox then apologized for having to exit the elevator, and I might have said something in return had Elizabeth not told her that Mommy was waiting for us and we had to go.

I didn't even bother correcting her snarky tone.

"The ladies really like you, don't they?" Michael asked with the most serious look on his face, and I had to laugh, which Emily (who had quickly become my parrot after the Great Spaghetti Incident) mimicked from her perch on my arm.

"If they do," I replied as the elevator finally stopped on floor ten, "I have no idea why."

Michael and Elizabeth continued to chatter as we walked down that hall towards the condo, and I never dreamed I had to bang on the door to get Talia to answer it. What the hell? My anger was close to spilling over when I heard a frantic "Just a sec!" before the rattling of the doorknob, and finally...

"Mommy!" Michael exclaimed as he ran in. "You gots sleep!"

Talia was pulling up her hair in a messy bun as our two oldest flew past, chattering about whatever movie it was that they'd brought back and how they were going to watch it. Damn it, she was in those yoga pants... those sassy pants of hers that hugged her hips, accentuating her ass as she bent over to pick up their bags they'd merely tossed on the ground.

Wasn't I supposed to say something to her?

Oh... just a camisole on underneath that little jacket that she'd just thrown on. I resisted the urge to reach out and fix where the hood in the back was half tucked in and...

"What?" she asked.

"Excuse me?"

"You're staring." Her expression was set in a light scowl. "I'm sorry I didn't get the buzzer, or... um... the door right away... What?"

I felt the corners of my mouth lift up in a smile.

"I'll see you," was all I could say.

"Wait just one minute," she called after me, and I turned back towards her.

"What?" I asked innocently.

Only when she held her hands out did I realize Emily was still on my arm. Em shifted slightly and leaned towards Talia, who gathered her up close. I grinned sheepishly as Talia shot me a glare, my stomach taking a dive when her gaze softened.

She looked so sad...

My phone began ringing, its tone indicating it was Chris, who was probably in a panic. "I have to go," I said softly.

"Okay." The word sounded almost like it was stuck in her throat, and my heart constricted just a tiny bit.

I wanted to stay right there, in her presence... I wanted to pull her into my arms, if she'd only let me, and kiss away all the hurt I'd caused. I wanted to beg for forgiveness, and I wanted her to say yes... yes, she forgave me, and that while it wasn't okay we'd get past it, and we'd give us a shot, our family a shot.

"Jase..."

"I'm ... staring, I know," I stammered, my face getting hot under her gaze. I looked down at my shoes, so dark against the light tan carpeting, and shrugged slightly. "Wednesday..."

Wednesday, that was my next day to see the kids, and I just... I wanted to see her, I wanted her to come with us, and I wanted so badly to ask, and...

And my stupid fucking phone rang again.

"Yeah, um... "

"You have to go, I know," she said softly, and I stole one more glance up at her face. So beautiful, but so stricken...

"I'll see you Wednesday?" Why did I make it sound like a question? Fuck! What was my problem?

"Sure," she replied.

I hadn't realized I was holding my breath until that moment, when I felt it leave my body. I stood there for one more moment before I smiled slightly and walked out the door.

"What do you mean, she's on my flight?" I demanded. I had parked my car at the airport and was walking towards the terminal, my bag over my shoulder and my phone up to my ear.

"You were supposed to be at the airport over an hour ago, we had to scramble to change your flight," Chris said, his tone showing his annoyance. "You're lucky we could get you on this flight."

"So I'm stuck in the air on a non-stop flight from L.A. to New York with Bree. That's just…"

"Are you out in public?"

"You think I fucking care who hears me?" I asked angrily.

"I'm sure you won't be seated together," he continued, ignoring my question. "However, you both are in first class."

"Great," I muttered.

"Just keep it professional, and if she is anywhere near you tell her it may be best for everyone involved if one of you changes seats."

Well, in a perfect world I wouldn't have to worry about that. But this is L.A, and this world is far from perfect. So instead of being seated far away from her in a rather deserted first-class section, she exchanged her seat with the person who was originally next to me so that he could sit next to his new bride on their way to their honeymoon destination. Just once I wish I could bring myself to be an asshole and say no.

Not that it was my call.

But when Bree flashed that smile at them and said, "Oh, I'm sure Jase won't mind, will you, Jase?" what was I supposed to do? So the new Mr. and Mrs. Whatever were happily seated together on the other side of the cabin, and Bree was sliding into the seat next to me.

"You haven't called," she pouted.

"I've been busy."

"You were never too busy for me before, Jase." She leaned towards me and the faint scent of cigarette smoke lingered around her. "Why are you avoiding me?"

I sighed heavily, looking over at her face, somehow unaffected by the tears swimming in her china blue eyes. Perhaps it was because I knew how easily she could make herself cry; she'd shown me on more than one occasion, bragging about how she used it to get her way. "I'm …" I stopped myself from lying that I hadn't been avoiding her, and instead stuck with the truth. "I'm trying to do the right thing."

"It's a bit late to think about right and wrong, don't you think?" she asked quickly, settling back into her seat.

"Thanks for the reminder," I mumbled, reaching in my pocket for my iPod.

"What, you don't want to talk with me?" she asked incredulously.

I sighed as I looked back over at her. "You know, Bree," I said in an exasperated tone, "if this was... a couple months ago, if... if I hadn't screwed up so royally, if we were really friends in the way we should have been, then I wouldn't mind it at all." I kept my voice low, leaning in to try and keep others out of our conversation. "But you and I both know that it went too far,"

"And you're making *me* out to be the villain," she cut me off. "And just for the record, we are friends, or at least I thought we were. Or do you need reminded that I am the one who has been there for you for most of this past year when your *wife* was too preoccupied?"

I closed my eyes briefly, refusing to answer as I sat back in my seat. My jaw was clenched rather tightly as I looked forward at a spot on the wall in the front as if it were the most interesting thing in this world.

"Jase," she said softly, reaching out and placing her hand over mine, "I still want us to be friends. You need someone on your side through this, you know. You don't have to be alone."

I tried pulling my hand away, but she wrapped her fingers around and squeezed a little tighter.

"The damage is done," she continued, leaning over and placing her head on my shoulder. "The media... everyone is tearing us both apart, and everyone's being so cruel. To both of us, you know? Have you been reading it?"

"No," I said, then quickly added, "Bree, sit up."

"I do love you," she said softly, turning her face and leaving a kiss on my cheek before she sat back. "I'd do anything for you. Can you say the same for Talia?"

Once upon a time I could...

"You don't have to be sad or lonely anymore."

I closed my eyes, Talia's face filling my mind... her hair framing her beautiful face as she hovered over me, her hands caressing my face as she leaned in, brushing her lips across mine. So soft... so sweet... so full of love...

"Sir."

I jumped as the flight attendant woke me. Damn, I hadn't realized how tired I was. She was instructing me and the still-groggy Bree, who was tucked up under my arm, that we needed to sit up because the plane was getting ready to land. I quickly removed my arm from around Bree's shoulder, glancing at her warily.

"You don't need to look at me that way," she said haughtily as she flipped out her compact, checking her makeup and hair. "You're the one who pulled me up against you."

"I shouldn't have," I replied. "And I'm sorry."

She narrowed her eyes as she looked at me. "You know, Chris had me under the impression you wanted to speak with me, but he apparently lied."

"He didn't." I took a deep breath. "But this is hardly the…"

"Well, since you're bound to avoid me like the plague until the show, now is a good a time as any."

"I just wanted to ask you to not say anything." I kept my gaze steady as she shot me a nasty glare.

"So I'm not supposed to defend myself?"

"All you need to say is… 'no comment' or… or tell her you don't talk about speculation or rumors, or… damn it, Bree, don't look at me that way. Don't do this."

"Tell me, Jase, why? Why is it that you don't want me to tell them the truth?"

"Sure, by all means—tell them we didn't sleep together. That *is* the truth," I reminded her.

"We would have."

"No, Bree, we wouldn't have. Or do you need me to refresh your memory about how I'd said no?"

Perhaps that was the wrong thing to say, with the anger that flashed straight at me from her cold eyes. But less than a moment later, she rolled those eyes and muttered, "Sure, Jase. Whatever you want."

"Bree,"

"I said I wouldn't say anything, and I won't," she snapped, wiping one of those bullshit tears away.

I breathed a sigh of relief, allowing myself to smile for the first time since I'd talked to Chris at the airport. "Thank you, Bree."

"Don't mention it."

So with that out of the way, I took the rest of the evening to sit alone in my hotel room and stare at a blank piece of paper, unable to write a thing, and wonder what next step I should take to win my family back.

CHAPTER 9

TALLI

I am so embarrassed. I swear I don't just sleep through anything, and yet I slept through eight missed calls, the buzzer, and almost through the pounding on the door

"Hey, Mommy, d'you want to see the dress he bought Em?" Elizabeth asked excitedly.

"In a minute, honey," I replied, still preoccupied.

How am I supposed to explain this to him?

"Mommy, Daddy couldn't... he couldn't find Em's puppy," Michael added as he ran into the room, still full of so much energy. "Is that what you're looking for?"

"No, baby, it's not," I said, still sifting through my remaining boxes.

I've already failed as a wife, I'm failing as a friend... am I failing as a mother, too? How am I supposed to take care of them if I can't hear that annoying buzzer?

"And Em didn't want outta the bath, either!" Elizabeth exclaimed.

"And Daddy gave...he gave her another bath today," Michael added. "What are you doing, Mommy?"

No... no, it was just a fluke, me sleeping through that buzzer. That's what it was.

Emily whined, her little bottom lip sticking out as she toddled into the living room.

"You miss your puppy?" Michael asked.

"Don't mention it to her, dummy!" Elizabeth snapped, and Emily instantly began to cry.

And... and Jase had just stared at me. He must think I'm some kind of... well, unfit something. But Emily seemed content enough in his arms.

Color me jealous.

"You can have one of Sis's toys," Michael offered as I continued sifting through the next to the last box.

No, I'm not jealous. And I'm not angry that Emily warmed up to him. I'm actually rather pleased, relieved even. It meant the world knowing that the children were happy. That was all I could ask for, at least now, and...

"You can't just give my toys away!" Elizabeth said forcefully

"You do it to mine!" Michael yelled back.

"Kids, stop, please!" I said, finally turning away from the box, its contents scattered.

"I want my Daddy!" Elizabeth screamed at the top of her lungs before stomping out of the room, slamming her bedroom door firmly behind her.

So do I...

Oh, fuck.

What am I doing?

I... I am having papers served to him... papers that end our marriage. Papers that essentially say that I don't love him anymore, and that's just not true.

"Dase," Em squeaked.

And... and those papers, they say that I don't trust him with our children, and I do. I really do. He's so good with them, so patient,

And... and...

"It's Daddy, silly," Michael laughed at her, taking her chubby hand in his and leading her to his bedroom. "I gots boy toys, but you can have one if you want, okay?"

"Dase," she replied.

Oh, the look on his face when he was here earlier... okay, maybe I'm reading too much into it, but... but... what if he still loves me?

No, I don't think he does.

But maybe, somehow… maybe he could love me again someday. Or… or maybe if he can't, he could just tell me what I did wrong, why he doesn't love me anymore.

But that smile…

Did I jump the gun?

Maybe I should call the lawyer's office in the morning and ask them to wait, just until I talk to him on Wednesday. And I will talk to him.

I must be insane.

But love does make you crazy.

So crazy, in fact, that I seem to have misplaced an entire box. And not just any box—this had my certificates from school, the kids' baby books, and the paperwork… the paperwork for the star, for our Angel.

It was like losing our baby all over again.

"Mommy, I don't wanna go to daycare tomorrow," Elizabeth announced, opening her bedroom door.

"But you have to."

"I wanted to stay at Daddy's, but Daddy said he had somewhere to go, and besides… I said you'd be too mean to let me."

"Thank you, Baby Girl," I muttered. "I love you, too."

"Daddy said you weren't mean, though."

I stopped in my tracks, my eyelids sliding shut at her words.

"Mommy, if you and Daddy say nice things about each other, why can't you say nice things to each other?"

I glanced over at our oldest daughter, her face so solemn as she looked up at me, and sighed. "I don't know, Baby Girl. I just don't know."

I have never been a fan of Monday mornings, but this particular one saw me waking up with the worst case of anxiety I had felt in ages. It was going to be one of those days, one of the days where I wanted to stay curled up in bed and let the world go on about its axis, forgetting for one day that I existed.

Emily's morning screech when the alarm wasn't shut off before waking her reminded me I didn't have that luxury.

"I'm getting, I'm getting," I mumbled. I picked her up on my way over to the dresser where the alarm was singing some old 80s tune. What the fuck was... oh, right.

Hands to Heaven.

Same damn song that I watched Jase and Kaitlyn dance to.

Okay, so that something completely unfounded, but the song still brought the worst feelings back to the forefront. So it wasn't Kaitlyn, and our relationship wasn't new... but...

Why the hell was my phone ringing at five a.m?

"No, no," Emily said plain as day, pushing the phone away as I picked it up.

"You're such a comedian," I mumbled to her before answering. "Hello?"

"Talli?"

"No, it's Esmeralda of the Dumas family." I said with a roll of my eyes. "What's up, Jaden?"

"Well, um... you."

"No stalling," I said, cradling the receiver as I opened the bedroom door the rest of the way and walking out towards the kitchen.

"Just... can you promise me you won't look at the internet this morning?"

I sighed, letting Emily down to walk over to the refrigerator where she stood and hit the door repeatedly. "Ah, what have they dug up this time?" I asked with a laugh, then before she could answer I added, "You know what? Don't tell me. I... I don't think I could deal with the internet today."

"Good," she replied with a sigh. "I mean, not good that you can't deal, but good that I don't have to argue with you."

"Oh, that's nice."

"Well, I love you, Talli, but let's face it— you're not the easiest person in this world to reason with."

"Thanks, I love you, too," I said as I pulled down a clean sippy cup for Emily, filling it with milk and handing it to her so she'd be appeased while I got her something to eat.

"Just... can you promise me?"

"I can promise you that I'll try," I answered.

"I suppose I'll just have to live with that."

"Hey, Jaden... did you happen to see this... box?"

"I saw lots of boxes out there," she replied. "Let me guess, your eyebrow is up and you're glaring."

I touched my forehead absentmindedly, wondering if she had the house bugged as I lied, "No, it's not, and I'm not."

"Whatever. What box are you looking for?"

"It has paperwork."

"Oh, that's real specific."

"My school paperwork, transcripts... um, and the kids' baby books, and... stuff."

"No, I sure didn't," she said, and I smiled as I heard Pete's voice in the background. How wonderful it must be to have that normalcy of family life... I missed it so much...

"I must have left it," I mumbled, making a mental note in what was left in my mind to search for it at the house during Emily's party.

Oh, I could just hear it now, him going off about how I could lose something so important.

And of course, it bothered me all day.

It bothered me as I left a message at the lawyer's office for someone to get back to me, praying that they called in time.

It bothered me as I repeatedly ignored my screaming curiosity that kept telling me I wanted to look online, check *Celebrity Gossip*, check any gossip paper I could find.

"Are you okay?"

I jumped as Paul... Dr. Coffman walked past me in the hallway.

"Hmm? Oh, yeah... yeah, I'm just busy today is all..." My voice trailed off as a couple of young nurses walked past, their conversation ceasing as they both stared at me, one with contempt, the other pity. Just as soon as they passed, they turned to each other, chatting again in their hushed tones about whatever it was that held them so intrigued.

"I just wanted to check," he said with a grin.

"No, I'm..." Another group of employees walked by, eyeing me before returning to their conversation. "Okay, this is not a coincidence."

"Talia,"

"And you apparently know what's going on, too, so…"

"No, listen… I'm sorry, I thought…"

I couldn't hear what the rest of his explanation was because I had picked up my pace, pushing past people in the hallway and going back to the clinic where my office sat down the middle of the first hall. To hell with staying away… if people were going to point and stare and…

My cell phone was buzzing in my pocket, and I hesitated.

Jase.

No. No, I had to know first, before I talked to him, I had to know what everyone was so wrapped up in, and…

He left a voicemail. Well, good for him; I'll be sure to listen sometime after I found out what the hell was going on.

"Talia," Amy, one of the medical assistants, said as she stuck her head in my office, "your husband has been trying to get ahold of you."

"My…oh." Seriously? Did I just have some kind of a brain flux where I couldn't figure out who she was talking about?

"Yeah, he wants you to call him right away," she continued, standing in the doorway, popping her gum as I hit the button on my computer, cursing that it had actually been turned off. "Maintenance," she explained, still standing in my doorway.

"Thank you," I murmured, rolling my eyes as my phone buzzed again, this time indicating a text.

"He's called, like… ten times or something crazy like that."

What do you know? The text was from Jase.

Please call me.

I could feel the tension, the anxiety building as my computer finally finished booting up. I clicked on the button to bring up the internet as my phone began buzzing in my pocket again. I pulled it out, determined to click on that silence button until I noticed it was Sherise Adler's office calling.

"Hello?" I said, as friendly as I could.

"Hello, Talia?"

"Hello, Ms. Adler," I said, hearing my lawyer's voice through the phone.

"Oh, please, call me Sherise."

"No, I… um… I…"

"Is there something you needed, Talia?" she asked, her voice thick and saccharine sweet.

But I couldn't answer.

No, see, because staring at me on the front page of *Celebrity Gossip*, were pictures... oh, the pictures...

She was in his arms.

"I was wondering about this message you left, saying you needed to talk with me."

I did?

Oh, right.

Because like a fool I'd almost fallen for that smile, that charm all over again. But, no... no, now I could see... oh, look more pictures. My, how cozy they looked on that plane. Elizabeth had said he had to go somewhere...

"Talia?"

"Have the papers been delivered yet?" I asked, snapping out of my trance.

"No, not yet. Would you like to be informed when they do?"

One tear escaped, running down my cheek as I clicked that little red 'x' at the top. "Yes," I said with a sigh. "Yes, please."

"Will do, then. Is there anything else you needed?"

"No," I replied, thanking her for her time before I hung up the phone, which immediately buzzed in my hand.

Another text from Jase.

Talia, it's really important. Please call me.

Call you, you say?

Fuck you, Jase.

Fuck. You.

JASE

I don't handle stress well. I never have; that's one of my vices, if you will. Monday had been one of the most stressful days of my life, and Tuesday wasn't starting much better.

"I won't be on the same fucking airplane as her again," I said to

Chris as I walked through the terminal, all eyes seeming to be on me.

"You're not, Jase, but I tried to tell you…"

"Just handle the fucking spin… the damage control… the… whatever, okay?" I cut him off.

"Alison and I are working on it," he replied, a little too calmly for my tastes. "Have you talked with her?"

"Why the hell would I talk with that…"

"Talli, Jase. Have you talked with Talli?"

I swore under my breath, my frustration overwhelming. "No."

It wasn't for lack of trying, either. I'd lost count of how many times I'd called, how many messages I'd left, how many different placed I had tried to reach her at. The longer she avoided talking to me, the more convinced I was that she'd seen the picture.

And the show hadn't even aired yet.

When that happens, when that gets back to Talia… oh, God…

I had my headphones on while I was on the plane, trying to stay calm, focused. Instead, all I could see were those pictures popping up on that monitor backstage as I was getting ready to leave, followed by that smug look on Bree's face.

"Don't worry 'bout any of those 'boos,' hun. I can always have them edited out," Stella said as the crowd showed their displeasure.

One of the girls close to the front row yelled out, "Homewrecker!"

And Bree… that eyebrow of hers raised up, that fucking smirk still on her face as she said, "There would have to be a home to wreck, sweetheart."

What. The. Fuck?

She was saying some bullshit about pictures being worth a thousand words as I struggled to get back down that hall and out on that fucking sound stage. Of course, Bubba the Bodyguard stopped me from entering, stating that they were taping so no one was permitted through.

Seriously?

And I knew… I *knew* they'd edit this just so, spin it even more. And one or both of the songs would air after Bree's interview portion, even though they'd both been taped before.

"And that song, 'Everything'?" Stella asked, gasping and placing her hand over her heart. "What a beautiful love song!"

I was cursing under my breath as Bree merely smiled, crossing her slender tanned legs.

If I hadn't been raised right, I wouldn't think twice about slapping the shit out of her over this.

See, that was a song I'd written one night in Memphis, in that motel room right after Talia had called with the news that Emily was sick. That was the first time she'd made that call, so while I was disappointed, I wasn't angry. I hadn't realized that this was just the beginning, that Talia was pulling away from me... but, I had this inspiration to tell her how I felt, what she meant to me.

And Bree fucking knew it.

It wasn't a song I was going to have on my album, even though I planned on recording it someday. But Bree had convinced me to let her record it, having me on backup vocals, and the result, I have to admit, was beautiful.

So I let her put it on her album.

And now I was adding that to a list of regrets that I had that has reached at least a mile long.

Now Bree is insinuating this is about her...

The beginning, where I wrote about falling in love with a voice on the phone... and there Bree sat explaining how we'd talked on the phone for a couple of weeks before we met in Memphis.

Please... please, Talli, remember us. You have to know this song is about you...

But the public... they don't know that. They knew we'd met as teenagers, and then found each other years later. They just didn't know how.

And then, the lines in there... damn it... the lines about how I'd been so sure about what I wanted until she walked into my life...

No... please, please don't think that, Talli, please...

Of course she would play this game. She knew her album sales were liable to jump, she knew her name would be googled more often once this aired than it was on a normal basis. And would she care what would happen when Talia saw this, when she watched how much passion I put into that song?

Of course I would.

Because I believe that song with everything in me, because that's what she is…

Everything.

And she has to listen to me. She has to answer the phone.

She has to talk to me.

Jackie was calling nearly the moment I turned my cell back on when I was walking into the terminal at LAX. "What's up?" I asked as I answered the phone.

"Same old same old," he replied. "I hadn't gotten the call; do you need me there when you get home?"

"I think Chris and Alison got the damage control," I said, hoisting my bag over my shoulder.

"I wasn't talking about damage control."

I took a deep, shuddering breath. "I appreciate it, Jackie, I just don't think I'll be very good company."

"Are you sure?"

I growled, holding back a curse as the vultures descended, their shutters clicking.

"Positive, Jackie. But thanks."

It was a fight to get past the paparazzi, but luckily a couple of security guards helped me out to my car, wordlessly standing by as I closed my door and revved the engine. I blasted the air conditioning hoping it would cool down quickly. July in California was sticky, hot, humid, thick, and it didn't help my throbbing head.

Were they harassing Talia, too?

Please… please no. They wouldn't care if our children were there or not. Trying to reason with them about the kids would only fan the flames, so I stayed silent.

No matter how much it was killing me.

I hooked up the headset to my cell, preparing to listen to the messages left while I was in the air. I should have known better than to wish that one of them would be from Talia, at least acknowledging that she had received my messages. Of course, she hadn't called.

First, there was Chris, telling me when he'd be at my house. He kept droning on about how he was unsure I should say the song was written for Talia without being asked the question directly. I made a mental note to tell anyone who would listen, regardless of the consequences.

Next was my Nan, telling me she wished I'd talk to her.

Then there was Pete. I was half expecting a shitty message, but he sounded tired more than anything, asking me to call him. And I needed to, I know that.

Alison was next, telling me a copy of the statement would be sitting in my inbox, and asking if I could have Talia contact her also. I almost laughed at that. Hell, Alison, I can't get her to call me back!

Damien wants to make music.

Tom is working on a surprise that I'd planned months ago, and I just didn't have the heart to call and tell him it wasn't necessary anymore.

And last...

"I don't see why you won't talk to me."

That's okay, Bree; I don't see why you don't comprehend that I don't want to.

"I was defending myself, and you would have done the same thing in my shoes."

Would I? I'd like to think I wouldn't.

"Besides, I mean... I miss you, you know? We were really close, and I miss that. And I can't help but wonder what if, you know? What if the situation was different?"

Well, it's not. And do you really have to say *you know* all the fucking time?

"I do love you, and I'm sorry I've made you angry."

That's not love, and angry doesn't begin to cover it.

"So, you know..."

There it goes again.

"You preach about forgiveness and... I'm hoping you have some left in your heart for me."

Way to throw my words back in my face.

"I'll see you tomorrow, when we fly out for Thursday's taping."

Not on your... wait. What? Tomorrow? Taping? You've *got* to be fucking kidding me! Didn't my team get this shit canceled? I have to pick up my kids tomorrow... tomorrow is Wednesday, and after all of this, Chris and Alison had to find me a way out of it. I just... I couldn't, not after everything else that had happened. And I couldn't tell Talia that I wasn't picking up the kids... not now. Please, please not now.

I was even more of a wreck by the time I got home, knowing that stupid fucking show was already on. I can just imagine if Talia sees it before she talks with me...

Chris was already there waiting for me in my office, where he'd gone after Linda let him in. He was sitting in the office, rubbing the back of his neck as he glared at the television, where the interview was airing. "They're apparently airing 'Everything' after they air this garbage," he said, gesturing towards the screen.

"I should have listened," I admitted.

"I should have gotten you out of it," he countered, then he glanced over at me. "Have you reached Talli?"

I sighed, dropping my bag to the ground. "No." I rolled my eyes at the screen, asking Chris, "Can you get me out of the taping that we have tomorrow?"

"You actually signed that contract, Jase," he replied. "I'm so sorry."

"Chris, my *kids*," I pleaded.

"Maybe after this it's best for you and Talli to keep your distance..."

"No, it's best for me to not be anywhere near THAT bitch!" I yelled, pointing at the screen.

"You know how T gets when she's upset," Chris tried reasoning.

"I know that she needs to *listen* to me, okay? How am I supposed to tell her I can't come pick them up after... after that?"

More pictures were shown on that screen, one of Bree holding my hand, another of us asleep with my arm around her. This just... this can't get any worse...

"Mr. Warner?" Linda said as she came to the doorway.

"Please don't Mr. Warner me, Linda," I mumbled.

"There... there is someone at the front door."

"No..."

"Not press... not paparazzi." Linda looked so troubled as she stood there, wringing her hands.

"Do you need me to get this?" Chris asked, and I shook my head.

"I can do this," I answered. I sighed slightly as I left the room, thankful to get away from that broadcast, pulling out my cell and dialing

Talli's number as I bounded to the front door. Was it some kind of sickness that made me want so badly to get in touch with her? Her line was ringing as I came up to the front door, standing in the frame and looking outside at the gentleman standing there wearing a suit and a pair of wire-rimmed sunglasses. "Can I help you?" I asked, clicking the end button on my phone when it went to voicemail.

"Mr. Jason Michael Warner?" he asked, completely business-like.

"Yeah…"

He pushed his arm forward, shoving an envelope into my hand. He muttered his thank yous as he walked away, leaving me bewildered, staring after him as if he'd grown a second head.

Whatever.

I scrolled down, redialing Talia's number for the millionth time as I tore open that envelope, its contents thick, folded, on a heavy paper that…

Oh…

Fuck…

No. No, no, no, no, this wasn't happening… I thought, I really thought that we had a chance to…

"What?"

I jumped when Talia finally answered her phone, her voice constricted, the telltale sniffles giving her tears away.

One glance at the screen showed the pan across me and Bree as we sang an acoustic version of 'Everything'.

And I could hear it in the background of the phone…

"What?!" she demanded more forcefully. "What the hell do you want now?"

My eyes scanned over the papers in my hands, where she had filed for divorce from me, my heart laying in shards at my feet as the words on the pages blurred. I clicked the end button without saying a word, without even being able to tell her I was sorry, without saying everything I had meant to say…

How could I tell her I love her?

How could I tell her I was sorry?

How…

"Jeeeeezus." Chris Pete the word out as he walked up to me.

116

"Jase… are those…"

I shoved the papers at him, walking away as I hastily wiped my eyes, remembering all the times I'd promised her she'd never be alone, she'd never have to worry about anything, I would make sure that they were safe, they were secure…

"Jase…"

"Give her whatever she asks for," I choked out, grabbing my keys and heading to my car.

"Jase…"

But I didn't hear the rest of what he had to say.

I just had to get the hell out of there. I had no idea where I was going, no idea what I was doing, no idea how I could make it another day without my wife, without our kids, without my family that I'd tried so desperately to keep together.

I drove aimlessly for hours, pulling up to a spot that I had to know I was heading to all along.

She was going to hate me for this.

How many times could I screw up, how many times would I go searching for solace before…

"What took you so long?" Kaitlyn asked as she opened the door to her home.

But I couldn't speak.

I didn't know what to say.

All I could do was bury my face in her neck…

And cry.

CHAPTER 10

TALLI

Their song?

Their song?

'Everything'... that was ... for her?

Was it a blessing or a curse that I'd ended up with that Tuesday off work? I mean, if I'd heard or seen and been around everyone, there's no way I could have held it together. Then again, here I sat at home, with that show on, curled up on the couch with a box of tissues beside me. Perhaps I'm a glutton for punishment; I should have known. And yet, here it was, right in front of me.

No wonder Jase had been trying to hard to reach me.

Really? Do they have to show them singing this? Does he have to look like that, like he's pouring his heart into their song? No fucking wonder he didn't want to record it himself, no wonder he let her record it and put it on her album.

And there he is again.

That's... that's IT! That's it, I've fucking HAD it!

I grabbed my cell phone, hitting that accept call button, and I snapped, "What?"

Nothing. Fucking pussy.

"What?" I nearly shouted into the phone. "What the hell do you want now?"

Are you going to tell me she's lying? Are you going to swear that

118

song was for me, about us? Are you going to grovel, plead, tell me it wasn't what it seemed?

But no.

Again, he said nothing.

I hit that end call button, tossing my phone onto my couch, bitterly wiping my tears away as I did so. If that was what he wanted, then so fucking be it.

Oh, and Bree... you silly little girl. That little comment you made when you were asked about you reputation for dressing too provocatively? *"If some frumpy housewives can't stand that their husbands wish they were more like me..."* Yeah, I know, the paparazzi are going to come out to play now. I've played this game longer than you've been in this business, cupcake.

Am I going to break out that little black dress? No. Emphatically not. But this... this just wouldn't do anymore.

I looked down at my t-shirt and sweatpants that hung on my size six body. I could make it to a four, I was already on my way down to a four. Did I have trampy clothes? Well, of course I did, but I had kids now, and I had enough class to not try and look like a street walker.

But a frumpy housewife?

Those days were over.

"Mommy, are you crying again?" Elizabeth asked as she came out to the living room. I clicked that television off as I stood up and placed a kiss on top of her head.

"Not anymore, Baby Girl," I replied, tossing my tissues in the trash on my way to my bedroom.

"Did Daddy make you sad again?" she continued, following behind me.

"You have no reason to worry your pretty little head over it," I said, opening my closet door and giving the clothes in the front a once-over. Oh, this would never do. All of my cute, hot clothes that had Jase on his knees had been pushed all the way to the back of the closet.

"Are you feeling okay, Mommy?" she asked warily.

"Of course I am." I began pulling the clothes out of the back of the closet, placing them on my bed for me go look over. I didn't have to wear scrubs when I wasn't on rounds or scheduled to L & D. Why did I have so many... drab things? Why so many dark colors, so many loose-fitting things? Oh, right, because I haven't been able to stand looking at myself since having Emily. It's not the same; I'm not the same, no matter how much I work out, no matter how much I try, no matter how many pounds I lose, no matter how much I cut back on my eating, I cannot stand to look at myself.

And I certainly didn't want anyone else to look either.

But... I've lost another five, possibly even more, pounds since moving out here. Maybe I could handle seeing myself in these clothes, in these colors again.

Maybe... maybe I could do my hair like I used to. I haven't bothered to straighten it in a while either, or make it look sassy.

And makeup... I haven't done too much in the makeup department, either. I know that Jase said I didn't need much, but I didn't even wear what I used to. I kept it simple, kept me simple.

Kept me invisible.

Did I need to do the makeup like I did in Vegas, or like I did when I was a teenager? No. But... but I could get the colors back out, I could start wearing the gloss again, I could show that I'm no frumpy housewife.

My phone began to ring again, and I knew that it wasn't Jase calling by the ringtone. I set down the clothes I had in my hand and walked out to the living room to retrieve my phone, Elizabeth following me and chattering on and on behind me.

Fuck, had she been talking to me this entire time?

I picked up the phone, biting my lip when I saw it was the lawyer's office. "Just a minute, Baby Girl," I said to Elizabeth as I answered. "Hello?"

"Talia?" came the voice through the line. Oh, wow, once again—a call from Ms. Adler herself. I really do rank.

"Yes?"

"I just wanted to let you know the papers were served."

Oh...

Oh, fuck.

That wasn't supposed to hurt... this is what I want... this is what he wants...

"Talia?"

"Yes... yes, thank you for letting me know," I stumbled over the words as my hands began to tremble.

"Not a problem. Of course, the media will pick up on this now, so be prepared. And I'll let you know any response his team comes back with."

Of course you will, it only pushes your bill through the roof, doesn't it?

"Be prepared for him to fight back," she continued. "And he may fight dirty."

My eyes narrowed as I thought of that little tramp spending any more time with my children then she'd already weasled her way into.

"Let him try," I said, my voice even once more.

"There's my girl," she replied with a laugh. "So, as soon as we hear from their camp, I'll let you know their counteroffer."

I thanked her, setting my phone down only to meet the worried look on my oldest daughter's face. "Mommy?"

"I'm fine,"

"Don't worry 'bout you, I know, but..." I blinked a couple of times, taken off guard by her words. Suddenly, she smiled at me. "Can we play dress up?"

"I'm sorry?"

"You gots out your clothes... we can play dress up!" she said excitedly, her smile beaming.

"Dress up, huh?" I asked, pasting my smile back on.

"Yeah, and... and you can get out all your colorful stuff! You need to... to wear blue to Em's party, Mommy. Daddy likes you in blue."

My eyebrow shot up as Elizabeth continued her rambling.

"And sassy pants, Daddy tol' Damien that your sassy pants make him..."

"My sassy pants aren't exactly birthday party material," I cut her off, trying to keep the conversation away from the subject of him.

"But... what about those pants, Mommy?" She pointed to another pair of black pants, dressier, clingier than the ones I'd been wearing lately.

"Those?" I asked, contemplating if I could fit into them now.

"And... and this shirt," she continued on, pulling out a teal colored top that tied around my neck, showed lots of cleavage, and clung to my midsection before ending right at the top of my pants... when I was thin enough, that is.

"I can't wear that to her party! There's going to be... kids! Lots of kids, and... young lady, are you going through my drawers now?"

"If you don't wear that, then... this?" she asked.

Oh, wow.

My black spaghetti strapped tank top. THE black spaghetti strapped tank top, the one I'd worn to the Cleveland concert.

"I still have this?" I asked, holding it up.

"But you need color, so don't wear that," she said, taking it out of my hands.

"Is that so?"

"Blue... blue... or red! Why not red, Mommy?"

"I don't know, why not red?" I asked, a bit amused.

"Yellow!" Michael added when he ran in.

"You look good in yellow, too!" Elizabeth agreed. "Do you have yellow?"

"Not orange, though," Michael said.

"Mommy doesn't have anything orange."

"Blue?" Michael asked.

"Tha's what I was saying! Blue! See, Mommy? Blue."

"That one!" Michael said, pointing to the top Elizabeth had pulled out earlier.

"No... no, no."

"Chicken," Elizabeth said, her arms crossed in front of her.

"I am not a chicken, I am an adult, and..." I groaned as my phone rang again.

"Wow, you's popular today, Mommy!" Michael said as he followed me out to the living room.

"Sure," I mumbled. "Where's Em?"

"Asleep on my bed," Elizabeth replied as I picked up the phone. Well, huh, that was odd.

"Hello?" I asked, recognizing the number as Sondra.

"Hi... Talli?"

"Yeah, Sondra, it's me."

"How are you?" she asked.

"As good as can be expected," I said, trying to motion for the kids to be quiet as the kept rambling on about colors and what I should wear.

"Talli... I... I really hate to do this."

"Fuck," I muttered. "What?"

"Jase has to be in New York..."

"So he should have fucking stayed there," I snapped, then immediately felt guilty. "I'm sorry, Sondra, it's not your fault."

"No, I... fuck, I just work for the guy right now, okay? I would love to kick him in the balls. I... don't know where he's at right now, or I'd do it. But he... won't be there to get the kids tomorrow."

"Wonderful, I have to disappoint them again. And he couldn't call me himself?"

Oh, fuck.

That's probably what he was calling for.

"Not ... not after the... Talli, it's going to get bad. Really bad."

"So people keep telling me."

Michael ran out carrying a royal blue short dress that clung to me like I'd been melted, poured in, and forgot to say when. Would I ever feel comfortable in that again?

"If you need anything, just... call me, okay? Will you do that?"

"I don't think that would be..."

"As a friend, Talli," she cut me off. I smiled wistfully, remembering how much fun we had before all of this mess happened.

"Sure," I mumbled, wondering if I really would ever call her.

It was doubtful.

"Jase will be there to pick them up for his weekend, though... his next weekend."

"I'm sorry?" I asked.

"His weekend, the weekend of Emily's party. I will be there for her birthday... you know, I actually think Chris and his family will be there, too!"

"You're kidding," I said with a half-smile.

"No, no kidding. But since Jase will have the kids that Friday, do you want to get together? Watch a movie?"

"Um... we'll see, okay?" I said, avoiding telling her everything.

Jase wouldn't have the kids that Friday, see... he apparently either hadn't read everything over very carefully, or he hadn't told everyone what was going on. But I wasn't going to tell her that; I wasn't going to go into all of my reasons for limiting his visitation, I didn't even want to think about that bitch and her frumpy housewife comment.

Hell, I wasn't even a... a *wife* anymore... or I wouldn't be... not after...

"Mommy!" Elizabeth ran out, holding up a crimson red sleeveless button-down shirt and carrying a pair of jeans... not just any pair of jeans, Jase's favorite pair. She was smiling, wiggling her eyebrows up and down, and I had to laugh.

Oh, my.

Frumpy, huh? You think I'm frumpy? Why, because I wear conservative business suits, little to no makeup, and rarely do much of anything to my hair?

Okay, fine. So she had a point, and of course he would go looking elsewhere.

But on that day, the day of Emily's party, frumpy will be the last fucking word he'll have to say about me.

"Are you sure about the jeans?" I asked her. "Not the black pants?"

"The jeans, Mommy. You never wear jeans anymore."

Well, okay. So I'm a frumpy soon to be ex-wife who's now taking fashion tips from a five year old child.

"Please, Mommy?" she asked, her blue eyes full of hope for the first time in so long.

What the hell. Why not?

JASE

"Here."

Kaitlyn was shoving a bowl under my nose, its contents bringing the first smile to my lips in the thirty minutes that I'd been there.

"Mint chocolate chip ice cream," I said with a smile, accepting the bowl. Kate sat beside me, her own bowl with a different flavor for her. "You don't like mint chocolate chip ice cream. Is this something Jack left?"

"His name is Jase, and the answer is no. When the news about you and Talli broke, I bought that disgusting crap for you." She shot a sideways glance at me before reaching out and tousling my hair. "You're lucky I love you, Warner."

"I've never deserved your love, Kate," I said softly, stirring the melting contents in my bowl.

"Eat up. I've heard it's the cure for whatever ails you," she said, ignoring my self-depreciating comment as she picked up the remote.

"Says who?"

"Says some schmuck who used to bring this crap to my room all the time, whenever he was trying to mend his broken heart."

"Hey, this is not crap, okay?" I said, hastily wiping my eyes once more. "This is… this is the epitome of heaven in a bowl."

"Oh, that was cheesy," she teased, still messing with her remote. "So tell me," she began, finally placing the remote down, "what did take you so long?"

Of course she'd ask a question just as I took a bite of my ice cream. I held up one finger and I swallowed, then turned my hand to flip her off as she laughed at me. "Damn, Kate, give me a minute, would ya?"

"You're been here long enough to answer the question now."

"I didn't want to bother you with it," I admitted with a shrug. "I figured you were going through enough. Which, by the way, you never came to me with."

"What, because Jase and I separated?" she asked, raising one of her perfectly sculpted eyebrows, her chocolate brown eyes boring in to me.

"Just give me the word; I'll gladly kick his ass again."

"After what he did for Elizabeth?" she asked, and I immediately felt the color drain from my face. "I'm sorry… I'm sorry, Jase. I know you were just joking. I shouldn't have brought that up."

"At least you remember," I mumbled, turning back to my ice cream, my eyes resting on the big screen TV. "Hey…"

Kate let out a soft laugh as the opening of *Almost Famous* filled the screen. "I figured you would need this, too."

"What about you?" I asked, turning to look at her. "I… fuck, I'm so sorry, I've been so wrapped up in everything going on in my world…"

"Hey, I'm good," she replied with a shrug. "I married a narcissistic bastard who occasionally has a God complex. Don't get me wrong, he's a great guy. Just a lousy husband."

"Why did you split up?" I asked suddenly. She chewed on her bottom lip, seeming to contemplate how to answer. "You don't have to tell me if you don't want to."

"He's… well, we just didn't work," she said with a shrug. "I'm set in my ways, he's set in his."

"Kate…"

"He's just very, very career oriented. Not that that is a bad thing, you know."

"Way to soften the blow there, Evans."

"And that's another thing," she added, licking her spoon. "His ego. We've had problems with everything. I don't want to change my name. Where is the law that says I have to change my name?"

"There's not," I answered, not that she listened.

"Kaitlyn Evans is known as a very successful wedding planner. Not Brooks. Evans."

"Besides, I like calling you Evans," I added with a grin as she continued.

"And god forbid I talk about my career with him! Apparently being a wedding planner is sooooo insignificant compared to being a doctor."

"So is being a musician," I muttered, reminiscing over a past discussion I'd had with Brooks.

"But you remember hearing about Kiefer Sutherland's wedding? That huge one where he married that attorney?" she asked and I nodded. "The one where the original wedding planner ran off with their money and had done nothing? I fixed that. I walked in there and handled their wedding in three days, Warner. Three days. I have Kiefer and his wife promising me if there's anything I ever need, all I have to do is call!

And you know what Brooks said?"

"Nothing?" I asked, grinning at her.

"Exactly. And excuse the hell out of me for not wanting to be barefoot and pregnant!" she continued. "Did he think I was kidding? Seriously?"

I took another spoonful of ice cream, annoyed at Brooks and amused at Kate as she kept going.

"I know I want children someday, but not..." Her hands were waving, gesturing, as if she were trying to find the words.

"Not on someone else's terms," I finished for her.

"Exactly," she said with a sigh. Her spoon clinked in her bowl as she set it down on the table. "And do you think I'm wrong?"

"No, it really is something that the two of you should agree on," I replied, remembering how Talia and I had both agreed upon us wanting children, and when. Okay, so Emily was a surprise, but she was such a happy surprise and worth it—so, so worth it.

"Exactly, and I'm just... I'm not ready."

"Was that it?" I asked. She sighed, pushing her dark brown hair back.

"Only a tiny piece." She turned her head towards me and smiled softly. "I'm sorry, Jase, I'm sure this is the last thing you want to hear."

"That's what friends are for, right?" I asked, smiling softly.

"Right." She settled back into the couch, her legs drawn up as she concentrated on the film. "I guess I've been... I don't know." She fidgeted slightly, like she always did when something bothered her. I could only imagine the asinine things Brooks would say to undermine her confidence.

There was no need for insecurity.

Kaitlyn is easily one of the most beautiful women I know. Time has been an even greater friend to her, the maturity in her features showing what a strikingly beautiful woman she'd become. Perhaps the best part of it was how she was so unassuming, so unaware of it.

"What?" she asked.

Busted.

"You look good, Kate," I said, grinning slightly.

She smirked and said, "Being on the verge of divorce could do that for you. See? No loss."

Wow... oh... wow.

I felt my face fall at the mention of that lovely 'd' word. Fuck. That just... that hurt. I turned towards the television, blinking back the tears that were threatening, feeling her eyes on me the entire time.

"God, you really love her don't you?"

I chuckled softly at her question, glancing sideways at her. "Is it just hitting you now?"

She shrugged. "I always thought it was just the hair thing. Your brief obsession with redheads or something," she said nonchalantly, and I had to grin.

"Nah, I think it was the, we have kids thing, and she changed my life thing. You know, the usual."

Kate shook her head slowly. "Then why'd you let her go, dork?"

"I..." The tears spilled over once more, Kate's face blurring in front of me. "I didn't, Kate. I didn't."

I felt her take the bowl from my hands as I closed my eyes against the torrent of emotions. My hands were shaking as I brought them up to my face, rubbing it roughly.

"I don't understand, Jase."

"I... I didn't let her go, Kate. She left me." I couldn't even bring myself to look at Kate, so I kept my eyes on my hands. "She took the kids, and..."

"Why?"

I swallowed, the guilt more overwhelming than anything. "I can't blame her. I... I fucked up Kate."

"No."

"I did, I fucked up, and I have to live with it, live with myself, and..."

"I don't... Jase, you didn't. You... you wouldn't do that."

I was quiet as I sniffled slightly, shrugging as I continued looking at my hands. "I've done a lot of things that I thought I'd never do," I finally said.

"You..." She sighed and I felt her hand run through my hair. "I didn't think... I still don't. Jase, you wouldn't sleep with someone else."

I looked over at her, brushing a tear away with the back of my hand as she continued.

"Even with everything that has gone wrong... ever... with... with anyone, with us, you don't cheat. You're not a cheater. You would never... never sleep with someone else, and..."

"I didn't," I interrupted her.

Oh, that felt so good to say that.

"Oh, thank god," she said, placing her hand over her heart. "Because I was about to feel really stupid if you'd said that..."

"I may as well have, Kate. Just because I didn't sleep with her doesn't mean I didn't cheat."

"What happened?"

"I just... I know I was wrong, and... OW!"

"Stop beating around the bush and tell me!" Kate said, holding the pillow she's hit me upside the head with.

"Bree." I cringed saying that word, her name. "But... but it didn't start with Bree."

"What did it start with?"

I bit my bottom lip as I tried to come up with it. Was... was it when I left? Or was it before? I mean... I don't want to blame anything on...

"When Em was born," I finally said. "God, Kate, it started... way back... then." My eyes were wide as I let it sink in. "I... I love that baby, and I'm not sorry that she's here, and..."

"Okay... go back then, okay? What changed?"

"Everything," I said, my voice soft. "But... but we still tried, not that we really talked about it, and then I went on the road, and..."

"And what?" Kate asked softly.

"And Talli... stopped trying. She just stopped, and it was like she was waiting for me to leave so she could push me away, and... and I was working with Bree, and... it didn't just happen, I let it happen. OW!"

"What do you mean you let it happen?" she demanded.

"I thought you were supposed to be my friend."

"I am being your friend." She put the pillow behind her back. "I'm sorry. Continue."

"There's... not much else to say," I replied. "Talia and I..." I sighed before continuing, my pride shredded to pieces already. "Kate,

129

when I came back, Talli was sleeping in Emily's room."

"Why?"

"She said it was because Emily wasn't sleeping well."

"And you accepted that?"

"Kate..."

"I'm sorry, I'm sorry. You gave up, then what happened."

"What am I supposed to do, fight for someone that doesn't want me anymore?" I sniffled again, wishing I had a better grip on my emotions.

"You say you didn't let her go."

"I didn't."

"So then why did she leave?"

My hands were shaking, my voice wavering as I began to tell her. My eyes stayed on my hands as I began with the plan, how Talli was going to bring the kids to Texas, and we were all going to be together in the hotel suite all weekend.

I told her about getting the message that Talli wasn't coming.

I told her about going home, and Talli and the kids being gone, and the pain was every bit as fresh as the day it had happened.

And I kept going on, no matter how unbelievable it sounded, and I left it all out there on the table to the girl who had been my best friend, my first everything, who had always believed in me no matter what. And I waited for her to stop me, I waited for her to tell me that there was no way I was telling her the truth, even though I was, and... and...

"Okay, listen..." She reached out, placing her hand over mine.

Here it comes.

"Does Talli know you didn't sleep with Bree?"

I hadn't realized I was holding my breath until that moment I let it go. "No," I said softly.

"And she left after that?"

"Yeah, as soon... as soon as she could. Please, Kate, I don't think I can talk about this anymore."

"Okay, then don't talk. Listen." I felt her hand gently touch my face, turning it towards her, and I died a little more inside as it hit me that I didn't know how long it had been since Talia had done that, just... touched me, or let me touch her. Even the simplest touch would mean the world to me...

"Jase?" Kate's voice brought me back, and I raised my eyes to meet hers. "Okay, now... listen. I... I may be totally off base here, but what if... what if she was reacting, rather than just acting?"

"What?"

"She left after what she... saw, okay? You said you didn't tell her, and yes you have a point that right then it may not have mattered."

"Thanks."

"I'm being honest with you. This is coming from someone essentially in your shoes, someone who has filed the divorce papers herself. When did those come?"

"Today," I replied. "And...I ... I couldn't take it anymore, I can't take it anymore, Kate. I'm supposed to get on some damn plane tomorrow and perform on a stage with someone who I'd rather... I can't even say it."

"So, don't go."

"It's not that simple," I disagreed.

"The hell it isn't. Listen to me... and I will pull out that pillow if you interrupt me again, got it?"

"Fine, Evans, please... go on."

"I saw the interview."

I cringed when she said that, knowing what it looked like, and...

"And I could smell the line of bullshit from a mile away."

I know now why I love Kate so much.

"But I'm not emotionally invested in this, and let's face it... Talli may know you're a cuddler with her, but she probably doesn't know that anyone within arms length when you fall asleep is fair game. I have almost an album full of evidence that I have taunted you with for years."

"Not if I burn it first. OW! Damn, Evans, fine! I'm shutting up!"

"Thank you," she muttered, placing the pillow on the floor beside her as I rubbed the side of my head. "Now... the papers. What did the papers say?"

"I don't know," I admitted.

"What do you mean, you don't know?" she demanded.

"I... just handed them to Chris. OW! You asked that time!"

"That was for being a dumbass," she said. "Okay... okay, we can fix this."

"What do you mean fix, and what do you mean 'we'?"

"First thing, you're sick."

"Thanks, I love you too."

"No, no no... dork, you're... ill. Deathly? No, not deathly... let's avoid karma here. But... you're sick, and you are unable to go on this trip."

"I wish..."

"No, you will," she cut me off. "And then, Mr. 'Obligations', you're going to get your priorities straight, and take a... a... sabbatical."

"What?"

"A break. You need a break, for personal reasons, and it's not a lie. Tell Chris, tell Alison, tell Jackie...yes! Tell Jackie, and he'll make it happen, okay?"

"What then?" I asked, shrugging.

"Well, that depends... first we look over those papers she had you served with."

"Chris took them, though. I told him to give her whatever she asked for."

"Have you lost your damn mind?" Kate asked. "Without looking at them?"

"I promised her I'd take care of her, and... and I'm going to."

"And you've just essentially told her you don't give a damn."

"Would she have filed the papers if she did?" I asked, eyes narrowed. "She wants out."

"Just read the... never mind. Let me read them."

"Why? You think there's something in there that you'll understand that I won't?" I asked, sinking back into the cough, my eyes back on the movie.

"Yes," she answered matter-of-factly. "And when I prove it to you, you're going to owe me."

"What are you going to prove?" I asked, rolling my eyes back in her direction.

"That she still loves you," she replied, looking a bit too confident in herself. I couldn't hold back the scoff.

Love, huh?

If that's what love is, if that is what it does to you, then I don't think

I can deal with it anymore.

"Yes, you can," Kate said, and I looked over at her, confused.

"I can what?"

"I know that look on your face, Jase. You can deal with this, you will get through this, and it will all be okay, got it?" She handed me a frame that she'd pulled off her end table, and with one glance down I felt the corners of my mouth pull up in a smile.

My family.

The picture was taken the day Kate came to see us at the house just before I left on tour. Elizabeth had a big cheesy grin on her face, Michael was making a face at the camera, Emily was looking at Michael like he'd grown a second head...

And Talli was curled up next to me. Her head was on my shoulder, her nose crinkled up as she smiled... she was probably getting ready to laugh. I knew that look on her face. I missed that look.

I wanted to see it again.

"You're going to see this again," Kate said.

"Would you get out of my head?" I asked with a soft laugh.

"Never, Warner. Never." She kissed my cheek, reaching for the frame that I held in my hand. I pulled it away slightly, and I shook my head.

"Can I?" I held it close to me, smiling down at it.

"Absolutely," she said. "Hold on to it as long as you need."

I am not entirely convinced that there was no double meaning to her words. Knowing Kate, I'm sure there were. But I did hold onto it, as I called Jackie and I told him to spread the word that I was sick and wouldn't be going. I held onto it as I stuck to my story with Chris. I held onto it as we continued watching the movie we'd watched together so many times before.

And I believed.

CHAPTER 11

TALLI

I think I'm going to throw up.

My hands are shaking, my stomach is in knots, I'm staring at myself in the mirror, and I... I don't recognize me anymore. This is a stranger staring back at me.

"You don't need to pack the dipie bag, Mommy. Daddy has all that stuff," Elizabeth informed me as she whizzed past the washroom for about the millionth time in the past five minutes.

"I... still want to... to take it."

Oh, yeah. I am definitely going to be ill.

We're supposed to be there in a half an hour, and there's going to be a house full of our families, our friends.

And Jase.

Jase, who I haven't seen since he buzzed through here dropping the kids off, apparently on his way to the airport with ... her.

Jase, who had one of his assistants call to say he couldn't get the kids because he had to go back to New York.

Jase, who didn't go to New York because he was 'sick'.

Jase, who finally read the divorce papers, and... and...

"Mommy, Em's presents!" Michael squeaked as he ran into the bathroom. "Mommy, where's the red top?"

"I... I can't, baby."

I was back in a brown business suit that I mostly wore to work. And the hair... the hair that I had taken the pains to make it look like I hadn't taken pains to do it... the hair that was just... sassy, with loose tendrils around my face... no, it didn't fit with my clothes at all. Nope, I needed to just take it down and pull it all back into a knot and...

"Mommy Christine, you get in there and change this instant!" Elizabeth was in the doorway, one hand on her hip, the other hand pointing towards my bedroom.

"Young lady..."

"Don't take that tone with me, Mommy, we had a deal. If you don't want me to have an attitude today, you'll get back in there and change."

Oh, great. My five-year-old has turned into a blackmail artist. Perfect.

"I just don't feel comfortable in it," I mumbled, not quite sure why I was arguing with my child over it. I was the adult, damn it! It was up to me how I dressed for Emily's first birthday party. And why the hell would Jase care, anyhow? I mean, I'd gotten that call from Sherise Adler's office telling me that he wouldn't be contesting the divorce, so this was obviously what he wanted.

And would someone please explain to me why that hurt so badly?

But... but I'm not holding my breath, see. Because after I'd heard that lovely bit of news, I figured it would be safe to answer the phone when Jase called. But this last call was bad. So, so very bad.

"I didn't see you in it, Mommy," Elizabeth reminded me, her bottom lip sticking out. "Can I see you in it?"

"Me too?" Michael chimed in.

"Fine... fine, I'll let you see me in it, then I'll change back, okay?" I caved, pushing past them to change into that sleeveless red top and jeans. It just... I just... well, they fit. I can admit that they fit, but that was the problem. They fit. The jeans weren't skintight, but they hugged my ass, which was not covered by the shirt that ended just below the waistline of my low-rise jeans. And the shirt was tailored just so, tight enough to show the swell of my breasts without gapping in between the buttons, and the sides of the shirt curved along my waist, tapering in around it before flaring out just slightly at the bottom to rest on the tops of my hips.

Oh, this just wasn't going to do.

It was bad enough that he's so pissed off, I don't need him pissed off AND looking at me like... like...

Well, I guess I don't have to worry about that now, do I?

My hands shook as I smoothed them over my blouse, recalling his words, his tone...

"Why?" he'd asked as soon as I answered the phone.

"I think it's fairly clear why I would file..."

"Why are you doing this, Talia?"

"As I was trying to say..."

"They're our kids. Ours. You know I would never do anything to hurt them, to harm them, damn it, you know that."

"I... don't know that anymore, Jase," I'd replied, cringing at the lie.

This wasn't about him, and I knew it.

"That was the one damned thing we could agree on, and it could work. It... it was working, or are so you so fucking bitter that you couldn't see that?"

"Oh, bitter. Bitter... that's..."

"The truth," he cut me off.

"You know, I don't have time for this."

"Of course not, Talia. You never had the time for this, or us, or me. Of course."

And my blood began to boil every bit as much as his was.

Where the fuck did he get off turning this around on me? I wasn't the one running all over the country with someone else, flaunting my affair in his face, fucking someone else in our bed!

I told him to take it up with my lawyer if he didn't like it, and even though I haven't heard from Ms. Adler's office I'm sure he will probably fight back now. Just like she said he would. Just like I feared he would. And that tiny part of me... no, that big part of me, that part that was drug through the mud when he and I first got together, the part that he promised would never be brought up again... I had a feeling that it would.

And when he said in that ominous tone of his that we would talk at Emily's party, I could feel every single skeleton from that graveyard in my closet come creeping back, reaching out for me, taunting me.

He... wouldn't.

Please, god, tell me he wouldn't.

"Mommy, let us see!" Elizabeth's voice filtered through the door.

I pasted a smile on my face as I opened the door. "See?" I said. "It's…"

"Awesome!" she exclaimed.

"Mommy, you look so pretty!" Michael added, reaching out and taking my hand, and I fought against the tears stinging my eyes.

"Guys, I have to change back."

"No! No, Mommy, don't!" Michael said, holding my hand just a little tighter.

"We hafta go, Mommy," Elizabeth said, her expression completely serious. "Come on, we're gonna be late."

"Baby girl…"

"Mommy, everyone's waiting!" she continued, her arms outstretched in pure drama queen fashion. "Jaden's even there! And Jaden will tell you that you look… spet… septatcul… she'll tell you that you look great." By this time, Michael had drug me to the living room, where Elizabeth was holding up my keys and my purse.

"I need the diaper bag," I caved, reaching for it.

"Em! Time to go!" Michael called after his baby sister, who came toddling out carrying one of his Transformer toys.

"Transformers? Seriously?" I deadpanned as I looked at my beautiful one year old daughter, who merely crinkled up her nose and grinned at me.

"Her puppy is at… at Daddy's house… and…"

"Slow down," I advised Elizabeth, who sometimes would speak so fast her brain couldn't keep up.

"Mommy, your boots! Your shitkickers!" Michael exclaimed, running over to me with them.

"Young man!"

"He's only repeating what he hears," Elizabeth reminded me, pulling that whole five-going-on-thirty routine perfectly.

"Whatever, mother," I said as I took my boots from Michael's hands, and Elizabeth had the nerve to laugh at me.

Did I have to give birth to someone who acted just like me? Seriously?

"Good call on the boots, though," Elizabeth added as she slipped her sandals on. "You never know who's poop you might need to kick today."

"Ew!" Michael said. "Tha's gross!"

I shook my head, adjusting my boots as the older children continued their discussion on literal and figurative speaking, and I turned to Emily when I was done. "You ready, Princess?" I asked, and she held up her hands to me.

Here goes nothing.

I hadn't seen the house since I'd driven away from it. I don't know if I was expecting some kind of creepy vibe to it, or for it to take on some Munsters quality or something, but no. It was still that house, and it still had the nerve to look warm. Welcoming. Inviting.

Such a shame I knew better.

"Jackie!" Elizabeth exclaimed as soon as I had unhooked her booster seat, and she ran straight up to the big, burly man who had come out to the front lawn to greet us. Michael soon followed suit, and he had them each hoisted up in his arms, squeezing them close. My heart constricted in my chest, and I turned back to my task of unhooking Emily from her carseat.

Nostalgia.

She's a real bitch.

Emily clung to me as I walked up the front lawn, a tight smile on my face as Jackie sat Elizabeth and Michael down. They scampered towards the front door, announcing as loudly as they could that they were there and looking for their Daddy.

Just like they used to whenever we'd come back from the store, or from one of Emily's appointments.

"Well, well, well," Jackie said as he stopped in front of me. "Look at you, Spunky."

"Let's not and say we did," I replied, a blush crossing my cheeks. Jackie put his big, strong arms around me, rubbing my back slightly.

"You are missed around here, T," he said softly.

Perhaps everyone else did, but the one I wanted to miss me I'm sure couldn't care less.

I swear my whole body was shaking as I stepped through the door into the entry way of that house. It had been my home for years. So much had happened under this roof, within these walls. So many happy times, as well as the sadness that had enveloped us, especially so shortly after I'd moved in.

Nan's voice could be heard from the great room as she gushed over Elizabeth and Michael, how big they were how they looked just like their Daddy. Except Elizabeth's eyes...

"I see Talia right there, in those eyes."

Oh fuck...

That was Jase...

And his voice, his tone... it was the same tone he always reserved for the kids. So loving, so sweet. If only he used that tone for me.

At the sound of his voice, Emily was pushing against my chest, prompting me to set her down. Her diaper crinkled as she ran towards the voices, which immediately became louder at the birthday girl's presence.

"Oh, look at you!" Nan exclaimed. I leaned against the wall, closing my eyes, my hand over my heart as I continued to listen.

"Hello birthday girl!" That was Lisa. I'm so glad she made it, she needs this, even though it's so soon after Jack's death.

"There's Mini-Talli." Chris? Chris was here? Huh.

But I didn't hear Jase.

I didn't hear what he had to say about our youngest child, all dressed in an outfit he'd bought for her when he was on the road, her curls pulled up on top of her head in a puff-ball of a ponytail. I clenched my eyes shut as the 'awww's filtered through, trying my hardest to calm my nerves.

Jaden... where was Jaden? I didn't hear her among the squeals and laughter and conversation.

But I could feel a pair of eyes on me.

And even before I finally opened mine, I knew who was standing there.

Damn it, did he have to look so... so... good?

Did his hair have to be tousled just so? And... and did he have to have just the tiniest bit of scruff on his face, maybe one days' growth at the most? Did he have to be in those jeans that had the tear right... there where I had been yanking at the button in haste to get them off of him? And that damned white button down shirt, opened enough to expose his neck and a tiny part of his chest... oh, he had nerve.

He had a lot of nerve.

And where did he get off raking his eyes up and down me like I was...

Like I was...

His wife?

Just as quickly, as soon as our eyes met, that look was gone. His jaw was set, twitching just slightly as his eyes turned stormy, dark, narrowing as he looked at me.

"Are you going to just stand there?" he asked, his tone harsh and sharp. Emily, who he was holding easily in his left arm, squirmed and fussed slightly, as if she could sense the tension in the air.

Oh, what an asshole.

"While it beats the alternative, I wouldn't miss the party that I planned for my daughter," I snapped back.

"Oh, your daughter, is it?"

"Okay, kids, let's keep this civilized," Pete said as he walked into the entryway. "Hey, T." He came straight up to me, giving me a big hug that I wasn't quite expecting. "Jaden's in the kitchen, and she has some questions for you."

"Good," I said, smiling at my brother-in-law. I walked with him, past Jase, involuntarily cringing and moving back as Jase reached out for me.

"Some things never fucking change," he muttered, pushing past us and going back to the great room, Emily still on his arm.

But he was wrong. He was so, so wrong.

If things had never changed, it wouldn't have to be this way.

JASE

Why?

That one word has been circling in my head for days now, going on just under two weeks. Ever since per Kate's insistence, I retrieved those papers back from Chris and read them.

And I mean *really* read them.

After my initial shock and all the tears I cried on Kate's shoulder, the anger began to sink in. She and I had agreed on this, damn it! These kids needed us—both of us—and we knew that it was imperative that we show them that no matter what was happening with us, they weren't to blame and they wouldn't be punished or kept from either one of us.

And now... now here I was waiting for Talia to bring our children to Emily's birthday party, even though the kids should have been here last night. I had a house full of people that I had to avoid the questions of... seriously, why would they ask anyhow? Weren't the details discussed on *Celebrity Gossip* or in some rag mag? Fuck, I should have read them, I should have watched the show. Maybe then it wouldn't have taken me by such surprise.

"She's late." I said those words through clenched teeth to the only person who hadn't turned on me in the least.

"She'll be here," Kate replied, walking up behind me and running her fingers through my hair. "Go change your clothes."

I pulled at the hem of my t-shirt and asked, "What's wrong with this?"

"Go put on your white button down shirt, and that pair of jeans that you were talking about earlier."

My face flared crimson as I berated myself from ever telling Kate the story of how that rip occurred. "No," I protested, scowling. "Not those jeans."

"Yes, those jeans. And no shaving. It's perfect, just like when you got married."

"Kate..."

"Besides, you have a house full of guests that you're attempting to avoid like the plague."

"Good point," I mumbled, scowling once more when she messed

with my hair again. "Quit!"

"I see you used the cucumbers on your eyes, though," she said, ignoring my protests. She placed her hands on both sides of my face, her knowing look striking another nerve with me. "That's what I use after a good cry."

"Great, go ahead. Rub it in. I'm a pussy who can't handle..."

"Jase, stop it, okay?" She continued caressing the sides of my face as she added, "You've been going through hell, and I know you're a mess knowing she's going to be here today."

"And I'm going to give her a piece my fucking mind when she does."

"No, you're not."

"Try and stop me, Kate! She's keeping my kids from me."

"She's upset, and she's hurt, and she's fighting back."

"You're squishing my face," I said, pulling back and rubbing my cheeks absentmindedly.

"There you are," Lisa said as she huffed her way around the corner.

"I'm going to get changed," I mumbled, turning and taking those stairs as quickly as I could. I had a house full of people, all right. The majority of them had some sort of condescending remark to make about how the layout wasn't how Talli would do it, or the house just wasn't the same without Talli and the kids there. Well, no shit. You're preaching to the fucking choir here. You think I don't know how different this house is, how empty?

How lonely?

And Lisa, of course, had to go on and on and on about how devastating her and Jack's divorce had been, like I need to hear that. You know what, Lisa? You and Jack didn't have any kids. You had clearly stated that when you divorced Jack you didn't feel the same way that you had when you married him.

I don't feel the same way about Talli either.

I love her more now than the day I had stood before family and friends, more than when I had danced with her in Lisa's back yard.

And all she wanted from me was to keep me the hell away from her kids and, according to Chris, about half of the child support she could easily get. No alimony. No parts of this house, or its contents, or... me.

We were a house divided.

Even here, this day, Emily's birthday... a house divided.

Talia's family, or those from her family that had shown up, were in one area of the house, congregated and gossiping away. Her friends and co-workers stayed with them also, I'm sure going on and on about what a lousy son of a bitch I am.

My family, for the most part, stayed in the great room, commenting on the pictures that still lined the walls, waiting for the birthday girl to arrive. None of them said one ill word towards Talia. None of them dared, and not because of her family and friends being present.

Because of me.

Because I had asked them not to.

Because no matter how angry I am at her, no matter how much I wish I could scream at her at the top of my lungs, no matter how much it hurts, I still love her.

So I'm standing here, looking at this stranger in the mirror, wondering how the hell I'm going to make it through today. And I have changed into those stupid jeans with that little rip in them from when Talli and I had barely made it into the house before the clothes were flying... only a few short days before I left on that stupid fucking tour. I had that white button down shirt on that she always loved, cursing myself for putting us in this situation, wishing that she would look at me—really look at me—when she finally got here.

Or just let me touch her.

Hell, why not go for broke and wish for both, right?

"She's still late," I said from my seat in the great room. My knee was bouncing up and down as I tried in vain to calm my nerves.

"She'll be here," Kate continued trying to reassure me, placing her hand on my bouncing knee.

"She..."

"You know, if you weren't gallivanting all over this country with Dial-A-Whore, maybe my sister would be here," Lisa said as she walked into the great room. "Maybe she..."

"Maybe you have about two seconds to shut the hell up," Jaden snapped on her way through to the kitchen. "And I dare anyone to start once those kids are here."

Pete grinned sheepishly as he got up to follow his wife. "Hormones," he said with a shrug before following her to the kitchen.

"You know..."

"They're here," Jackie cut off whatever Lisa was about to say. My heart began to race as Jackie made his way out the front door, and I instantly reached for Kate's hand, which I squeezed as hard as I could.

They're here.

My kids are finally here, the way they should have been all along.

And Talia...

She's here.

Here.

For the first time since she left, she's going to walk through those doors. And as angry as I am, as hurt as I am, I'm half-tempted to lock her in a room somewhere and never let her leave again, just so I can have her near me.

I miss her so badly...

I...

"Daddy! Where's Daddy?" Elizabeth's voice echoed as she and Michael came into the house, no doubt running through that front entryway. I felt Kate's hand on the side of my face, and only then did I realize that a tear had fallen down my cheek.

Fuck, what's wrong with me?

I have to pull it together, not just for everyone else here, but for...

"Daddy!"

Elizabeth and Michael came running into the room, past everyone else, straight into my arms.

I wanted to hold onto them forever.

"Nana!" Elizabeth squealed as she saw Nan, and she ran over to her. Nan was gushing over how much they'd grown, how beautiful they both were, how they both looked just like me.

"Minus those big blue eyes," she added, her hand firmly on Elizabeth's chin as she grinned down at her.

I was knelt down beside Baby Girl, holding onto her hand, speaking to no one in general as I said, "I see Talia right there, in those eyes."

Elizabeth is always so proud to have anyone tell her that any part of her reminds them of her mother. I tell her every chance I get the littlest things that remind me of Talli that she has—from her mannerisms, to the way she crinkles up her nose when she smiles, to those eyes.

"Oh, look at you!" I heard Nan exclaim, and my attention turned back to my little Princess who had entered the room.

I think it was Chris who called her Mini-Talli.

And he was right.

She looked so damn cute, running up to me with her little tiny ponytail... no, not even a ponytail, just a little cotton ball of curls on top of her head. And she was dressed in the cutest little yellow outfit... oh... oh, I bought this. I brought this home for Emily when I came home from tour. And Talia had... well, she'd made some remark about how I didn't even know what size Emily wore, and then I'd snarked back about how if she'd brought them around maybe I'd know.

Ah. Hindsight.

But here she was at her first birthday party, clinging to me and looking around at everyone, not the least bit happy about so many people being around. And I knew she was nervous, I knew she was looking for Talia, so I made my way through everyone who were fawning all over Elizabeth and Michael to look for their mother.

I didn't have to go far.

My breath caught in my throat as I saw her standing there, her eyes shut tightly, her hand on her chest.

She looked so different.

No... no, not different.

She looked like *my* Talli. My Talli, the one who had all but disappeared. She was wearing jeans, for fuck's sake. I hadn't seen her in jeans in forever. And oh hell, did they look good, and her ... her boots? Holy shit, she was wearing the boots she wore in Cleveland. My stomach took a dive as I remembered that game of... what was it, strip drink guessing? We hadn't gotten very far, but I remembered especially when she took off the second boot, the way she'd wiggled those cute little toes of hers...

And today... today she was in red. Red. Not brown, not tan, not beige... red. And this shirt, the way it clings to her in all the right places was making my mouth water. Her hair... and... and her makeup and...

Oh, God.

What was it Kate had said?

"Being on the verge of divorce could do that to you. See? No loss."

Of course she was moving on, and taking my kids with her, and doing whatever she could to cut me out of all of their lives.

Think again, sweetheart.

It almost didn't register that her eyes had opened, and I couldn't help myself, the anger and hurt were just too strong. "Are you going to just stand there?" I asked her. Emily began to fuss, and I immediately felt guilty.

Until...

"While it beats the alternative, I wouldn't miss the party I planned for my daughter."

You. Bitch.

"Oh, *your* daughter, is it?" I started, ready to let it fucking fly.

Of course Pete picked just that time to walk in to the entryway.

"Okay, kids, let's keep this civilized."

Fuck you, Pete.

But I thought about it, what Pete said. And he's right, at least today we should. But damn it, I am going to talk to her. I just want to know why.

Just... why?

They were walking past me, and I reached for her, my heart breaking just a little bit more as she, once again, cringed and backed away from me.

"Some things never fucking change," I muttered, pushing past her before she could see those stupid fucking tears that had sprung up into my eyes. Elizabeth and Michael were still with Mom in the great room, and Emily pushed against my chest signaling she wanted to get down and play.

"Jase?" Kate asked softly as I sat Emily down.

"Not now, please," I replied, just as soft. My hands were shaking slightly, and as much as I hated it, a beer was not just in order but needed to settle my nerves.

Oh, great.

Now I'm drinking at my daughter's birthday party.

Talia was out of that kitchen every bit as soon as I had walked in, and she was consoling Lisa over... well, whatever was bothering her, probably how our problems were reminding her of her divorce from Jack. Whatever, sweetheart. Jaden looked absolutely livid, but she'd been in a mood already.

"Jase, are you seriously..."

"Yes, I'm having a beer at Emily's birthday party. It's either this or go the fuck off on..."

"Would you let me finish?" she snapped, and I stopped in my tracks.

Wow, she really was pissed.

"Yeah, sure," I said with a shrug. Man, Pete was right. Hormones indeed.

"I love you both," she started, just like she always did.

"Yeah, and we love you, too."

"But this... *this* is wrong, and she's not listening to me, and..."

"This... what *this*?" I asked, needing clarification.

"She doesn't have the right to keep them from you."

It's a good thing I've had theatre training, otherwise I probably would have fallen over right then and there, dropping my beer and going into convulsions or something. Jaden Danielle Brogotti Warner, Talia's best friend, the one whose middle name was bestowed upon our youngest daughter, was siding with me?

Well... ish.

"Not that she doesn't have the right to be pissed off..."

"Of course not," I agreed, still looking at her like she'd come from another planet.

"But this is wrong."

"You... yeah. It's ... it's wrong."

"And you need to talk to her," Jaden continued as I took a long sip of my beer.

"Yeah... yeah, I do."

"And I'm going to help you make it happen."

I had no witty retort of any kind, so I merely nodded and took another drink of my beer.

"So, sometime today, it's going to happen. And Jase?"

"Hmm?"

Jaden stood up, her eyes completely dark and serious as she placed her hand on my arm. "Make her listen. Something's not right. Something about her is just… off, and… Just make her listen, okay?"

Jaden was right.

Something definitely seemed off.

Talia was so skittish as she fluttered room to room, occasionally speaking with people, but for the most part avoiding them. She barely spoke with my Nan, whom she'd been so close to. She eyed Kate the way she had back in Vegas, and where the hell that came from I'll never know. She wasn't outside playing with the children.

She was distracted.

Something… something was up.

I stood with my arms folded in front of me, my eyes narrowed as I watched her chewing on her thumbnail—something she never does—as she looked around the room full of people before disappearing yet again.

This time she was going down to the basement.

"Jase," Jaden whispered to me, and I nodded.

I walked over to the doorway that Talia had disappeared through, knowing she was all alone down there. I silently pulled that door open, stepping onto the stairs before closing the door behind me. I turned the lock slowly, stopping as I heard the 'click'.

We had to talk.

We *needed* to talk.

And it was time.

CHAPTER 12

TALLI

One would think that with a house full of people I would be able to inconspicuously slip away and look for that damn box. That box I need so desperately...

Then again, that ONE person thinking probably wouldn't be surrounded by tension, drama, a best friend who hates them, and a sister who won't shut up about her divorce from her late husband. Er, ex-husband. Whatever.

Oh, I sound like such a bitch, don't I?

But you know what? I can't help it. From the minute Jase shot me that dirty look and snapped at me, my day has gone from bad to worse. The only plus side is the kids are occupied and don't have to see me like this.

"What the hell has gotten into you?" Jaden asked when she caught up with me looking in an empty room. She'd already taken a turn at me early, and pregnant or not she was really pissing me off.

"You've already bitten my damn head off over my decision of what's best for my children, Jaden. I'm really not in the mood for round two."

"I'm not just talking about this stunt you've pulled..."

"It's a *stunt* now?" I asked, my temper flaring. "Tell you what, once your baby is born, you ship him off to Bree for her to raise, okay?"

I didn't wait for her reply.

Not that I would have wanted to have another argument, but Lisa was dragging me off, apparently in the nick of time as Jase was walking down the hallway.

All I wanted was to find that box, those damn papers, find our Angel's star so I could take her home with me. I just didn't want to ask Jase and have him give me more and more hell over everything I'd forgotten, or lost, or…

"Talli, are you listening to me?"

"Yes, Lisa, of course I am," I replied.

"So, if you would move the presents from the dining room to the great room…"

Presents? What? Oh, right. Lisa didn't like the way things were set up.

"You really need to take that up with Jase, okay?" I said, rubbing, my temple. Please, not another headache. Not now.

"You seem so distracted, Talli."

"Yeah, well, it's a difficult day."

"Do you need something?" she asked.

"Excuse me?" I turned to her, my eyes narrowed. Surely she wouldn't suggest…

"Did you fill your prescriptions? You look like… here… I have some…"

"Are you fucking kidding me?" I demanded, pushing her hand away from her purse. "No, I don't 'need' anything, okay? I'm doing just fine."

"Of course you are, Talli… but it's just anti-anxiety medication."

"Have you lost your fucking mind?" I asked and would have continued had Jase not walked in the room.

Damn, was he following me?

"Mommy, Daddy! Tristan's chasing me!" Enter Elizabeth to somewhat save the day, minus coming to both of us as Chris Webber's precocious son ran in behind her, his blonde hair damp with sweat, his big brown eyes sparkling with mischief.

"What'd you do?"

Oh.

Oh…

We asked it together. Simultaneously.

Just like we used to.

I could feel his eyes on me, but I couldn't bear to look at him. Nostalgia was wearing me thin, and I was close to my breaking point already. Tristan was talking excitedly with Jase about wanting water balloons so he didn't have to keep filling his cup to chase everyone around with, so I quietly slipped away.

The only place other than upstairs—and forget it, I wasn't going up those stairs—that I could think of that the box could be was the basement, down by the washer and dryer. We never had finished that basement the way we'd wanted to… everything else had gotten in the way.

The first opportunity I could, I made my way down those stairs. It looked pretty much the same as it had before, the sounds above muffled as I glanced around the room with a sigh.

Looks like Jase has been doing a lot of packing, probably ridding the house of things I had left behind. How the hell am I supposed to find that *one box* in the midst of…

"But you wouldn't dream of missing *your* daughter's party."

"Oh fuck!" I screeched as I turned around, Jase's voice frightening me to the point where my heart was racing. "Don't…do that!"

"What are you doing down here, Talia?" His glare was hard as he stepped closer. "You're so adamant that I can't be a decent father to my children, and yet here you are, in the middle of Emily's party, and…"

"Can it, Jase. I'm not in the mood."

"Why are you in my basement?"

I opened my mouth to protest, then quickly remembered…

"Hey, you're the one who said this house was a fucking prison, or did you forget?"

"Save the dramatics, theatre boy," I snapped back. "I was looking for…"

"Let me guess… you *forgot* something."

My mouth snapped shut, my eyes narrowing as he continued on, just like I knew he would.

"And yet *I'm* the…"

"You're the one who couldn't keep it in his pants," I cut him off.

Always back to that, huh? Funny, I recall keeping it in my pants for months, sweetheart."

"Oh, give me a fucking break," I scoffed.

"I already asked you nicely, Talia, now I want to know what the hell it is that you're looking for in my basement."

"You've been following me around all fucking day, Jase, just fucking spill it!"

"Oh, back to the 'fuck' words. My how you've grown."

"If you're not going to talk, then get the *fuck* out of my way," I said through clenched teeth.

"I'd tell you to move me, but you wouldn't dare, would you? It would involve actually touching me, and God knows you haven't been able to handle that in... how long now?"

"Oh, I get it! I see now!" I knew I was yelling at this point, but I didn't really care. "You're going to turn this around on me! Are you saying it was my fault you fucked Bree?"

"You know so much about what happened, don't you?" he yelled back, running his hand through his hair. "What was I supposed to do, *wait for you*?"

I swear he winced even before I picked up the nearest item and threw it at him, missing hitting him with the candle holder by a mere inch. It hit with a bang against a banister, the sound of it echoing as I screamed, "You BASTARD!"

"Is that the best you can do, Talli?" he screamed back, the veins in his neck beginning to show. "After all these months of being a heartless, emotionless, fucking zombie the best thing you can conjure up is calling me a bastard?" He ducked again as I continued throwing anything I could get my hands on at him, the glass from a frame shattering as it hit the back wall. "And *this* is the behavior of the same bitch who is taking my kids away from me?"

"Was she worth it?" I yelled as loud as I could, this time throwing what I swear was a dictionary that he deflected with his arm.

"What?"

No... no, don't you fucking dare just stop and stand there you fucking prick, you... you...

"Was... she... worth... it?" I asked through clenched teeth, ignoring the pounding on the basement door, the rattling of the doorknob. "Was that whore worth it?"

Don't you fucking dare cry, you rat fucking bastard!

"ANSWER ME!"

I hit him square in the chest with a folder, its contents seeming to explode on impact sending papers flying.

"Having your precious fucking Bree around was so goddamned important to you!" I continued, inching in closer even as Pete started calling down to us, yelling at Jase to open the door.

"It wasn't like that..."

"Stop lying to me!" I yelled at him, shoving him by his shoulders as hard as I could, getting even more pissed off when he barely took a step backwards.

"That's why you're... don't keep them away from me, Talli. Please."

"No...no, don't you fucking *dare* cry, do you hear me? You don't have the right to!" I continued poking his chest for effect as I kept on going. "*You* wanted this, Jase, you fucking *got* it. Now you answer me. Was she worth it?"

"Please don't do something you'll regret, Talli, because you..."

"Oh, that's just fucking RICH!" I backed away from him, my arms spread wide. "Me do something I'll regret. Like what, fucking someone else? Oh, wait... that was YOU!"

"Do you really think Bree was our only fucking problem?" he yelled back.

"Oh, things were so fucking bad, so unbearable for you, weren't they? When? When you were on the road, or when you were cozied up with your whore?"

"But you were a fucking saint through all of this, weren't you? You were always there for me, you wouldn't put anything in front of us, would you Talia?"

"You fucking hypocrite!" I threw another frame at him, which somehow he caught and sent hurtling into the side wall. "If you were so fucking miserable with me, you should have waited until I left!"

"You!" He was pointing at me, moving forward. "You are looking at the date you packed up that U-Haul and moved away from me. But you…" He stopped in front of me, placing his hand on my chest, over my heart which was hammering against my ribcage. "You…" His voice was soft now, catching in his throat as he continued. "You left me a long time ago."

It seemed a lifetime passed as we stood there, his hand firmly placed over my heart, our breathing in unison. Our eyes were glued to one another, mine glaring, his soft…

Why?

Why does he have to look at me that way?

He didn't so much as flinch when Pete kicked the door open and came bounding down the stairs. "What the fuck is going on down here?" he asked.

Jase's eyes finally lowered, along with his hand, as he turned from me. "Nothing to see, Pete," he said softly as he pushed past him and took the stairs two at a time.

"Jeezus, Talli, are you okay? Did he hurt you?"

Did he hurt me…

Wow, was that ever a stupid question.

"Talli?"

"Just give me a minute," I mumbled, turning towards the washer and leaning onto it with my arms.

"T, just…"

"Please, Pete?"

My mind was racing, the memories this room held crashing down around me. I remembered being down here, looking for my cell phone the day Jase had come home from tour. I remembered how we'd been back then, our hands always on each other, making love every chance we could… and that day, right here, right where I was standing…

My eyes slid shut as the tears came as other memories came rushing forward. These… these were different, not so pretty…

"Damn it, Jase, not now!"

"If not now, when? Can you answer that one, Talli?"

"Just… not now."

"Do you know how long you've been saying that to me?"

"Can't you see I'm busy?"

"Or you're tired, or you don't feel well, or the kids need you, or the hospital needs you. What about me, Talli? What about when I need

you?"

That very argument had also happened right here, right where I was standing...

And he'd left the next day for a weekend publicity tour, with *her.*

He didn't have to go, he'd chosen to go.

And now...

Now I could see why.

Oh, God. What have I done?

"What the hell has he done to you now?" Lisa asked, but I waved her off, stepping around her, around the broken glass...

The frame.

Our Angel.

Oh, God... what have I done?

JASE

She let me touch her...

I could feel every set of eyes on me as I rounded that corner, Pete hot on my heels, but I just didn't care.

She didn't flinch... she didn't push my hand away...

"What the hell is wrong with you?" Pete demanded as I entered my office, heading straight for my chair.

I didn't answer. I couldn't answer. He just... he just wouldn't understand.

I could feel her heart beating... no... no, it was hammering in her chest...

"I told you if you ever laid another hand on her..."

"Pete, could you excuse us for a moment?" Kate asked as she stepped in the room.

"Not now, Kate," Pete snapped, trying to step around her. I sunk into my chair, my hands covering my face, trembling ever so slightly.

Oh... I can smell her... the jasmine...

"Yes now," I heard Kate say, and I could only imagine the glare she shot him.

She's hurt. I... I hurt her, and it's killing me inside...

"You're damn lucky the kids were outside, Jase," Pete continued. "What were you thinking, locking yourself in that room with her like that?"

Right now I'm thinking I wish you hadn't interrupted us.

"Pete, the last thing anyone needs right now is another argument, okay?" Kate was saying.

She wants to know... No. No, Talli, she wasn't worth it, I swear. Nothing is worth losing you, and I'd take it all back if I could...

"I'm gonna check on T, and you damn well better hope she's okay."

Does she care? Is that what this all means? Can... does... oh, God...

"Hey," Kate's voice was soft as she sat on my desk, lightly running her fingers through my hair. I took a deep breath before I lowered my hands, and Kate took one of mine in hers. "I'm not really the type of person to say 'I told you so',"

"Liar," I said, feeling a grin tug at the corners of my mouth.

"She still loves you," Kate continued, ignoring my comment.

"I wouldn't go that far," I disagreed with her, squeezing her hand as if it could make me stop shaking. "How much did you hear?"

"Pretty much everything that was yelled at each other," she replied. "Along with the crashes, and the glass breaking. Are you okay?"

"Yeah, thanks for asking," I said with a slight laugh. "Oh... God, Kate, is she hurt? Did she get..."

"Jase, did you physically hurt her?" Kate asked, her eyes narrowed.

"No... no, there was just... stuff." I was waving my free hand trying to come up with a word, any word.

"You threw stuff at her?" Kate asked, smacking me hard on my shoulder.

"No! Damn! Let me finish, would you?"

"So, *she* threw stuff. Okay, that makes sense."

"Thanks," I deadpanned, pulling my hand back as I stood up and began pacing back and forth in front of the desk. "Fuck... fuck, what do I do now? What do I say to her? Is she... no, she wouldn't leave, would she? Not in the middle of Emily's party, right?"

"Are these rhetorical questions?"

I turned to Kate, shaking my head slightly before I resumed pacing.

"I don't know what to do now, Kate."

"Talk to her civilly?"

I let out a short laugh, running my hand through my hair. "Yeah, I wasn't very civil," I admitted.

"But you're hurt, too."

I felt my resolve break, the tears threatening at Kate's words.

Because they were true.

So, so very true.

"No, don't you dare. You are not shutting down, got it?" Kate's hands were on my shoulders and I opened my eyes to find her big brown eyes staring at me. "You get out there, you paste a smile on your face if you have to, and you give your daughter a wonderful birthday. And that smile that you're pasting on? You make sure you use it for Talli, too. And if you get the chance, if you feel you need to, you apologize..."

"She won't listen..."

"Apologize about today. Don't bring Bree's name into it again, not today, okay? Apologize for losing your temper."

"But..."

"And don't expect an apology from her."

"Ouch, way to tell me I was in the wrong, Kate," I said, grinning at her.

"I think you both were, for the record." She smoothed my shirt front, reached up and messed with my hair, then returned her hands to my shoulders. "Come on, Daddy, your little girl has presents and a cake on the way."

"The cake's not..."

"The cake is here, you know what I'm talking about. Come on already." She tugged on my hand, leading me towards the door. I faltered slightly as she opened it, my nerves getting the best of me.

"I can't." I stepped back, shaking my head, chewing on my thumbnail.

"Jase..."

"She hates me, Kate." My voice was so small, like a child, and I bit my lower lip to keep it from trembling. Kate shook her head slightly, her smile attempting to reassure me.

"You, sir, are mistaken. Now come on."

Time to face the music...

I didn't know whether to be happy or disturbed.

From the moment I went back downstairs, with the party in full swing, every single adult there was acting as if nothing was wrong. Eric was handing me a beer, a huge smile on his face as he brought his hand down on my shoulder, and if he was an actor, I'd swear that smile was fake and he meant to nearly knock me over.

Lisa walked in the kitchen about that time, and instead of some lecture about alcohol and violence, she said, "Boys," in a mom-like tone before laughing and walking out.

Had I stepped into Bizzarro World?

The great room was more of the same.

Emily sat on my nan's lap making silly faces, giggling when Nan made them back. Pete was hoisting Michael up on his shoulder, having my boy hang half upside down, as he ran towards the back door, both of them laughing and carrying on as if they didn't have a care in the world. My cousin Tom had finally made it, and he walked up to me, pulling me in a huge bear hug, along with that slap on the back that would have choked me if I hadn't swallowed my beer.

"Got another one of those?" he asked, pointing at my hand.

"Right here," Jackie said from behind me. He was handing a beer to Tom, who smiled and nodded in his direction.

Jaden was sitting in one of the big, comfy chairs, with Elizabeth leaned over her. Baby Girl had her head resting on Jaden's belly and was laughing saying that the baby was kicking her. I turned away quickly, remembering her doing the same thing with Talia when she was pregnant with Emily.

I missed that so badly.

"I can't believe she's in college!"

My head turned sharply to the far corner of the room, Talia's voice echoing in my soul. She was huddled up on the tiny loveseat with Tish and Cass looking at something on the computer that sat on Tish's lap.

"Is she enjoying it?" Cass asked.

"She's eating it up with a spoon," Tish replied. I felt a smile tugging at the corners of my mouth, knowing they were talking about Moira who was studying at the University of Toronto.

"Why Canada, though?" Talia asked, her lips going down into a pout that set off the butterflies in my stomach. "That's too far away."

"It's closer to me than California," Tish replied, raising an eyebrow in her direction.

"Oh, well, you're just gonna have to get over that," Talia said, her eyes still on the computer.

"Mommy, Daddy, are we gonna do Em's presents?" Elizabeth asked, and Talia's eyes came up, wide with surprise as if she didn't know I was in the room.

Of course she didn't.

When those big blue eyes rested on me, she immediately looked away, pushing herself to a standing position and walking around the sea of people towards our oldest daughter. She was intentionally avoiding eye contact with me, I'm sure of it... but there was no avoiding contact when the crowd of people shifted slightly causing Talia to lose her footing, sending her straight against me. I swear it was an accident, or instinct maybe, that had my arms circling her, preventing her from falling.

It was heaven.

That brief moment where her body was up against my chest before she giggled... actually giggled, pushing herself away to reach Elizabeth. And then... then she looked over her shoulder at me, her grin and shrug her only communication, but I understood it completely, just like I used to.

What was my opinion? Did I think it was time for Emily's presents?

This day was going to be the death of me before it was over.

All I could do was smile and nod, and I suppose it was a good thing she comprehended and started gathering the troops because I could have easily just placed my hand over my heart and melted to the floor.

"What'd you get her, Daddy?" Elizabeth asked me as she grabbed my hand, tugging me towards the dining room.

"You'll find out soon enough," Talia answered for me before briefly closing her eyes and shaking her head. "I'm sorry... habit."

"I'm sorry, too," I said softly—so softly I didn't know whether or not she heard me. The only indication that she may have heard me was the way she blinked her eyes quickly as she turned away.

Way to go, Warner. Way to ruin the moment by...

"Sorry I'm late, babies!"

The room fell silent minus the music playing in the background as all eyes turned to look at the one person who had no business being there.

"It was a little difficult to read the start time on these hand written invitations," Bree continued as she walked into the room, her hips swaying from side to side. "But I must admit, they are rather... quaint? Is that the word I'm looking for?"

"Ms. Hamilton, you need to come with me," Chris said as he stepped forward.

"Oh, no... I'm so here for the birthday girl. Hi, Princess, how are you?" Bree leaned over as she waved at my little girl, her breasts nearly falling out of her halter top.

"You're right, Mommy, those shirts aren't 'porpriate for Em's party," Elizabeth said as she looked up at Talia, and I couldn't help but smile. Several others heard Elizabeth's comment and began laughing, closing the circle around Talia and the kids as Chris began to pull on Bree's arm.

"I'm not leaving," she was protesting.

She was bound and determined to cause a scene, make things more uncomfortable, rip my family even further apart than we already were.

I couldn't let her.

I wouldn't.

I turned towards the doorway, motioning for her to follow me. She smirked back at the rest of the guests, not bothering to notice that Chris had followed us, and I will be forever grateful for that.

"Well, hello stranger," she said as we stopped in between the entryway and the staircase.

The list of things I could have said to her at that moment was longer than said staircase, I'm sure. I opted for the nicest thing I could come up with. Pointing at the door, I said the one word I could conjure up.

"Leave."

She sighed, holding her invitation out in front of her. "I was invited here by the birthday girl's mother, you know."

I yanked the invitation out of her hand, ripping it in little pieces as I said, "I told you I didn't want you here. I told you that you were not welcome here. I told you that you were to stay the hell away from my wi…"

"You're still calling her your wife even though she's divorcing your ass?" she cut me off, her voice raising.

"Ms. Hamilton, you were told to only be here in a professional capacity, and since Mr. Warner has cancelled all appearances in the foreseeable future, it's time for you to leave."

"You don't look sick to me," she said, ignoring Chris's statement.

"Do not engage in a conversation or argument with her, Jase," Chris intervened, his hand on my arm. "And Ms. Hamilton, you were instructed to leave."

"Is everything okay here?" Nan asked as she walked towards the entryway.

"Well, hello Nan!" Bree exclaimed, extending her hand. "I'm…"

"Not welcome in this house," Nan cut her off. "And just so we're clear, you're lucky it wasn't my house you pulled this stunt in. I would physically throw you out."

"Daddy?"

Michael was wandering into the entryway, his voice conveying his concern over the sudden change in the atmosphere of the party. I turned towards him, lifting him effortlessly and placing a protective kiss on his cheek. "It's okay, Little Man," I said. "Let's get back to the party, okay?"

"Aren't you going to say hello to me?" Bree asked, presumably in Michael's direction, and I felt my blood begin to boil. My eyes narrowed as I glared at her, and just as another reminder that this bitch was NOT Talia, she began to cower away.

That's what I thought.

"We can't do Em's presents without you, Daddy," Michael said in a scolding tone, his expression so serious that I had to smile.

"Is that so?" I asked as I turned my back on Bree and her antics, the way I should have months before, and walked back to the dining room.

But the faces there were no longer friendly.

There was no more pretending that this was a happy family, that there was nothing wrong. That aura had been sucked out the minute that bitch walked into this room. And I had no one to blame but myself, and I know that. I'm the one who wasn't completely honest from the beginning. I'm the one who knew what Bree wanted, the one who kept lying to myself that so long as nothing happened it didn't matter. I was the one who let her into our lives, I was the one who turned to her. It was all my fault.

I looked at Talia, who was now intentionally avoiding my gaze, her back turned to me as she gathered Emily's presents for her to open.

In that one moment I knew that the words 'I'm sorry' would never be enough.

CHAPTER 13

TALLI

"Sorry I'm late, babies."

With those four words the illusion that everything was going to be okay came crashing down around me

I tried my hardest to not look, to keep her out of my line of vision. But when Elizabeth made the comment about how those shirts weren't appropriate, I couldn't help but glance over.

Why... why did I do that?

Why did I have to see that perfect little Barbie in her perfect size zero clothes with her perfect small breasts right where God intended them to be? Did she have to be so beautiful? Did she have to look *belong* here?

I tried swallowing over that lump in my throat as that moment stretched into eternity, where Chris was telling her she needed to leave.

But it shouldn't be Chris telling her.

Jase... please. Please just once, tell her to leave, tell her to go away. Right here, right in front of me—who gives a damn about everyone else—but in front of me, show me that she doesn't mean anything to you. Tell her...

Oh... God.

My heart shattered into a million pieces, every tiny shard of hope that I'd felt from the moment he placed his hand over my heart... all of it, gone as Jase walked out of the room with that whore right on his heels.

I should have known better.

I handed Emily to Lisa, ignoring Em's protests as I quickly made my way out of that room, and I kept going until I was out the back door of the house. Standing on that back patio, right by the furniture we'd relaxed in so many times over the years, I felt the first tear fall, my hand clamped over my mouth to keep as quiet as I could.

I can't believe that I had come up those stairs, demanding everyone put their happy faces back on.

I can't believe I had dared anyone... dared them to say one cross word to Jase.

I can't believe I had thought that we'd be able to talk, we could make progress, he cared about me.

About us.

I'm such a fool.

"Talli, please come inside." Jaden was standing beside me, the curve of her baby bump touching me slightly. I shook my head slightly, choking back a sob. "Talli..."

"I can't breathe."

Did those words just come from me?

"God, T..." She put her arms around me as the tears fell freely down my face.

"I can't stay here, Jaden. I just can't... all I... all I see is her... her face, in this house... every room... this is... she belongs here, I don't."

"That's not true, Talli."

But I knew better. I knew it was true. I wasn't the glamorous Hollywood type; I never had been. And she'd been completely at ease, completely comfortable in this house, with his management team, with his friends, with...

"Talli, let's... let's just get you inside, and ignore him, and just get through this party, okay? If you think you can't talk with him now..."

"I can't see him right now, I can't look at him right now."

All I could see was him with *her*.

"Presents and cake, Talli... then you can leave."

And that was my intentions.

Presents and cake.

And avoid Jase like the plague until it was time to go.

My oh my how the mood had changed. Michael was clinging to Jase like glue, which he normally did when he was upset about something. Emily was more than happy to stick with me, opening up her gifts that Elizabeth was helping hand to her.

What a spoiled little girl she is.

The adults were completely focused on the children, which helped tremendously. I don't think I could have handled a single 'how are you' because I probably would have fallen apart, and I can't do that. Not now, not in front of him.

"Wait, wait... one more." Jase, with Michael on his hip, walked over to our youngest daughter, who was eating all of the attention up with a spoon. He handed a package to her, which she proceeded to beat on with brute force.

"I told you, she's a drummer!" Pete exclaimed from his spot across the table, his hands massaging Jaden's shoulders.

Did they have to look so happy?

I tried to avoid looking at Jase as he kneeled in front of Emily, helping her rip the paper, laughing with her as her bottom lip quivered at the sound of it. "It's okay, Princess," he said softly. Did he just sniffle? No... no, he didn't... "Here, let's pull it back... this way."

"New bath toys!" Elizabeth said excitedly, jumping up and down. My eyes traveled down to Elizabeth and Michael, who were now laughing at Emily's reaction to her treasure by clapping her hands.

Over bath toys?

Emily lunged forward, reaching for Jase who scooped her up into his arms, holding her close to him. Why did that hurt so much? Aren't I supposed to be happy that Emily has finally warmed up to her father? Just because he was replacing me obviously didn't mean he was replacing them, and...

And I couldn't watch.

I busied myself with cleaning up the paper and trash as Beth brought the cake in from the kitchen. "Where are the candles?" she asked.

FUCK.

Fuck me, I forgot...

"There's one in the drawer by the fridge," Jase answered his mother, and I cringed as I waited for it.

Come on, rock star. Go ahead. Berate me, belittle me for forgetting something like a candle for our daughter's cake. Why would having everyone around matter? It hasn't before.

"Got it," I heard Nan say as she walked back in. I continued on my task, taking the trash out to the large bins in the garage, my hands shaking uncontrollably.

I thought I could handle this. I really thought I could. How hard was it supposed to be to be surrounded by friends and family, celebrating Emily's birthday? There are so many others here that his presence shouldn't make me fall apart, right?

But I was falling apart. I was shaking, feeling like I could vomit at any moment. My heart was hammering so fucking hard that I felt close to passing out, and...

"Talli?"

"Not now, Lisa," I said as I knelt beside Jase's car, the car that used to bring me comfort and joy whenever I saw it pull up. Now all I could see was Bree sitting in the passenger seat, waving as they drove off to the studio or wherever they were actually going, and...

"Listen, Talli, I'm not trying to dictate what you should do, and I know that you have had problems with this in the past." She sat beside me on that garage floor, taking my hand in hers. "But right now, you are falling apart."

"I'm not..." My voice faltered as I couldn't even finish the lie.

"Today, you need help. Even if you don't need help every other day, today... today, you do."

That little voice in my head was screaming at me, telling me no... no, don't do it... you don't need help, you can do this without any help...

But could I make it through the rest of the day without it?

Could I walk back into that house, could I see him looking so happy when I was dying inside?

Could I?

"Just today," Lisa said, her hand on my shoulder as she offered one of her prescription pills.

"We've been looking for you," Jaden said as I walked into the dining room a good fifteen minutes later.

"It's a big house," I replied, my voice soft and controlled. "It's easy to get lost in."

"Always the joker," Eric laughed as he came up behind me, giving me a huge squeeze. I swear that mountain of a man could easily kill someone with his bare hands.

"Who's joking?" I mumbled, pushing back a stray curl that had fallen into my eyes. I held my head up as I looked across that room, locking eyes with Jase for the first time since Bree had waltzed in. "People tend to lose themselves in this house all the time."

Don't you dare look sad at that comment, you asshole.

"Okay, Emily's in her high chair ready for some cake... who's singing with me?"

I don't even know who asked that question.

I do know I didn't sing, though. I was too fixated on my little girl, her red curls so similar to mine, her blue eyes looking adoringly up at her Daddy, whose voice carried across the room straight into my heart.

And I hated him for it.

I hated that he looked so happy, so... smug when Emily smiled at him. Seriously, where the hell did he get off? It wasn't as if he'd been there this whole...

"Cake, Talli?"

I smiled and shook my head, declining the cake that someone was offering me, feeling stifled and a bit claustrophobic in that room. I quietly excused myself, walking out to the back porch once more, taking in a deep breath of fresh air, or as fresh as the air was going to get here.

Ah, there it was.

My sanctuary.

I kicked off my shoes, letting the grass tickle my feet as I crossed the lawn that I'd once shared with Jase. The fountain was still going, the water trickling and bubbling as I sank down beside it. This was where I'd gone whenever I needed to think, to reflect... and yet I hadn't been out there since Emily was born.

I could still hear the giggling and talking, even though it seemed worlds away. It seemed just like yesterday that I'd been sitting out at this fountain, feeling lost and confused, wondering why I'd flown all this way to be with a man who was so out of my league. And now as I ran my fingers through the cold water, I wondered why I'd stayed.

"Mommy! Mommy, come see Em!"

Elizabeth's voice brought me back to the present, reminding me why I'd stayed.

And why it hurt so badly to leave now.

Even with as sad and as selfish as I know it sounded, I didn't want to go back in there. I didn't want to see him looking so happy that his little Barbie had shown up, even if he escorted her out to...what? Save face with me and everyone else there? Please, too late.

"Mommy, hurry!"

With a heavy sigh, I forced myself back up, my legs feeling like they were weighted down and treading through sand. *Time to paste the smile back on, time to be Mommy again, time to play...*

No, there was no more playing the doting wife.

Wait... had I just... played the part?

I chewed on my bottom lip absentmindedly as I took in the surroundings, our friends and family each enjoying cake or a drink, smiling and laughing at my little Em.

"Oh, Em."

Jase was shaking his head at her appearance, her entire face looking like it had been painted with chocolate frosting. Everyone around me was laughing, smiling, while my heart was racing in my chest...

"Talli, are you okay?"

Eric was beside me, I know he was... but I was so disoriented I merely grabbed at his arm, clinging helplessly as I plunged into darkness.

But the darkness, it wasn't so bad.

In the darkness, I felt loved. I felt safe and secure. In the darkness, there were arms there to hold me, to comfort me. In the darkness, there were soft lips on my forehead, a kiss to take away the hurt.

In the darkness, he still loved me.

JASE

"Move...just...move. Out of my way."

I didn't give a damn how much of an asshole I was being.

My heart was in my throat as I pushed my way into what I had long ago dubbed Talia's room, my eyes resting on her as Eric laid her on the couch. She looked so pale, even against the cream-colored cushions.

Please, no... not again...

I was trembling uncontrollably as I passed Kaitlyn, who was giving Lisa ten tons of hell for not wanting to call the paramedics. "Have you lost your mind?" Kate was asking, and I didn't bother telling her that Lisa's mind had been gone for years.

I couldn't.

Because right at that moment, all I could do was drop to my knees beside Talia. I leaned over, studying every feature of her face.

She couldn't do this to me.

Not again.

"Please... open your eyes," I whispered, gently pushing her curls back from her damp forehead. I placed a kiss there before burying my face in the side of her neck, my hands caressing her arms.

"Lees, maybe we should call someone," I heard Eric say.

Yes... yes, call someone, she needs help, she needs...

"I love you, baby," I murmured softly in Talia's ear, praying she'd hear me. The memory of her lying so still in that hospital after Elizabeth was born was all that kept replaying in my mind, ripping me in two. It had only been maybe a couple of minutes since I'd seen the color drain from her face as she clutched to Eric, who only noticed when I'd called out her name... I know it had only been a couple of minutes.

I couldn't help but panic.

"Wake up... please. Baby, just open your eyes, okay?"

I felt her slowly begin to stir, a tiny groan of protest escaping from her as she turned slightly. My eyelids slid shut from the pure ecstasy coursing through my veins as she nestled in, slightly nuzzling my neck.

Oh... God...

"I had the worst dream," she mumbled sleepily, curling her arms up as if she were cold, her hands twisting in my shirtfront, pulling me closer. I knew I shouldn't... but the memories of all the nights she'd curled into me, just like this, came crashing back. I cradled her upper body in my arms as I kneeled beside her, dropping soft kisses on her temple, her cheeks, everywhere but her lips, no matter how badly I wanted to. "Mmmm, come to bed." I felt her smile against me, and I tried to stifle the sob, I swear I did, but this was my own personal hell that she was putting me through. I knew the moment she was coherent she'd be pushing me away.

I tightened my arms around her, biting my bottom lip as she placed an open-mouthed kiss on the most sensitive spot on my neck. *God, baby, please don't do that... I've been without you far too long...* My breathing became more labored as she kissed up my jaw line, my heart skipping a beat as her lips settled over mine...

"Hey, is everything okay?" Eric asked rather loudly, and I felt Talia's body go completely rigid.

Fuck.

I pulled back slightly, my arms still around her so I was unable to wipe the tears away before she saw them. Confusion was etched in her features as her eyes passed over my face, settling on my lips, then my neck, and then trailing down to my arms. Slowly, reluctantly I pulled away, our eyes locking once more as the chaos around us began creeping back in.

My mind kept screaming at me to say something, but I found myself stunned silent as the moment dragged on. She had to know... she had to...

"Talli, do you need to go to the hospital?" Kate asked, sounding exasperated from having to deal with Lisa.

I already knew Talia would decline.

"I... I'm fine," she said, lowering her gaze, a blush crossing her cheeks. I was surprised when she didn't add the 'don't worry about me,' and I narrowed my gaze, drinking her appearance in.

She was pale... I'd already noticed that... and the curls that had come loose hanging in tendrils around her face were damp from the cold sweat she'd broken into. But there was something... else. See, I'd seen her in these jeans, in that top before, but today... I mean, she was beautiful, she's always beautiful, but she's just so... thin. Too thin.

When the hell did that happen?

Why the hell did that happen?

"I just..." she licked her lips nervously, averting her eyes from anyone's gaze.

Talia, what's going on?

She stood slowly, amidst the protests of nearly everyone but Lisa who piped up with, "All she needs it to get the hell out of this house."

"Here," Jaden said as she walked in, carrying a plate with a sandwich and some fruit. "Eat this before you do anything."

"Thank you," Talia and I said to her in unison as she accepted the plate, and Talia's eyes darted back to me, still knelt beside the couch. I tried in vain to smile at her, but she quickly looked away and walked over to her papasan chair, flopping into it like she used to, one leg curled underneath as she picked at the food on her plate.

"Michael and Elizabeth are with Pete," Jaden said, snapping me out of my daze.

The kids...

"Did they..."

"No, Little Bit, I got you out of there quick," Eric interrupted Talia's question.

Oh, thank God...

"Emily's gonna need a bath, though," Jaden added with a smile.

"I've got it," I said quickly, and Talia looked over at me, her cheeks still too pale for my comfort. "You... you eat, okay?"

She looked down at her plate of food, a frown on her face as she continued pushing the plate's contents around.

"The quicker you eat, the quicker we can get you the hell out of here," Lisa added, and I couldn't stop the glare I shot at her. As much as I would have enjoyed giving her a piece of my mind, I resisted the urge to do so.

Today had already taken its toll, on all of us.

"Jase," Eric said, gaining my attention. He motioned for me to follow him as he walked out of the room, and with one glance back at Talia, I did. He spoke in hushed tones as we walked back towards the dining room. "Talli, she's... she's just not herself, Jase."

"None of us are," I reminded him.

"You know what I'm saying," he added. "She's... distant, she's moody..."

I know she is, and it's all my fault.

"...and now she's... she's losing weight and passing out. I mean..."

"You insinuated before that you thought she was using again, when your mother died," I said, my eyebrow raised as I looked up at him. "And you were wrong."

"Jase, *look* at her."

"She's... she wouldn't, okay? She *wouldn't* do that." I said the words with such conviction, through clenched teeth. "Not with as far as she's come, not with the kids, not with..."

"Not with what? You?"

We were stopped at the end of the hall, trying to keep others from listening to our disagreement, and I felt myself clenching and unclenching my fists at his words. "Damn it, Eric, I know..."

"Before you say you 'know' her, are you that oblivious to the fact that you're practically strangers now?"

Fuck... are we? How... when... why did that happen?

His words were still resonating in my head as he continued. "When was the last time you really looked... and I mean really looked at your wife?"

"Daddy, are you gonna give Em a bubble bath?" Elizabeth interrupted us as she ran up to me, her big blue eyes sparkling.

"Yeah, of course I am," I replied, lightly tousling her hair. "I'm coming to rescue Nana."

"Jase," Eric called out as I began to walk away, and I glanced over my shoulder at him. "Think about it."

I merely nodded, then continued walking down the hall.

"You are getting water everywhere!" I couldn't help but laugh as Emily splashed extra hard, sending bubbles and water spilling over onto me, splattering my already drenched shirt. She scrunched up her face as I continued gently washing away the chocolate frosting, her bottom lip sticking out when I had to hold her still. "Come on, Princess, I know you're in there somewhere."

She responded by bringing both hands down forcefully, squealing with delight as the bubbles splashed up onto my face. "Yeah, yeah. You think you're funny, I know. Here... hands. Daddy needs to wash your... hands... don't pull them away, Stinkerbell." I knew she would fight me, fussing as I held her hands still, so her squawks of disapproval were no surprise.

"Everything okay in here?"

I jumped slightly at the sound of Chris's voice, which caused Emily to giggle. Figures. Women.

"Yeah, yeah, it's fine. You taking off?"

"In just a minute. I know you're occupied in here, but mind if I talk to you for a sec?"

"Nah, just... if you don't want to get wet you may want to stay back."

"That's fine, that's fine. Um... Jase, I know the timing sucks, and it's an unpleasant subject."

"Then must you bring it up now?"

"For the sake of your children, yes."

"You haven't been talking to Eric, have you?" I asked as I continued washing the frosting from every fold and hiding place Emily had gotten it into.

"No, I haven't. He said he talked to *you* and that *you* would handle it."

"Good. Let's keep it that way."

"Jase, in less than an hour your soon-to-be-ex-wife will be driving across this city with your children in that car, after she'd passed out, after she'd refused medical attention. Doesn't that worry you in the least?"

I faltered for a moment as I was wringing out the washcloth.

I hadn't thought about that.

With my silence, Chris continued on, stepping in and shutting the door in case of unwanted listeners. "Jase, this isn't a personal attack against Talia, okay? This isn't about she and I not getting along. This is about a mother who is expecting full custody, only granting you limited visitation, who can't even handle the simple task of taking care of herself."

"Stop it."

"Jase, she's always been absentminded, okay? I can give her that much leeway. But when she is the sole provider, the one person that these children have to depend on, she has to be physically and mentally capable of the job."

"She's a nurse practitioner, you can't say she's not capable…"

"That's not what I'm talking about, Jase, and you know it."

My jaw clenched as I continued washing Emily, who was now looking curiously up at Chris.

"Jase, is she…"

"Not another fucking word, Chris."

"You can demand a drug test, Jase."

I sat silent, contemplating his words as he continued on with is legal jargon. Something about demanding that she get checked out, bringing all of this up in court, or just having the lawyers handle it, and…

"If she refuses, you can demand temporary emergency custody of the children."

"I can't do that to her."

"This isn't about revenge, Jase. This isn't about not wanting to upset her. This isn't about trying to win her back. This is a health and safety issue, regarding your kids. You need… Jase, look at me."

I kept my hand securely on Emily's arm as I glanced over my shoulder at him.

"You need to answer her petition of divorce with one of your own."

"I don't want to…"

"I know." He bent his knees, lowering himself closer to my level. "It's written all over your face whenever she walks in the room, okay? I know. And if some day you two do work this out, I'm going to be the first one in line to congratulate you. I know you don't want a divorce, and that's… you're not coming out and saying you do, you're fighting her petition. At least in the end, if you can't work this out, you can demand equal time with the kids."

I looked back over at Emily, who'd bent down and proceeded to nibble on my fingers thinking maybe that would convince me to let her go.

But I couldn't.

I couldn't… I couldn't let them go.

"Okay," I said softly. "Okay, do it."

I had to change clothes myself after Emily's bath, she had me drenched from nearly head to toe. After she and I were both dried and dressed, I hoisted her up on my hip to take her back down the stairs where there were still a few stragglers left after the party. My little Princess was completely wiped out, her head resting on my shoulder as I walked into the great room where Talia and Jaden were packing the gifts in bags.

"Are you about ready to go?" Lisa asked.

"We've got this, it's okay," Jaden said softly to Lisa.

"I brought my DVD's with me to watch on the plane," Cass added as she walked in the room. "I'll just bring them over, I'm sure you have the popcorn, girl."

"Of course," Talia replied, her voice so soft I could barely hear it.

"And I left a message with Mark telling him I'd be at your place for a while, so he shouldn't call the hotel room," Tish said, stepping around me and entering the great room as well. Talia glanced up, noticing me and Emily standing there.

"Oh, I'm so glad that fits," Lisa said, walking over to adjust Emily's clothes, prompting Em to scowl at her and snuggle closer to me.

"She looks exhausted," Talia commented, her eyes fixated on our daughter.

"Hell, Michael already knocked out," Jaden said with a laugh, pointing to where Michael laid across Pete's chest, drooling on his shoulder. "Elizabeth is only staying awake by talking Nan's ear off."

"I should get them home," Talia said, taking Emily from my arms, ripping another piece of my heart to shreds.

This is their home...

"Talli, you could just..."

"No."

Fuck, she wouldn't even let me finish.

She turned her back, walking away from me, Emily's head now on her shoulder.

Don't... don't fucking cry. Not now, Warner. Quit being such a fucking pussy.

"We're just doing a girl's night... um... *in*," Cass said with a smile. She was always so nice to me, no matter what transpired at any given time, and I'll be forever grateful. "You know, movies... popcorn... gossip."

"Great," I said with a short laugh, lowering my head and messing with the back of my hair.

"Actually," she continued, linking her arm around mine, "as a golden rule, we avoid the subject of whatever's upsetting us. Or we try to."

I could only imagine what had already been said.

"And we're gonna stuff popcorn and ice cream down her throat and hopefully she'll feel better."

"Thank you," I said softly, trying not to get too choked up.

I didn't know how much more I could take.

"I wanna go with Nana," Elizabeth announced as she walked over to me. "Mommy said no."

Oh, she always did this.

Whenever Talia told her no, she'd come running to me. Up to a certain point, I would always side with Talia, tell Elizabeth to do as her mother asked her to. But as Talia grew more distant, and I felt more unreasonable, I'd began to one-up her, allowing Elizabeth to get away with more, letting her do things that Talia had refused to.

Had I really resorted to that? Getting to Talia through the children?

"Daddy, I know you'll say…"

"Baby girl, you need to go with Mommy. She wants you to go with her, okay?"

Elizabeth stood in shock at my words, her mouth half-hanging open at my audacity to deny her something she wanted. Once she realized I wasn't changing my mind, her lower lip began to tremble, and big tears filled her blue eyes. "Mommy's right. You don't love us anymore."

What the fuck?

Before I had a chance to respond, demand to know what she was talking about, she'd run from the room screaming about the unfairness of it all and how she wished she'd never been born, prompting Michael to raise his head off of Pete's shoulder.

"Wha's her plob-lem, Daddy?" he asked me and I merely shook my head and smiled. "Oh. Women. Right, Daddy?"

"Right, Little Man," I replied, holding my arms out to him.

"You okay?" Pete asked me, and I shrugged in response.

No point in lying now.

Talia was coming back in with Elizabeth screaming on her heels about how she never got to see her Nana, and how she'd be going to school in the fall and wouldn't have as much time to. Talia kept on walking, one eyebrow raised even as Emily looked at her sister like she was off her rocker.

"Man, Daddy," Michael said with a shake of his head. "I just wanna go bowling for my birfday, okay? Just bowling."

I couldn't help but laugh, and one glance at Talia, with the side of her mouth twitching as if she were trying to keep from smiling, I know she heard him, too.

"Just bowling," I promised.

"I gots to go now, don't I?" he asked, his arms draped around my neck.

"Yeah... yeah, bud, you do."

"You take me to the car, Daddy?"

"Of course," I replied, walking slowly out to Talia's car, which was being loaded with most of Emily's presents. I didn't say a word about the bath toys, which were now drying off in the upstairs washroom. I wanted those here, for us, for when she was home.

Because this was her home.

Their home.

Even as I watched them drive away, my stomach in knots as I remembered Chris's words, it just felt wrong. They shouldn't be twenty-two minutes from this house. She shouldn't be going anywhere but down the hall to her room, or maybe to the media room, for girls' night in. Our kids should all be lying down right now, in their beds, in their rooms. They shouldn't be driving farther and farther out of my sight, the taillights disappearing as she turned the corner at the end of the street.

"She still loves you," Kate said as she stepped up beside me, wrapping her arm around my waist. My arm settled right across her shoulders, squeezing her for just a tiny bit of comfort.

"I wish I could believe you."

"Jase, I saw what happened."

"And it wouldn't have if she..." My voice trailed off at the painful memories from earlier. "Kate, do you think she's okay?"

"More okay than that batty sister of hers," Kate replied with a sigh. "Although I suppose I have to give some room to Lisa, considering she just buried her ex-husband a few weeks ago."

"Yeah, she's…"

I blinked a couple of times, stopped dead in my tracks.

"She is a bit one off, and I kinda remember her being that way from the wedding, too," Kate continued. "And that was him… Jack… that sat with her there, wasn't it?"

"Jack… Jack's…" I turned to Kate, looking her square in the eye. "Jack's dead?"

"Well… yeah. That's why Talli went to Ohio. Was that him? The one that…"

"When she went to Ohio… you mean just… just a few weeks ago, right before she…"

"Right before she left, yes. Jase, was that…"

"Holy shit, I don't believe it."

I turned from Kaitlyn, running my hands through my hair as I began pacing back and forth on my front lawn. This… it made perfect sense. Of course it would take something like that to have Talia and the kids leave, to make them go back to Ohio! Of course she wouldn't just up and go, after she'd told me that she couldn't come to Texas.

But… but…

"Kate, why didn't she tell me?" I asked, my hands outstretched. "Did she think I wouldn't want to know? Did she… did she just not want me there?"

"I don't know, Jase," Kate replied. "I… think they're under the impression that you knew. I certainly was."

"But I didn't."

I didn't know.

And it was all so confusing to me. Was this good? Was this bad?

Did it matter?

Or was it too late?

"I have to get going," Jaden was saying as she walked out the front door.

"Relax, they won't start without you," Pete quipped, and Jaden stuck her tongue out at him.

The nerve of happy couples.

"Hey… Jaden?" She was right by me when she stopped, turning towards me, her eyebrows raised as if she was waiting for me to continue.

What do I say? Why didn't I know? Or... why didn't she want me in Ohio? Or...

"I'm sorry, Jase, but I'm already late and..."

"Take care of my girl," I said softly. She smiled and nodded before walking towards her rental car.

I needed her to look after Talia.

Until Talia would let me back in to do it myself.

CHAPTER 14

TALLI

I... kissed him? Seriously?

"Talli, your ice cream's melting!" Cass exclaimed with a giggle. I stared down at the contents of my bowl, now looking like green soup with bits of chocolate.

"I guess I'm not wanting ice cream right now," I mumbled as I settled down a little further into my papasan chair.

I'm so embarrassed... how many people saw me do that?

"I'll take care of that," Tish said, standing up to take my bowl. "You three decide which movie we're going to watch."

Even in my own home there's no escape. That... that couch they're sitting on, would they really want to know everything Jase and I had done there?

"I'm Harry Pottered out," Cass said, shaking her head slightly.

"No to Harry," Jaden noted as she flipped through the DVDs that Cass had brought. "Um... do we want action, drama, or comedy?"

It wouldn't be so bad if he had at least kissed me back. I mean... gah, it was just so humiliating! First the passing out, then the practically throwing myself at him, to have him just... reject me.

"Talli?" Jaden asked. I guess the decision had been given to me.

"It doesn't really matter," I replied with a shrug. I'd changed into yoga pants and a t-shirt so curling up in my papasan chair was as comfortable as having the girls around me. "Hell, we could watch QVC for all I care. It's been too long."

At least with them there, I wasn't sitting here driving myself absolutely crazy going over and over everything that had happened at Em's party.

Cass raised her eyebrow, turning to Jaden who merely nodded.

"What?" I asked.

"Comedy," they said in unison.

Whatever.

I'm only driving myself half-crazy this way, see. I'll have a little bit of distraction so I won't have to think how good it felt to have his hands on me, his lips under mine...

"*So I Married an Axe Murderer?*" Jaden suggested.

"No," I said a little too quickly. I haven't been able to watch that movie in weeks. All I keep replaying in my mind is rocking Emily while watching that movie as Bree stood in the entry way of my room, asking if I really didn't mind her 'stealing' my husband for the evening to go to the studio. As if that's what they really did, right? Jase and I had spent the entire day fighting, so at that point I'd been relieved to hear that door close.

Why?

Why had I been so stupid, so blind?

"Talli, you're not helping us here," Jaden said, nudging my foot with hers. She was standing beside me holding out two discs, *While You Were Sleeping* and *13 Going On 30*.

"Is this oldies night or something?" I asked, making a mental note to stay away from romance as well. And anything with Mark Ruffalo, especially *13 Going On 30*, since Dr. Paul Coffman could pass as his twin. Creepy.

"Why not?" Cass asked, her eyebrows hidden beneath her blonde bangs. "It could be fun."

"If we're going for oldies, why not... um... *Breakfast Club*?" I suggested. "Or... or *Pump Up the Volume*?"

"*Pump Up the Volume* is not a comedy," Tish said as she walked back into the room.

"Oh!" Jaden exclaimed, pulling a disc out of the booklet, holding it up as if it were a treasure. "*Drop Dead Fred*!" She flashed a cheesy grin, and I had to laugh.

"Please don't ever make that face again," I said, still giggling.

"If it makes you laugh, I will do this face over." She did it again, the bitch. "And over." She got a little closer, grinning again. Dear. Lord. "And over." She leaned right down in my face, the cheesiest grin she could conjure up.

"You're helpless," I said, pushing her back slightly.

"You'd push a pregnant girl!" she exclaimed with a wink as she made her way back over to the couch.

"Not just a pregnant girl," Cass reminded her.

"An Italian gypsy pregnant girl," Tish said, taking the disc from Jaden and walking over to my entertainment center.

"Fuck all of you, okay?" She stretched out, placing her feet on my coffee table.

Just like Jase used to do.

"You okay, Talli?"

I don't even know who asked. I merely smiled and said the usual.

"I'm fine; don't worry about me."

But I wasn't fine.

It was time to accept that.

Mondays suck egg rolls with shrimp. Especially Mondays after a difficult weekend. The kids themselves had been relatively unaffected, other than Elizabeth and Michael asking repeatedly why they couldn't stay with Jase. I didn't expect them to understand, but I didn't want them subjected to that... thing he was messing with any more than they had to.

Wow. Bitter much, Talia?

Anyhow, everyone had gone home, and it was back to just the kids and me. The condo seemed even smaller, and yet even emptier than before. I'd gotten up in a rush thinking I had to be at work, and then had to chastise myself for forgetting that I'd taken the day off... you know, since Jase wasn't here to chastise me.

Damn, stop it, Talia!

So, I settled down to VH1 where, of course, one of Jase's videos pops up while I'm drinking my coffee. I almost changed the channel but decided against it as nostalgia crept in.

I remembered helping him get ready that morning, since I'd kept him up practically all night. I even talked him into shaving, which about made the producers of the video have a heart attack but, in the end, had done wonders since his fans loved it. Wait... here it comes... here it comes... yep, that's where he stretched out on the bed, and where his eyes... slid... shut.

Fuck.

I better change the channel.

About the time I reached for the remote, my phone began to ring. It caught me a bit off guard, but after checking the number I figured I better answer. Seeing my lawyer's phone number on the caller id wasn't helping the anxiety that was beginning to build.

"Happy Monday to you," Sharise Adler said, although her voice wasn't showing much joy.

"Isn't that an oxymoron?" I asked before taking a sip of coffee.

Oh, great. She sighed. This cannot be good.

"Jase has filed his own petition for divorce."

With that one sentence it seemed the air had been sucked from the room. I mean, I should have seen this coming. I should had been able to spot it from a mile away. Of course he was going to file.

No wonder he didn't kiss me back.

And what the hell is up with these tears in my eyes?

"Oh... um, okay," I said softly. "So, what do I do now?"

"Well, Talia," she began, again with a heavy sigh, "you should get in here as soon as possible this morning. I'm sending a car for you to pick you up, preferably before they've served you. We need to come up with a strategy."

"A strategy?"

"Jase has filed for emergency temporary custody of the children."

Oh... God...

He wouldn't do this. He wouldn't take them away from me. He... he just...

"There are several demands they're making," she continued on, "and if you could get to my office immediately than we can comply and file a motion before they take physical custody of the children."

Physical... oh, no... no, please tell me this wasn't happening...

"Is there anyone who can keep the children until we've averted this... well, glitch?"

"Why is he doing this?" I asked quietly, not realizing I'd asked it out loud until she answered.

"My guess is revenge."

Revenge? Is this what it has come to?

"They're demanding a drug test, among other things."

A drug test? Why would...

Oh.

Oh!

"And a complete physical... it seems you had an episode sometime this weekend."

An episode. Of course. Had I so naively thought he wouldn't use that against me? Did he really think he could use that as an excuse to take the children?

Oh, fuck... could he?

I was in a panic, wondering what to do, who I could trust with the children. I couldn't call Linda or Sondra; they'd take them straight to Jase. Had Jaden gone back to Missouri? It didn't matter; I couldn't get her involved. Pete would take them to Jase, anyhow.

Who could I trust?

And suddenly, I knew.

"How long do I have until the car gets here?" I asked suddenly.

"Due to traffic, it may take a little bit."

"Okay... okay. I have to call someone, but I'll be ready for when that car gets here."

I'd often wondered why I'd been tortured with the latest hospital gossip. Seriously, did I need to know who was dating whom, or who was screwing around, or who was getting a divorce? No. I particularly sympathized with the gossip subjects having been repeatedly raked over the coals for years. But today, I was thankful I'd been subjected to the myriad of stories, one in particular. It was one of a doctor whose actress wife had filed for emergency custody, leaving him blindsided and scrambling desperately to get his children back.

It wasn't just his advice I needed.

Dr. Paul Coffman answered his phone with a pleasant tone, or hint of laughter in his voice. I heard a small child's voice in the background and cringed slightly. *He's probably too busy, and I'm just inconveniencing him... I mean, who in their right mind would get in the middle of this?*

"Um... I'm sorry, I..."

"Talia?"

I was a bit surprised that he recognized my voice, but I recovered as quickly as I could. "I'm so sorry to bother you, Dr. Coffman."

"We're not at work, Talia. It's just Paul."

"Just Paul, right. Um..." I was trying to not stammer, not show the desperation I was feeling. "I... I need... help. I need help, please."

"I heard about the birthday party," he said softly. "Are you okay?"

"I'm fine... seriously? You heard about that? I thought you were on vacation."

"I'm not immune to the gossip mill, though."

"Great," I muttered.

"Seriously, though... what do you need? Do you... hell, tell you what. If you need a break, say the word, I'll gladly take the kids off your hands while you get some r and r."

"It's not... r and r I need. Not... exactly."

"I don't like the sound of that."

Did he have to be so friendly?

"I... um, I've been told I have a decent shoulder, too, if that's what you need. I've been there, Talia. I know."

No... no, don't cry. Because if I start crying, I'll never stop and there's so much for me to do.

"Talia..."

"He's trying to take them." I nearly choked on the words, my emotions boiling over. "He... I just... I forgot to eat, and I was stressed,

185

and I'm on this diet anyhow, and it was hot, and…"

"Did you get checked out?" he asked, the tone of his voice mixed with a bit of concern.

"No, I'm fine, but…"

"But he's using it against you."

"Yes," I replied, my voice trembling.

"Did he file for emergency custody?"

"Yes, but I… I haven't been served yet, and they're still with me."

"You moved into the building my sister's in right? The one I told you about?"

"Yes… yes, it's great here, thank you so much for the tip."

"You're welcome. I'm about five minutes from there, is that enough time?"

"Enough…"

"I'm coming over. I'll take the kids down to my sister's apartment on the sixth floor, you come get them when the coast is clear."

I hadn't even asked.

"Talia…"

"I don't know what to say."

"Then don't say a word."

"I… I don't want to put you in the middle of this, I just… I don't know what else to do."

"I wouldn't wish what I went through on anyone… Bren!" he yelled out, probably to one of his kids. "Get your shoes on, and help your sister, okay? We're gonna see Aunt Mary."

Mary. Ah, Mary Coffman, now that made perfect sense why she was so nice to me. Damn, was I that absentminded that I couldn't even get that straight?

"I'll be there soon," he continued talking to me. "You do what you have to, get to that hearing…"

"Hearing?" I asked, my eyes wide. "There's a hearing?"

"Unless your lawyer gets you out of it, but you may need to go in front of the judge, show the judge that you're capable of taking care of your kids."

"Wow, I guess it's a good thing I forgot I didn't work today," I mumbled, looking down at my suit. Maybe… maybe the black one would be better, though. The one with the thin skirt, and the jacket, and...

"Take a deep breath, okay?"

"Taking a deep breath," I mumbled.

"I'll be there as soon as I can."

"Emily can be a bit... difficult," I said suddenly. "Just... you know, for a warning."

"Thank you for that warning. Five minutes, okay?"

"Okay. Okay... I... I need to change, and get stuff together, and..."

"Five minutes, Talia."

"Five minutes."

Five minutes and my reinforcements would be there.

JASE

My phone was ringing repeatedly, over and over, beginning again almost immediately after it stopped. I groaned, rolling over and glancing at the receiver, its battery running low. Damn... stupid crick in my neck. This sofa isn't always the most comfortable. I held my neck with one hand and reached for the receiver with the other.

Chris Webber must be a morning person.

"Dude, this better be good," I grumbled into the phone.

"Make sure you're at the courthouse by one and it just might be," he said.

"What?"

"Wear a suit and tie."

"Chris, what the hell is going on?" I sat up, rubbing my eyes, waiting for his answer.

"Get your house ready."

"My... house? For what?"

"Your children."

I swear my heart stopped altogether for a fraction of a second before taking off at an alarming rate. My... children? Were... they coming home?

"The hearing for emergency custody is set for one thirty," he continued. "A half hour is plenty of time to get you up to speed; all you need to do is sit back and let your legal team do its job."

"Emergency... Jeeezus, Chris, what happened? Are they okay? Where's Talli? What..."

"Slow down, slow down. They're fine. Nothing's happened, not since Saturday at the party. And this very well could go your way, so..."

"You said we'd make her get checked out... did they find something?"

"She hasn't been served her papers yet, but her lawyer has been made aware of the situation. Your legal team decided it was best,"

"No."

"...to go full force..."

"No."

"...show her you mean business, and..."

"NO!"

"Jase, she has got to take care of herself, she has to be physically capable of taking care of those children, and..."

"I know that, Chris, but bullying her isn't going to accomplish anything other than making her more pissed off."

"So it's okay for her to keep the kids from you?"

Ouch.

"No, it's... I just..."

"Don't play the martyr here, Jase. Two wrongs don't make a right."

"So adding a third wrong to the mix will make it all better?" I asked, my bitterness showing in my tone.

"Jase, even if you don't retain physical custody of the children, you have the chance today to demand that the original visitation plan be implemented again."

I could see them more, just like Talli and I had agreed on...

That would be better, so much better than the bullshit agreement her lawyer had come up with. The only problem was... yes, I wanted them with me. All the time. This... this is their home.

But I didn't want it like this.

Not like I was using them to get to Talia.

This...this is something Nan had discussed with me, when I was finally in a place where I could talk without breaking down like a fucking sissy boy. She'd explained in detail the great pains that she had gone through to ensure I was unaffected as possible and how I was never used as leverage. And I had turned out okay...

Right?

But I don't want to be a part-time father. It's bad enough that I already feel like one when I'm on the road, but damn it they were still in my life, still in my home then. I shouldn't have to feel like I'm intruding when I want to call and see how they're doing. I know I was in the wrong, I know I screwed up, but losing Talia was hell enough. Losing the kids... I just...

It just hurts.

And I know what it's like to have them taken away. I wouldn't wish that feeling on my worst enemy.

Why the hell would I do that to someone I love more than life itself?

"Jeez, Jase, what is going on?" Kate asked when she called me later in the morning.

"What do you mean?" I asked, cradling the receiver as I maneuvered the razor across my jaw line.

"Well... okay, so I occasionally glance at *Celebrity Gossip*, and..."

"Occasionally?" I interrupted. "It's as if you live on that website lately."

"Only when they're practically crucifying my best friend," she replied.

"Well, that's been going on since... well, since before Talia left." I sighed as I rinsed the razor blade before continuing. "So what are the sharks saying now?"

"That you're expected at the court house this afternoon."

"Damn, that was quick. They actually got something right?"

"What's going on, Jase?" she repeated. I was silent as I patted my face dry, feeling as if I was looking at a stranger in the mirror. "Jase?"

"It's an emergency hearing," I finally said. "For custody."

"God, Jase, what happened?"

"No, it's... about Saturday," I replied, grabbing my bottle of water and walking into the bedroom, eyeing my suit that I'd laid out on the bed. "Chris and the legal team seem to think it may force her to take better care of herself or some shit like that."

"I... well, I see the point, but you're just asking for more trouble, more drama, you know? I mean, her lawyer would chop your balls off if Talli would let her."

"I have to do something, Kate."

"Hey, here's an idea..."

"If you're going to suggest that I talk to her, I need to remind you of what happened the last time I tried that."

"You weren't exactly lily white in that one, either."

"Thanks."

"What about... a... mediator?" she suggested. "Or... or counseling?"

Counseling.

Talia had brought up counseling once, in passing, when she'd talked about Lisa and Jack. I remember scoffing at her about how that had done so much good for them.

Fuck, had she been... suggesting it? For us?

"It really would be a good idea, you know?" Kate was saying.

"I think it's a little late for that," I mumbled.

"Listen... do you want some company? Some moral support?"

"I'd like that," I replied.

"Okay, I'll be over as soon as I can, okay? Oh, and Jase?"

"Yeah?"

"Wear the Armani. Knock her socks off."

I glanced down at the Armani suit, grinning softly. "One step ahead of you."

"Good. Give me a few minutes, okay?"

"Okay."

"And Jase... you're doing the right thing. I mean, you could do more, but..."

"Bye, Kate," I cut her off with a laugh.

I was fully dressed, minus the jacket and tie, as I made my way down the stairs. Kate hadn't arrived yet, but I heard Linda as she made her way around the kitchen. "Hey," I said to her with a smile as I walked in.

"Hello," she said, doing her best to return the smile. Our relationship had become strained at best since she'd found out about Bree, not that I can blame her for that. Still, she stayed, her stoic presence reminding me every day that she was there how much I had done wrong.

Like now, with the look she was giving me.

"Lunch date?" she asked as she wiped down the counter.

"Court house date," I replied softly, looking down at my shoes.

"Ah."

That was it. Just 'ah'. I looked up as she walked over to the door that led to the basement.

Oh... the basement. I'd been unable to bring myself to go down there, and I didn't want to burden Linda with the task of cleaning up the mess.

"Hey, Linda?" I called out to her, and she looked over her shoulder at me. "Don't... don't worry about the basement, okay? I'll take care of it." I was beside her then, my hand on the doorknob, a tight smile on my face as I shrugged. "I'd meant to earlier, I just didn't get around to it."

"There's a lot you haven't gotten around to," she remarked, stepping away from the door.

"I... I deserve that, I know." I opened up the door to go down, survey the damage, see what I could pick up while the minutes ticked away.

"Their birth certificates are down there," she said as she went back to wiping non-existent stains off the counter. "In a box, along with a frame that I'm sure she was looking for."

Of course... I knew Talia had to have been down there for a reason. She needed their birth certificates, probably other important papers as well. I nodded, thanking Linda, and made my way down the stairs. Was it crazy of me to want to find the papers and bring them to her? I mean, it wasn't like it was going to win any brownie points in the least, not on a day when she'd consider me the lowest of the low.

No, wait.

I'd already achieved that in her eyes.

Fuck it.

She needed them.

I groaned as I glanced around at the damage we'd inflicted upon that room. Books were thrown about, a stored lamp toppled over, the contents of a folder scattered across the floor.

"Oh, Talli," I sighed as I stepped around as much as I could, "you're lucky I love you."

I stopped abruptly, hearing the crunching of glass under my feet. I looked down, moving a few of the papers out of the way with my feet, my heart constricting as I saw what was underneath.

Our Angel.

She'd been looking for... our Angel?

I knelt down, picking up the shattered frame and its damaged contents in my hand, wincing as a tiny shard of glass punctured my finger. Reluctantly, I set the frame back down before pulling the piece of glass from my finger, sucking on it when it began to bleed.

"Holy shit, Warner."

I jumped at the sound of Kate's voice, glancing over my shoulder as she walked down the steps. "Hey," I said softly. "Yeah... we... um, we made quite a mess down here."

"Are you okay?" she asked, pointing at my hand.

"Yeah, it's just a little cut. Nothing big. Careful down here, though."

"Oh... Jase," she said as she looked down at the frame. She gingerly lifted it, sadness etched in her features. "I know someone who could take care of this, fix this."

"It's just a frame," I muttered.

"Can you get another certificate?" she asked and I shrugged in response.

"It's no big deal," I lied.

"Yes it is; I know better." She shook some of the excess glass from the frame, holding it out away from her. "You need to fix this. Not just for Talli, but for you, too."

"And there's no double meaning behind those words, I'm sure," I said, grinning at her when she raised her eyebrow at me. "I know, Kate. I know."

"Just cleaning up?" she asked, and I shook my head.

"I'm also looking for a few things... birth certificates, shot records, the title to her vehicle..."

"Like all of this?" she asked, gesturing towards the papers on the floor.

"Oh... great."

"Here, let me get this upstairs and I'll help you shake the glass out of those."

"Nah, I can do it," I said. "Thanks, though. Hey... can you get me a folder from my office for these? Linda will have a key."

"Sure," she replied, smiling softly. "Be careful, okay?"

"Always," I mumbled, sifting through the documents, most of which were completely unscathed.

But the memories...

Oh, there was Elizabeth's birth certificate, her name bringing back some of the hardest memories of all. Elizabeth Christine, my baby girl who almost didn't make it. To look at her today, no one would ever know. I still have a problem with her birthday, and it was something I'd believed that Talli had understood. This year, though... this past one, she carried on as if it was like all of the other kids birthdays, leaving me with my anxiety, a bottle of Jack, and...

I shook my head, moving on as I picked up the next one.

Michael James Warner, my little man, born on the hottest day in August, no problems, no drama, so easy that Talli and I had both asked if that was it. He let out one short cry before opening his eyes, and he seemed so mesmerized by his surroundings that he couldn't be bothered complaining. The first time I held him, he stared up at my face, watching my mouth as I talked to him. I'd told Talia that he was going to talk early, and she'd laughed at me until he was nine months old and asking questions.

Ah, the title to Talia's minivan. I remember the wide-eyed expression she'd had when I told her we were trading her old car in for that brand new fully loaded minivan. "Oh... God... I'm... an old lady!" she'd said, not wanting to listen to reason when I told her we needed the room. We'd just been surprised to learn that our third child was on the way, and we needed a vehicle that would fit all of us. To this day, it was still just referred to as her 'car', the word 'minivan' stricken from our vocabulary. Hell, when Elizabeth had graduated up to a booster seat from her car seat, Talli had just put all three of them together on that bench seat, leaving the back unoccupied. Sometimes—no, a lot of time—I didn't understand this woman.

And the shot records... there they were... yep, for all three of them.

Talia's transcripts from college were underneath the shot records. Wow, she had graduated with a 4.0. I mean, she'd told me she had, but sometimes I just had to wonder.

Fuck, stop it, Warner. She has a brilliant mind, it's one of the million things you fell in love with.

Just one more...

Ah, Emily. Emily Danielle Warner. Elizabeth had come up with her first name, and Talli gave her Jaden's middle name. Em was the first baby I had no say so when it came to her name, actually, but that was fine. I remember how my heart had just melted at the sight of her, the tiny copy of her mother. I just couldn't get over her face...

I still can't.

There was an envelope over to the side, and as I picked it up, a few pictures fell to the floor. The first one was an older picture of Pete and Jaden, taken in Paris when they'd flown out that June, so very long ago. This was on Talli's birthday... I could see the two of us in the background of the picture, where she'd slid on my lap and was whispering in my ear.

Oh, I remembered that.

And there was one... oh, wow, I should get rid of this one. Kate and Brooks at one of our... Christmas parties, I think? I kept flipping through them, shaking my head. What was with all of the couples pictures? Timmy and Cheryl, Chris and Nancy, Tish and Mark, me and...

Bree?

What the...

This was ... it was in this house, during one of our 'meetings' we'd all had that became more drinking sessions than anything. Oh, God...

we... we had our arms around each other, making goofy faces at the camera, and... and way off, in the background was Talli, her face sad, her eyes downcast. What had Talli said to me that night? Oh... oh, she'd said that I was blind if I thought Bree saw me as just a friend. And I'd argued with her, it had actually turned into a huge shouting match as I'd told her it was in her head.

All in her head.

And I knew better.

I knew, because Bree had told me from the moment that Talli didn't show up in Memphis exactly what she wanted.

I knew, because in Tallahassee she'd kissed me.

I knew, because in Toronto, she'd stayed in my room, holding me through the night when my wife had to cancel our plans again.

I knew, because in Chicago she'd told me she was in love with me.

And I said nothing.

I ripped that picture into tiny pieces, each one a fraction of my heart that I'd allowed to grow so cold towards the only one who could warm my soul.

Talli... I'm so sorry... I don't even deserve your forgiveness...

One more picture laid at my feet, face down. I bent over and picked it up, turning it slowly, as if I was afraid of what it may have in store. Please... please, no more reminders of...

Oh.

Oh.

Talli and me.

It was a picture that a fan had taken, just before Talli had gotten pregnant with Em. We'd been out at a club seeing Timmy's band play, having so much fun, enjoying life, enjoying each other.

And she looked so happy.

She looked so very happy, with me.

And she had been.

We had been.

There was that glow about her, the same glow she always had, and the most beautiful smile ever.

I miss that smile.

I miss my girl.

"One folder at your... um... service?" Kate came down the stairs holding the folder out for me.

"Thank you," I said, taking it from her and placing the documents in it. "I think I got all of the glass out of them."

"You don't have any on you, do you," she asked, and I shook my head 'no.' "Good. You need to get your jacket and tie, it's about time to go, okay?"

"Yeah... yeah..." I was a bit distracted, looking around, trying to see where I'd put that picture. I just... I just wanted to hold it, keep it with me. "Where did I put that?" I mumbled, mostly to myself.

"Put what?" Kate asked.

"Nothing," I replied, doing my best to smile. It must have been a sign. "It's about time, right?"

"Right."

I took a deep breath, calming my nerves as best I could, praying that today would do more good than harm.

CHAPTER 15

TALLI

"Why can't I go with you?" Elizabeth pouted as I gathered their things together.

"This isn't somewhere little kids can go," I replied.

"You look pretty, Mommy," Michael said, a sleepy smile on his face.

"Thank you."

Donna Karan suit, Manolo pumps, hair now down, just a slight wave in it, make up now fitting what I was wearing, yet not so dark that I'd look like a street walker- yeah, I was ready to go.

"Do you have a date?" Elizabeth asked, her tone uneasy.

"No, Baby Girl, I don't."

"Then who's *that* guy?" she asked loudly, pointing to the couch, where Paul sat reading over my hurried instructions. He smiled over at us and waved, seemingly unfazed by the question.

"That's Dr. Coffman…"

"Paul," he interrupted, correcting me.

"Sorry… *Paul*, and you kids are going to stay with him, or go with him, to his sisters."

"Mommy says not… not to get in… da car with strangers," Michael said to him as he looked at him suspiciously.

"Well, we don't have to get in a car," Paul explained. "We get in the elevator and go to floor six."

"Why?" Elizabeth asked again, her eyes narrowed. "Em's not gonna

197

like him."

I groaned inwardly, thankful that Paul laughed at her statement. "Mommy has things to do today."

"So call Linda."

"Not today."

"So call Daddy."

I faltered just outside of my bedroom door before walking in to get Emily. "Not today, Elizabeth," I repeated, taking a sterner tone with her. My cell began ringing, and I glanced down at the unfamiliar number, almost afraid to answer it.

"That might be whomever was sending a car for you," Paul's voice carried easily from the living room.

"Good point," I agreed, answering my phone. "Hello?"

"Mrs. Warner?"

I cringed at the thought of losing that title... no, not the title itself, but everything it had meant to me. "Yes... yes, this is."

"This is James Wilson, from Sherise Adler's office. I'm out in the parking lot, parked illegally I believe, to pick you up."

I couldn't help but laugh. "Give me just a minute and I'll be down. Or, make it closer to five with the way these damn elevators are running."

"Yes ma'am," he replied, and I shuddered.

I'll never get used to that word.

"Don't worry about waking her up," Paul said to me after I'd hung up. Emily had apparently decided today, of all days, she wanted to sleep in. "My kids are with my sister downstairs, so they're okay. I can just stay here until she gets up on her own..."

"She's going to freak out on you," Elizabeth singsonged from her spot in my papasan chair.

"I can handle it," Paul said to her as I stood and walked towards me. "You have everything?"

"Yeah," I replied, grabbing my purse and checking to see that I had my keys.

"You do what you have to do," he said, placing a hand on my arm. "They'll be right here waiting for you."

"I can't thank you enough," I said softly.

"Sure you can. You can thank me later."

"I'm... um... what?"

He laughed at my stammering, not in a mocking way but in a completely friendly, platonic, make me feel at ease kind of way. It was... nice.

"You can thank me later by sitting down and actually talking," he explained. "That's what friends do, Talli."

Friends.

"Good," I said with a slight smile. "I mean... good, because of the friend thing, and... and I need that."

"I know." He removed his hand from my arm, pointing at the door. "You, go. Give 'em hell."

Hell.

Oh, boy.

Here we go.

"Okay, so we know you had an incident on Saturday," Sherise was saying, looking over her notes. "I need... everything, Talia, *everything* you can think of."

"Well, it's... I mean, I forgot..."

"Not forgot," she cut me off. "Leave the word 'forgot' out of it, okay?"

"Okay," I said slowly. "I hadn't eaten since that morning, though."

"You were there for what occasion?"

"Emily's birthday."

"And you'd agreed to have it at his house because?"

"Because all of the plans were already made, and people were coming in town, and..."

"Make sure you specify that you had made the plans," she added.

"Okay, but... can we just do this? Please?" I rubbed my temple that was beginning to pound. "I've done the physical thing with the independent doctors, they've drawn my blood, I just... I mean, if you'd just come face to face with the thing your husband was screwing around with..."

"I'm sorry, did you... Breeann Hamilton was there?"

"Yeah... yeah, she was there. She showed up when we were opening presents. I didn't say that before?"

"No, you hadn't, and... and this is perfect. Perfect."

"Speak for yourself," I mumbled, picking at my roast beef sandwich. "That was the last thing I needed."

"So seeing the woman that your husband is having a rumored affair with at the party would cause undo strain and stress."

"I thought we weren't bringing this into the divorce," one of her assistants said.

"I thought so, too," I spoke up, my eyes darting back and forth between the two of them.

"And you thought that your husband would never bring your past drug use into this, either," Sherise pointed out, placing the documents in front of me. "Are you telling me that you still don't think he is?"

I looked over the papers, the request of toxicology reports, the psychological evaluation that was being ordered, the comments about 'bizarre' behavior and references to past indiscretions...

Yeah, that asshole was airing all of my dirty laundry.

My jaw was clenched as I handed them back to her. "I... I don't know what else to do. I'm not... I haven't used drugs in that capacity since I entered rehab. And he's making me out..." I shuddered, cringing at the thought.

"So if he wants to destroy your reputation, you need to point out that, if not for your entire marriage, at least since the children were born you have never been seen intoxicated in a public setting... not even any reports of private settings, correct?"

"Correct, but..."

"Thank you, *Celebrity Gossip*," the assistant added, placing printed off photos and documented accounts of Jase being publicly intoxicated, numerous photographs of him with an alcoholic beverage in his hand.

"And thanks to you as well," Sherise added, nodding towards the photos printed off of my camera from Emily's party, at least three of them at different intervals showing Jase with a beer in his hand.

"He's not an alcoholic, though."

"And you're not on drugs," she replied quickly, her eyebrow raised. "And these gems here…"

I felt the bile raise up in my throat as she laid out the numerous pictures of Jase with Bree, including ones that had been taken on the plane.

"Mr. Warner isn't going to know what hit him," the assistant said.

"Oh, of course he will," Sherise disagreed. "His legal team would be fools to not see this coming. They know that they're opening the can of worms, opening the door to bring Breeann Hamilton and all of her… thank you again, *Celebrity Gossip*… baggage…"

"What is that?" I asked, pointing at the printed article in Sherise's hand.

"Oh, this? This is where Ms. Hamilton was arrested for public intoxication, lewd behavior, indecent exposure… would you like to read this?"

"When did this happen?" I asked, feeling the scowl creep over my face.

"This was within the past two years," she replied. "It was actually before she met and became involved with your husband. I'm surprised it hasn't surfaced in the wake of all of this," she said with a wave of her hand.

"Are you thinking what I'm thinking?" the assistant asked Ms. Adler, who sat back and smiled her most perfect, pristine smile.

"Talia, my love," she said, grinning at me, "I do believe your worries are over, at least for today."

"Maybe they're not actually trying for physical custody, though," the assistant… what was his name?… added. "Maybe this is their scare tactic, their way to say 'give more visitation time or else'."

"Well, Talia? Do you want to cave, go back to the old visitation agreement?" Sherise asked me. I glanced down at the pictures of Jase with Bree, the account of her arrest, the way she snuggled up to him on the plane…

"No," I said quickly. "No, I don't."

It was just after one when we arrived at the courthouse. Even though the hearing wasn't set until one thirty, Sherise Adler wanted us there. Ready.

I wish I had a friend with me. Like... like Jaden, even though she had no business being there, since she was married to his brother. Or... or Tish, who was admittedly busy with her own family. Or Cass, who was trying to get a big promotion at her job.

Or even... Paul.

But I would be fine, see. I'm beyond capable of holding my own. I can command attention at any given time with merely a glance; I know this, I've worked the rooms of parties for many years, long before I'd ever gotten involved with one Mr. Jase Warner.

But this was different.

This wasn't for me.

This was for my children.

I held my head high as I walked down that hallway. There were no more shutters clicking, no more flashbulbs going off in my face the way they had on the way in, but I still felt eyes on me, as if every move I made was being scrutinized.

Like I said, I knew how to work a room.

And today, it was once again a good thing.

"We're going to be in a private room on the left," Sherise said to me. "Due to the number of cases they have going on today, we will try to hammer out as much as we can before we go in front of the judge."

"We're all going to be in that room?" I asked, expertly keeping my tone even.

"Yes," she replied, "and we have contacted Mave, a co-worker of yours, who was at the party. She's agreed to come in as a witness."

"A witness," I repeated the words.

"I received a call from a friend here who let me know that Mr. Warner arrived with a witness of his own."

What the hell?

Who did Jase bring with him? Who else was so adamant that I wasn't fit to raise my own children?

"Kaitlyn Evans is apparently rather reputable," Sherise said, but dismissed the comment with a wave of her hand.

"I'm sorry… did you say… Kaitlyn Evans?" I asked, stunned.

"Yes, I did," she replied. "But since she's an ex-girlfriend we can show definite bias, especially when we can prove he already has a penchant for messing around."

She continued rambling on and on about how to discredit the perfect, immaculate Kaitlyn Evans as we walked into our private area, my heart slowing only a fraction when I saw that Jase and his team were not in the room just yet.

But…

Seriously.

Kaitlyn Evans.

Kaitlyn, who had helped me finalize details for our wedding. Kaitlyn, who had held Elizabeth during the ceremony. Kaitlyn, who has asserted herself into our lives, and put up the ruse of being my friend.

Kaitlyn, who had once said I wasn't good enough for him.

And now she was going to help her ex-boyfriend, her first love, her first everything take my children away?

Not even if hell froze over.

"I know that you're not exactly on board with all of this, Talia," Sherise added.

"Oh no," I disagreed. "No, I am on board one hundred percent."

My eyes narrowed as Jase's legal team began entering the room one by one. All male, all dressed starkly in black. Sherise smiled at me… a bit of a reassuring smile, showing me she wasn't the least bit intimidated.

And then…

Jase walked in.

I set my jaw as I attempted to keep myself from glaring at him, ignoring my racing heart at the sight of him. His hair was perfectly tousled in all the right places, the highlights catching in the light of the room. His eyes were a stormy gray, matching his Armani suit that he had the audacity to wear, the fucker. He knew what seeing him in that damn suit did to me.

And you know what? Even with as pissed off as I was, even with as much as I wanted to just shove my Manolo pumps straight up his ass, my body still had the nerve to betray me.

But I can hold my own.

I can always hold my own.

My gaze was still hard, steel-like as he took his seat, directly across from me, his eyes glancing my way briefly... just for a flicker of a second.

What's the matter, Warner?

Oh, right.

There you go.

Bring your eyes right back this way... yep. It's me.

Oooo, good one, way to pretend to be shocked, surprised. You've seen me in this before, remember? And... there it is, the obligatory eye flicker up and down... yes, Warner, my breasts are still there. And they're, what, ten times the size of your little toy's?

Eat your heart out.

"And the witnesses are in the hallway?" Sherise's question caused Jase to quickly look away, over at the head of his legal team.

"If they're so needed, yes," Jase's lawyer replied.

Great. Wonderful. Kaitlyn fucking Evans is here to help her first love take my kids away.

A muscle in Jase's jaw twitched slightly, but he didn't bring his eyes back to me, so I focused my attention on my lawyer instead.

Let the games begin.

JASE

I was a bundle of nerves when Kate and I arrived at the court house, wishing I'd had someone else drive us. At least then we could have gotten out and walked only a short distance to the front doors. But no, I'd mistakenly thought we'd avoid the circus and drove my own car myself.

Screw up one for me.

"I have the folder," Kate muttered as we made our way towards the doors, the clicking of the shutters grating on my nerves. Even though there were roughly only a dozen of the sharks out there, it was still incredibly uncomfortable.

"Thank you," I said back to her. "I thought I'd left it."

We were silent the rest of the way, not that I could have heard her over the shouts of my name, and the questions they were firing at me.

"Jase! Will Bree Hamilton be joining you today?"

"Is this Kate? Are the two of you an item again?"

"Where are the children? Is it true you feel they're in danger?"

"Jase! Is it true your wife is back on drugs?"

A security officer finally met us at the steps, helping us the rest of the way in. Once inside, I removed my sunglasses, placing them in the pocket of my suit jacket, my eyes adjusting to the indoor lighting.

"Are you all right?" Kate asked.

"Peachy," I replied dryly. "Chris said I'd be meeting Robert in room 213, before we meet with Talia's lawyer." I glanced down at my watch, seeing the 12:30 staring back at me. "They asked me to be here by one."

"So you're early." Kate smiled tightly. "Is it really coming to this?" We paused by the elevators, and I sighed as it hit me how many times I'd asked the same question. "You know what you need to do?"

"My guess is you're about to tell me," I mumbled as we got on the elevator.

"You need to just... stop the meeting, or hearing, or whatever, and tell her you don't want this," Kate stated, and I let out a short laugh. "Jase, I'm being serious. This... this isn't like my divorce, and not just because I don't have any children. The two of you love each other. Beyond rhyme, beyond reason, beyond..."

"I used to think... you know, that love was enough," I cut her off. "But all the love in the world didn't make her happy."

"Neither did you acting like you were single. Hey! I call them as I see them."

"That wasn't the start of the problem," I reminded her.

"Do you want this, Jase?" she asked, placing one hand on my arm, making me long for the days when Talli would do something that sweet, just the tiniest gesture.

Hell no... no, I didn't want this. I didn't want a divorce; I didn't want my family away from me.

But I didn't want the way we had been living either.

"Jase?"

The doors opened, the bustling of activity on the second floor greeting us. "This isn't what I want, not this."

But there wasn't much I could to about that, was there?

"Just sit back and let us do our jobs," Robert said to me as I sat in room 213. "Your friend here… Kate? Is that your name?"

"Yes," she responded.

"We actually need you to sit out in the hall. There are a few private things we need to discuss."

"Really? She can't be in here?" I asked, a bit surprised. "We're just going over some details before we meet with her lawyers, right?"

"Yes, but…"

"She can stay in here then, right?"

"Fine," Robert said with a sigh. "We don't have time to argue right now. I can tell you that she won't be able to come into the conference with us, though."

"It's quite all right; I don't want to be.."

"You're no trouble," I cut her off.

"We received word that Talia was picked up earlier this morning and has already had the physical done, the results of which will be brought with them, minus some of the blood work."

"Good," I said softly. "Good."

"But I really do believe that Sherise Adler is going to come after you, both guns blazing. She'll bring up Breeann Hamilton, I'm sure."

"I thought that… I thought that she wasn't mentioned anywhere."

"Well, when we demanded the tests, we left that open. Chris informed us that Ms. Hamilton showed up at the party. I guarantee that they'll bring that up."

"Where is Chris?" I asked.

"He'll be here for the hearing," Robert replied. "He can serve as a witness for when Bree showed up, since he was with you when you told her to leave."

"Why does that matter?"

"Because I guarantee they'll make seem as if she was invited."

"She was. Kind of."

"How so?"

"Talli made the guest list a long time ago."

"So they can't really say anything about her being there," Robert stated, filing that paper on the bottom of his list.

Somehow, I doubted that.

"We do need to go over in detail about her bizarre behavior over the past year, though."

"What do you mean, bizarre behavior?" I scowled as they put a few papers in front of me. "Is this the... is this what you had served?"

"Chris said that you may have a few problems with the way the papers were worded, but I assure you that this is all in the best interests of your children."

My children.

"If you want to have your children with you, or at least have your visitation modified, this is what has to be done."

Kate was looking over the papers with me, scowling as well. "Jase," she whispered, "don't... don't do this!"

"Is there a problem, ma'am?" Robert asked.

"Are you kidding me?" Kate replied, looking over the papers.

"Kate, don't."

"You're... you have no idea what you're doing," she continued, ignoring me. "Jase, if you go through with this, you're asking for World War Three."

"We have gone through with this, and believe me, ma'am, I know more about this that you do. Now, Mr. Warner, as I said, just sit back and let me do my job."

How many times was I going to have to hear those words today?

I had a bad feeling about this.

The more that Robert shoved the 'for the good of the children' down my throat, the more I thought that going after Talia was the worst possible thing in this world. How was that going to be good for our children? I felt like we were taking her out to slaughter, and Robert... he was so pleased with himself, acting like the cat who swallowed the canary, asking me if I had my house ready for my children to come stay with me.

And through it all, my heart ached for her.

It hurt knowing what was bound to happen just an hour or so from the time we headed into that conference room where Talia and her team of lawyers sat.

Wow

This is what it had come to.

Us and our teams.

I tried my best to keep my composure as we filed into the conference room. I recognized Sherise right away, remembering how many times I'd seen her in various news blips, if that's what they could be called, from various different high-profile divorces. Her record was impeccable. So was her taste in clothing, as well as the clothing of the rest of her team. Wow, guess they would score well in a fashion show, especially the one in…

Oh, God.

Talli.

Wow… wow, she looked… amazing. Amazingly pissed off as well, but… amazing. Damn. I recognized her Donna Karan suit, remembering how she'd giggled when she came home from buying it.

"You just don't get it, Jase… me! In a Donna Karan suit? Gah, I have to call Jaden!"

Jaden, who giggled right along with her.

And here Talli sat today, her team against mine, and…

Witnesses? Did someone say something about witnesses? Oh, right, Chris was going to be here. But Kate… Kate was in the hall, too. They couldn't be talking about her. Hell, how would they even know Kate was here? What would it matter? She had only come as a friend for me.

Breathe, Jase. Breathe. Sit back, let the lawyers do their job.

"Ms. Adler, your client made up the guest list, she clearly didn't mind Ms. Hamilton being there, so…"

"Can it, Robert, you and I both know the list was made up before your client was caught in bed with her."

Wow, she was a pleasant one.

I felt my face grow hot, knowing Talia's eyes were probably on me right at that moment. Jeez, was this really going to be brought out in that court room?

"Where's your proof?" Robert retorted.

"There has already been a confirmation of the affair from Ms. Hamilton herself on Stella Black's show. We do have transcripts available for the judge. And the undo stress placed on my client due to Ms. Hamilton's arrival..."

"A good forty minutes to an hour before your client collapsed..."

"...so you're saying had she fallen out in front of her husband's mistress it would be okay? We all know that stress takes its toll on the body."

"Yes, let's see the reports, shall we?"

"Her physical examination was conducted at the hospital of your choosing, so there would be no conflict of interest," Ms. Adler continued, handing over the report. "And you can see that while my client's heart condition is for the most part benign..."

Oh, God...

Her heart.

How could I be so fucking stupid?

"If your client is in poor health..."

"Are you blind, Robert? It's in black and white. She's a healthy person under an unhealthy amount of stress that your client and his *mistress* have placed her under."

"The toxicology reports will determine if that's truly the case."

My eyes slid shut as I remembered the first time that I'd been with her, when her murmur had acted up. It was years ago, before we'd ever gotten married, when we'd lost the baby. Who was it they had called back in Ohio? John... they'd called John.

I had to call him later.

I had to... I had to talk to someone about this.

"If she's under so much stress, then perhaps a break..."

"A break?" Sherise Adler's voice was loud as she barked the word at him. "Taking her children from her isn't what is considered a break, Robert. Are you really prepared to..."

"Ms. Adler, if the court finds it unnecessary to remove the children from your client's care, then we will be asking for the original visitation agreement. Surely you agree that…"

"So it would take stress away from my client to hand her children over to a man who spends a good deal of his time drinking and seeking the company of other women?"

Wait…

What?

My eyes narrowed as Sherise Adler began setting out pictures from various sources of me in various states of sobriety.

What the fuck?

I looked sharply across the table at Talia, and was surprised to find her eyes on me.

Oh, they were so cold.

They were two pieces of ice as she stared me down, her glare piercing as her lawyer began arguing with mine about my chosen lifestyle.

Oh, is that what it is now? Not my career, but my chosen lifestyle to spend so much time away from home.

"Ms. Adler, bringing up something that happened before they ever met is…"

"Exactly what you're doing to my client," Sherise finished for him.

Oh, nice one, Talia. Bring up Pete and me dancing on the bar. Thanks for that, babe.

"My client hasn't had to spend time in rehab."

"And my client has walked the straight and narrow since giving birth to their children. Can the same be said for yours?"

Their heated debate continued as Talia and I sat across the table from one another, sizing up what we had become.

For all the polish, the designer clothes, the fancy cars, the team of over-priced lawyers, nothing could mask the cold, hard, ugly truth of this day.

This day, my entire world was slipping through my fingers.

And I was powerless to stop it…

And too angry to want to.

CHAPTER 16

TALIA

An impasse.

That's what Sherise Adler announced that we were at when we refused to give in to Jase's demands.

There would be no peace, no compromise before we stepped in front of the judge, before the fate of our children was handed over to someone who didn't know them. Didn't know me. Didn't know Jase. Someone who had the power to say that Jase's whore was more suited to be a mother to my own children.

When our 'meeting' adjourned, and Jase and his team exited the room, I could feel... it, whatever that 'it' was... it was slipping away. We were one step closer to irreparable damage- hadn't that already happened?- and I felt powerless to stop it. And Jase, the look on his face, that cross between anger and despair... it's exactly what I was feeling.

I wonder if our expressions were the same.

"We have a really strong case here," Sherise said, shuffling papers before putting them back in her briefcase. "We haven't even brought out everything. Hell, by the time I'm done with him, he'll be having supervised visitation only."

"No."

I said the word so quickly I had to blink back my surprise, but I recovered and continued.

"Don't do that; it's going too far."

"Talia, that's exactly what he's trying to do to you."

"Ms. Adler," her assistant began, "perhaps... if we approach this by showing her generosity by *not* asking for supervised visitation..."

"Ah, good point, Todd," she said.

Todd. His name was Todd. Her assistant that was as determined as she was to completely emasculate my husband... soon to be ex-husband...

"Just to forewarn you, though," she continued, turning back to me, "if I do my job properly, the judge will automatically revoke his visitation."

I swallowed over the lump in my throat, wondering what the hell I'd gotten myself into.

"Not to worry, though." Sherise stood with the precision of a super model, smiling down at me. "If the judge is the one who mandates it rather than you asking for it, you can hardly be seen as the bad guy, right?"

Oh wow.

If that's what she really thought, she didn't know Jase at all.

"How is it going?"

The question that Paul asked when I called him was so very simple, and yet so loaded.

"It sucks," I found myself admitting, rubbing my temple. "I just needed to hear a friendly voice."

That was about the time I hear Emily let out an ear-piercing scream that she followed with a very dramatic my-life-is-over cry.

"Fear not," he said as I heard Em's cry get louder. I could tell he'd picked her up by her shriek of protest.

"She doesn't like you," Elizabeth's voice sounded in the background.

"I'm so sorry," I said in a rush. "I... I can call someone, if you need me to."

"It's no big deal, Talli. I'm going by your instructions and putting her cranky butt down for a nap."

"NnnnoOOOO." Wow, was that word ever clear from her.

"Your mom tells me no all the time, and guess where I'm at," he said to her in the sweetest voice, bringing pangs of nostalgia as I remembered Jase putting our children to bed.

And then his words sunk in.

"What?" I asked with a laugh.

"Caught that, huh?"

"Yes I did." I smiled softly. "Thank you, Paul. I really appreciate this."

I felt a pair of eyes on me as Paul told me that it was really no problem... just a creeping sensation up my spine that turned my blood to ice. I turned slowly, peering over my shoulder.

Oh, hell no you don't have the right to stand there and glare at me, Mr. Warner. Not standing there in your Armani suit, leaning against the wall, arms crossed, looking at me like *I'm* a piece of cheating scum. No, jackass, that title belongs to you.

I turned my body completely around, holding the phone up to my ear, one eyebrow up as I silently challenged him.

Say something, asshole. I dare you.

"Talli?" Paul's voice filtered through the phone.

"Yeah, I'm here," I said, my voice smooth as silk.

Jase had the audacity to roll his eyes and shake his head before walking away, towards his team of lawyers and...

Kaitlyn.

Kaitlyn who reached out and squeezed his hand.

Fuck you, Warner. Fuck. You.

"Ah, I take it he's by you."

I winced as Paul once again saw right through me. "Yeah, he was," I replied. "Sorry."

"Don't sweat it. Was or is? Because I can feed you lines to say to me that..."

"Seriously?" I cut him off, again laughing at him.

"There. There, now I feel better

Oh, that hurt me.

Jase used to do the same thing, all the time. He'd call and know just by the sound of my voice when something was wrong, and he'd never end the call until he'd made me laugh at least once. Or, when I would come home from work all stressed out, he'd wrap his arms around me, holding me, letting me vent, being the calming force in my life.

Why had he stopped?

Oh, right.

Because I had.

Was Bree before or after that?

Did it really matter?

This was bad. This was so, so very bad. This was... crawl in a hole and hide, never emerge bad.

And the worst part?

It was really going in our direction.

"Where is the proof that Mrs. Warner is taking illegal substances?" Judge Spencer asked as she peered down her nose at Jase's lawyers.

"The toxicology report isn't in, however..."

"So you have no proof."

"Your honor, Mrs. Warner lost consciousness for an extended period of time..."

"So I see. Are you suggesting that every parent who has had a fainting spell have their children taken away, sir?"

And of course, bringing up my fainting spell brought up the wonderfully unpleasant subject that I had wanted most to avoid.

"Your honor," Sherise said, raising her eyebrow for effect, "Mr. Warner's team is failing to mention the extenuating circumstances regarding my client's fainting spell."

"And just what would those extenuating circumstances be?"

"Breeann Hamilton," Sherise said, smiling at the objections being thrown from the other table.

"Breeann Hamilton is not an issue here..."

"You brought my client here on the basis that she was on drugs; I'm showing the circumstances that led up to her fainting spell, therefore yes Breeann Hamilton is an issue."

Why did I have to see Jase's expression out of the corner of my eye? Why did I have to see him bow his head, looking as if he were in silent prayer?

"Your honor, I'd like to submit transcripts from the Stella Black show where Breeann Hamilton admitted to an affair with Mr. Warner, on national television no less."

More shouts from both sides.

More pain in my heart.

More accusations thrown back and forth.

Why?

Why did it come to this?

"Mr. Warner doesn't even attempt to hide his decadent lifestyle, his excessive drinking... binge drinking, even."

"Oh, come *on*, Ms. Adler, is that the best you can do?"

"I've had enough of your outbursts!" the judge barked at Jase's attorney as she surveyed the evidence that Sherise had brought in. The pictures, the articles, the home photos... each one of them making me feel just a little sicker to my stomach.

I knew my day had started out bad. More than bad, actually, knowing that I'd had to fight tooth and nail for my children. It was almost gut-wrenching to actually have to call someone who had been insisting that I needed a friend and ask him for help. Watching Mave break down in the court room, proclaiming her love for the both of us, absolutely broke what was left of my heart. And Kaitlyn? She seemed reluctant to say much of anything.

But the lawyers, oh they had plenty to say.

And so did the judge.

"I hardly think that Mr. Warner is one to point fingers of blame, label anyone else as an unfit parent when parenting has been the lowest of his own priorities."

Sherise sat back, a satisfied smile on her face.

Jase's face fell, his eyes filled with tears as the decision was made.

Oh, God.

This isn't happening.

JASE

Have you ever found yourself in the middle of a complete clusterfuck, knowing that you'd created it, knowing that you thought your actions were right, only to have it completely blow up in your face?

I mean, I'd told them I didn't want to do this. I told Chris that the only way I wanted a hearing for emergency custody was if Talia's tests came back positive. I had to know that my children were safe, I *was* looking out for their best interests. I needed to know that Elizabeth, Michael, and Emily weren't going to have to suddenly fend for themselves, because God knows they were far too young to.

I'd never said that Talia was a bad mother. Quite the opposite, you know? She's... she's so good at it, she loves them so much that sometimes she doesn't know how to let go. I know, because that was part of our problems, one that she and I just couldn't see eye to eye on.

But this?

I never wanted this.

I cringed every time they brought up her past drug abuse, the affair with Keith... especially when they tried to use that to cancel out what had happened with Bree. What the fuck were my lawyers thinking? And don't get me started in on Bree, okay? What she'd done in her past was quite honestly none of my business, hardly being the saint myself, but I'd had no idea about her arrest, and I certainly had no idea the judge was going to hold it against *me*.

Yeah, everything about my life was shredded to pieces too. My 'decadent lifestyle,' as they so sweetly named it, was on display, each piece of it making me look like a man whose children were merely accessories.

And that's not true.

Fuck, that's so not true.

And Talia, she knows that. She knows how much I love them; she knows that they're the center of my world. I would do anything for them, damn it, and if Talia didn't want me to drink around them, all she had to do was say something.

Just... say something.

But who am I to judge, right? I mean, did I try and talk with her after the incident at the party? No. I let her have her space. I let her go off to her condo, with my children, to sit around with her friends and just have her own space. And I'd told Chris to make sure my children were safe, and... and...

I glanced over at Talia, the stricken look on her face as our lawyers continued tearing each of us apart tugging at my heart strings. Hell, at that point I had no idea why she looked so sad. She was coming off as some patron fucking saint while I was the big bad wolf trying to destroy the innocent minds of my 'accessories'. How sick was it that I just wanted to gather her in my arms, tell her it was all going to be okay? Until...

"Mr. Warner, you have shown no just cause for your request of emergency temporary custody."

Okay, that's all well and good.

"On the contrary, if these children need protection from anything, or anyone, it would be your actions, the company you choose to keep, and the lifestyle you choose to live."

You don't know shit about my lifestyle, lady, and sans Bree the company I've kept are some of the most incredible human beings on the face of this Earth, and Talia *knows* it.

"Therefore, it is in my opinion that the children remain with their mother..."

That's fine, that's fine... she's a good mother, she's good with them.

"... and that the visitation rights that you have acquired be removed..."

What?

"...until such time as you have proven to the court..."

Oh God... don't do this... don't do this... don't take my babies away...

"...that you are willing and able to have a safe, stable environment for the children to be in."

How much safer and more stable can you get than their *own damn home?!*

"The court hereby orders that Mr. Warner's visitations be supervised, in a controlled environment, with a court-appointed liaison present at all times."

What the hell just happened here?

I felt like all the air was being sucked from my body, the room was closing around on me, the faces starting to blur as I did my best to keep the tears away. I couldn't... I *wouldn't* give her the satisfaction of seeing me cry. I can't let her know how much she's broken me today. I just... I can't.

"I believe that's what's called... backfire." Sherise Adler's voice was like nails on a chalkboard to me at that point.

"This isn't over," Robert promised.

Damn straight it wasn't.

Damn fucking straight this wasn't over.

I saw Talia's legs as she passed by me, but by the time I glanced up it was too late to see her face, see her expression, and that was just fine by me. If I'd seen the triumphant gleam there, I probably would have gone the fuck off on her. But I don't have the right to, see? Because I started this. And this was exactly what my lawyers were trying to do with her.

"Jase,"

"Chris, you fucking *asshole*, I told you..." I muttered those words softly between clenched teeth as he came up and placed his hand on my shoulder.

"Let's get you out of here."

I shrugged his hand off of me and stood, holding on to the last shards of my composure as I hurried my way out of that courtroom, past the knowing glances of the people who were out in the hall.

"Jase, let's go back to the conference room, and..."

"Fuck you, Chris," I hissed at him.

"In light of everything that's happened, you have got to get a grip on yourself," he replied.

Get a grip on myself? Was he fucking kidding me?

"Jase..."

That was Kate. I knew that voice. Without missing a beat, without looking for her, I reached out and she took my hand, walking along as we approached that damn conference room where I'd tried to tell them the first time that this was a mistake. And what was their response?

Oh, right.

Let them do their jobs.

And look what it cost me.

I heard the door click shut, and before Kate could say anything, before anyone could stop me, I was in Chris's face, his back up against the wall. "Are you fucking happy now? Are you?"

"Jase, calm down."

"Fuck you!" I yelled at him, shaking Kate's hand off my arm, ignoring her protests. "You handed this over to the lawyers, you practically gave them carte blanche to go after her, and I *told* you to wait!"

"Jase, listen…"

"But what the hell do I know? I'm not a fucking lawyer, right? No, I'm just a father who has lost his kids!"

"What?" Kate gasped beside me, only then reminding me she'd left the courtroom after they were done with her.

"We can fix this."

"You… you damn well better hope and pray that you can, Chris."

"There are a few things…"

"I don't give a fuck what it takes!" I cut him off, backing up only slightly. "I don't fucking care. Get my kids back."

"Jase, you are asking for…"

"She wants a war?" I cut Kate off, looking over at her for the first time. "She's fucking got it."

"Are you sure you don't want to pull over? I can drive."

I glanced over at Kate, who was looking at me with pity. Have I mentioned I cannot stand when someone looks at me like that? I was in a foul mood to begin with, that was the last thing I needed.

"I'm fine," I muttered, my eyes now back on the road.

"You're just driving like a mad man, that's all," she commented with a sigh. "Okay, fine, Mr. Destructo-Boy, you want to drive? Have at it. Please remember, though, that you *do* have a passenger."

"We're almost at the house, Kate."

"Do you want me to…"

"I'm not really good company, and I don't think ice cream is going to fix this."

"Hell no, ice cream won't fix it. And neither will two packs of lawyers going at each other with your children caught in the middle."

"What the hell else am I supposed to do, Kate?" I snapped. "She made it clear she doesn't love me, she moved out, took them away, filed for divorce... hell, she has everything she fucking wanted! And who the hell is Paul?"

"Paul?" Kate asked, and I could tell by her tone she was confused. "What the hell are you talking about?"

"It doesn't fucking matter, Kate. Just... well, it would make sense, wouldn't it? Why she'd pulled away from me? She wants to throw Bree in my face, and yet..."

"Jase, don't jump to conclusions, okay?"

I clenched my jaw tightly at her words, thinking to myself I had every right to jump to conclusions. What the hell was Talia trying to hide from me? Why had she moved that far away, so quickly? Why, after agreeing to a generous visitation schedule, had she pushed it to where I had to have supervision to see my kids?

My kids?

"And before you go off about what Talli has done... or what her lawyers have done... Jase, please remember that it's exactly what you were trying to do to her. And it sucks, doesn't it?"

"I didn't want to take them away from her, Kate," I finally said. "Not unless she was using again. Because I swear to God, if she is..."

"Jase, come on. Please. Just..."

"Just *nothing*, Kate! Just... fucking... nothing! Let me find out she's using again, and I swear on all things holy she'll regret the day she kept them from me. Fuck, she's going to regret it any way."

"Don't talk like that... just... take a step back and..."

"How many kids do you have, Kate?" I asked suddenly, stealing another glance at her before taking the exit to my home.

"If you're implying that my not having children would cloud my judgment, then you are sadly mistaken," she said coolly. "And I know that you're upset, so you should be grateful that I'm taking that into consideration instead of knocking you upside your thick skull."

"What if she is? Huh? What if she is?"

Kate took a deep breath and sighed. "Well, from what I know, they may not find what they're looking for in the toxicology report."

"What do you mean?" I asked, my heart beginning to race.

"Jase, she never used illegal drugs, never abused them anyhow. Everything she took was *legal*. Do you know what they're looking for?"

"I don't understand all that medical jargon bullshit."

"Then what you need to do is… well, first, run over those pricks in your driveway."

"Gladly," I muttered, honking my horn and revving my engine as I made my way towards my house. Jackie stepped outside, standing by the garage door to ensure that none of the creepy fuckers got inside as I gunned it up my driveway into the garage. "Damn. I missed." Hitting the button, the garage door closed behind us, the muted light and noise level contrasting against my frayed nerves.

"Better luck next time," she said, then took off her seatbelt and turned towards me. "Jase, you need to talk to someone who would know."

"Know what?" I asked, squinting slightly as I looked at her.

"If she's using. Is there anyone you could call?"

"What am I supposed to do, call Eric? Or Lisa? Lisa won't talk with me, and if she sneezes wrong Eric thinks she's using."

"What about Jeff?"

"No… no, I'd rather not call him."

"Tish? Cass? Jaden?"

"Tish might know," I said, remembering how Tish had been the one to help intervene when Talia had begun to spiral out of control.

"So call her."

"Or…" I shook my head. "Nah. Nah, that would be ignorant."

"What would be?"

"Nothing; I'll just call Tish. And hope she talks to me."

Kate smiled at me, squeezing my hand. "It will be okay, you know? Let me talk with Rebecca, see if this is something she might be interested in."

"Rebecca?" I asked, not knowing who the hell she was referring to.

"Rebecca St. John, the attorney who married the actor Kevin Bauer. Remember?"

"Kinda," I said with a sigh. "Fuck, this is a mess."

"Yes, it's a mess, and yes she's a rather pricey attorney, but she specializes in custody cases, Jase, specifically ones involving fathers' rights."

I contemplated this for a moment, but only a brief one knowing that Kate would never steer me wrong. This sounded just like what the doctor ordered; someone on my side who would fight to get my children back, someone who handled cases similar on a regular basis, and *knew* how to win them.

Someone who could beat Sherise Adler at her own game.

"She's good?"

"She's won against Ms. Adler before," Kate replied.

"Then do it, Kate. Please. And I don't care what it costs, okay?"

"I'll call her as soon as we get in there," she promised, placing a hand on my arm. "This is just temporary. It, too, will pass."

"Yes, Zen Master," I mumbled, my heart not even close to being behind the words, hoping with everything inside of me that maybe she was right.

I didn't want to consider the possibility of her being wrong.

She has to be right; this has to be temporary.

It just... has to be.

CHAPTER 17

TALLI

I kept my eyes straight forward, blinking back my tears as I followed Sherise Adler out of the courtroom. I couldn't look at Jase... I just couldn't. One glance, and I know I would have broken.

How did this happen?

He's not a bad father. He has always been so patient, so kind, so gentle. The only exception had been during Emily's outbursts after he had come home, and even then, he'd taken it out on me, not the children. And now some stranger has decided that's not good enough for them?

I was still holding back tears as we stepped out into the hallway, trying to ignore the lingering paparazzi that hadn't been chased off who were trying to act as if they weren't taking pictures. Sherise was gloating, repeatedly congratulating herself and the team on their win, each word bringing another wave of nausea. My hands were shaking ever so slightly, and I felt myself begin to break out into a cold sweat.

Oh no... not again.

"Talli!"

What the hell does Kaitlyn fucking Evans want with me?

"Talli, wait!"

"Do not stop, do not speak with her, do not even make eye contact," Sherise barked at me.

Oh, hell no.

I'm not your fucking flunky.

I stopped dead in my tracks, glaring at the back of Sherise's head as she continued walking down the hall.

"Here."

Kaitlyn was beside me, putting a blue folder in my hand. I looked at it, then back over at her as if she'd grown a second, or perhaps even a third head.

"Jase said you needed those."

Oh he did, did he? Lucky for Jase, I was unable to find a trash can in the immediate vicinity. I nodded slightly and continued down the hall towards where Sherise Adler stood, arms crossed, a look of disgust on her face.

"Talia, when I tell you…"

"I am *not* your employee, Ms. Adler, so if you have a suggestion for me, you may want to ask nicely," I said, my tone cold and even as I channeled my inner Chris Webber. Her nostrils flared slightly before she flashed a curt smile in my direction.

"So noted," she said before motioning to Todd to open the conference door. What, was her hand broken? She stood to the side, making sure that I walked in first before they entered behind me. I slowly lowered myself into one of the large black chairs, placing the blue folder in front of me, avoiding looking inside. I was tracing unseen patterns on that folder as the team took their various seats around the table. I flinched slightly as the door clicked shut but recovered quickly and maintained composure.

"Congratulations everyone on the first of many victories for this case," Sherise said, and my head snapped over in her direction.

Victory? Was she fucking kidding me?

This is her idea of a victory?

"I must remind everyone in here that this is merely the beginning. There is sure to be appeal after appeal until we get the actual court date set for the divorce."

Appeal? You know what? Good.

"Talia, they're bringing the car around for you."

"If this meeting isn't over, I'm not leaving," I said, and there was no mistaking that she wanted to roll her eyes.

"Talia, go home to your children. Bask in the glow."

"What glow?" I snapped. "How... how can all of you consider this a victory?"

"How can you *not*?" she asked incredulously.

"You want to know how?" I asked, my voice rising. "Because I have to go home and tell my children who think the sun rises and sets with their daddy that they can't see him anymore. That's how."

"They get to see him..."

"And don't preach to me about them getting supervised visitation. They're just children. They're... they're babies, they're our babies, and they won't understand."

"So make them understand," Sherise said in clipped tones. "Or would you have preferred that you be sitting in his shoes? Do I need to remind you that you're here because he was trying to do this to you?"

Of course not. Of course I didn't want them to go with him, I didn't want to lose them. But this... this just wasn't right.

"Fix it," I said through gritted teeth.

"That would not be in your or the children's best interest. Now Talia..." She walked over to the door and opened it. "Your car is waiting."

I stood, my jaw clenched as I kept eye contact with her, my gaze as unwavering as my voice. "There will be no more decisions made, no motions filed, nothing else done without my approval."

"As you wish."

As I wish. Fuck you, you arrogant bitch.

I made a mental note to thank Chris Webber if I ever got the chance, as I sincerely doubted I could have pulled it off without so many years of observing him.

Ah, hell. Paparazzi. Still. Like I fucking needed this. I clutched that blue folder to me, planting my sunglasses on my face as I stepped out to the blaring sun and popping camera shutters.

"Talia! Talli!"

Dick, you have no right to use my nickname.

"What's the verdict?"

"Is it true you've retained full custody?"

"What are your thoughts on Jase's relationship with Bree Hamilton?"

"Has he moved on now with Kate Evans?"

I'd never been more thankful to crawl in the back of a car in my life, which under any other circumstance would sound bad. As it was, I was slumped slightly down in the seat, pulling my sunglasses off and phone out, sighing as I stared at it.

I didn't feel like talking with anyone.

I didn't want to discuss what happened. There was nothing to be happy about, nothing to celebrate.

What was I supposed to say?

There were no messages, so everything must be going okay with Paul and the kids. Probably much better than things were going for me.

Forget about me.

What about Jase?

I stared down at that phone, wishing I could call him, tell him I was sorry, promise him that somehow, some way we could fix this. There must be a way to fix it.

I thought of the kids, and how they always talked about how much they missed him.

For them.

I have to fix this for them.

"Mommy!" Michael bounded up to me, throwing his arms around my legs as I walked in the door. I dropped my purse and the folder on a table.

"Hi, Little Man." I swung him up on my hip, placing a kiss on his cheek. "Have you been good?"

"They've been very good," Paul said as he walked into the living room. Emily toddled behind him, holding her sippy cup, fresh tears clinging to her lashes.

"'Cept she's been crying lots," Michael added, pushing slightly against me until I set him back down. Emily kept walking towards me, giving me the evil eye of death.

"I take it you're mad at me," I said to her as she turned her nose up and walked away.

"She'll get over it," Paul commented, grinning at me. "Oh... oh, did today not go so good?"

"I… um…" I glanced to see that all of the kids were out of earshot. "I retained full custody."

"Hey, that's great!" he exclaimed, pulling me into his arms for a quick, friendly hug that I just wasn't prepared for. My arms were by my sides still when the first sob broke free, followed quickly by another, and the tears… oh, the tears. I couldn't stop them once they'd started. "Hey…" He held me closer as I gave in, holding on to his shirt and crying as if there were no tomorrow.

Crying for a love lost.

Crying for our children.

Crying for the way things should have been.

"What happened?" he asked, his voice soft and soothing.

"It was so… so awful."

"Talli, what did he do?"

"That's just it." I pulled back, wiping my eyes. "Technically nothing, other than the whole starting this shit to begin with. I mean… I know he was trying to do this to me, but it doesn't make it right."

"I don't understand."

"They took…" I swallowed, taking in a deep breath. "Paul, they suspended his visitation."

"They must have had good reason to."

"Oh, they certainly came up with a good enough reason." I kicked my shoes off, grabbing a tissue as I passed the end table. "He's a good dad, Paul. He really is."

"You've always said that… here. Come on, sit."

"Thank you for inviting me to sit in my own home, Paul," I muttered. "I'm sorry… I'm so sorry."

"No, no… I apologize." He sat down on the couch as I took my normal perch in the papasan chair, one foot tucked underneath me.

"You're just being nice, and I'm getting off track, and…" I waved my arms around, trying to come up with the words. "Supervised visitation."

"So at least they'll get to see him."

"Yeah, you try reasoning with them about that. You tell Elizabeth that she can't curl up on her Daddy's lap without someone scrutinizing it, or tell Michael that he can't go back to what was his home and... and play football with him. Or... or you step in between Em and Jase now that she's warming up to him. She *hates* strangers."

"So I've noticed."

"She'll tweak the *entire* time." I wiped away the tears that continued falling, unable to stop them. "And it's for two hours every Saturday, and that's it."

"I know the drill," he said softly. "So, was this not something you wanted?"

"No... no, I just... I thought that Sherise was just going in there to defend me, defend my actions, make them see that I'm capable of taking care of them. And then she comes up with this grandiose scheme to one-up them, and the next thing I know they won't let Jase see the kids."

"Welcome to the wonderful world of divorce lawyers," Paul deadpanned. "I know that you mean well, but right now just... relax. Let this play out a little bit, and when he comes for an appeal, then just... you know, make it go away."

"I can do that?" I asked, sniffling slightly.

"Absolutely. Your lawyer might have a problem or two with it, mind you."

"Oh, fuck her. I'm so pissed at her right now I can't even fucking see straight."

Paul simply grinned at me and began to chuckle. He shook his head slightly and sighed. "I knew that you were in there somewhere, Talli."

"Huh?" I asked, taking the box of tissues that he handed to me.

"It's going to take some time, but you can bring yourself out of PPD."

"I don't have PP fucking D, Paul."

His head dropped back as he laughed heartily. "Okay, I'll play along. But in the meantime..."

"What do I do?" I asked, shrugging my shoulders. "How... how do I tell my kids they can't see their Dad?"

"*What* did you do?" I'd never heard so much venom spewed forth as I heard in those four words as they were screamed at me by my five year old daughter.

"Baby girl..."

"What did you do?"

"Elizabeth, your Mom didn't do anything," Paul said, ignoring my hand that was trying to shush him.

"You're not my Daddy!" she screamed at him, her face turning beet red as she began to shake. "You... tell me what you did."

"Young lady, I am your mother and you will not speak to me that way."

"*I want my Daddy*," she said, her voice low as tears filled her eyes.

"Baby girl, please..."

"I want my Daddy!" The tears spilled down onto her cheeks as she stomped towards me with much more force than a five-year-old should have. "You promised me I could see him when I wanted."

"Elizabeth,"

"You promised all of us before you took us away from him. You get my Daddy *now*!"

"Excuse us," I mumbled to Paul, who merely nodded and smiled at me. Does he have to be so underfuckingstanding? I stood and took Elizabeth's hand, and when she protested I picked her petite frame up in my arms and carried her back to her room, shutting the door before I placed her on her bed.

"I hate you," she spit out at me. "I hate you for what you've done, and for taking us away, and for making us live here, and for not loving my Daddy..."

"I will always love your Daddy." I stopped her tirade with those words, smoothing back her soft hair that had darkened to a light brown away from her face. "And I know you're upset. I'm upset, too, okay? But that doesn't excuse your behavior."

"I... I want Daddy." Her bottom lip quivered as she threw herself towards me, burying her head in my chest as the sobs racked her little body.

What was I supposed to say? I mean... I knew exactly how she felt, exactly how much she missed him, even if it was in a different way. I missed him too, so much that it hurt, so much that I was fighting the urge to pull out my cell phone and call him and tell him how sorry I was, and ask him if he'd ever find it in his heart to love me again.

But would that ever be enough?

I heard some commotion coming from the living area, and Elizabeth's muffled voice carried up to me. "Your friend was ordering pizza for us."

"Oh... OH. I better go pay for that then," I said, wondering for a brief moment how the hell I was going to be able to afford to after all of the added expenses this month. "Are you okay?"

"Peachy," she sniffed, her arms folded tight to her body. "Can I wait to come out?"

"Until you're over your 'tude?" I asked, and she nodded. "Okay, but don't take too long."

"Sure."

Hmm. She sounded a little too happy that I was leaving the room. This is never good. I'll give her all of five minutes before I'm back in there telling her to get washed up for dinner, which by the time I made it out to the living room was paid for.

"How much do I owe?"

"Nonsense, this is on me." He was cutting a piece into tiny Em sized bites and pulling out plates for everyone. "I do have to go after this, though."

"I... I can't thank you enough, for everything."

"You know how you can thank me?"

"Don't tell me to join your support group, please." I actually smiled slightly. "I'd get torn to shreds."

"Just... talk to someone about this, okay?"

"Like a shrink? I don't need one."

"Talli, in light of..."

"Mommy!" Michael shrieked from the top of his lungs. "Mommy, Lizbeth wont gimme the phone!"

I looked over at the counter, the receiver for the phone still firmly in place, then patted my pockets for...

Oh, that sneaky little... mini me! What was I going to do with her?

I started to walk towards her room, demanding she hand over the cell phone, berate her for being so deceiving, but hearing her words nearly brought me to my knees.

"What did I do wrong?"

I stifled back a sob, knowing exactly who she was talking to, exactly what she was thinking.

"But... but Daddy, I'll be good."

It's not about that, Baby Girl... if it were only that simple...

"Don't you want me anymore?"

I had to explain this to her, I had to tell her that's not what was happening, that it was a bunch of stupid games that a bunch of monkeys in suits played that never should have went down, and...

"Then fix it, Daddy."

...and I knew I had to talk to him, even if he wouldn't listen right at that moment.

"I wanna talk, too," Michael whined, holding onto my leg, and after wiping my eyes I motioned for him to go in to Elizabeth's room. "Mommy said I could talk."

"Talli?" Paul's voice made me jump slightly. I turned towards him, embarrassed to be crying yet again, but he merely put his arms around me, holding me in a comforting embrace. I hesitated for a moment before my arms loosely went around him, returning the hug. "See? I don't bite." He stepped back and took my hands in his. "Now... let them have their time, okay? You. Eat."

"I don't do well having orders barked at me," I mumbled, walking towards the kitchen.

"I somehow knew that about you."

"Em... Em, baby, don't get into that," I said, walking quickly over to the end table that I'd left the blue folder on.

"Dase."

"Oh, great. You, too?" I picked her up with one arm, quickly shuffling the papers back into the folder with the other.

"I put hers on her tray," Paul said.

"Thank you," I mumbled, setting her in her highchair, her protests ceasing when she saw what was on her tray. "Kids, dinner."

I almost immediately regretted yelling that out.

I didn't want to seem as if I was intruding.

"Where's your plate?" I asked Paul, who was grabbing his things.

"I've intruded enough into your personal space."

"But..."

"Talli... dinner is on me, okay? Some night we can sit down, but right now I think my kids are chomping at the bit." He smiled again, and this one I returned.

"I'm sorry for…"

"Not another word." He held up his hands and gestured towards the door. "I'll just see myself out."

After the door closed, I let out a long drawn out sigh, staring down at the pizza and the plates. I fixed Elizabeth and Michael's plates, setting them at their usual spots before taking a deep breath and walking towards Elizabeth's room.

"I love you too, Daddy," I heard Elizabeth say.

"Me, too, Daddy!" Michael called out.

I opened the door slightly letting them know that dinner was on the table.

"Pizza!" Michael exclaimed, running from the room.

"Dinner time, Daddy. I love you." Elizabeth was walking past me as she said this, then placed the phone in my hand, still on.

Still connected.

My heart was hammering as I looked at it perhaps a fraction too long before bringing it up to my ear.

Still connected.

"Jase?"

I could hear him breathing, I knew he was there.

"Jase, we need to…"

Click.

I knew I didn't deserve any more than that, not at that moment.

With a resigned sigh, I placed the phone back in my pocket, promising myself I would try another day.

JASE

I can't remember the last time I felt this alone. I mean, even when Talia had packed everyone up and moved, I still had my visitation with the kids to look forward to. But today, when that judge made me feel like the lowest form of scum before taking my last shred of hope away… yeah. Today I truly learned the meaning of the word 'alone'.

And it *sucks*.

No, that doesn't even describe it.

They were my lifeline, my heart, my soul. I would have given up anything... *anything* for them, but I'd been so blinded by my own stupidity, by my own pettiness, that it had cost me everything.

I sent everyone away, telling Chris I'd deal with his ass later, telling Kate I wasn't in the mood for company, telling Jackie I appreciated his concern but I couldn't talk about it. Hell, I didn't even want to *think* about it. I couldn't walk up those stairs and see their bedrooms, their toys, their belongings, without knowing how long it would be before they'd be here. I couldn't stay in the great room or common room or what the fuck ever we were calling it that week, with all of our pictures smiling at me, taunting me, reminding me that I'd had it all and lost it.

And for what?

"Fuck you," I muttered to my cell phone, its display flashing Bree's name. Ignore button, you are my friend. Oh, and guess what else Bree... home number has been changed and your ass doesn't have it.

"How fucking ignorant can one man be?"

Apparently ignorant enough to wander aimlessly room to room around an empty house talking out loud to himself. Yay me.

My breath caught in my throat as I entered Talli's room, my heart constricting in my chest. How could I stay in here now? How could I sleep in here, on that couch, using her blanket after what she had done to me? What was it she had said when we discussed the children before, when she had announced she'd found a place for them?

"They're our children, not weapons."

Good one, Talli, Good one.

"Fuck." I drew the word out as I sank into the recliner, holding my head in my hands. The one place in this house where I'd found sanctuary, where I could hold myself together, where I could pretend there was a tiny shard of hope, and now... now it was forever tainted because of this day.

Like I had room to bitch about it.

Hell, we were at that fucking courthouse because my lawyers thought this stunt would get me if not full custody, at least more visitation. Backfire indeed, Sherise Adler, you must be awfully fucking proud of yourself.

I need a beer.

What are you gonna do about it, Talli?

My first beer was gone in two long drinks, my second took about five minutes, and my third—which I really didn't want but decided to have out of spite—was in my hand as I walked down the stairs to the basement.

What a fucking mess.

God, that's what this all was. A fucking mess. And it had been, before I'd made that fatal mistake of getting too personal, too friendly, going too far with someone who would never be who or what I wanted them to be.

She'd never be Talia.

But Talia didn't want me, she didn't want this life.

Every place I went, every corner I turned, there was a piece of her, a piece of our life, memories that we held as we built our life together. This was our home to me, but to her it had been a prison, and here I sat weeks after she'd taken that final step to remove herself from here keeping everything the same, as if holding a piece of her... hostage, for lack of a better word. She was alive and kicking twenty-two minutes from my house, but her ghost was here haunting me at every turn.

In so many places I could think of in that house, every sweet memory had been tainted, tarnished.

It was time for an exorcism.

Starting with this fucking basement and the remnants of our fight here.

Oh, speak of the fucking devil. Look who's calling me. What, to gloat? I don't fucking think so.

"I have nothing to say to you," I snapped and hit the end button before she could start in on me. I couldn't listen to a fucking word of it, not then. I shoved my phone back in my pocket, taking a trash bag and beginning to fill it with the broken objects scattered about the floor.

Son of a bitch.

"Did I fucking stutter?" I yelled, hitting the end button once more. Damn that woman, she wouldn't stop until she'd fucking killed me, would she? I picked up a paperback book, ready to shove it in the bag, faltering as I saw what it was.

'One Flew Over the Cuckoo's Nest.'

The book I'd been reading at that hospital in Illinois. The book she'd borrowed from me and refused to return.

She'd had it in that box?

She'd wanted to… to take it with her?

Why the hell was she calling me again? Was it that fucking important that she just had to rub my nose in it?

"What?" I demanded, my breathing heavy, my jaw clenched in anger, in hurt as I waited for…

"Why are you mad at me, Daddy?"

"Oh…God, Baby Girl, I'm so sorry." I couldn't stop the sob that escaped from me at hearing her voice, I couldn't control the overwhelming guilt over her hearing what I'd meant for her mother, I couldn't stop my heart from breaking knowing she thought it was for her. "I didn't know it was you, I swear, and I'm so sorry."

"Who are you mad at, Daddy? Is it Mommy?"

Elizabeth, you don't need to be in the middle of this. You're so young, you're just a little girl, you should be happy and playing and annoying your brother like always.

"No, no… don't worry about that. What's…" I swallowed over the lump in my throat, knowing that she'd been crying, somehow knowing that she'd been told. "What's wrong?"

"Michael, stop it!" I heard her say and heard his subsequent whine and I had to smile. I missed that so much. "Daddy, I'm running away."

"Baby girl…"

"No… no. I'm… I'm *your* girl. I'm… I'm *Daddy's* girl, and… and Mommy said I can't see you anymore, and she can't say that 'cause I'm your baby girl, and… and I can stay with you, and… and you won't be alone and you won't be sad and no one can say that… that I can't… see you."

She spoke in such a rush, each word seeming to trip over the next, as if she had the whole master plan taken care of. And as much as every word she said broke my heart, it was nothing compared to what I had to say to her.

"I… I'm so sorry, baby, but… you can't."

I shut my eyes tight as the pain rushed through me at my own words, her strangled "Why?" bringing on a new onslaught of tears.

"Baby Girl, you just can't..." I sniffled, wiping away my tears, wishing more than anything I could drive those twenty-two minutes down the road and gather her into my arms. "You can't come stay here."

"What did I do wrong?"

Oh... God...

"Baby, please..."

"But... but Daddy, I'll be good."

I'm so sorry... I'm sorry for all of this. I'm sorry I was such a bullshit excuse of a husband that I was so fucking weak. I'm sorry I didn't tell my lawyers to fucking drop their quest today. I'm sorry I can't be there for you right now.

"I know you would be, but..."

"Don't you want me anymore?"

"Oh, hey... hey..." I nearly choked on the words as I sat on those stairs. "I wish... I wish I could come there and... and pick you all up and bring you home." My hands shook as I ran one of them through my hair, feeling so horribly weak, so fucking pathetic to be telling this to a five-year-old child instead of her mother who could give a fuck less. I couldn't put Elizabeth in the middle, it wasn't fair. "Some... sometimes things just don't work out that way."

"Then fix it, Daddy."

I couldn't help but chuckle at that, no matter how much it broke my heart. She always held me in such high regard, thinking I could fix anything from a boo boo to a broken doll house, to... to this.

"I'm working on it, I promise."

And I meant it with everything in me. I was going to do something about this. No one... no judge, no set of high-priced lawyers, no bitter hell-bent on revenge woman, *nobody* was going to keep my children away from me. Come hell or high water, each and every fucking one of them were going to eat my fucking dust, kiss my ass, put in whatever analogy or pun... it was going to happen.

Because this?

"I'm... I'm not... I'm not gonna eat no more til Mommy takes me to see you."

Wasn't going to work.

"Elizabeth Christine, you *will* eat," I said, trying to use that Daddy tone even through my tears. "You will eat, you will do what your mom tells you to. You will be a good girl,"

"Not til she lets me see you."

"You'll see me Saturday," I said quickly, wondering how much else she knew.

"I'm coming home Saturday?"

"No… they… Mommy will bring you to see me." *In a strange place with a strange person watching, taking notes, critiquing every fucking thing I do or say.*

"At home."

"No… no. Not at home."

"Then I can go home with you? When Mommy brings me there?"

I took in a shaky breath, choking out the word, "No."

"What happened, Daddy?"

I tried to look out for you and she threw it back in my face.

I sighed, glancing over at the bottle of beer resting on top of the washer, where I had set it when I brought it down with me.

"You don't need to worry about that, okay?" I said, the anger over the vile, bitter attack that Talli had her lawyers release on me bubbling up once more. This was revenge, pure and simple. This wasn't looking out for our kids, this was getting even with me for something I didn't even fucking do. Hell, at this rate I should have. Why not? I was paying the price either fucking way.

"Mommy said I could talk," I heard Michael say in the background.

"NO," Elizabeth said, her voice firm and harsh.

"Baby Girl, let him talk, okay?"

"Fine," she said in a near huff. "Only 'cause you're his Daddy, too."

I had to smile at her reasoning, wiping away another fucking tear that had fallen down my cheek. "And Em's too," I reminded her.

"Yeah, but Em's out there with Mommy and Paul."

An icy grip took hold over me at the mention of this Paul person. Oh, I couldn't be around my kids, but he could? And who the fuck was he? Was this the reason she'd been so quick to find a place? Or had it not been quick, had it been something she'd had in the works while I'd been away?

"Here, boogerhole," Elizabeth said, and I heard a commotion before Michael's voice came over the line.

"Hi, Daddy! I played... I played with big stuff today and was helping with Em too."

"Hi, Little Man," I said with a smile, his excited voice warming my heart. He was so young; he wouldn't understand what was going on. But he shouldn't have to be put through any of it, damn it! He should be up in his room, messing up this house, putting his greasy fingerprints all over that kitchen island. "So..." I swallowed, holding back the new tears. "You had fun today?"

"Yeah, Em cried a lot, though. She don't like Paul."

Don't smile at that, Warner. It isn't something you should take pride or some kind of sick pleasure in.

"Paul was here, and Mommy wasn't."

What the fuck?

"So me an... and Lizbeth help-ded with Em."

I heard Elizabeth correct his speech but was so focused on the fact that she left another man there with my kids the same damn day that she decided I wasn't good enough.

"You... that was good, that you helped," I managed to say, my pulse hammering so fucking hard I was sure my heart would come flying out of my chest.

"Yeah, an... but he didn't bring his kids this time."

How fucking lovely. He has kids too. Something for them to have in common and sit around and talk about, the way she used to fucking talk with me.

"He's getting us some... some pizza."

"That's..." *Infuriating. Frustrating. Not his place.* "...good."

"He said we had to be nice to Mommy, but Lizbeth isn't."

"I am too!" I heard her say defiantly, but somehow felt that Michael was telling the truth.

"Both of you, be nice to your Mommy," I said softly, not wanting anything more to fall on their shoulders.

"Because of..."

"Because you should," I said quickly, not wanting to hear anything else about what this Paul character had to say, my blood boiling at just the thought of what could be.

Don't think the worst…

Who was I kidding? Of course, I was going to think the absolute worst. Isn't that what we had been doing all along?

"I wanna talk now," Elizabeth said in the background.

"I not done," Michael replied, before saying to me, "When I come back home, I think I left my football here but it's okay so we can play, right? Can you play with me?"

Little Man, I'd give anything to have you here, tossing that ball in the back yard, trying to keep you from throwing it in the fountain… but it always end ups there, doesn't it?

"Daddy?"

"I promise," I said, sniffling slightly, praying that Elizabeth wouldn't say anything to set him off. I just couldn't take it; I knew I'd be on my way over there, and God only knows what kind of problems that would stir up, and I'd been drinking which would only reiterate what a horrible influence I am for our children. "I promise as soon as you are here, we are going out back and just… play."

"Like fools," he added, and I couldn't help but laugh.

"Like fools," I repeated. "I…" I held back, damning the tears that just wouldn't fucking stop. "I promise."

"Okay, Lizbeth wants to talk now," Michael said. "You have to be good too, okay Daddy?"

"I will," I said, cursing the day that an almost three-year-old child had to become the man of the house.

"I miss you."

"I miss you too, Little Man." *And I'm going to fix this.*

"I'm back, Daddy." Elizabeth was now on the line, sounding a little more like her old self, as if hearing from me was enough to help her.

I knew exactly what that felt like.

Because hearing from her, from them… it renewed my resolve.

No one was going to take my kids away from me. Not if hell froze over, not over my dead body, not some judge, not a pack of lawyers, and definitely… *definitely* the only other person on this Earth that should know exactly what they meant to me.

"You heard me, right? You're going to be good for your Mommy."

No more ammunition, no chance that she'll say that I'm trying to influence them to give her a hard time.

"I will."

"I love you," I said with absolute conviction. "And I'll be there, at the center on Saturday to see you."

"I love you too, Daddy."

"Me too, Daddy!" I heard Michael say.

There was so, so very much I wanted to say to them, to try and convey exactly how I felt, promise them that everything was going to be okay. But there wasn't enough time, there never was.

Michael was saying something about pizza, which meant my little man was on his way out of that room, away from the closest that I could be with him, out to that dining room table where that Paul character was probably sitting, maybe even at the head of the table, in my place.

My fucking place.

"Dinner time, Daddy. I love you."

I could tell by the way her voice trailed off that she was setting the phone down, leaving me alone there, hanging on the line, my heart going a million miles a minute.

No... no, don't go, baby girl! I... I'm not done! I didn't get to tell you that I love you again, or ask you what you'd done today. I... I didn't get to read or... or tell you a story. I didn't get to tell you one more thing about you that reminds me of your mother, even though I wouldn't get to see your face, see how proud it would make you. I... I didn't get to blow kisses to you through the phone, or... or play the guess what I'm thinking of game. I didn't get to...

"Jase?"

You fucking bitch...

Damn you, Talli... why?

Why did you take away the only reason I had left to move, to function, to breathe?

"Jase, we need to..."

I hit the end button.

I... I hung up on her.

I'd never done that before, not... not intentionally, not since that first call all those years ago, that fateful wrong number that led us...

Here.

Taking a deep breath, I stood and shoved that phone in my pocket, returning to the task at hand, praying I could make it to another day.

CHAPTER 18

TALLI

I honestly can't pinpoint the exact date when I'd stopped turning to Jase, stopped reaching out to him. It had probably happened slowly, gradually, over a long period of time. I'm sure it hadn't started out maliciously; it was more than likely started just out of the blue, out of circumstances being just so, one random day when he'd been too busy or I'd been too tired, maybe even both. It had escalated, though, broadening the gap between us until we were virtual strangers who shared a last name that had somehow acquired three children.

Even through everything, though, there was always some form of safety net, some way that I felt he'd still be there for me, even through the whole Bree fiasco. I'd always believed back in the recesses of my mind that if I reached out to him, he'd respond, we'd find a way through the darkness, and even if he didn't want to be with me we'd still find a way to do the right thing. Together, we would make sure our children hurt as little as possible.

That one sweltering Monday in July changed everything.

When Jase hung up that phone, severing that one special tie between us, it ripped what was left of my heart in two. This was it. I knew it was; I'd known it for a long time. But this was just *different*. This was his way of telling me that he was done. No more trying, no more pretending.

It had gone too far.

I had pushed too hard.

After the kids were in bed, I moped around the rest of the evening, that stupid cell phone on me at all times. I debated with myself over and over whether or not I should call or maybe just send him a text message. Hell, I even contemplated turning on that damn computer and risk seeing any 'breaking story' about us to just send him an email.

But what would I say?

Seriously, was I going to apologize for his plan to take the kids from me backfiring? That would go over wonderfully. Should I try and strike a deal, tell him if he stayed away from Bree, I would drop this, go back to the original visitation plan? Hell, knowing Jase I'd probably just pushed him right into her arms. Go me.

That night I was just lonely. Incredibly lonely. I was in mourning for a love lost... no, not just a love lost, for also losing what was once my best friend, my closest confidante, someone who knew me so well he could tell by one glance, one syllable out of my mouth exactly what my mood was.

I missed him.

I missed...

I missed Not John.

And I found myself staring at that clock when it was showing 2:35 in the morning, knowing that technically it was three hours off since he called at 2:35 Ohio time, but wishing my phone was ringing.

Or...

Or that I had the nerve to call him.

And I almost did. I scrolled through, selecting his name, just staring at it willing myself to hit the call button.

And then the clock said 2:36.

And I lost my nerve.

Just like I had lost him.

––––––––––––––

Tuesday morning brought about a phone call from Dr. Stewart telling me that their office was being staked out and asking me to not come in that day.

Just fucking lovely.

"You goin' to work, Mommy?" Elizabeth asked sleepily as she

wandered out into the kitchen.

"No, Baby Girl," I said with a sigh. "Not today."

Today I'd be stuck, a prisoner in my own home, wondering if my darling soon to be ex-husband and his size zero slutbag were going to cost me my job. I'd already fielded a call from the apartment manager, who was so very proud of himself for calling the police to try and keep the paparazzi from sneaking into the building when random tenants came in. And I'm sure that everyone in the building was absolutely thrilled to be reminded not to let anyone they didn't personally know into the building.

With a sigh, I opened up my computer, hoping to avoid any sensational stories about Jase and/or me, with no such luck. This time, though, we were in a random piece about messy Hollywood breakups, musicians and actors alike in this crowd. Great. Now we weren't just a breakup, we were a messy breakup apparently with the makings of one of the nastiest divorces that Hollywood had seen in ages.

My cell phone began ringing, an unknown number popping up, and for just one moment I resisted answering it. Then it kind of dawned on me that there were many phone numbers that I'd left behind in that house, that perhaps it was someone I needed to speak with.

I should have gone with my first instinct.

"Listen... I don't need some bitter old hag dragging my name through the mud."

Breeann Hamilton was the last person on the face of this Earth that I wanted to speak with.

"Where the fuck did you get this number from?"

"Where do you *think* I got it from, the tooth fairy? You know what you saw, your eyes can't be that deceiving to you."

I swallowed down the bile that had crept up in my throat, trying to stay as calm and as rational as possible. "If your name is in the mud, through the mud, over the mud, covered in mud, it is of your own doing. Not mine."

"Why the hell are your lawyers bringing my name up?"

"Why the hell were you in bed with my husband?"

She bit back a laugh as I felt my heart racing a million miles a minute. I'd never... never demanded answers, never questioned her.

Why the hell was I doing it now?

"Your husband." I could just see her rolling her eyes as she was lighting that cigarette that I heard her take a long drag off of. "Sweetheart, you abandoned your husband. He was tired of the nagging, the bullshit excuses for you not sleeping with him, so he came to me. And believe me, I took very good care of him. If you were that concerned about your husband, you wouldn't have filed for divorce from him, now would you? So... you've lost your right to lay any claim on him. Now..."

"One, I'm not your fucking sweetheart so unless you want my foot crammed straight up your ass you will never refer to me in such a manner again."

Whoa. Where the hell was this coming from?

"Two, you and I both know that I didn't abandon my husband. I can only begin to imagine how you manipulated every single situation, and my guess is soon he'll see right through you, if he hasn't begun to already."

I recognize the voice. I mean, of course I do. It's mine. But... but...

"And last, but definitely not least, you are not the kind of person who needs to be in any way, shape, or form involved in my children's lives, so when it comes to you? Yeah, that shark I hired? She has carte blanch. And believe me when I tell you, she knows exactly what can and cannot be said, and will be damn sure that every little tidbit out in the public eye will be nothing but the truth and therefore cannot come back on me. So calling my number? Telling me to stop my lawyer from exposing you for the run of the mill scum on the bottom of my shoe gutter whore that you are? That was, if not your worst, then at least your latest mistake. Any questions?"

Silence.

"That's what I..."

"One question, Talli. How did it feel to see *your husband* on top of me?"

"The first thing that went through my mind was that I didn't want whatever STD you may be carrying," I replied, the venom flowing freely through my veins.

"You little..."

"You do *not* call me, you do not attempt to contact me in any way, and if you have a problem with your dirty laundry airing, take it up with my lawyer."

"Oh, you want dirty laundry?"

"Goodbye, Bree."

I hit that end button, seething, blood boiling, wishing I could reach through that line and choke the living shit out of her.

But you know what?

No. There was someone else that needed the living shit choked out of him.

Who the fuck did he think he was, giving my phone number out to his whore? Seriously? Of all the things he'd done to me, this was one of the lowest. He knew... he knew how I felt about her, and the fact that I'd caught them in bed together wasn't bad enough... no, now he goes and gives my phone number out to that bottom feeder?

"Mr. Jason Michael Warner, you sir... are about to get... a piece of my mind."

I hit the call button on my cell phone, recalling at the last moment how he normally wouldn't get up this early. Oh, no...he was probably still in bed, even if that bitch was there.

"Hello?"

Yeah, I just woke his ass up.

"Why the hell did you give that bitch my number?"

"Wha... Talli?"

"You have no business giving my phone number out to your whore."

"I... fuck you, Talli."

Excuse me?

"You have no right..."

"Rights?" Oh, he was awake now. "You want to call my number, talking to me about rights? Fuck you!"

"Where do you get off..."

"You... you filed for divorce, you wanted this. I remember very distinctly when I wanted to talk with you, you telling me to take it up with my lawyer. It's time you take your own advice. If your number shows up on my screen, it damn well better be the kids."

"If you think that it's okay for you to..."

The line was dead.

My hands were shaking slightly as I set the phone down. Oh, he had a lot of fucking nerve! First, he gives out my phone number to Bree of all fucking people, and then he has the balls to go off on me? And tell me that I couldn't call him, that I had to contact his lawyer to tell him to quit giving out my fucking phone number?

I don't think so.

I picked that phone back up, refusing to lie down and take his shit any fucking more. Scrolling down, I reached his cell number again, hitting the call button, ready to let it fucking fly.

Oh, great.

Straight to voicemail.

If he wanted to play that game, I could play it.

I scrolled back through the contacts, cringing as I realized I still had it listed as 'home'.

That was not my home.

I hit the call button, still seething with anger over his outburst, wondering where the hell he got off not only hanging up yet again but also for giving out my phone number. Perhaps I was a glutton for punishment, perhaps I'd just... had it.

I'd just... had it.

I wasn't his fucking doormat. I wasn't someone he could speak to any damn way he chose, the way he had been for quite some time. I wasn't someone he could treat any way he chose.

I was his wife.

I was the mother of his children.

And the days of him treating me with complete disrespect, complete disregard, were at an end.

And...

The number I had reached has been changed to an unpublished number.

Perfect.

"Are you okay, Mommy?" Michael asked as he walked into the living room.

I smiled as sweetly as I could. "I'm..."

I glared at the phone that now sat on my countertop.

"Perfect."

JASE

Talk about a rude awakening. It was bad enough that I'd barely gotten any sleep as I'd ended up curled up on that stupid little sofa in my office. But then to wake up to Talli bitching me out over... hell, I don't even know what... was the icing on the fucking cake.

It was going to be a bad day.

I groaned as I looked at the time on my cell phone, shutting it off so I could attempt to get some more rest. Did it work? Hell no.

At least the basement was done. I'd stayed up until four a.m. purging that room of everything I could. A lot of it ended up in the trash, but there were two large boxes that I had marked of things that belonged to Talia.

That book was not in there.

She'd taken it from me years ago, and occasionally I'd see her curled up in her papasan chair with it. But it was mine. It was one of a long list of things that she'd taken from me that I was demanding back.

I just wish I knew what she'd done with my heart when she didn't want it anymore. I could use it right about now.

"Good morning."

Linda nearly scared the hell out of me as I rounded the corner. I'd forgotten she would be there again today. I half waved at her, shuffling over to the coffee pot to get it started.

"I can get that for you."

I recognized the tone of her voice. I didn't need her pity, and I certainly didn't want it. I reminded myself, though, that it was Talia I was pissed off at, not anyone else.

"Thanks, but..."

"Cinnamon," she said softly. I looked over my shoulder at her, confused. "That's what Talli puts in it, that's what the boys liked so well."

I nodded, faltering for a moment. Linda gently reached over taking the carafe from my hand before gesturing to me that she'd finish.

Why the hell would something so simple as that affect me in that way? It was just coffee. Sorry, cinnamon in the coffee. Why would it matter that Talia would do something so… special?

Unique?

Damn it, I… I can't break. Not now. Not anymore.

"Hey, Linda… that furniture store you were talking about, do they haul away the old stuff?" I asked, glancing over at her.

"They did when J… um, yeah."

"What…what's this?" I asked, my tone as light as I could get it.

"Nothing," she replied, blushing slightly.

"Noooo, you made the 'J' sound," I teased.

"Don't you have to get dressed or something before Chris and Jackie come over?"

"Jackie… what's up with you and Jackie? Oh, come on, Linda, how many years have you two been going back and forth on this?"

"You… oh, just… mind your own business."

I finally had something to smile about as I bounded up the stairs, almost thankful that Talia had called and woken my ass up. I'd completely forgotten that Chris and Jackie were coming over, to discuss business of all things. Or the lack of business, as I was pissing people off left and right by trying to lay low. Man, today really did have the potential of getting ugly. Good for me that I had something to give Jackie shit about.

Once out of the shower, completely cleaned up and at least slightly presentable, I walked down the hallway to my office where the catalog for that furniture store set on my desk. I thumbed through the pages, making notes on what might work, what I would like, what would purge this house of things that didn't belong there anymore.

It had to be done.

"Are you up for saving the world?"

I glanced up, grinning at Jackie as he walked in. "Well, hello Alfred, so nice to see you. Come. Sit."

"I don't pry into your personal business, you know."

"That's such a blatant lie. Soooo… you and Linda what?" I asked.

"A gentleman never answers that question," he said with the straightest face before breaking down and chuckling softly. "We gave up one mortgage is all."

"Living in sin, then?"

"Is there any..." he stopped, his face growing somber. "No... scratch that. There are other ways."

"Jackie, don't." My voice was soft as I looked back down at the furniture catalog, placing it over to the side. "Is Chris here yet?"

"Um... yeah. Yeah he is."

"Well?" I held my hands up, silently asking where the hell he was, and the look Jackie shot me, telling me I didn't want to know, made me decide I better go find him.

"Man, just... give it a..."

"You can't tell me that I can't go up there and see him."

Bree was at my house.

See? A bad day.

"If you have to babysit us, then..."

"What the hell, Bree?" I asked tiredly, going down the stairs. It wasn't even noon and she looked like she was going to a club. "Why are you here?"

"You." She pointed at me accusingly. "You tell that hag you're divorcing to stop talking shit about me."

"Hag?" I asked, one eyebrow raised, my eyes raking over Bree, my mind wondering what the hell I'd been thinking.

"Did I stutter?" Bree snapped, and I heard Jackie stifle a laugh behind me.

"Um... no, but... you're going to have to call Sherise..." My voice drifted off as I recalled the brief bitchout session Talia had given me earlier. "You called her?"

"Oh, she already reported back to you? Poor thing can't handle hearing from me?"

"Oh, fuck."

That came from Chris, who rolled his eyes and put a hand up to his forehead before turning away.

"You called Talia this morning," I repeated, letting it sink in.

"God, what is *wrong* with you? I just told you I did, didn't I? *You* need to tell her..."

"That was really stupid."

Was I honestly starting to laugh?

"Excuse me?"

"You obviously didn't get the chance to tell her what you wanted to say."

Jase, you are just going to make this worse… don't crack a smile. Don't… laugh at Bree's expression… this is not a comical situation, this chick just made things that much worse for you.

"Can anyone get a word in edgewise with that bitch?" Bree asked, one hand on her hip.

Chris, whose face was now buried, was trying to stop his shoulders from shaking. That fucker was laughing, too. That was not going to help me in the least.

"I can," I said without thinking, my mood sobering almost immediately.

"Exactly, which is why I'm here, and…"

"Don't touch me," I said, pulling my arm back.

"Apparently you can act just like her, too," Bree retorted, her dig hitting right where she knew it would.

"Ms. Hamilton," Chris spoke up, all business like once more, "if you have a problem with Talia's lawyers and what they do, you need to speak with them. Here is a business card with Sherise Adler's office number on it." He held it out to her, refraining from rolling his eyes when she snatched it out of his hand. "But I might suggest having your legal team handle this."

"Why can't…"

"Jase's legal team does not represent you," Chris cut her off.

Yeah, they're not representing me very well either.

"Hey…" Jackie, motioned at me to follow him up the stairs, which I was more than happy to do.

"I'm not done talking with you," Bree called after me, but I left it to Chris to handle. Let him earn his damn paycheck, right? We headed back to the office, where I sat at the desk, my hand gently touching the picture of the kids on my way to the chair.

"This really is ugly, isn't it?" Jackie asked, and I nodded. "I didn't get a chance to tell you that I'm sorry. It isn't right, Jase."

"I kinda asked for it though, didn't I?"

That was a loaded question. I knew it was. I mean, I asked for it, for trouble, when I stepped over the line with Bree. And I asked for even more trouble when I let my lawyers go after Talia, even though they hadn't taken the route I'd asked them to.

"That doesn't make it right," Jackie said softly. "I just… you can get as pissed off at me as you want over this, but it doesn't sound like something Talli wanted either."

I opened my mouth to protest but found I couldn't. I mean… the more I went over and over the whole scenario in my mind, I didn't remember her team ever once stating that I should be kept away from the children. Of course, with the job that Sherise did on me they really didn't have to, did they?

Stop it, Jase. Stop reading into this. She filed for divorce, she wanted this over with. Stop trying to find the silver lining of that cloud, there is none.

"You know," Jackie said with a laugh, "I would have loved to listen in on that conversation. I… I wonder if she did that whole countdown thing."

"Where she numbers the things that piss her off?" I asked softly, one short laugh escaping. "Yeah, that…" I frowned, picking up the furniture catalog to take my mind off of it.

"What are you doing?" Jackie asked, gesturing towards the magazine.

"Purging," I answered with a shrug. There were so many things that just needed to go, to be replaced.

One room…

One room needs gutted altogether.

"Jase…"

"Don't. Please."

"Are you sure?" he asked, and I looked him in the eye.

"Yeah."

He didn't understand. I'm sure he couldn't. No one could unless that saw what I did, through my eyes.

I just couldn't take it anymore.

"Okay, first off," Chris started as he walked into the office, shutting the door behind him, "she's annoying as hell and I apologize profusely for ever coming up with the idea that you should collaborate with her."

"Apology accepted," I said softly, knowing Chris wasn't to blame for my actions.

"Secondly, please reiterate if you hear from her again that she isn't to come over here, okay? She's not listening to me."

"Is this where Talli got her numbering shit from?" Jackie asked, and one corner of my mouth lifted up in a smirk.

"And... that's not funny... last, we have got to talk about you taking this damn sabbatical from your work."

He was sitting directly in front of me, looking almost like death warmed over, or at least death fucking with his head a bit. I sighed and shrugged.

"I... I can't right now, Chris."

"Jase, you have contractual agreements..."

"That get changed all the time. Chris, please." I didn't want to sound so vulnerable, I didn't want to sit there and beg for some private time away from the press, away from prying eyes, away from questions about my kids, about Talli.

He nodded once, looking down at the papers in his hand. "I'll see what I can do. There will be a lot that will have to be rescheduled, which will put more on your plate later. I'll give the message to the powers that be, hoping they are as understanding. And just for future reference, I'll probably ask you about it every time hereafter, got it?" After I nodded, he asked, "Have you been writing?"

I let out a short half-laugh. He was kidding, right? One would think that I would have a plethora of material from this, have several heart-wrenching albums for the mass public to either eat up with a spoon or crucify me for causing so much hurt to begin with.

"Jase..."

"Could you?" I asked quickly, looking up at him, and he shook his head.

"I have let Ms. Hamilton's management know that your professional relationship with her is on permanent hiatus. Before yesterday they'd disagreed, but since the hearing yesterday and the leaking of certain information, they're now also wanting the distance. Hopefully they'll convince their client also. All that remains is the okay from the record company since they were so gung-ho about it in the first place."

"Whatever sells records," Jackie muttered so softly I barely heard him.

No more working with Bree. No more being hassled over refusing to work with Bree. Somehow this wasn't enough to brighten my mood.

My eyes clouded over as I glanced up, that picture of the kids catching my eye.

I missed them terribly.

They... they should be pounding on the door, or running in unannounced trying to get me to settle some argument, and I...

Oh, God.

Talli, I swear I'd never yell at you to control them, to keep them out of here again. I'm so sorry...

So sorry.

"I guess that's all I've got," Chris said. "What about you, Jackie?"

"Um, I have a few messages from people who don't have your new home phone number," Jackie said, handing me some small slips of paper.

"Sorry," I muttered, cringing when I saw that one of them was my mother. Why didn't she call my cell? Oh, shit, this was from this morning. My cell was still off. I reached into my pocket, pulling it out and hitting the 'on' button.

"Yeah, try not to do that anymore," he said, pointing at me. "Oh, and I have a message sent basically through the media to you."

"Oh, fuck," I groaned, holding my head in my hands. "Go ahead, lay it on me."

"Rebecca St. John has announced that she's taking over your custody case."

My head snapped up, my eyes wide. Holy shit, Kate did it.

"What did you say?" I asked, my heart pounding in my chest.

"Rebecca St. John has..."

"Wow," I cut him off, sitting back in my chair.

I smiled then... a genuine smile as my gaze once more fell on that picture of my children.

This wasn't such a bad day after all.

CHAPTER 19

TALLI

It was Thursday morning when I made my way back into my office, ignoring every single phone call from Dr. Stewart and every one of her associates. I was not going to be kept away from my job by some blood hungry sharks, they would not keep food out of my kids' mouths or take the roof off from over their heads. I piled everyone into the vehicle, fighting my way through traffic, and dropped them off at the daycare that I'd already paid for before pushing my way through the front doors of the practice, strutting my way through that waiting room and down that hallway towards my office.

"Talli, wait," one of the receptionists called after me, but I waved her off. Their waiting room was full, and I knew that part of that reason was they had continued to reschedule my patients around everyone else's schedule.

That was far from necessary.

"Talia." Dr. Stewart sounded so surprised to see me. "I... um..."

"If you're going to fire me, then do it now, but by God you better have just cause," I said right to her in the middle of that hallway. She silently nodded towards my office door, which I went into, dropping my purse in the chair nearest my desk. I picked up my stack of messages and began thumbing through them, placing them in order of importance when she walked in behind me and shut the door.

"I know you're going through a rough time right now."

"Do you?" I asked, looking up at her. "I don't have any more leave; I've used every bit of it up with the move and every single illness that Emily has had. I will not let a bunch of assholes looking for a story keep me prisoner in my own home, and I won't be bullied into leaving a job that not only do I need to support my children, but I deserve. I've worked my ass off for you, and you *know* it."

"Oh, Talli," was all she would say, tears brimming in her eyes. I stood momentarily stunned as she walked over to me, throwing her arms around my shoulders and pulling me into a hug. "It's so good to see you."

"See me?" I asked, confused. "I was just here on Friday. It's your own damn fault I haven't been in since Tuesday."

She laughed, pushing back, placing a hand on the side of my face. "Oh, girl. You just don't get it. Still."

"I think you've lost your damn *mind* is what I'm thinking," I muttered, stepping back from her. I was still looking at her like she'd been transplanted straight from Mars when I asked, "What's on the agenda for today?"

"Well, we're overbooked, as you can see."

"Mmm hmm, I see that," I said, placing my messages to the side.

"We've rescheduled your patients for next week, but it would be such a tremendous help if you could handle pap smears today."

"Oh, goodie," I deadpanned. "Yeah, not a problem. When's my first?"

"They're getting her prepped in exam room two."

"Thanks. I've got this."

"That's so good to know," she replied. "See you at lunch break?"

"Of course."

"Good. And Talli?"

I looked up at her, waiting for her to finish her thought.

"Welcome back."

"Wow." I jumped slightly as Dr. Paul Coffman appeared beside me in the lounge off to the side of the cafeteria. I paused from taking a bite of my apple to peer over at him.

"What?" I asked.

"You look absolutely stunning today," he said, sitting down in the chair next to me.

I looked down at my black tailored pants and teal blue shirt, then back over at him. "Um... thank you?" I smiled as he laughed. "No, seriously, thank you. You've helped me so much this week."

"Your kids are adorable, even if your youngest hates my guts."

"If it's any consolation, she hates *everyone's* guts," I replied, setting the apple down and opting for my salad instead. "And you're just gonna have to deal with me eating. I'm fucking starving."

"Really? Do I know him?"

"Oh, ha ha." I rolled my eyes and gave him a slight kick in his shin. "You only think you're funny."

"I know I am. Oh, by the way... speaking of funny..."

"This should be good."

He held out two tickets that I squinted at, then my eyes widened in surprise.

"*Spamalot*? How did you manage that?" I asked.

"I know people," he answered with an easygoing shrug. "Or, my ex-wife knows people who like me better than they do her, I should say. It's for next Friday evening, and I think I know one feisty little redhead who's due for some fun."

"Oh, yeah? Who's that?" I asked, and he raised his eyebrow at me. "Oh... me? Really?" My voice was softer as I looked at the tickets, then back at him.

"As friends, Talli."

I could use a friend.

"I'll behave myself, I promise."

"Well, yeah, 'cause you'd be ball-less if you didn't," I said without thinking, then put my hand over my mouth, my eyes wide. "Oh, I'm so sorry."

He didn't even hear my apology, he was laughing so hard. Good one, Talli.

"My, you are a spunky one," he finally said as he calmed down, and

I felt my face fall.

Spunky.

That was one of my nicknames... one that Jackie had given me.

"I'm sorry, are you okay?" he asked suddenly.

"Oh, yeah... yeah, I'm fine," I replied, covering. "I just..." I pulled out my phone that was beginning to buzz in my pocket. "Oh, I'm sorry, I really need to take this."

"Go ahead," he said with a grin as I stood and walked over to the corner of the lounge, answering the phone call as quietly as I could.

I really hate my personal business being out in the open.

"Hey... what's up?" I asked in the most cheerful voice I could conjure up.

"Not too much," Tish responded through the line. "I've just been worried. I haven't heard from you since I came back to Ohio, and there's plenty of crap being splashed all in the tabloids about you."

"Yeah, you know how it goes," I said nonchalantly. "They're looking for a story, what can I say?"

"Room full of people?"

"Damn, you're good."

"So I've been told. Hey... are you okay, though? I mean, physically?"

"Yeah, yeah. I had a complete checkup and everything," I replied, a bit confused until I remembered she'd actually been at Emily's party. "I really am fine."

"You just haven't been yourself lately... I know, I know, I wouldn't be either," she cut off what was sure to be my reply. "Look, I'm just going to ask you this straight up. Talli, I love you; you know I do. I don't think the answer is yes, but I'm not living there so I don't know. Are you using again?"

I felt my face flame red at her question, my temper flaring. *Keep it in check, Talli. Room full of people, which she probably counted on. Count. One, two, three...*

"Talli..."

"No," I said quietly. "And you of all people should know better than to ask me, since you were there before."

"I had to ask, Talli. I don't know you anymore."

Oh, wow.

I thought of that statement the rest of the day. I thought about it as Paul agreed to let me ponder whether or not to go to see a play with him. I thought about it as I talked with Jaden about her baby shower, relenting when she insisted that she was buying tickets for me and the kids to come out. I thought about it as I closed up at the office, finishing my paperwork before picking up the kids and driving home.

Tish, one of my oldest and dearest friends, didn't know me anymore.

But I'd heard that so many times, from so many people over the past year.

I'd heard it from Mave that day at the courthouse when they took visitation away from Jase.

I'd heard it from Sondra, who'd told me to stand up for myself when I caught Jase with Bree.

I'd heard it from Jackie when I just couldn't pull myself out of bed one day.

I'd heard it from Linda, from Chris, from Pete.

I'd heard it from Jaden too many times to count.

And Jase.

I'd heard it from him, too. And I'd told him he was imagining things, he was making shit up in his head, he was too wrapped up in himself.

Seriously? I had said that to him?

And the truth is, as I sat there that night, washing the makeup off my face after putting the kids to bed, I was staring in the mirror at someone who'd become a virtual stranger. I had shut myself off from everyone... *everyone*, just like I'd sworn, and promised I would never do again. One by one I had isolated myself from the people I loved the most, from the people who loved me.

And I had no idea how to fix it.

I had no idea how to fix me.

And the saddest part? The first person I wanted to call was Jase.

I just want to tell him I'm sorry.

I'm so very sorry.

The phone ringing jarred me from my pity party, my heart jumping into my throat over my wishful thinking, but it was just Paul.

No, not *just* Paul. Paul who had befriended me, stuck by me and given me unwavering support Paul.

"Is everything okay?" he asked.

"Yes and no," I replied with a shrug that he couldn't see.

"Is it anything you want to talk about?"

"I... I do need to talk about it. Just... not with you, please don't take that the wrong way."

"No... no, I won't. Are you saying what I think you're saying, Talli? You're ready?"

I nodded through my tears.

"I can't hear you."

"Yes," I finally said before burying my face in my hands, letting go of a sob.

"That's wonderful news. I'm..."

"If you say you're proud of me I'm so kicking you in some place that will hurt a lot more than your shin," I cut him off, and he laughed.

"Fine, I won't say it. When are you going to go?"

"As soon as... as soon as I can," I said, wiping my eyes hastily.

"I'm not going to let you back out of this, you know."

"Oh, Paul. You silly boy. When I make my mind up, that's all she wrote."

"I've heard that about you. Haven't seen it for a while, but I've heard it."

"Fuck you," I muttered with a half laugh.

"I thought... no, never mind, bad joke coming on."

"You seem full of them," I deadpanned, sniffling slightly. "Paul, thanks... for not... for not giving up on me."

"Talli, I don't think anyone has given up on you."

I choked back a sob as my mind drifted to the boy with the beautiful eyes... the one who'd stolen my heart, only to hand it back to me in tiny shards.

I'm sorry, Paul.

This time, you're wrong.

JASE

Ms. Schwartz, the court appointed liaison assigned to our case, has absolutely no sense of humor. Nada. None. When she showed up Wednesday afternoon unannounced, she glared at the cold beer in my hand. She was even less receptive to the fact that it was my fourth of the day. I joked that it didn't matter since they were keeping my kids from me anyway.

Bad first impression, I know.

She seemed a bit alarmed at the number of trash bags, which I found disturbing. Who the hell cares how much I was throwing out? Okay, so there were a lot of *broken* things in the rubble, scattered pieces of pictures I'd destroyed strewn about, but they'd all make the trash eventually, right? She also counted the number of empties in my recycle bin, and didn't think it was the least bit amusing that a lot of those came from various people during my daughter's first birthday party. Count those against me, too, sweetheart. By now I'm used to it.

My cousin Tom was in town, helping me shovel out the old and bring in the new, which was great for me in most ways. Not so much, though, when he joked about the 'throw down' that Talli and I'd had in the basement. Oh, great, now she's going to think that we were like that, that *I* am like that.

Neither was the truth.

I did get brownie points for donating furniture, though. I mean, why the hell not? I certainly didn't need it, there were too many soured memories associated with every piece I was hauling away.

All in all, though… a big negative. Huge.

"She was not digging on your sense of humor, dude," Tom was saying later as we sat out on the back porch in the furniture that would be leaving the next morning.

"No, she was not," I half-slurred. "She needs to grow a sense of humor of her own."

"Amen, brotha," he agreed, holding up his bottle, which I semi-gently hit with mine, sending a bit of beer splashing onto the table between us. "Dude, alcohol abuse."

"I'm not," I paused as a slight hiccup left me, "I'm not licking it up. It can stay there."

"That sounded…" His voice trailed off as he threw his head back in laughter.

"Don't go there, man. Don't do it."

"You're so hard up you'd go for a *table* know."

"I don't 'cause you won't tell," he commented, suddenly serious, glancing over at me as he took another drink of his beer. "What happened?"

I felt my mood sour as I glared at my bottle, like it was going to change anything. "I don't know."

"Oh bullshit, dude," Tom said with a laugh. "One minute you're all having me bust my ass to get this glorious surprise for her, the next she's moving out and filing for divorce. You still..."

"Yes," I cut him off, hating how my mood had shifted, hating how she could still get to me when she wasn't even here. "She's... she'll love it," I finished quietly, without adding how I wished she still loved me.

"One word that I have to say, and I don't care how pissed off at me you get."

"What's that?" I asked without looking over at him.

"Bree."

I felt my jaw clench at the sound of her name.

"And I just got my answer."

"What do you mean?" I asked, finally looking over at him.

"You didn't split up for you to be with Bree."

"Fuck no," I said quickly with a shake of my head. "I didn't want her to go."

"I hear ya."

For the first time since he'd gotten there, I remembered that Tom had been through a divorce as well. Man, did I ever feel like an ass.

"I'm sorry, Tom... I didn't ... fuck, I don't want to bring up bad memories or any shit like that for you."

"No, I'm okay," he said with a shrug. "And I mean that, you know? She's happier, I'm happy for her, we've moved on. That was how many years ago?"

"Five," I said. "Right about five. Talli was pregnant."

"With Elizabeth, fuck that's right dude! Damn, you have a good memory."

"Most of the time. You know, when I'm not killing my brain cells." I grinned, trying to suppress the memories.

Fuck.

I'd thrown away the best thing that ever fucking happened to me, and here I was sitting getting shitfaced in my own back yard, drinking to try and forget her.

And I was never going to.

"Man… just… *talk*. Just do it. It's not going to go anywhere; it's not going to leave my lips once I leave this house, you know?"

"I don't know what I did wrong." I heard the words coming from my mouth, I just didn't recollect saying them. "I mean… before Bree. Before all that shit, because that wasn't the beginning."

"Wow." He was quiet for a moment. "No offense, but I didn't know anything was up until all this shit hit the tabloids."

"No one did, except us."

"Well, you both deserve Oscars then, because I never would have dreamed you two had fallen out of love."

"I haven't."

I said it with such conviction that it almost scared me.

"But you think she has?"

"Yeah," I replied, taking a long drink of my beer. "Can we change the subject?"

"Sort of," he said, and I raised an eyebrow at him. "This lawyer chick, the one that announced she's taking over your case, the one that Kate helped get for you."

"Rebecca will be here tomorrow," I replied with a grin.

"So, why is Kate doing this for you?"

I shrugged, a soft smile as I said, "She's my best friend, my oldest friend. Not that she's old, but…"

"Yeah, I know what you mean."

"But this lawyer, man… I googled her and shit, right? She… she's won against Sherise fucking Adler, and she's all about fathers' rights and shit. And she fights fair. Totally, one hundred percent… fair."

"It's kinda weird, though," he commented, leaning back and looking up at the night sky. "Talli has the ball crusher, and you have someone who's known for *not* playing dirty."

"I don't want to play dirty," I said sullenly. "It doesn't pay to."

"Yeah, it bit you in your ass there, didn't it? Hey, I call 'em like I see 'em."

"Thanks, asshole."

"You'll get your kids back, though," he added. "I don't think Talli would want you to not be a part of their lives."

"Are you saying…"

"I said Talli, not her lawyer, whatever the fuck her name is."

"Sherise," I said with a roll of my eyes.

"I think…" He paused as he finished his beer. "I think the first chance she gets, she's gonna let you see them. She's gonna make it happen, that's what I think."

"You're talking gibberish."

"I'm gonna get another one. Want another?" he asked as he stood.

"Hmm? Oh.. .um, nah, I'm good. Thanks." I half-smiled at him as he started to go inside for another beer.

"Jase?"

"Yeah?"

"You're right about one thing. She's going to love her surprise."

I smiled wistfully as I stared out at the fountain, hoping he was right.

———————

I groaned as I glared at my cellphone that was buzzing, signaling a text message from a well-known number.

On our way. Have beer ready. Kate

What the…

Holy fuck, what time is it?

I groaned again as the clock came up. Ten thirty. Ten fucking thirty in the morning. Damn, it was a good thing Kate knew me so well, but this Rebecca person didn't. And beer? With my new lawyer? I sat up, rubbing my neck. That stupid sofa in that damn office just wasn't going to do anymore. Wait, hadn't I said that the night before? And… the night before that?

I just…

Ugh.

I stink.

I grabbed a quick shower, throwing on a t-shirt and jeans as my doorbell sounded. Fuck it, if it was a beer meeting, it was a t-shirt and jeans day.

"How are you holding up?" Chris asked as he came in wheeling the large case that contained the divorce and custody files behind him. I shrugged in response. "If nothing else…"

"I see my kids in two days, yes I know."

"I admit, we underestimated Sherise Adler," he continued, following me into the office.

"You think?"

"No, I … know, what's going on in here?"

All of my files were in boxes along the far wall, my desk the only thing that still had objects on it. "I'm getting new furniture," I responded.

"The front room looks nice," he commented.

"Thank you. Front room? Is that another name for it now?"

"How many does that make?" he asked as he sat down, setting the rolling case beside him. "Great room, common room, front room…"

"Entry way."

I turned towards the familiar voice, smiling at the sight of Kaitlyn Evans filling my doorway, a sweet looking girl with soft brown hair behind her. This must be Rebecca St. John, her hair back in a ponytail and an AC/DC shirt and faded blue jeans on. She smiled as she walked in, holding her hand out.

"Hello, Jase. I'm Rebecca St. John."

I stood, shaking her hand. *Wow. Very firm. I'm impressed.* "Thank you for taking this case…"

"Rebecca. Just Rebecca."

"Thank you, Rebecca. And *you…*" I pulled Kate in for a warm hug, giving her a soft kiss on the cheek before I pulled back. "Oh, Rebecca, this is…"

"Chris Webber," he said, shaking her hand.

"Ah, we've spoken on the phone. Don't let this fool you," she said, gesturing towards her clothing. "Believe me, I'm all business and can put the darling Ms. Adler to shame. And who is this?" she asked, her eyebrow raising as Tom entered the room.

"Tom Warner."

"My cousin," I said, since Kate was too busy giving him a hug.

"Cousin who comes bearing refreshments. I like." She took the freshly opened beer from his hand, drinking about half of it as she crossed the office towards the case. "Files?"

"Um... yeah," Chris said as I shrugged towards Tom who left the room with Kate.

"Good. First beer." She raised her bottle as she turned to me. "Then we get started."

"Got a plan?" I asked, scratching the back of my head uncomfortably.

"Of course." She sat and smiled warmly. "The plan is simple. You do as I say, you have your kids back. Any questions?"

"Uh... no. No, I have none. Do you?" I asked as I looked at Chris, who shook his head. "Okay, then," I said with a grin. "It's a plan."

"Have a seat," she said, patting the chair beside her.

And as I lowered myself into that chair, I could feel it.

The hope was back. It was alive.

"Rebecca?" I said suddenly as another thought popped into my head.

"Fear not," she replied, seemingly reading my mind. "I won't make a move without getting your approval first."

I couldn't help but smile, feeling my luck was finally beginning to change

CHAPTER 20

TALLI

"One of my best friends thinks, or *thought*, I was doing drugs," I said softly as I picked at my salad. The kids had eaten already and were playing before bath time, and I was on the phone spilling my heart out.

To Paul.

"Jaden?" he asked.

"No," I replied, giving up on food and settling in the papasan chair with my Diet Pepsi. "No, it's Tish. I've known her for close to forever, but she... she said she didn't know me anymore."

"So that's what did it?"

"Pretty much, yeah." I turned off the TV using my remote, not in the mood to listen to any celebrity gossip. "My appointment is on Tuesday. Providing I don't chicken out, that is," I added with a laugh.

"I won't let you."

"Whatever. Oh, it also depends on if Jase's new lawyer gets us back in the courthouse."

"Are you nervous about that?" he asked, and I sighed.

"Not nervous about the lawyer, no. Sherise said she's familiar with her anyhow. I'm... I'm nervous about seeing Jase tomorrow."

"Ah, the first supervised visitation. What time do you have to be there?"

"At one, which is going to be just... great," I said, my voice dripping with sarcasm. "It's during nap time, and Emily is going to have an absolute meltdown. I can feel it."

"You can't reschedule?"

"Oh god, no," I said quickly. "No, I... last time I called him, he said..." I sighed again before I continued. "He said he didn't want me to call him anymore, that if my number showed up it better be one of the kids."

Wow, did I ever sound like I was pouting. Then again, it hurt like hell.

"You have to see where he's coming from, though," Paul began. "I know how hurt I was to be absolutely blindsided, losing my kids with no warning."

"I know, I know, and I'm trying to take all of this into consideration."

And I was, I really was. It's just... I couldn't explain this *urge* in me, this sudden need to reach out to him, equally to comfort him and just...

Talk.

I just wanted to talk with him.

I understand completely that he doesn't want to speak with me, and I can't blame him for being hurt. I've pushed and pushed, never given and inch, all of the times he tried to talk with me. But damn it, he... he started this, so holding it against me was completely unfair. I just wanted...

Hell, I don't know what I wanted.

Maybe I just needed to tell him I was sorry it had come to this.

I couldn't help being nervous about seeing him. And the circumstances were going to be less than desirable. I couldn't. turn to Jaden, I just couldn't burden her with it, not in her condition. And... Tish was right, we didn't know each other anymore. I'd pushed all of my friends away, and it left me so isolated, so alone.

It was wonderful that I had Paul to talk with.

But somehow it made the ache more prominent.

Paul wasn't Jase. He would *never* be Jase.

Day by day, moment by moment, I was creeping closer to being myself again. The downside to it? The more I felt, the more I hurt. It was like I was grieving all over again, or maybe even grieving for the first time. It didn't mean I could go back—I couldn't live that way...

broken trust, hateful words, seeing Bree at every turn.

But it's... it's like I just... gave up. I should have fought for him, before it escalated. And I mean really fought for him, not just agreed with him when he bold faced lied to me. And Bree, I should have confronted her. I should have refused to let her in my home. I should have told her to her face I could see right through her.

And there it was. Along with the hurt, my anger was up threefold. I could just... strangle him. Chop his fucking balls off. Kick his ass up one side and back down the other.

Then I want to cry.

On his shoulder.

If only he would let me.

Of *course*, Em would fall asleep on the way. That child is the epitome of evil when she's woken up. Wow, was Jase ever going to have fun with this.

Yep. There it is. The ear-piercing, blood curdling scream that had everyone in the parking lot looking in our direction. Thank you, Princess, we are already damn close to being late.

"Why are we here, Mommy?" Elizabeth asked.

"This is," I attempted to say over Emily's howling, "where you're going to see Daddy."

"Why here?"

"Because..." I sighed, shifting Emily to my hip, grabbing her with my other arm as she tried throwing herself backwards. "Because that's just the way it is, Elizabeth."

"That don't make sense," she mumbled as she shuffled along beside me.

"Well, I... where's your brother?" I asked, looked around. Michael was standing back by the vehicle, pouting. "Damn it." I turned back towards him and gestured for him to hurry up.

Of course, he shook his head 'no'.

Fuck. Me.

"Michael James, get up here *now*."

Of course, that would make Emily scream louder. And, of course, Michael began to cry as well. I took a deep breath and walked back towards the car, taking Michael's hand and trying to make him walk with us, but he didn't want to budge.

Oh...

Oh fuck...

My heart began racing, dropping me to my knees, leaving me gasping for breath.

No... not now, please not now... Deep breaths, Talli... come on...

"Do you need some help?" I heard a stranger ask, and I almost shook my head no but thought better of it.

"Yeah, I just... I must have pulled something," I lied, trying to smile. She looked friendly enough anyhow, and I wondered if she was here at this center for the same reason I was.

"Here, let me..."

"She won't go with you," I said quickly as Em clung to me, her screams muffled by her face being buried in my shoulder. "But... Michael?"

His lower lip was trembling, but he accepted this stranger's hand after seeing me nod. I slowly stood, praying that I wouldn't pass out here, now. That would be my luck, though, wouldn't it?

"Are you sure you're okay?" the kind stranger asked, and I nodded. I smiled at her shirt.

"Aerosmith?"

"One of my favorites," she replied with a smile. "Let me guess... nap time?"

"Yeah," I said, sighing. "That's probably his problem too."

"They don't take much into consideration when they set these up, do they?"

"No, they don't," I said, perhaps a bit too harshly. "I'm... I'm sorry, it's just..." I was quiet as I took the three front steps up to the doors, trembling slightly. *Please, heart... please slow down... I know that's his SUV, right over there. I know he's in here...*

"But it's what's best for the children."

"Oh, God, no." I stopped, leaning up against the railing to catch my breath.

"Are you sure you're okay?" I felt her touch my arm, and just out of habit pulled back.

"I'm... I'm fine, I really am." I smiled weakly. "I'm just nervous."

"Understood."

"Do you work here?" I asked as she opened the door, ushering Elizabeth and Michael inside, and continued holding it open for me.

"No," she replied.

"Did you... have to bring your kids here for..."

"Here... over here... sit down."

She guided me over to a bench, which was such a good thing. I sunk down into it, leaning my head up against the wall behind it. Emily was still sobbing slightly in my arms, clinging to me, but thankfully Elizabeth and Michael were too mesmerized by the fish tank to pay much attention to me.

"No offense, but you look like shit."

"I feel like shit," I said with a laugh. "I'm probably coming down with something."

"And it doesn't help that you don't have help with them."

"I don't need help," I said with a wave of my hand. "I've pretty much done this on my own from day one. Except..."

Except when Jase had been there, back when he wanted to be a husband and dad, or at least back when he wanted to be a husband. Things changed when he'd tired of me.

"I... need to get them to room 104." I sat up, a wave of nausea hitting that I held down.

"It's right down this hall. I can take them, really."

"No, that's okay." I conjured up all the strength I had and stood. "No offense, but I don't know you."

"None taken. Here." She gathered up Elizabeth and Michael, helping to usher them down the hall to the room, a small sign with its number on a plaque, three hours blocked out with the name "Warner" written on the schedule.

That was so wrong.

"Daddy!"

I stifled a sob as Elizabeth and Michael ran up to him, and he dropped to his knees, pulling them both close as he always did. He was dropping kisses on their faces, smiling and laughing with them, his hands so protective around them.

Just as he always did.

And his eyes, they were so kind, so full of joy...

Until they rested on me.

I could have crawled into a hole at the glare he shot me, the way his nostrils flared, that muscle in his jaw twitched.

But I wasn't going to crawl away. I wasn't going to hide. I held my head high, attempting to set Emily down, which thanks to the liaison or whomever she was didn't go over so well.

"Here, let me..."

"Oh, you don't want to..." I tried to stop her, but it was too late.

There Emily went again.

I held her close, trying to soothe her, when Jase's words cut through me like a knife.

"This is *my* time, Talia."

I'm well aware of that, asshole.

He stood and walked over, taking her from my arms as she continued screaming and fighting to come back to me.

But Jase was right.

It was *his* time. And I was intruding.

I walked swiftly back out into the hall, choking back tears as the sound of Emily's broken heart, a bit surprised to see the kind stranger out there waiting for me. I smiled slightly as I made my way back to that bench, sinking down onto it to gather myself together before leaving.

"Do you think," she began as she sat beside me, "that it would help if the time was changed? Make it earlier? Say... ten until one?"

"Yeah," I said with a short laugh. "If you could do that, you'd be my new best friend."

"Well, I can, but I doubt the best friend part. Although you and I, we both want the same thing."

"Pardon?" I wiped away my tears as I looked at her curiously.

"Talia, my name is Rebecca St. John. I am representing your estranged husband, and just like you I want what's best for those children."

"You're kidding," I deadpanned. "No, I mean about... the... *you're* his lawyer? Oh, that sounded wrong, but..."

She laughed at my rambling, and it was a genuine laugh not one of those forced ones that Sherise Adler was so well known for. It was the kind of laugh that kept me from going ballistic over sitting next to what was essentially the enemy. "Yeah, I get that a lot. But... yeah, I am his lawyer, and I can get the times changed for next week, okay? And if it's Jase's reaction you're worried about, I think he'll agree too." She smiled a little wider. "He was just telling Ms. Schwartz in there she was probably going to have a headache before the first hour was up."

I laughed again, able to picture him saying it, when it occurred to me exactly what Jase's lawyer had witnessed.

Oh... fuck, oh no, she would probably...

"I want you to know," she added quickly, "again, I need to reiterate that I'm working towards what's in the best interest of the children." Her eyes were so earnest, so honest as she continued. "They need *both* of you."

I felt my eyes fill with tears once more as I nodded. Without saying a word, I stood and began walking towards the door, leaving Rebecca St. John in her Aerosmith t-shirt and ripped up jeans sitting on that bench. As I reached for the handle, I turned back towards her.

"I didn't want this," was all I said before I left the building.

JASE

I don't like Mondays; I don't think I ever have. I especially don't like Mondays that start off with a major headache that's not even alcohol induced. Someone up there *really* doesn't like me.

I held my head in one hand as I made my way from the office to the kitchen, fumbling around the cabinets for a moment before remembering I didn't have Excedrin Migraine meds anymore; Talia had taken that with her. Great. Ah, well, I still have the Motrin. I grabbed a handful of them and a Dr. Pepper out of the fridge before heading back up to my office to make it more presentable.

The headache was still in full swing when Rebecca and Kate showed up about an hour and a half later, a bit late but judging by Rebecca's suit and shoes she'd been all business that morning. "Give me a minute to go change," she said as she walked past me, the sway in her hips much different in the three-inch heels that made her taller than me.

"Sure...thing," I said, shrugging when she didn't wait for my answer. I closed the door, making sure it was locked before going with Kate up the stairs to my office.

"I like the new furniture," she said with a grin. "A sleeper sofa? In your office?"

"How'd you know it's a sleeper sofa?" I asked, then grinned back when she shot me her 'bitch, please' look. "Yeah, well, you never know."

"With all of the rooms here, I hardly think it's necessary for you to sleep in your office Jase." She sat down with a beer that she'd obviously gotten from my refrigerator while I was showing Rebecca where to change.

"Oh, and these?" Rebecca said, walking in wearing a t-shirt and form fitting jeans. She pointed to the bottle of beer in Kate's hand, one eyebrow raised. "I suggest you get rid of them and the rest of the alcohol in your house, at least for now."

"Fuck, seriously?" I groaned. It wasn't that big of a deal, other than the stubborn part of me was still pissed off.

"Put it this way," she began, walking past Kate to stand by me, "right now you need to make Mary Poppins look like a crack whore, and not because of anything your estranged wife did, get that look off your face right *now*."

"Fuck, damn, fine." I was still scowling, though. "You sound like *her*, though," I added, pointing at Kate.

"Is that a problem?" Kate asked. "And... I can leave if..."

"No, I already told you, you are free to be in on this. All of this. I have nothing to hide from you."

"Am I interrupting the two of you?" Rebecca asked, her grey eyes twinkling.

"No, sorry," I mumbled.

"Sorry," Kate added.

"This has to do," Rebecca continued, "with you being stone cold drunk when the court liaison showed up for her unannounced visit."

"I wasn't stone cold drunk," I protested. "I was... buzzed, but not drunk."

"Jase..."

"Don't use the 'mom' tone with me, Kate" I said, a smirk on my face. "And you're interrupting her now. That's rude."

"Sorry," Kate said again, and Rebecca let out a soft laugh.

"So, enjoy my beer, bitch," I said, winking at her, then turned back to Rebecca. She was holding a picture frame she'd picked up from my desk.

"Just so we're clear," she said, turning towards me and handing me that frame.

My kids.

"I know, I know." I took the frame from her, smiling down at it. "They're worth it, you know. All the bullshit I've gone through, all the shit I'm bound to still go through. They're worth it."

"They're adorable," she commented.

"Not to sound biased, but... yeah. Yeah they are."

"You love them very much."

I could only smile in response.

"And their mother... you love her, too."

And the smile was gone.

"Let's not..."

"I'm simply stating what I've observed," she interrupted me. "That is my perception, and if I'm wrong then by all means tell me. But if I'm not..."

I felt my face flame as I thought back to Cleveland, and to Vegas. To everything that had gone so wrong.

And everything that had gone incredibly right.

"No, you're right," I said softly.

"Now, to the business at hand."

"Something tells me this isn't good."

"It's... semi-good?" The lift in her voice caused me to look up at her. "You're sure it's okay for Kate to be in here?"

"Absolutely," I repeated.

"Okay, so no overturning the initial ruling *yet*... I'm stressing the *yet* here."

"My fault entirely."

"Not gonna lie and say it wasn't. However." She stood up a bit straighter. "There will be no fewer than two visits from the court liaison per week. One on Thursdays at two, one or more unannounced."

"Yippee."

"You're *going* to say yippee, because guess what else. Nope... nope... wait for it..." She grinned as I stood there bouncing on my heels like a child. "Two weeks from today you will be back in front of that judge, and I will be pleading your case. Oh, and have I mentioned that I'm working on it being a new judge?"

"What? Why?"

"Are you complaining?" she asked, one eyebrow raised.

"Um, no, but why?"

"It seems your judge had a meeting with one of the people from Sherise Adler's team before everyone went into the court room, and if I can show bias in any way, voila. New judge. I told you, I don't play dirty and I won't let anyone else play dirty either."

"Fuck, would Talli..."

"There's where you need to stop."

And that did stop me, cold. I looked at her curiously as she continued.

"I don't think your estranged wife had anything to do with that, at all."

"Don't be so sure, Rebecca. You don't know her. She's hell bent on revenge."

"I can understand why, after everything we've discussed, but listen. I only had a brief moment to speak with her on Saturday, but I truly believe that she does not want to keep those children from you."

"She changed the visitation on me to begin with, limiting my time with them. You can't say she didn't want to keep them from me."

"That may be where the spite came in, but this supervised visitation? That's not something that she wanted. She even told me so."

I took a deep breath at her words, my heart picking up its pace slightly. "When..." I licked my lips, finding them suddenly dry. "When did she say that?"

"Right before she left. You know, she really didn't look like she was feeling well. How did she look when she picked them up?"

"I... I didn't really look at her," I admitted. "She said that? Really?"

"No. I'm lying to you." Wow, I could see why she and Kate had become such quick friends, they were so much alike. "*Yes* she said that. Did you think I would make it up? Oh, and on that note... your visitation is now nine to twelve. I tried ten to one, but they have some rule about their lunches being at twelve or something."

"Seriously? You did that?" I asked excitedly. "That's... that's so good, that's between wake up and nap times, and... wait, Talli's gonna get pissed over that."

"Um... no, she won't."

"You don't know her," I reminded her.

"She told me if I could change it, I would be her new best friend."

Stunned silent once more, I could only stare at Rebecca as if she'd been transplanted from outer space.

Talli would do that?

"She," Rebecca continued, "like you, wants what's best for the kids. As far as they are concerned, once we get over this bump in the road, most things regarding the children should be smooth sailing."

I felt my hands begin to tremble as my thoughts raced a million miles a minute. I didn't know whether to laugh or cry, celebrate or grieve. Was she giving up, or was she compromising?

And did it really matter?

"Oh and mark your calendar for November 19."

"What's November 19?" I asked.

"The tentative date for the final divorce hearing."

And just like that, it felt as if all of the air had been sucked out of the room.

November...

November was such a good month for us, always. We'd go to Groves Point, spend time with family, start out the holidays. And we had so much fun, always. She was big on tradition, big on making sure everything was perfect and that everyone was happy.

This home... this home was always filled with love and laughter, and she'd start baking her ass off, leaving the smells of cookies and pies lingering in the air. I'd give her hell over it every year, telling her I could just walk in the house and gain ten pounds.

And the kids were always so excited. They'd help get out the Christmas lights—the same lights I'd had up in the back yard the night I proposed to their mother—and they'd hang the decorations on the tree. And they'd promise to not run through the media room during the big football games, but they would anyway, leaving a trail of spilled popcorn behind them.

And Christmas morning... that was the best of all, to watch them get so excited over everything that was under the tree and in their stockings. And Talli, I loved to watch how she created special traditions just for us, for them, she always did so much for our children.

So much for me.

But this year... this year it would all be gone.

On November 19 I lose everything.

"Jase, are you okay?" Kate asked, walking over to me. I nodded silently, swallowing down the lump in my throat.

"You don't think that court liaison will be here today, do you?" I asked.

"Hell, I doubt it," Rebecca answered.

"Good. Good." I glanced sideways at her, completely serious as I said, "I need to get rid of the alcohol in the house, right?"

"Yeah, I'm afraid you do. And on that note, my husband is expecting me, so..." She placed her hand on my shoulder. "It will all work out," she said softly.

"Thank you," I murmured. "Um, do you..."

"I can show myself out. I'll call you with the rest of the details, okay? And Kate?"

"Saturday," she said, giving my new lawyer a quick hug.

"Jase?"

Kate turned to me once we were alone. I pointed to the beer in her hand.

"Feel like finishing it with me today?"

She smiled sadly, reaching over and pushing my bangs back out of my eyes. "Yeah. I can do that with you."

278

"Thanks," I said with the best smile I could conjure up. I began walking towards the door when I noticed I was still holding the frame. I signaled to Kate I'd be down in a second, turning around and placing the frame back on my desk.

I stared wistfully at it for a moment, wishing I could turn back that clock, take back everything I'd said and done that had gotten us here.

But wishful thinking never did any good.

"I'm sorry," I whispered as if they could hear me, then turn around and left the room.

CHAPTER 21

TALLI

Dr. Paul Coffman, you are a genius.

"Are you enjoying yourself?" he asked softly in my ear halfway through the first act of *Spamalot*. I smiled in response, a genuine smile that I hadn't been able to give anyone in so long.

This was definitely what the doctor had ordered, no pun intended of course. The laughter was wonderful, so long as I could keep my mind focused. I have to admit it was a bit difficult.

My life had been in absolute shambles for so long that I'd forgotten how good a smile and laugh could feel. This evening out, as friends, no strings attached had allowed me some space to be me, Talia Christine Em... *Warner*.

I'm still Talia Warner.

But tonight, I wasn't Talia the Mommy, or Talia the Nurse Practitioner, or Talia the wife, or Talia the... whatever other label was bestowed upon me at the moment. I was Talia, the woman who'd been denying herself the simplest pleasures for so long that I'd forgotten what it felt like to do something for *me*.

So I smiled and laughed as I let myself get lost in the show, forgetting all about the court appearance that was coming up. I was pleased it was coming along so quickly, for the kids' sake, as even with the earlier hours Emily was still Miss CrankyPuss whenever that court person, Ms. Schwartz, was around, even when she'd made a surprise visit to my home. Luckily the only thing out of place was that stupid blue folder that I kept forgetting about… so when did I remember to look at it? During the middle of the play, of course. Which meant that without a doubt I'd forget again before I got home and relieved Linda of her babysitting duties.

Linda, who was all too happy to come over and gush over the children and how much they'd grown. She even brought her two boys and asked if it was okay if Jackie stopped by with them, he'd missed the kids so much. I only wish I'd been there when he did; I missed him, too.

Talli, you are out having a fantastic time. Stop thinking about everything else.

Renovations.

Linda said Jase was doing renovations to the home.

Of course he would. I mean, he couldn't do it any time I'd asked, could he? No, he waited until the old hag was out of the way, so I wouldn't taint anything new he brought in. I wonder if the decorations will be as cheap and gaudy as…

Stop it, Talia. This is a funny part. You're supposed to laugh.

I really was having a good time, though… when I allowed myself to, or when a song came up that would completely take my mind of a pair of smoldering kaleidoscope eyes that should be on me right now, but instead…

Instead I smiled again at Dr. Paul Coffman, his brown eyes so very kind as they looked at me.

At least therapy was going well. Or counseling, or whatever it was being called. I mean, I wasn't taking any medication for this depression that they are so sure I have to take. I was progressing, and the progress was evident to everyone who saw me regardless of whether I told them my plight or not.

Or, at least they noticed if they bothered to look.

Jase won't even acknowledge my presence in a room.

Fuck it. He made his decision; he can stick with it. He's moving on? Wonderful. So am I.

At least sort of.

"Sorry," I whispered to Paul after I jerked my arm away when he'd involuntarily brushed up against it. "Habit."

"Old habits die hard, Talli," he whispered back with a wink.

That they do.

Intermission found us down in the lobby getting drinks. I was going to have just a Diet Pepsi, but this place was all Coke products, no thank you.

"How about some wine?" Paul suggested, and I smiled.

"I'd love to."

It had been forever since I'd actually had a glass of wine, and this one was, again, what the doctor had ordered. I could feel myself relax as we sipped on our drinks during that intermission.

"So you have court in two days?" he asked, and I cringed.

"Yeah, thanks for reminding me. I don't think it's that big of a deal, though; it's just Jase and his lawyer trying to regain his visitation."

"Which you don't have a problem with?"

"No," I replied honestly. "I don't have a problem with it at all. They miss him."

"You're a good mom, you know that, right?"

I blinked a couple of times, taking a deep breath before I answered. "I try to be. I... just want them to be happy, to know that they're loved, to have everything they need."

"You act so surprised that someone would say that to you."

I blushed, shrugging as I looked away. "I... haven't been told that in ages, Paul. I honestly couldn't tell you when. Hell, I..." I laughed softly. "I don't even know if he's said it at all, to be honest with you."

"Talli..."

"But that's okay," I added quickly. "Because it doesn't really matter, you know? I know I'm nothing like my mom. She had six and I can barely juggle three, right? But..."

My words trailed off as he placed a soft kiss on my temple.

Probably not the wisest thing for him to do.

"Don't doubt yourself, Talli. That's all I'm saying."

"Thank you," I murmured softly, taking an uneasy sip of my wine.

"I don't want you to feel uncomfortable around me," he said softly as he moved in closer. "Let's just use the rest of tonight to let go of everything else out there. No court, no kids, no ex's or almost ex's, no siblings getting on our last nerve. Tonight, we're just... here. To enjoy the rest of the show. Deal?"

"Who says I haven't been..."

"Talli..." he cut me off, one eyebrow raised.

"Okay, fine. Deal."

I swear I felt like I was twelve again as we stepped out of that theatre, somehow ending up with the crowd that was marching down the street singing "Always Look on the Bright Side of Life." Stranger things have happened in the heart of Los Angeles, believe me, but the smile on my face was genuine as Paul pulled me into a small café on the corner.

"Coffee," he said simply.

"To keep me up the rest of the night," I added with a giggle.

"To keep you sane when Emily gives you ten tons of hell for going out tonight," he replied, and I threw my head back in laughter.

"Okay. Coffee."

I sat at a table towards the side of the coffee shop, right by the windows like I hadn't been able to do in ages, taking in the sights of the city. As crazy as this place was, as much as I wished I was raising my children somewhere saner, something about this city had grown on me. Sure, I could do without the bullshit that came with it, it wasn't the most comfortable place for someone who wasn't blonde, tan, and a size zero. I loved the history, though... the insane amounts of it that you could get on any street corner in L.A., or especially in Hollywood. And there were times when Jase and I could go around practically unnoticed, or at least not bothered, due to the insane amount of celebrities that lived in this area.

As that thought crossed my mind, I frowned slightly.

"Penny for your thoughts," Paul said as he slid in the seat in front of me, handing me my cappuccino.

"Let's not and say we did." I smiled tightly, then sighed. "Thank you, so much. I really did need this."

"You are very welcome. Thank you for being incredible company." I opened my mouth to protest, but he stopped me. "Seeing you smile for a change has been wonderful."

"Yeah, well don't tell all those people that work that think I'm a she-zilla. You might ruin my reputation."

"Your secret's safe with me. So..." He held up his coffee. "Here's to smiling, and to friends, and to Monty Python, and to coffee, and to... new beginnings."

I contemplated this for a moment before raising my cup as well. "To... everything you said." We touched cups, and I took a short sip of my coffee, wondering when the last time I'd actually gone out for coffee was.

I couldn't remember to save my life.

"Do you have someone to watch the kids? On Monday, I mean, when you go to court."

"Yes, I do," I replied. "As a matter of fact, I think you saw to that when you asked your sister, and she called me and offered." I laughed as a blush crossed his cheeks. "Thank you for that, Paul. I can only hope that you warned her about Em."

"She knows she hates all people that are not you or..."

I know he was going to add Jase's name, but instead he smiled at me.

"I'm happy that she could help you."

"So am I, but I do want to add that I... really... well, I don't need saved." I bit my bottom lip, wondering how to continue, but deciding just being blunt Talli was the best bet. "I have to be able to do this, take care of things. I did for so long, all on my own, I suppose I just grew complacent with having Jase there. I know I am capable of solving my own problems without having to rely on him, or his... people, you know?"

"Weren't you essentially running that household on your own to begin with?"

"Well..." I thought carefully before answering. "Yes and no. I did run the house, I did plan the parties, I did take care of the children. But there was always a backup. Always Linda, or Jackie, or Sondra, oh... God, even Chris, if I needed help. I don't have that now, and..."

"You have me."

I took a deep breath, looking straight into his kind brown eyes. "As much as I appreciate that, there are certain… things I have to do on my own. I'm not a helpless little girl. Believe me, I've pulled myself out of a lot worse."

"So I've heard."

"Yeah, well…" Wow, nothing was sacred anymore, was it? Oh, right… my graveyard had been exposed when I'd first moved out to Los Angeles, and now…

"But this is different."

"To say the very least." I sat up a little straighter, smiling softly at him. "But I can fix this, too. Me, you know… I… I can fix me."

And I meant it, with everything in me. I can fix me. I have the drive, the conviction, the determination to get back to the person I was before. And maybe, just maybe, if I could love myself, then someone else could love me. Because me, like this…

I still felt disconnected, even if just a little bit. And as Paul walked me to his car and drove us to the condo, I still felt a little like I was merely going through the motions. Maybe it's because even with as much as I was happy to be out, I couldn't help but wish, but think 'if only'.

If only I would have reached out to Jase instead of pulling away, not that I noticed it then but now… now I could really see.

If only Emily hadn't gotten sick on a regular basis.

If only Jase would have listened to me, been honest with me.

If only I had just bitch slapped Bree and gotten it over with.

If only I had…

Stayed?

No.

I couldn't have done that. I couldn't have lived the lie, not after what I had seen. Besides, if he'd wanted me to stay, he would have said something.

Right?

The children were all asleep when I made it home, walking into that condo all by myself to find Linda sitting there alone watching television. She smiled up at me as I walked through the door.

"They were angels."

"Really?" I asked, kicking my shoes off and walking over to my papasan chair.

"Absolutely. And Jackie says he's sorry he couldn't stay. He misses you."

"I miss him, too," I said with a wistful sigh. "Where are the boys?"

"He took them home with him," she replied as she stood, grabbing her purse.

"So, he's babysitting...no, they're older, they... Linda, what's with that shit eating grin on your face?"

"I keep forgetting you're not in the middle of the gossip there," she said softly.

"Shut up, are you two really shacking up?" I asked quickly, standing and squeezing her as tight as I could when she nodded. "I'm so happy for you!"

She stepped back, wiping her eyes slightly. "I'm... well, I wish the same happiness for you." She patted my cheek slightly, then handed that damn blue folder to me. "Em wouldn't leave this alone."

"Oh, thank you... I keep forgetting about this thing. Are you sure you have to go?"

"Oh yes, church in the morning and all."

"Yeah, I can only imagine how much you need that with who you work for," I teased, then my smile fell. "I'm sorry; I shouldn't have said that."

"It's all right," she said, smiling back at me as she opened the door. "Jackie's not the only one who misses you, Talli." Without waiting for my answer, she walked out the door, shutting it softly behind her.

I could lie and say that what she'd said didn't affect me in any way, but what was the use? My hands were shaking slightly as I sat back down in that papasan chair, the blue folder on my lap. I mean, this was so important that he'd sent Kate down that hall to give it to me, so it must be something important, right?

Oh...

It was...

Most of what I'd been looking for, that day during Emily's party.

Tears touched my eyes as I looked over the kids' birth certificates, remembering what I could about Elizabeth, and everything under the sun about the other two. What I remembered the most was how...

How I wasn't alone.

How he'd been there, every step of the way. Well, minus when I'd opened my eyes to see Kate standing over me after the Elizabeth incident, but he'd been with our baby girl, so I forgave him for that. But with both Michael and Emily, he'd held my hand, encouraging me, shedding tears of joy when they came into this world.

He'd told me Michael would talk early... and he'd been right.

And Em... with Em, he'd just held her, marveling over her, saying he couldn't get over her face. I caught him more than once singing softly to her that song... what was it? That Roberta Flack song. I couldn't recall the name, but I could hear the melody.

Ah, the title to my vehicle. Yeah, I kinda needed that.

And the kids shot records. Oh, thank god, I needed those to enroll Elizabeth in school, which I had to do in the next couple of weeks. Wow, was she really going to start Kindergarten?

Out of the corner of my eye, I saw a small rectangle fall to the floor. I could tell once I looked at it that it was a picture, and as I reached for it I never dreamed I would turn it over to find...

Us.

A picture of us.

And I certainly wasn't expecting to feel my resolve crack, feel the tears fall freely, feel the sobs being ripped from my soul.

God, I missed him. I missed us, the us we'd been back when this picture was taken. The us that was so very happy with our lives, with each other. The us that had stood up against the world that seemed so against us at times. The us that stole every minute that we could to spend it together. The us that reveled in the passion, the us that embraced the security that our love brought.

The us that had stood before God and man, swearing with everything in us that we'd love one another, forsaking all others, 'til death do us part.

I held that picture up to my chest, covering my heart as if it could help it heal some way.

But I knew better.

JASE

She was beautiful.

She was smiling, laughing, blushing.

And every picture ripped my heart out.

So this is how it felt, or how it would have felt if she'd cared. This stabbing, this ache that held me in a stranglehold. It was like a train wreck looking at those pictures, reading the short article, but I just couldn't look away. Even without seeing the captions I knew exactly who this guy was.

Paul.

But was he just any Paul? No. No, this guy was a doctor, yay me. How could I compete with someone who has so much in common with her? Oh, look... not *just* a doctor either, but a doctor who was involved in a high-profile divorce from his celebrity wife. Super.

This was the guy she trusted my kids with.

This was the guy she was laughing on the phone with.

I glared at the picture of his hand on the small of her back, my imagination going into overdrive. My stomach began to turn at the thought of his hands on her, making her moan and sigh the way she used to do for me...

"Hey," Kate said as she sat beside me, glancing at the scene unfolding before my eyes as I browsed the 'net from my phone. "Jase, in less than an hour you're going to be in a court room with her. Just... close that browser, okay?"

"I'm a big boy, Kate. I can take it."

"It could be nothing, you know? Like us eating pizza and having ice cream."

"Except she's all dressed up, out on the town. An obvious date, Kate... to the theater no less. Let's just call it like it is, okay?" I hit the end button on my phone, shoving it in my pocket. "But she points the finger at *me*."

"I love you, Jase, but she had a reason to and you know it."

"Let me find out this guy was..." I stopped myself, closing my eyes and inhaling deeply. I didn't want to believe that Talli had turned to someone else before she'd left... but I had no room to talk if she had, did I?

I heard the clicking of heels coming down the hall, and I knew without even turning my head that Talli was there. I kept my eyes down, my jaw clenched shut as she walked by, not acknowledging my presence. My oh my, how some things just never change. My knee was bouncing, just like I always did when I was seething, and Kate placed her hand on it to try and calm me down.

No such luck.

"Is he here?" I hissed as quietly as I could. Kate looked around as inconspicuously as she could, then shook her head 'no'. "Good."

"Jase," Kate began, but the next thing I knew I heard another set of heels, this time turning to look.

Rebecca St. John meant business today.

"We have a private conference room right up this way. Hello, Kate," she said as she walked up to us.

Kate and I followed Rebecca down the hall to the private conference room, where I sunk down into a chair, that scowl still firmly on my face. It was bad enough that I felt like my world was crumbling, but to see it happen, knowing I was the one who had been the catalyst was devastating in its own right.

"Okay, first off... there won't be a need for witnesses today," Rebecca began after we were all seated.

"I'm just here for moral support," Kate said quickly, and Rebecca smiled at her.

"Good. Second, there will be no mention of anything that was in the tabloids about Talia and her anonymous date."

"I told you it was a date," I muttered to Kate.

"You don't know that," she replied.

"And his name is Paul; he's not as anonymous as he may want to be," I said, still seething.

"I don't care if his name is Paul or John or George or Ringo, we won't be bringing him up today. Got it?" Rebecca asked, her eyebrow raised as she looked at me. "Above the board. You catch more flies with honey than with vinegar."

"Fine," I mumbled, still pouting, for lack of a better word.

"Can you give us a moment?" Rebecca said, and I know she was talking to Kate, who quickly agreed and left the room. After the door shut, I felt Rebecca's hand on my arm, and I looked over at her, still upset over everything I'd seen and read.

"I know; pull myself together."

"And I need you to trust me," she said. I nodded slightly, taking in her appearance in her unbelievably expensive suit tailored fit to her, absolutely incredible shoes... I think they were Manolos... and her Louis Vuitton briefcase. What a far cry from the girl who came to my house in her concert tees and ripped up jeans.

"You and I both know that the chances are slim to none that the original verdict will be completely overturned, but I am accelerating this process. I want to ask for extra time with the children..."

"Do you think I can get it?" I asked, my eyes wide, my heart thumping with anticipation.

"I think that these past two weeks have shown good faith, so you may. And if they say no to unsupervised, I will ask for a continuance in thirty days. In the meantime, *this* is where I need you to trust me."

"I will... fuck, Rebecca, whatever it takes."

"I want to suggest mediation."

I blinked a couple of times, confused. "Isn't that what we're doing?"

"No, we're doing... *litigation*, if you will. There will be a third party brought in and..."

"I want *you* handling this."

"Jase, listen to me..."

"No, see, I let someone else handle it and... and I've had a whole nine hours with my kids since then. And Em has cried almost all of it, and Elizabeth doesn't understand, and Michael just wants to play and have some more time with just us guys, you know?" I felt the tears threaten, but I kept them at bay, even with my voice wavering. "I can't leave it in the hands of someone who doesn't care."

"You're not," she said, removing her glasses, setting her papers aside. "You're leaving it up to you, and to Talia. The two people who care most about those children, and whether or not the two of you want to admit it, but you're also the two people who care most about each other."

"But the mediator?" I asked, ignoring her last comment.

"The mediator is simply someone who helps the two of you come to a decision."

"The two of us," I said, my stomach in absolute knots.

"Jase, you would need to be able to set aside any differences that you have with her, don't think about the past, don't think about what the papers have written about either of you. You have got to walk into this with a clear, sound mind with *only* your children's best interest at heart. Can you do that?"

Could I?

I thought back to all of the hateful words shot back and forth between us, the accusations that my guilty conscience kept pushing aside. I remembered her absolute indifference when she finally had her proof, the way my brain and my heart were just screaming silently, begging her to care. I remember wanting to scream at the top of my fucking lungs when I walked in, hearing her call our home a prison. And the fight in the basement, the way it had felt so good to let it all out in the air, only to have my hopes thrown away a mere few days later. And the pictures flashed once again in my mind. The ones of Paul, and how happy he seemed to make her where I'd failed so miserably, how devastating it was to see, to know.

And then...

Then I thought of Elizabeth, who fought so hard to live. I thought of her spirit, her spunk, that spark that ignited into a full-blown flame whenever she would walk into the room. And Michael, whose baby pictures could so easily get mixed up with mine. I thought of his eyes, and how they glowed when he opened his first guitar this past Christmas, even though he was just over two years old, and how he told me he was going to be just like me some day. And Emily... my sweet Princess, it wasn't her fault she didn't know me. It was mine, and I take complete responsibility for that. But it wasn't always that way; she was my girl, through and through, rarely spending a moment with anyone else the first three months of her life. I wanted that closeness again. And not just with Em; I wanted it with all of them.

"Jase?"

"I can do this," I replied, sitting up just a little straighter. "I will do this."

"Okay," she replied, a soft smile on her face as she pushed her glasses back in place. "Game on."

I'm not going to lie and say that I wasn't a bundle of nerves when we stepped back into that court room. I was rather pleased to see it was a different judge, although this one seemed to be in a rather foul mood. She was as unimpressed as Ms. Schwartz was with the initial home visit, but Rebecca put on an impassioned plea on my behalf.

"Your honor, my client was grieving what was essentially the loss of his children," she'd said on my behalf. "Does that excuse his behavior? No. But my client has expressed regret for his actions and has gone to great lengths to make the changes requested by the court. Which, I might add, was made without my client having ever been in any legal trouble, and without him having ever put his children in harm's way."

There was some banter back and forth about black and white, and shades of gray, and the whole time I'd kept my head down. I didn't want to see the judge's condescending glare, or risk looking over at Talia for fear that I'd see the same thing. Besides, there was something coming up that I was truly dreading her answer to.

The judge denied our motion to set aside the previous ruling, which I'd expected. She did agree to reevaluate again in thirty days, which was frustrating but I could accept it. She denied the additional supervised visitation due to the scheduling conflicts, which broke my heart just a little, but that wasn't what I was the most on edge about.

"Your honor, while I am acting as my client's attorney in his divorce proceedings..."

Oh, God. Here it comes.

"...when it comes to resolving the matter of custody and visitation, my client requests that the two parties meet with a mediator and come up with a solution that is in the best interest of the children."

"Ms. St. John," Sherise Adler started up, and I felt my insides turn to ice, "there is no need for mediation when your client has no visitation."

"That's going to change, Ms. Adler, and my client feels the best people to come up with an amicable decision, one that benefits all parties involved, are the two people who care the most about the welfare of these children."

Please... please, Talli... give this a shot...

"Why, so he can play on my client's sympathy?"

Fuck you, Sherise Adler.

"I can hardly see how..."

"Yes."

My breath caught in my throat at that one word, so very strong, overpowering.

And it came from...

"Yes, I... I agree."

Talli.

I stole a sideways glance at her, where she stood in a navy blue suit, her red hair straightened, pushed back behind one ear. Gone was the smile she had in those pictures and in its place was a stoic, calm expression that was so very familiar with her. But the words from her...

"I am willing to meet with a mediator, for a new visitation agreement. As soon as possible."

My eyes slid shut at her words and I prayed for the strength to keep the tears away. And even though the first meeting wouldn't be set for at least two weeks, it was still something.

Hope.

That's what it is.

Hope.

Even if it wasn't for us, even if it wasn't for what should have been, it was still hope.

It was more than I'd ever dreamed I'd have again.

CHAPTER 22

TALLI

I officially dubbed that Thursday after the hearing as "Blast from the Past" day.

The day started off odd to begin with. I could literally count on one hand the number of times that my children had all gotten up early, not given me any hassles, and behaved like absolute angels towards each other. I even checked Elizabeth's temperature before we left the condo that morning. She and Michael hadn't argued one single time, and I couldn't think of the last time that had happened quite honestly. He was so laid back and compared to her impatience the two just didn't mix. But somehow, Michael had actually gotten ready on time, even putting his clothes on correctly, and Elizabeth was just sleepy enough to not be in a rush.

Emily... I was so sure I was going to have to deal with her screaming, or crying, or fussing when I got her ready. Again, she was rather subdued, so I checked her temperature as well. Thankfully she wasn't running one either, but she was quite the sneaky little thief. She'd decided that picture of Jase and me was hers, and there was no convincing her otherwise. Michael and Elizabeth were rather patiently trying to teach her to call him 'Daddy' instead of her usual 'Dase' but I think at least for the time being it's a battle they are not going to win.

I had to change clothes twice to find something that wasn't completely hanging on me, so my diet was working. And the counseling or whatever they were going to call it for my so-called depression must have been working too, because I was in no mood to have drab colored clothes just hanging off of me. I ended up in light colored pants that were tailored to fit just right and a pastel green colored top, which the kids were eating up with a spoon.

"You're so *bright* today, Mommy!" Michael exclaimed as I grabbed my comfortable shoes, and I had to smile at him.

"Why thank you, Little Man, I'm feeling rather bright today."

"Bright has more than one meaning, too," Elizabeth added, and instead of arguing with her, Michael asked her what she meant, which led to a rather lively, yet oddly intelligent, conversation between the two of them. It didn't take long for me to come to the conclusion they both had their father's intelligence. Okay, maybe a little bit of mine—I was in the medical field and had graduated with honors—but it was their style of speaking that so reminded me of Jase.

And, speak of the devil, the radio station was playing, of all things, *Hard to Believe* as I started up the vehicle. The children were so very excited, so for their sake I didn't change it, no matter how the lyrics alone got to me. Add his voice on top of that? I was automatically wishing I could call him, talk to him. I knew that he was going to act as if I wasn't in the room when I dropped the kids off; he'd done that since the one time he'd snapped at me. But maybe… just maybe…

I looked down at the stack of birthday invitations that I had to mail out that day. I was so very late getting these out, and most everyone had already been called with the invite anyhow. Jase, however, had made it very clear that he didn't want to speak with me, and that if anyone called from my number it had better be one of the kids. And I just didn't want to leave it to any of them to ask, risk them having their heart broken if he refused.

But he wouldn't… would he?

Michael was getting ready to turn three, and all he wanted was to go bowling. He didn't want a huge party with a bunch of people. He'd been very specific about who he wanted there. The only other children he'd asked to come were Paul's two kids; he didn't even ask for anyone from his daycare. He also wanted his grandparents, his great-grandmother, and Pete and Jaden there, even if Jaden had a 'screaming baby' with her, but he was relieved to hear that Jaden's baby wasn't due for about six weeks after that.

But there was one thing that Michael wanted, above everything else. Above his handheld game that he was asking for, above the movies, above the toys.

Michael wanted Jase there.

As the kids sang along to their father's voice on the radio, I remembered how Michael had said that's all he wanted for his birthday, was for his Daddy to come to his party, without the court liaison there, without having to be under lock and key, without having to go to that building to see him.

Who was I to say no?

I'd printed out address labels for everyone, since I could type much faster than write, and although they didn't have return addresses on there (I'd forgotten those in true Talia fashion), they were all stamped and ready to go. Inside each and every one, I'd put in the directions to the bowling alley along with directions to the condo for pizza afterwards, just in case it got too hectic out in public, and so I could put Emily down for her nap. Inside one, though, right on the invitation itself, I'd written two simple words.

Please come.

I didn't want to beg or plead; I shouldn't have to, it's his son. But at the same time, I knew that with the court order he may think it was some kind of a ploy, something to get him in trouble, and that couldn't be further from the truth. He needed to be there, and not just because Michael wanted him to be.

I wanted him there, too.

And it was killing me, because every time I'd get there, to that point where I would start to miss him so terribly and wonder why I'd left, I'd be reminded why.

Like when Bree's latest song came on right after Jase's.

"Change it, Mommy," Elizabeth said tiredly. I'd tried to shield them from everything, but I knew above all others she could sense my mood swings.

"You got it, Baby Girl," I replied.

So what was on the next station? *Faithfully*, by Journey. The song that Jase had sung softly in my ear, the one that was on the radio when he'd proposed to me. I took a deep breath, sucking it up, the memories bittersweet, but I could deal with it today.

I wouldn't be able to see Jase the next two Saturdays as I had to work, but Paul's sister would be bringing the kids to the center for his visitation. Next Sunday was Michael's birthday party, and three days after that, on that Wednesday afternoon, Jase and I would be sitting in front of a mediator, just the three of us in that room, with Jase and I actually having to speak to one another, come up with a visitation plan that was suitable for everyone. I didn't want to walk in there absolutely cold, not knowing what he wanted out of this, so I easily justified my strong desire, for lack of a better word, to have Jase there.

It was important, for the kids' sake.

Right?

Dropping the children off at daycare was just as uneventful as getting them ready that morning had been, which I took as a positive step. The only thing that could possibly go wrong was…

Damn it.

There it went.

My heart began racing again, with no warning, and this time no trigger. Hell, it hadn't needed a trigger the past couple of days, it simply had a mind of its own, speeding up, slowing down, making me nauseous, causing me to break out in a sweat. I made my way to a bench along the walls by one of the offices and lowered myself slowly, closing my eyes and taking several deep breaths.

"Talli?"

I looked up towards where the familiar voice was coming from, spotting none other than Mr. Dimples himself walking up.

"John! How the hell are you?" I stood, against my better judgment, and gave him a warm hug.

"Um… better than you, and I'm not talking about the tabloid shit. Sit," he commanded. I raised my eyebrow at him, which he countered with one of his own. "Sit," he repeated, pointing at the bench.

"I'm fine, I really am," I lied as I took a seat. "I've just been under a lot of stress, that's all. But you! I haven't seen you in ages! How the hell are you?"

"Wonderful, wonderful," he replied, taking my hand in his, like I couldn't tell he was checking my pulse. "Sara and I just found out we're having another baby." His smile was radiant, genuine as he said this, and I couldn't help but smile myself.

"Who woulda thought that Dr. John Craig would be such a family man?" I teased.

"Not I, not I," he said softly, his smile fading. "Talli, I need you to sit still for a moment, don't talk, okay?"

"Okay," I said with a resigned smile. "But what brings you out to California?"

"Talli…"

"If you tell me, I'll quit talking." I grinned again, just needing the distraction, something to focus on, to wrap my mind around.

"Fine, if you must, I'm here visiting Brooks. Shut it now, young lady," he added quickly when I opened my mouth. "Just taking a breather before the conference next week. Sara's visiting her mother, so I came out here to see how Brooks's holding up, which turns out quite well before you ask so you can stop. He and Kate have agreed to everything, and they don't have any kids."

Yeah, and Kate has my husband to find solace in.

"Don't think anything of it, Talli," John said, as if he could read my mind. "When was your last EKG?"

"You are on vacation, stop worrying about me," I said, pulling my hand out of his reach.

"Your pulse is 128, now if you're not going to tell me as a friend then tell me as someone who once was your cardiologist. Is it like this all the time?"

I sighed before saying, "No, it's not."

"When did this start?"

"I… well, I had a few dizzy spells, but… nothing big until Em's party. I… I thought it was just a fluke." I shrugged slightly. "But I was checked out, and they didn't find anything."

"You said your last EKG was a while ago, Emily's party wasn't."

"Oh, potato, potahto. I had everything but the EKG." I threw my hands up. "Like I said, I thought it was a fluke. You can relax, though, and save playing 'Daddy' for your kids. I see my new cardiologist this afternoon."

"Who is it?"

"I'm so not telling you," I said, raising my hand. "You are on vacation, and..."

"Talli..."

"And I'm not your patient anymore, okay?"

"Fine. I'll just ask Jase," he said, pulling out his cellphone.

"Damn it, all right. It's Dr. Mendez, now put that phone away."

John pushed the cellphone back down into his pocket, but his features showed just how serious he was. "In all fairness, this is something he needs to know. It could end up affecting him, too."

"Let me find out what it is first, if anything. Damn, no need to jump to any conclusions! Besides... who says I wouldn't tell him?"

John didn't say a word, he merely raised an eyebrow and stared at me.

Damn, was I that transparent?

But I wasn't lying; I did have an appointment with Dr. Mendez, scheduled right after my lunch with Paul at the deli down on the corner. I was so tired of hospital food and gossip, and it since that was all our hospital had to offer, I just wanted to be elsewhere. Due to the gossip, though, I told him I'd just meet him there, so that we didn't have to listen to it walking down the street. After mailing out the invitations to Michael's birthday bowl-a-rama, I was sitting at a table inside enjoying my sandwich and writing in my little agenda where John and Sara would be dropping by to see the kids before they headed back to Ohio, minding my own business as I normally do.

"Talli?"

Although in Los Angeles, sometimes that's easier said than done. I sighed, glancing up from my agenda to see who would interrupt my lunch.

"Well... huh," was all I could say.

If I thought that seeing Dr. John Craig was something out of the ordinary, imagine my surprise when Keith Anderson stood by my table.

"I thought that was you," he said, a soft smile on his face. If I didn't know better, I'd almost swear he was happy.

"Yeah, it's... what are you doing in California?" I asked quickly, all at once thinking wow this was I and remembering the rumor mill talking about how he'd settled down with Stella Black.

"Um, Stella's doing some remote shows from out here... may I?" he asked, motioning to the empty seat in front of me.

Fuck it. What the hell.

"Sure, go ahead," I said with a tight smile. "But nothing here is on the record, okay?"

"No... no, I'm not here for... " He stared at me for a moment, his eyes almost sad. "I'm sorry, Talli. I really am. Divorce sucks, I know firsthand, but... no one deserves to go through what you are right now."

"Some people seem to think I deserve it," I said, eyeing him suspiciously. "As if it was karma paying me back for all those years ago."

"You and I both know I wasn't honest with you back then. And again, I'm sorry."

"My situation today doesn't concern you," I said softly. "I know that sounds mean, but..."

"I... meant I'm sorry for *then*," he explained. "I'm sorry about lying to you about my marriage, and I'm sorry that I sold you out to gain a quick buck."

"Looks like you gained more than a buck out of it," I said nonchalantly, and he actually blushed.

"Yeah... I'm actually getting married again."

"To Stella?" I asked, grinning at him when he nodded. "Um... well, I could say something really snarky, but I won't."

"What, like we deserve each other?" he asked.

"Pretty much, yeah, but that's mean and... apology accepted anyhow. Life's too short..."

"If you can't forgive?" he finished for me, but it was more like a question.

I sighed, looking down at my sandwich. "That's... one... " I looked up at Keith, someone who'd known me at one time better than anyone else, someone who'd seen me at the lowest of my lows. For as bad as things seemed now, at least I had my sanity, and my sobriety, and my children. I had something to hold onto, even if it wasn't what I wished it was.

That's why I wasn't with Jase.

Because I just didn't know if I could ever forgive him.

"Think about it, okay?" was all Keith said as he stood, nodding at Paul as he walked up. "It was good to see you."

"It was..." I hesitated only for a moment before saying, "It was good to see you, too."

"Now see?" he asked with a wink. "Was it that hard?"

Yes it was, Keith. It was harder than you could possibly know.

"Are you okay?" Paul asked as he sat down, his eyes darting over to Keith, who was exiting the deli rather quickly.

"Relatively speaking," I replied. "Don't be surprised if that ends up all over the tabloids, by the way. Or, this. Us being here together."

"I'm okay with that," he said, and I smiled at him. "Is he a friend of Jase's?"

"Oh no," I said with a laugh as I remembered their 'meeting' on Stella's show. I also remembered, ever so briefly, Jase's reaction to seeing him on the red carpet.

And then I remembered later that night, in the hotel elevator...

"Wow, you're really flushed," Paul commented, which only resulted in me actually blushing more.

"I'm fine," I mumbled, rubbing my temple slightly.

But even as I sat there smiling at Paul during lunch or arguing with my new cardiologist that I didn't have six weeks to take off work, I knew I wasn't fine. And it wasn't the physical ailment that Dr. Mendez said he wanted to correct with Cardiac Ablation. No, it was my head... no... no...

It was my heart.

But in a different way.

It was that stupid, wistful, wishful thinking, wondering if he ever thought of me that way anymore, wondering what would happen if I just showed up out of the blue and asked him to hold me, asked him to take this hurt away.

But it wouldn't be fair.

Because I knew... I knew even if he thought of me, thought of us that way... when I closed my eyes, all I could see was him with her.

And I just wasn't strong enough, wasn't a big enough person to forgive him.

Which I'd said about Keith as well, although now I know I truly could and had forgiven him.

But not Jase.

Not yet.

JASE

I was at that point, the point of conceding, the point of accepting that this separation, this divorce was what she wanted. Did I agree with it? No. Could I change it? No. How did that saying, that prayer go? Oh, right. I just needed the strength to accept the things I could not change.

And I couldn't change her heart.

One would think that reaching that point would make my life simpler. Unfortunately, somehow, it made the wound that much more painful, fresher. Holding my tongue when she walked in the room, refraining from reaching out to her. I knew, see... I knew I'd end up a fucking mess, and I couldn't let her see me like that.

So I avoided looking at her, looking into those beautiful blue eyes, at those curves that my hands longed to trace. God help me if she passed too close and I smelled that jasmine scent lingering behind; I'd end up hard as a fucking rock until I could find my release, closing my eyes, her name falling from my lips like a prayer.

Wasn't time supposed to heal all wounds?

But no, I had that ache in my chest still, and sometimes it gripped my heart in a vice, like when Michael talked so excitedly about his birthday party. The same birthday party that he'd told me he wanted, the one I knew I wasn't permitted to attend. And I couldn't call Talli, beg her to let me be there, listen to all the reasons why she said I couldn't. I wasn't about to say anything to the kids about it either; there was no need to put them in the middle, have them asking their mother if I could go too.

"You, sir, look like you lost your best friend," Kate commented as she placed a bowl of ice cream in front of me. I was looking through photographs at the time, trying to choose which ones to put in the front room, now that the family portraits no longer portrayed the truth.

"I have," I mumbled, my fingers tracing over a black and white photo of Talli with Emily.

"Thanks a lot," Kate said with a laugh, swatting my arm before taking a seat beside me.

"You know what I'm talking about," I said, frowning.

"Yeah, yeah, I know. Oh, these black and whites are nice."

"They're pictures that Jaden took, before…"

Before I'd fucked up so royally, even though I had already begun that path of destruction.

"They'll go really well with the new furniture you picked out," she said, reaching for the picture I held in my hand. "Jase…"

"Don't, okay? I *know.*"

I know that I shouldn't put up any pictures with her in them, even though she was their mother, even though she still had my heart. As much as it killed me, there wouldn't be any pictures of Talli in that front room, the way there had been since she'd moved out there.

"They're delivering more furniture this afternoon, right?"

I nodded at Kate's question as I piled the pictures together, placing them back in the envelope that Jaden had sent them in. I tossed the envelope back onto the growing pile of mail that I had yet to go through.

"How was your visitation today?"

I shrugged. "It was good, I guess," I mumbled, standing and rubbing my face hard. "She had to work today, again, so at least I didn't have to deal with *that.*"

"She? She's just *she* now?"

"I really don't want to talk about it."

"Okay."

"But, see, Michael's birthday? It's this Thursday. And… and I can't see him, I can't be with him. I can't do anything except take his present to him in that godawful fucking room next Saturday, because I fucking forgot it today."

"No… no, wait, you'll have your mediation before then, right?" Kate asked.

"The day before, yeah."

"So, *ask* her."

I rolled my eyes at Kate's suggestion, refusing to comment. I considered myself damn lucky that she would even agree to the mediation, I wasn't about to push it.

"Speaking of that... thing," I said with a wave of my hand. "I'm supposed to go over that with Rebecca today, get everything ironed out that I want to ask for."

"On a Saturday afternoon?" Kate asked, her tone showing her disbelief.

"Yes, on a Saturday," I replied, grinning at Kate in spite of myself. "It's okay, *mother*, I think I can handle going over this stuff with my lawyer."

"You don't think that's odd?

"It's no odder than you questioning my relationship with every single person of the female persuasion for the past, what... thirty years? Besides, you're the one who handled her wedding."

"You make me sound like some old shrew," she pouted. "Oh, and you're welcome."

"For what?"

"For me talking her into taking your case."

I smiled softly. "Thank you. Again. And you don't sound like a shrew, Kate, you sound like my closest friend." I smiled at her, adding, "You've always had only my best interests at heart, right?"

"I also thought you were the biggest player on the face of this planet."

"Proved you wrong, didn't I?"

She sighed, her eyes narrowing as she chose her words carefully. "Yes and no."

"What the hell is that supposed to mean?"

"You... well, you... okay, don't get angry, this is merely an observation."

"Oh, this should be good." I put my bowl down and leaned back, crossing my arms. "Let's hear it, Evans."

"You had this problem of... well, when you couldn't get what you want, you went to the next warm body who was willing. There. I said it."

"What?" I asked.

"You have an entire journal written to me that proves it, don't you?"

"Yeah, but I... I didn't..."

"No, technically you never cheated on me. You apparently decided to save that honor for your wife."

"Fuck you, Kate," I said quietly, my amusement immediately disappearing.

"No, listen to me, and because I love you the way I do I am being completely honest. When you and I weren't... you and I, you ran to anyone you could."

"Way to make me sound like an asshole."

"Well, you were. You should have said something."

"No, really?"

"Fuck you and your attitude if you can't take it, Warner. After me, you bounced from girl to girl. And Talli was different, because like you said... you love her, and you had that connection. She wasn't a rebound. She was never a rebound."

"No... she wasn't," I agreed, looking down, not wanting to have this conversation anymore.

"This is why I... could tell there were problems," Kate continued, and I felt her hand on my arm. "Because you turned to someone else."

"There's no justification for what I did, Kate," I said, looking her dead in the eye. "So please, don't try and make me feel better about it."

"Okay, point made. But in the end, there's no need to be a martyr over it either. That's why I'm glad you've decided to redo the house. It's time to move on."

But she didn't understand, and I didn't want to explain it to her.

With a heavy sigh, I dumped the remaining ice cream down the drain and continued my task of finishing my home.

"So, we have the copies of Talia's physical," Rebecca said as we kicked back in the office later that evening. "And they noted that there were no illegal drugs found in her system."

"She didn't take illegal drugs," I said, rolling my eyes as I set the paper aside. "See, this is why I wanted to handle this, go over everything before. But they jumped the gun."

"And we're getting everything taken care of now. So you're saying she abuses prescription drugs?"

"I don't know," I said, throwing my hands up. "I... well, she did, at one time. That's what I was trying to see. If she was doing it again."

"And you obviously didn't get your answer."

"No, I didn't. I mean, I called someone, but they never got back with me. I just..." I took a deep shuddering breath. "I'm afraid to even bring it up, Rebecca. What will happen if I do?"

"Tell you what." She kicked her converse off and sat cross legged in her chair. "You pay really close attention to her on Wednesday, and get back with me, okay?"

"Yeah... okay."

"Do you think she would agree to shared custody? Stating that she's the primary caregiver, of course, so that the children go to school in her district."

"I... I don't know," I stammered. "What would that mean?"

"More time, of course," she replied with a smile.

"But with Elizabeth in school, I just... I don't want to push it."

"Stop being such a chicken. Here." She pulled a six pack out of her oversized bag she was carrying. "Have one, help yourself grow a pair."

"Fuck off," I said with a short laugh, but accepting her offer and taking a cold beer from the package. "This should go over well with Kate."

"Why do you say that?" Rebecca asked.

"Oh, she's coming over for movie night later. Kind of a... thing we do." I sighed as my mind once again went back to Talli. "Does everything have to be in black and white? My schedule can get pretty dicey. Can't I just ask if I can call and just... you know, see them?"

"You don't want to ask for joint custody, but you want to just... call and ask if you can see them whenever the hell you want?" Rebecca asked, her eyebrow raised.

"Yeah, I know." I pouted slightly. "I just want what we'd originally agreed to. With, you know... some leeway with my schedule."

"I'd say that was fair. Did your visitation go well today?" she asked.

"Yeah, as well as it can. She had to work, so…" I ended with another shrug.

"She won't have to work all the time; you will have to learn to get past this, get to civility."

"I can be perfectly civil," I said, taking a long drink of beer.

"When you don't have your pouty face on, I'm sure you can. So she's feeling better, then?"

"What do you mean?"

"That day, the first visitation, the one I was at. She looked like death warmed over. I mean, she looked better at court, but… what?"

"What, what?"

"What's that look for, the one that says 'I've seen a ghost'?"

"I just…" I bit the inside of my bottom lip, wondering what the hell was taking so long to get my answer. I had made the call weeks ago and was promised they'd get back with me. Still… nothing.

"Anyhow, I think we've done everything we can here." She left my notes on my desk, returning the rest to her briefcase. "Go over that, and make sure you are in a decent mood when you walk in there on Wednesday, got it?"

"Got it," I muttered. "So… you're leaving?"

"Yeah, I'm meeting my husband at a friend's not far from here. Say hello to Kate for me, will you?"

"Of course," I agreed, looking down at my buzzing phone.

It was about damn time.

"I need to take this."

"That's fine; I can show myself out," she said with a wave, finishing her beer as she walked out of the room.

I hit the answer button, putting the phone up to my ear. "Talk to me."

"She's clean."

"And you're sure about this?"

"I'd know better than anyone else, Jase. That's why you called me."

"And it took long enough for you to call me back."

"I wanted to be sure. And believe me, I'm sure. There's something wrong, but hell that could always be chalked up to you breaking her heart."

"I didn't ask for…"

"I know you didn't; I'm just stating the obvious. But she's clean. I'd stake my life on it."

I contemplated the words for a moment, my nerves calming ever so slightly. "Okay. Okay. Thanks for letting me know."

"One more thing, Warner."

"What's that?" I asked, rolling my eyes.

"Don't be a fool… or, any more of a fool than you've already been."

"Don't even…"

"Trust me on this, okay? Look how long it took me."

I sighed, not really wanting to have this conversation either, which seemed to be the story of my life. "Thanks for letting me know, Keith," was all I said.

"Anytime. I owed her anyway."

I nodded, even though he couldn't see, shoving the phone back in my pocket when the call had ended.

"Everything okay?" Kate asked as she walked in carrying a box of microwave popcorn, and I smiled tightly.

"A little," I replied, releasing a pent-up breath as I left my office and followed her down the hall.

"Ready for movie night?" she asked.

"Oh God yes." I reached out, taking her hand. "More than you know."

CHAPTER 23

TALIA

I once thought that having a birthday party outside of the home made for less stress. Holy hell was I ever wrong. Then again, the party was going to be split between the bowling alley and here, so I still had to make sure that the cake was picked up and the pizzas ordered, to be delivered at the right time. I had the presents wrapped and sitting on the counter, and Michael had decided he wanted it left there, to go with other presents that people would bring.

It wasn't the presents he was excited about.

"Did he call, Mommy?"

I bit my bottom lip as my heart constricted in my chest. "No, Little Man, he hasn't." But I hadn't asked Jase to call; I'd merely asked him to come to the party.

"Daddy will be there," Elizabeth said, so sure of herself. "That Schwartz lady won't be there, will she?"

"No, she will not," I replied with a slight shudder that I hoped the children didn't see.

"Then he won't be there!" Michael whined, his bottom lip quivering.

"Hey... hey..." I knelt beside Michael, lightly brushing away the two large tears that had spilled over, dripping down his cheeks. "We invited him, okay? He'll..." I took a deep breath, hoping against all hope that I was right. "He'll be there."

"Are you sure?"

No. No I'm not sure. Not at all, and it's killing me to see what it's doing to you.

"I didn't give him... that... imbatation..."

"Invitation. And I mailed it, Little Man. I promise."

"But what if he didn't get it?" He looked so earnest, so frightened.

There was only one thing I could do.

"Here," I said, pulling out my cell phone. In lieu of his home number, which I still didn't have, I dialed his cell number, waiting for it to ring before handing it to Michael.

Well, fuck.

Straight to voicemail. At 10 a.m. on a Sunday morning. No, not just any Sunday morning. The Sunday of our son's birthday party.

"It's going to voicemail," I said softly, holding the phone out. "Do you want to leave a message?"

He smiled, taking the phone from my hand. "I'll wait for da beep," he said, holding his hand out as if he thought I'd take the phone away.

"It's okay," I said, standing up and continuing to get everything ready. I wanted to give Michael his space, not make him feel as if I was hovering, trying to listen in.

Please tell me this is just a fluke. Tell me you won't let our son down.

"Mommy, you can't wear that," Elizabeth scolded as she passed by. I looked down at my khaki colored tailored dress pants and soft blue button-down shirt, then back at my precocious five-year-old.

"What is wrong with this?"

"Mommy, *puh-lease.*" She had one hand on her hip, practically turning her nose up.

"It's not black, gray, or brown. You should be happy."

"Blue jeans. Go. Now." She pointed to the bedroom as my jaw went slack.

Seriously?

"Young lady..."

"And a cute shirt. A sassy shirt, even if it's black."

"There is nothing wrong with my clothes."

"Not for work, but this isn't work." She took my hand and led me to my bedroom. "What would you do without me?"

"Apparently without you I'd be comfortable at the bowling alley. And that shirt?" She stood on tiptoe and pulled out a cute emerald green top, one that hugged across my breasts then billowed down to my waistline, not too tight, not too loose.

"Yes, this shirt. You can bowl in this."

"I can bowl in the shirt I have on."

"Are you arguing with me Mommy?"

I put my hand up to my mouth, stifling a giggle. It was no wonder she spent a good half hour choosing her outfit every morning, for daycare no less.

"You need to look more pretty than normal."

"Why would I... oh, thank you, Baby Girl." I glowed, smiling down as she laid the outfit down on my bed.

"You're welcome," she grinned back at me. "And you need to look more pretty for Daddy."

My smile immediately fell.

"Elizabeth... baby... I think,"

"Please, Mommy?" Her big blue eyes were filled with hope as she stared up at me. She grinned sheepishly then, biting her bottom lip, looking like a small, soft, feminine version of Jase, and it made my heart hurt.

"Baby Girl, I'm... I'm not trying to be mean, or to hurt your feelings. It's just... your Dad and I..."

"Love each other," she finished for me.

"No! Um... I mean *yes*, but... but no."

"Yes but *yes*, Mommy. And I'll get you more shoes and a purse."

"They're both by the door."

"No, silly, you need different ones. Ones that will go with this outfit. Oooo!" She pulled my Doc Martens out of my closet. Hello blast from the past. "Wear these!"

"Didn't I give those away?" I asked to no one, just out loud.

"Obviously not, duh." She put them next to the jeans and the top, then nodded.

"Okay, fine," I caved, throwing my hands up. "Go, make sure your sister isn't destroying anything. And tell your brother to stay out of the presents! They're for after bowling."

I don't know how, I don't know why, but for some reason it just... fit. That top with those jeans... I never would have done it, but little miss thing had made up her mind. And it worked.

Damn.

My five-year-old was a genius.

"Don't say it," I said with a teasing glare in her direction when I stepped out, surprised that the Doc Martens still fit as well as they had all those years ago.

"Just let me find you a purse, 'kay?" She ran back to my room as I finished throwing a few odds and ends in Emily's diaper bag. I glanced around, trying to ensure that I hadn't missed a thing, spotting Michael sitting on the couch, a firm pout on his face.

Please Jase... please don't do this to him. Not today.

Eleven thirty sharp was when I glanced at my watch. It was officially the time that I'd put on the invitations. It was the time that Paul and his kids made it by. It was the time that Jaden and Pete arrived, coming straight from the airport. It was the time Emily toddled up to Paul, merely staring instead of screaming.

It was the time I started cursing Jason Michael Warner.

"You okay?" Jaden asked as I wrapped my arms around her as best I could.

"I'm wonderful," I lied. "I should be asking you."

"I can't see my feet," she said as she stepped back. "I have no ankles, my boobs are leaking, I have feet in my ribs at all times, and heartburn 24/7. I couldn't be happier."

And I believed her.

She was absolutely glowing, so very happy with her pregnancy, her life with Pete. I held her hands in mine, smiling at my best friend. "Motherhood agrees with you, my Italian gypsy."

She threw her head back in laughter, pulling me close once more. "I'm not there yet. I may really suck at this."

"Puh-lease," I said, channeling my oldest daughter. "You'll be wonderful. Trust me. Okay?"

"If you say so." She stepped back, still smiling. "I'm thinking cheese fries. Cheese fries?" she called out to the kids, who all agreed, including Emily who smiled and clapped along with everyone else.

"We're having pizza back at the condo."

"This little one isn't going to wait for pizza," she said with a wave of her hand, taking her wallet out of her purse and waddling towards the snack counter. "Oh, hi Paul." She waved at him as he walked over to me, then she concentrated on getting up to the counter to place her order.

"She looks cute," Paul commented, standing beside me and looking over at Jaden.

"She looks beautiful," I said, smiling so fully. "Thank you for coming, by the way. And bringing the kids. They're the only other children he asked to have here."

"Really?" he asked, acting surprised.

"Yeah. He's very shy; don't let his wit or charm fool you."

"I'll try to remember that. He seems really pleased that Pete's here."

I smiled over at Pete, who was holding Michael upside down while he squealed with delight and the other kids all clamored to be next. "He is. He adores him."

"And... um... well, the elephant in the room."

"The elephant obviously isn't here," I said flatly, my eyebrow raising.

"Have you heard from him?"

I didn't answer, my eyebrow still firmly high on my forehead, my annoyance palpable.

"Well, hello there, dearest sweetest sister-in-law of mine!" Pete said as he finally made his way over, scooping me up in his arms.

"Um... Pete..."

"You look incredible! Just, absolutely... wow..." He squeezed just a little harder, my feet now completely off the ground.

"Pete..."

"My brother's an idiot, you know?" he said softly, to where only I could hear him, but that was the least of my worries.

"Pete... oxygen... becoming an issue."

"Damn, I'm sorry." He set me down, patting my head slightly, smashing my sunglasses firmly into my scalp.

"Are you trying to kill me today?" I asked with a giggle.

"I don't think the wife would forgive me. Speaking of the wife... Babe! Another cheese fry!" he called out to her.

I smiled wistfully, remembering the time that this was Jase and me. Hell, I always thought that we had a better chance; we'd had a very concrete relationship for much longer than Pete and Jaden had. But apparently the concrete crumbled, and all the pieces scattered about, the dust still lingering in the air as it settled in ruins at our feet.

"I'm happy they let you two come out here," I said suddenly, trying to take my mind elsewhere.

"So am I, although we've been told this is the last time until he gets here."

"Do you have a name picked out yet?"

"Um... no." He grinned and shrugged. "I'd like to see him first."

Paul excused himself, perhaps feeling a bit left out, but he busied himself with helping the kids with their bowling shoes. Minus Emily, that is, as she walked up to me, holding her arms up. I picked her up, placing her on my hip where she held on to my shirt, eyeballing Pete.

"Wow, she's getting big," he said, reaching over and touching her hand that she instantly pulled away.

"I don't know how well she's going to do today. She's not fond of strangers, or crowds."

"How are you?" he asked suddenly. "And don't lie."

"Right now?" I asked, and he shot me that look that asked if I'd seriously just said that. "I'm pissed. He's late, his cell is going to voicemail, and our son is counting on him."

"Did you call his home phone?"

I sighed, feeling myself grow about ten shades of red. "I don't have it," I admitted, cursing the tears that threatened, not comprehending how something so simple would hurt me.

"Oh," Pete said, blinking a few times. "Well, I'll...I'll call him, okay?"

I nodded, my embarrassment keeping me from saying anything. As if she sensed I needed a break from the tension, Emily took a deep breath, blowing a raspberry right at Pete, who got quite the kick out of it.

"You tell him," he said, and she promptly did it again. "I'm gonna go make that call, okay?"

"Okay. And thank you."

"He's only about ten minutes from here, right?" he asked, and I nodded. "So no excuses."

"Hey, hot stuff! Cheese fries!" Jaden's voice floated across the room as she gathered her provisions from the snack bar.

"Gimme a minute," Pete replied.

"I wasn't talking to you, dork. Talli... cheese fries, front and center."

"No thank..."

"Now!" she cut me off.

"I wouldn't argue with her if I were you," Pete said to me.

"Okay, okay. Fine. I'll have one," I said as I started walking towards the table Jaden had set the treasured fries on that all of the children began to attack with vigor. I paused for only a moment to take a glance back at Pete, who was walking outside with his cell phone up to his ear.

Please let this work...please, if not another wish is granted... Jase, please don't let our son down.

JASE

For some unfathomable reason, I jolted awake about 10:00 in the morning on Sunday. There were no phones ringing, no kids running around, no doorbell to wake me from my slumber. I was simply lying there on the foldout couch in the office wondering what the hell I was forgetting. I had no appointments, nothing pressing, just a nagging, sinking feeling.

Must have been the beer.

The beer I'd consumed in the media room and accidentally spilt on my cell phone, frying the thing. Just what I needed, one more object to replace. At least I'd uploaded all of my pictures, completely on a whim. Talli had told me once that everything happened for a reason...

Talli.

I'd be seeing her on Wednesday.

Maybe that's what my mood, the anxiety I was feeling, was all about.

There was no sense in lying around thinking about it all damn day. I'd already spent a few hours the night before thinking about it, talking about it, obsessing over it. Over her. Hell, I know it got on Kate's nerves; she told me so. She also told me if I didn't quit talking about Talli, she was going to call her and just let her listen, or force me to call her and tell her myself.

I almost did.

I was only partially bluffing when I picked my cell phone up, scrolling through until I found her number, my thumb hovering over that call button.

But I set it down.

And then I spilled my beer.

It was a sign; I was sure of it.

I stared at the phone sitting on my desk, sighing heavily. No time to dwell today.

Besides, I had a room to finish.

There was much less to do than I had originally thought. The furniture had already been exchanged, the new stuff for the most part in its place. I wondered for a brief moment if I'd bought too much; it was just me now, no need for extras, right? But I'd seen it, and I knew it would help... somehow, it would help me.

I knew it needed done, this room above all others, but that didn't make it any less bittersweet. This room had seen its fair share of happiness, see. It had seen laughter, and triumph, and joy. We had shared so much here, and in one night I threw all of it away.

I understand why she left.

I can accept that now. I don't like it, but I can accept it. Now, I just have to get through until that horrid date in November and all will be well.

But with this house... it was time to start fresh. When the bad memories—the bitter part, if you will—outweighs the good, when there's no way to reverse it, it's time to move on.

With one last glance across the room, newly decorated in its muted blues, I knew I'd made the right decision.

I only hope it's enough.

It was nearly 11:30 when I finally got in the shower, washing the sweat and grime down the drain. I figured the cell phone place had to be open by then—I could take my shower, grab a new cell phone, maybe grab some take out, kick back...

And call her.

And apologize for being such a dick, and for telling her to not call me.

Because this house and its belongings wasn't the only thing that needed an overhaul, needed fixed, needed to be patched up in some way to make life bearable once more.

I don't know what it was that had a grip on me, where all of this nervous energy was suddenly coming from. Was it because my house was done? I wasn't sure. Whatever the case, whatever the reason, I needed to capitalize on it. First things first, though.

Clothes.

I kinda couldn't leave the house naked.

A light flannel shirt with its sleeves rolled up, a pair of blue jeans, and my Converse sneakers were the outfit of the day. I didn't much feel like doing jack shit to my hair, so I grabbed a ball cap and shoved it on my head. One dead cell phone in my hand, and I was ready to go out the door.

"Holy shit, Pete!" I exclaimed as I swung the front door open, startled to see my little brother standing there, arm poised, ready to knock.

"So you opted for fashionably late, or just to not show up at all?" he asked, obviously highly pissed at me.

"Um, hi. Nice to see you, too. And... what?"

"Man, don't play that fucking game, okay?" He pushed his way past me into the house, a pulsating vein prominent in his temple.

"Come on in," I said, my voice dripping with a bit of sarcasm. I followed him into the front room, and as I attempted to shove my dead phone into my pocket, it dropped to the carpet, bouncing once before sliding under a chair. I rolled my eyes at not only that, but the fact that my brother was there, in my house, absolutely laying into me.

"This just… Jase, this is really fucking low."

"What is, numbnuts?" I asked, crouched down, looking towards where the phone had come to a stop. I reached under the chair, pulling out my phone, a post card, and a small white envelope that had also found their way to this apparent black hole in my house.

"Do you know what today is?" he practically yelled as I sat in that chair, eyeing that white envelope curiously.

"Sunday," I replied slowly, carefully opening the envelope, pulling the colorful card out, a large yellow "3" on the front.

Oh… this… this was…

"She was counting on you, man. Really counting on… you… and… oh, you're fucking kidding me. Under the chair?"

Talli's writing adorned the invitation, two words written out where I could plainly see them.

Please come.

She wanted me there?!

"Man, isn't this fucking typical of your guys' luck, though?"

Sunday… today! At… oh… oh shit… it's already started…

"Come on! Let's go!" Pete exclaimed, tugging at my shirt as he passed by.

"Wait! Wait, I…"

I could get into so much trouble for this. Talli… she knows that. But she wouldn't… I know she wouldn't… and…

"Man, just…"

"I need to get his… his present," I said, my voice wavering slightly as I hurried to the hall closet. I grabbed the wrapped package that had sat there, waiting for him.

And I actually get to give it to him.

Today.

At his birthday party.

"It's at that bowling alley that we whooped your and Jaden's asses in, right?" I asked, pulling my keys out of my pocket.

"Yeah… just ride with me, man."

"No, I think I should drive myself." I grinned slightly and shrugged. "Just in case."

I couldn't believe it. It was a state of disbelief, a fog if you will, as I drove the familiar path to that little bowling alley. In just a few short minutes I would be there, I would show her...show them that I wouldn't always let them down. And...

Oh, come on red light! Seriously! I don't have all morning, you know?

Green. It's green now. And green means go, so... gas pedal.

But I'm not nervous. Not at all. I'm shaky as hell, my palms are a little sweaty, but it's just because I'm in a rush. I don't like being in a rush, and I'm not always the biggest fan of surprises. Some surprises, though... some of them are worth it. Some of them just make that edgy feeling so worth it.

Ah... there it is. Parking lot is not too full. That's a good thing, definitely. Hell, there's a spot right next to... No. No, Warner, don't park next to her van. Park away, way away so it doesn't look like I'm trying to be close. Because I'm not.

I'm not.

Being here is good enough.

No... it's better than good. It's better because...

"Daddy!"

...because I have them.

I dropped to my knees as Elizabeth and Michael ran up, throwing their arms so forcefully around me that I accidentally tipped back, taking them with me. But I laughed... we all laughed, because it felt so good, so right to be there, be with them. I kissed both of their faces repeatedly as I held them to me, as I always did when they ran up to me this way.

"Okay, guys... guys... let me up, okay?" I said, still laughing. I made my way back up to my knees, one arm around each of them.

"You need to shave, Daddy," Elizabeth said, a slight scowl in her features. Ah, my little fashionista.

"I love you too, Baby Girl," I replied, kissing the tip of her nose and making her giggle.

"You're late, Daddy," Michael spoke up, drawing my attention back to him.

"I'm sorry, Little Man. Happy birthday." I kissed the top of his head as I heard the distinctive crinkle of diaper approaching.

My heart skipped a tiny beat as Emily slowly walked up to us, the sweetest most impish grin on that beautiful face of hers. Her curls were coming out of the barrette that was supposed to be keeping her hair out of her face but was failing miserably.

"Well hi there, Princess," I said softly, not wanting to startle her into crying or running away. One chubby hand reached up, touching the brim of my hat tentatively. "Yeah, Daddy's wearing a hat. Hair's kinda rough today."

So what does she do?

She quickly grabs it, yanking it off my head, and begins to run away.

This, of course, makes Michael and Elizabeth giggle and cheer her on, even after I get back to my feet and start chasing her, one hand reaching for her the other trying to make the hair not look as bad as it did.

"Get your little butt back here." I picked her up from behind, her scream and squeals being more from delight and laughter than fright. I tried taking the hat from her hand only to be met with her pouty lip, so I sighed and caved, like I always did. "You're lucky you're so damn cute, you know that?"

She took a deep breath, her eyes growing wide as she did so, and then blew the biggest raspberry she could, spraying my face with her baby spit, causing me to throw back my head in laughter.

Oh, this was perfect.

This would only be more perfect if…

I felt Talli's presence beside me, making the hairs on my arms stand straight up. I glanced down at her, those sherry curls framing her beautiful face, held back by her sunglasses on top of her head. She looked different. Tired, strained, beautiful as always, but different. She reached up, trying to take the cap from Emily's hand, her hand brushing against my arm as she did, sending a shiver down my spine.

"No, it's okay. She can play with it."

Why the hell did I blush after saying that? She's my wife for fuck's sake, why should I feel nervous saying anything?

"She'll chew on it." Talli's words were soft, her eyes averted from me.

"I don't mind," I said with a shrug.

"It's gross," she replied quickly, crinkling her nose up. It was always so damn cute when she did that, and I couldn't help but laugh.

"It's just a cap, Talli."

"It's…" She paused, sighing softly as she looked up at me. "Can we not fight about this, please?"

I blinked a couple times, startled by her words. "I'm not fighting, I'm just…"

"You're late."

Oh. Well, that I could accept her being upset over. "I know that… well, it sounds a bit on the incredible or unbelievable side, but…

"The invitation had slid under a chair," Pete said as he walked up, a plate of cheese fries in his hand. "No lie. I was there. Witness."

I blushed a deep shade of red, the sheer embarrassment of my little brother knowing how little faith Talli had in me keeping me silent. I averted my gaze, grabbing a couple cheese fries to try out instead of having a war with her in the middle of the bowling alley.

"Oh."

I had to keep myself from snorting at her one syllable answer. Just 'Oh.' Great.

"You could have called before this, you know," I said before thinking, wincing at the tone in my voice. "I mean…"

"I… Michael tried. Earlier. It went straight to voicemail."

"Just today?" I said, trying to keep my voice low, level. "You didn't…"

"You told me not to call," she cut me off.

"Okay… children, this is why I came over," Pete said, stepping between us, which for some strange reason caused Emily to giggle. "You," he pointed at Talli, "should have called before today, regardless of what my bonehead brother has said to you in the past. And you," he turned to me, "shouldn't have said it to begin with for one, and should have given her your home number after it changed for two. Neither one of you has any excuse."

"I *did* give…" I stopped as both Talli and Pete glared at me.

Oh, fuck.

I didn't.

"I thought I... or..."

"Or you're used to one of your 'people' doing it for you, whenever our number changed," she said, her eyes just a little shinier, a little sad.

Our number... she said our number...

"Yes, I am," I admitted, my heart hammering in my chest. "And I'm sorry."

Her bottom lip began to quiver, turning my insides to absolute mush, making me want to spill everything to her right there.

I can't handle it when she cries.

Wait... she's... she's... crying?

"Talli," my brother said to her in a warning tone.

"I'm sorry, too," she said, her voice barely above a whisper. I felt my hand twitch slightly as I resisted the urge to reach out to her, pull her into my arms, hold her against me as I dried her tears.

But I couldn't do that.

"Everything okay here?"

That's why.

Paul. The Paul. The doctor who made her laugh and stayed with my kids was standing right beside her in his perfect clothes with his perfect hair smiling... perfectly.

I hated him.

No... I didn't hate him because I didn't know him, and besides, what a pussy reaction. What the fuck is up with me today? This guy is just that... a *guy*. Just because he took my wife out to the theatre and for coffee didn't mean anything. And neither did all the lunches they'd been spotted at, or all the whispers at the hospital that somehow still find their way back to me.

He was just a guy.

"Hey, there, little one," he said, poking at Emily's tummy. She stuck out her bottom lip and turned in to me, holding on just a little tighter.

Take *that*, perfect doctor guy.

"I... I'll be right back," Talli said, her voice still soft as she slipped past me, walking quickly towards the washroom. I knew why she was going there, to hide the tears, fix the makeup afterward. But I'd still be able to tell.

And it would still break my heart.

"Hey, where the hell did my cheese fries go?" I heard Jaden's voice behind me, and I turned to her, grinning broadly.

"Pregzilla!" I exclaimed, throwing my free arm around her and giving her a big sloppy kiss on her cheek. "You look gorgeous!"

"I believe fat, whale-like, swollen, and the whole pregzilla part. The beautiful? Not so much." She stepped back, caressing my cheek as she did. "Look at how she's taken to you again."

"Yeah, she's my girl again. I mean, she's always been my girl, but she is really coming back around." I sighed as I caught a glimpse of Talli out of the corner of my eye, leaving the washroom and walking up to the counter to get the bowling shoes. "She's really…"

"Oh, just go already," Jaden said with a laugh, pushing my shoulder. I grinned sheepishly, still holding Emily on one arm as I walked over to the counter where Talli stood.

"Hey," I said softly, trying to disguise the sharp intake of breath as she turned those blue eyes on me.

"Thank you for coming," she said, her voice just as soft, her eyes locked with mine rendering me speechless. "I knew the risks when I asked… that you wouldn't come, that we would both be in trouble… but it was worth it. I knew the moment he saw you, that they saw you. All…" She paused, smiling at our youngest child, content in my arms. "All of them."

I swallowed over the lump in my throat, trying to grin at her through my threatening tears. "Thank you for inviting me," I managed to say. "You didn't have to, and it… it means more than you know."

The corner of her mouth began to tug upwards in a smile, making the butterflies take off in my stomach, my heart race, my palms sweat. The silence between us as we stood there could have drug on forever and I wouldn't have noticed anything past those eyes, those sweet lips, the soft expression on her face.

Fuck, please… no more… not again…

Oh, who the hell am I kidding?

There's no *again* to it.

I've always loved her.

"Here you go. Size twelve." The gentleman behind the counter broke the spell, placing a pair of bowling shoes up on the counter.

Size… twelve?

I glanced down at them, then back up at Talli, who raised her eyebrows in a challenge.

"You have the bumpers up. That's cheating."

"Um, look again, Warner," she said, pointing down the alley at the two lanes beside the kids' lanes, where Pete was setting up.

"You know, you're a…" I stopped the automatic reply of telling her she was a Warner too, the blush on her cheeks reminding me of my boundaries. I glanced back down the alley, then over at her, smirking. "You think you can take me?"

One of those eyebrows of hers shot up, a smirk of her own on her lips. "I know I can."

"All right then." I stood up, taking the shoes in my free hand. "You're on."

CHAPTER 24

TALIA

Crisis averted. On our way.

Up until I received that text from Pete, I was absolutely seething. Of course, I was sure his excuse would be wonderful. He'd probably start in by saying that he thought I was trying to frame him or some shit like that, but damn it he should know better. He should know…

Well, we should know many things about each other. We keep forgetting, though, don't we?

I was so thankful that Jaden and Paul were there, keeping me sane, making me smile. That's what friends were for, most definitely. Between the two of them and the kids all running around like fools, we were in business. We'd gotten everyone's shoes, sans Jase's since I was still waiting for that text to come saying he'd changed his mind, and the kids were starting their first game on the lanes with the bumpers.

Elizabeth trying to help Michael with his ball made me smile, although a bit wistful, longing for the days when we'd bring the family here. Emily would sit in her little pumpkin seat while Elizabeth and I would play against Jase and Michael—girls against the guys—for a couple of games before we'd set them loose on the bumpers and play each other. Talk about bringing out the competitive edge, for both of us, and coming up with the prize was the best part.

King or Queen for the day.

Dinner and movie of the winner's choice, which normally consisted of torturing the loser with something they hated.

Whatever sexual favor the winner requested, no questions asked.

I shook my head to clear it, knowing I had to keep my resolve face on, no matter what. Today wasn't about us, it wasn't about me. It was Michael's day, and I would do everything in my power to make this day special for him.

I'd do whatever it takes.

"Daddy!"

I turned at that one squealed word, my heart taking off at a thunderous rate at the site of Jase jogging through that door looking so hurried, so concerned, and then so...

Happy.

So very happy.

No baseball cap pulled down would shield the pure joy on his face when he dropped to his knees, arms open wide as our two oldest bounded up to him, this time actually succeeding in knocking him over. I pressed my fingertips to my lips, trying to hide the smile at the scene before me, the laughter floating through the air, the love permeating the entire room. He still managed to get in all the kisses on their faces, hold them to him as he made it back to his knees, his eyes all squinty with his smiles and laughter.

I missed this.

They used to do this to him all the time, any time he would go out on the road. His homecomings would always be so full of joy, and it would set the mood of the entire rest of the day or night. Or it did until...

My heart fell slightly as the last handful of homecomings crossed my mind, how his smile would fade when his eyes would fall on me. He wouldn't want to listen about everything I'd had to do while he was gone, didn't even seem interested in all of the medical problems Emily was having, all he would do was bitch about the fact that I hadn't gone, or that I hadn't taken the kids out.

"Oh... Talli, look," Jaden whispered in my ear, pointing to where Emily was slowly walking up to Jase.

Please don't tweak on him, Princess...

Oh Lord.

I stifled a giggle as she grabbed his hat and ran away, partially over what she'd done and partially because his hair was a hot mess. He must have shoved that thing on his head when his hair was…wait, was it still wet?

Oh my, it was.

Mind out of gutter, Talli. Now.

And he's going to let her keep the cap. Ugh, Jase, really? You know she'll chew on that thing.

Okay, time to intervene.

Deep breaths, it won't kill you to be that close to him.

Oh, he smells so good.

My arm brushed against his when I reached for the hat that was in Emily's hands, and it was as if a jolt of electricity shot straight through my body. It sent a quiver through me, turning my insides to goo and my mind to mush.

Focus, Talli. Get the…

"No, it's okay. She can play with it."

I faltered at the sound of his voice, struggling to keep from trembling at the sheer force of the emotions flooding through my body.

"She'll chew on it," I tried to explain, avoiding looking up at him. Oh, I know what body wash he used today… and the shampoo… and…

"I don't mind," he replied.

Ew, seriously?

"It's gross," I said, instinctively crinkling my nose up. Seriously, Em could soak something in a matter of minutes, making it slimy and disgusting. Besides, this was a cap, for fuck's sake. Did he really want to put this thing back on his head with slimy baby spit on it?

"It's just a cap, Talli."

Jase, please… not today…

"It's…" I sighed, giving in and looking up at him, silently pleading. "Can we not fight about this, please?"

Oh, that was stupid, Talli. Stupid, stupid, *stupid*! He's going to think you're more nuts than other people think you are. Quick. Recover. Think of something more… what's the word? Acceptable?

"I'm not fighting," he said, the look on his face so honest, so open I instantly regretted saying anything derogatory to begin with. "I'm just..."

"You're late," I blurted out before I could stop myself, wanting to crawl into a hole and hide immediately.

He shifted Emily slightly on his hip, and for the first time I realized that she wasn't reaching for me. At all. She was safe, happy, content, and secure in her Daddy's arms, chewing on the bill of his ball cap, and it looked so natural, as if they hadn't spent so much time apart and...

Wait...was he saying something to me?

"The invitation had slid under a chair." Pete was beside us, and the smell of his cheese fries made my tummy want to grumble in hunger. "No lie. I was there. Witness."

Don't giggle, Talli. It isn't funny. It's typical, but not funny.

"Oh," was all I could say.

"You could have called before this, you know."

The tone of his voice brought me back to reality, reminding me that things between us were much different now.

"I mean..."

"I... Michael tried," I recovered as best I could, my heart hurting. "Earlier. It went straight to voicemail."

Why? Why had it done that, when you know that's the only number that I...that they can reach you at?

"Just today? You didn't..."

"You told me not to call," I reminded him, the flash of hurt in his eyes at my words causing tears to threaten just below the surface.

"Okay, children, this is why I came over." Pete stepped between us, and I tried... I really tried to not look at Jase, straight at his face, gauge his expression as Pete continued. "You should have called before today, regardless of what my bonehead brother has said to you in the past."

That must have been for me... must have...fuck, it obviously was. Focus, Talli!

"And you shouldn't have said it to begin with for one," Pete continued, this time obviously speaking to Jase. "And should have given your home number after it changed, for two. Neither one of you has any excuse."

"I *did* give..."

Jase stopped as I glared at him.

"I thought I... or..."

"Or you're used to one of your 'people' doing it for you, whenever our number changed," I said, my eyes filling with tears. It was as if I'd always been an afterthought; someone else would make sure I was informed, someone else would take care of giving me the details. Only on rare occasions did he ever offer up things of this nature to me, and normally it was only after I'd asked. Did he not think that would hurt?

"Yes, I am," he said, his eyes locked with mine. "And I'm sorry."

Oh...

Oh, fuck.

Did he not know what those two little words falling from his lips would do to me? And why... why is it that he could tell me he was sorry over a phone number, sorry over being late, sorry over something so trivial, but not once... *never* once did he truly say that he was sorry over Bree, over his affair with her.

I felt my lower lip begin to tremble, thinking over everything I was sorry for—for not making it out to him, for not speaking with him when I should have, for not fighting for him, for...

"Talli." Pete used his threatening tone that I could easily brush off, but not today.

Not today.

"I'm sorry, too," I choked out.

And I was.

For more than he could possibly know.

That hadn't gone well. That just... hadn't gone well at all.

I stood in the washroom, dabbing around my eyes with the little applicator from my compact, fixing where my makeup had begun to run. I fucking hate crying, and I hate even more that he can do it to me so easily.

But damn it, today isn't about me.

Or us.

It's about Michael, and the girls. They're so happy to see him.

Taking a deep breath, I stepped out of the washroom, walking past where Jase was talking with Jaden, my eye on the counter where I'd gotten the bowling shoes from. I should have gotten his to begin with; I know I should have, but I'd tried convincing myself that he wasn't coming. I should have known better, not just about that but about a lot of things.

"Size twelve, please," I said softly.

"Other member of your party made it?" the attendant asked, and I smiled.

"Yeah, he did."

"Size twelve, coming right up," he said with a wink, walking back through the rows of bowling shoes.

"Hey."

Every nerve ending was on fire at the sound of his voice, and I turned my eyes to him. It was time I said what I should have when he first walked in.

"Thank you for coming," I began, trying to keep my voice steady but it was so hard with those beautiful eyes shining so brightly as he looked at me.

Focus, Talli. Focus.

"I knew the risks when I asked," I continued, "that you wouldn't come... that we would both be in trouble... but it was worth it. I knew the moment he saw you, that they saw you. All..." I smiled at Emily, who had reached up and started playing with the ends of Jase's hair. What a lucky girl. "All of them," I finished, my eyes locked with his once more.

His eyes were shining, that boyish charm peeking through as he leaned in, our daughter still playing with the edges of his hair.

There he was...

"Thank you for inviting me," he said, his voice as smooth as silk. "It means more than you know."

...the boy I fell in love with.

The one with the kaleidoscope eyes, the heart on his sleeve.

Oh, how I'd missed him.

I felt a smile tug at my lips as we stood there in silence, pardon the Debbie Gibson pun but I was completely lost in his eyes. I could have stayed there forever, wishing he could read my mind, see into my heart, know how much I wished things were different between us.

"Here you go. Size twelve."

Guess we'll just have to settle for something else.

I raised my eyebrows, silently challenging him.

"You have bumpers up," he said, reading my mind as he used to be able to do so easily. "That's cheating."

"Um, look again, Warner," I replied, pointing down towards the other two lanes, where Pete was setting up.

"You know, you're a…"

Oh… oh, don't say it. Please don't say it, don't have me break down right here, right now.

He smirked at me then, that bad boy thinks he's Billy Bad Ass smirk, and I felt my knees go weak. "You think you can take me?" he asked.

Ohhhh hell…

I raised my eyebrow, thinking of all the ways I could take him, he just didn't even know. I shot back a smirk of my own and said, "I know I can."

"All right then," he said, pushing himself off the counter, standing straight up and taking those shoes in his free hand. "You're on."

Am I really?

Turns out the answer to that was a profound… yes.

"You… can't start dat one yet, we play together, 'member?" Michael asked as we walked up to the lanes that us adults were going to play at.

"We'll play together, easy there, okay?" Jase stepped in with ease, as if he hadn't missed any time at all. "You all continue your game there, and we'll start ours and…"

"You and Mommy will be all about winning and not play with us," Elizabeth said, raising her eyebrow and I had to stifle a giggle.

"We'll play with you, promise," I said. "Michael, take those cheese fries back up to that table, Elizabeth, get the pout of your face, and…"

She began to giggle and I raised my eyebrow, still looking at Elizabeth.

"He's making faces behind me isn't he?" I asked. She collapsed in a fit of giggles and I quickly glanced over my shoulder at Jase, who was mouthing the word 'no' to our oldest daughter. "Classy."

"Always." He grinned, attempting to put Emily down, but she clung to him like glue.

"Good luck with your game there," I said, turning to Jaden and winking before remembering that one, Jase and I weren't a couple anymore and two, Jaden couldn't play today. Hmmmm...

"So you think you and Pregzilla..."

"Oh, no. Jase, have you met Paul?"

He looked up, his eyes clouding over for a brief moment, turning to a smoldering gray as he reached his hand out. "It's nice to meet you," he said, his words clipped, but he quickly grinned as he shook Paul's hand.

"It's good to meet you too, Jase," Paul said in return, shaking Jase's hand briefly.

"Have I mentioned that Paul is on the top hospital bowling team?" I asked, batting my eyelashes.

"Ah, now Spunky, that's not fair," Pete piped up.

"No...no, it's okay," Jase said, patting his brother's shoulder. "See, because Paul's team isn't here to back him up. He's stuck with Talli."

"Hey...fu...scr..."

His eyebrows shot up in amusement at my attempts to censor myself.

"Oh, shut up," I finally said, turning and picking out my bowling ball.

"Careful there, Paul," Jase spoke up as Paul stepped up beside me. "Her ball handling is suspect at best."

"Oh, you think you're so damn funny," I muttered at the brothers, who were giggling like a couple school girl bitches on the bench. "Coming from someone who has trouble handling his balls whenever Em's around. Say, who is that attached to you today?"

"Ohhhhh, oh, is that where you're going?" he asked, still laughing as he tied his shoes. "That's cute, Spunky. Cute. When I beat your... when I beat you, you'll be singing a whole different tune."

"Keep telling yourself that, Warner," I singsong back, looking over at Paul who was laughing softly at us. "What?"

"Oh, nothing...nothing." He winked, picking his bowling ball and placing it with the others.

"What's da bet?" Michael asked, walking over and grinning up at us.

"Bet? What bet?" Paul asked, glancing up at me.

"Um... uh..."

"No, don't sweat it," Jase cut me off, then he turned to Paul. "I don't want to put her on the spot like that, have her lose so badly, make you pay the price too…"

"Oh, give me a fu…"

"Mommy," Elizabeth called over.

"A break," I corrected myself. "A break. Puh-lease, Warner, we can smoke the two of you." I turned to Paul, speaking quietly, "We can smoke them, right?"

"I… uh… I guess," he replied, his voice barely above a whisper.

"Give you a break?!" Jase scoffed, shaking his head as he once again attempted to set Emily down, picking her back up when she began to whine. "Tell you what, sweetheart…"

"Sweetheart?"

"In honor of the fact that I know I'm going to win…" He stepped a little closer, raising an eyebrow as his eyes raked over me, sending a shiver down to my soul. "Then you can choose."

"Me." It was more a statement than a question as I looked at him. He bit his bottom lip, looking down and then back up at me. Great. Now I need a change of panties.

"Yeah," he said softly. "You."

"Do it, Mommy! Do it!" Michael said excitedly, jumping up and down.

"Do… what?" Jase asked.

But, see… I knew exactly what Michael was talking about.

I licked my lips slightly, my eyes raking over Jase, pausing for just a moment to make sure…yep. He was wearing them. Good thing, too.

"When we win," I said, crossing my arms in front of me, "then you two boys…"

"Boys," Pete scoffed quietly.

"…will strip down to your boxer briefs…"

Jase's eyebrows raised, a smirk of his own on his face.

"…stand in the middle of this bowling alley…"

"And get arrested for indecent exposure?" Jaden quipped from behind me.

"…and sing *The Itsy Bitsy Spider*, hand movements and all."

Michael jumped up and down cheering, laughing hysterically since he was the one who'd come up with the bet eons ago. Actually, laughter was erupting all around us, including from Pete even though he was saying it was "so wrong". Jase and I, however, stood toe to toe, eyeing each other up and down, sizing each other up.

"Fair enough," he said, which of course caused everyone around us to cheer, and Paul promise to do his absolute best to help.

"Think you can handle it, Warner?"

"Oh, we're not through here," he said, stepping in close, his face so near I could feel his breath on my cheek as he spoke low, evenly, his eyes showing every raw emotion pent up within him.

God help me...

"When I win," he breathed, "I get five minutes... alone... with you."

Fuck. Me.

I know, I know...he wants to talk. We need to talk. And in the meantime, he really needs to not look at me like...

Composure, Talli. Composure.

"You're on," I said, smirking as I turned from him, my body betraying me, willing me to lose on purpose.

But I'd never do that.

"Daddy's gonna get naked!" Elizabeth giggled loud enough for couples a few lanes down to hear.

"Not in this bowling alley I'm not," he called back.

"Keep telling yourself that, Warner," I said, preparing as Paul picked up his ball and expertly threw it down the lane.

Steeee-rike one.

I grinned over at Jase as all of the children cheered beside us, their bumper lanes forgotten. He raised his eyebrow, returning my grin with a smirk before reciprocating with a strike of his own.

Oh yeah.

Game on.

JASE

"It shouldn't be this hard."

*She did **not** just say that.*

I stood up from my stance, absentmindedly pulling my shirt down in front of me, glancing over to my left where Talia stood. She was holding her bowling ball, smirking at me.

Sweetheart, you have no idea…

"I'm just saying," she added with an innocent shrug.

Now, I'm not stupid; I know she was talking about the game and not about what I was going to great lengths to try and hide from her. No pun intended.

But this game was going to be the death of me.

We were pretty much neck and neck, and while I wouldn't bat an eyelash to her dare, damn it I wanted that five minutes.

Alone.

It could accomplish so much.

But right now, I had to accomplish knocking down two pins, on opposite sides no less.

"It's called a split…"

"I know what it's called, Talia," I interrupted her.

"Oh come on, Warner. Just accept defeat."

I looked over at her once more, watching her expression change as she saw mine. "Not on your life," I replied, my voice low. As a blush crept across her cheeks, I rolled my ball down the lane, holding my breath until both pins fell.

Ha.

One step closer.

I smirked at Talli, silently challenging her to beat that. She shook her head slightly, rolled her ball down the lane, and…

"It's called a split," I said to her after the eight pins in the middle fell.

"I know what it's called, Jase," she replied with a roll of her eyes. Hell, maybe I should just let her win and strip to my boxer briefs in front of her, let her see exactly what being this close to her was doing to me…

"Oh, Daddy, you must be 'sausted," Michael said as he plopped down beside me on the bench.

"Oh, yeah. It's…" I tried to hide my smile as Talli only knocked down one of her pins in her second attempt. "It's very tiring."

"Come up here and get something to drink, Daddy," Elizabeth called out to me.

"On my way, Baby Girl," I said, picking up Emily as I headed up to get a drink, Michael right on my heels.

"It's Dr. Pepper, like you like." Elizabeth beamed with pride as she handed the cup to me.

"Get a move on, Jase. You're up."

"Already?" I asked, looking up at the score board. Pete had rolled a strike and followed up with nine more pins. I could have kissed him. I sat Emily in Jaden's lap, where she attacked the last batch of cheese fries with pure gusto.

"This is it," Pete muttered to me as I walked up to retrieve my bowling ball. "And if I have to drop my drawers because of you..."

"Don't sweat it, Pete." I grinned tightly as Paul picked up his bowling ball as well. "I'm gonna get those five minutes."

"Five minutes?" Paul asked.

"Yeah, that's what he's playing for," Pete said, gesturing towards me. "Five minutes with Talli, alone."

"To talk, numbnuts," I added, walking up to the lane.

Calm, cool, collected. You can do this, Warner.

"Did you suddenly forget how to..."

Talli's comment dwindled down to nothing as I looked over my shoulder at her, my jaw set. Her eyes clouded over for a moment before she mouthed the words, "It's just a game."

I shook my head slightly, mouthing back, "Not to me."

She sank back in her seat, her arms crossed in front of her, her eyes troubled for a brief moment before Emily climbed on her lap. Being the pro that she was, Talli changed her expression immediately, and I just didn't know whether to laugh or cry.

It's just a game?

Is that what she really thinks?

I turned back towards my lane, rolling a strike without batting another eyelash.

Who am I kidding? Of course she thinks it's a game with her little Prince Charming doctor boy bowling his near-perfect game, flaunting his perfect life in front of my kids. Damn it, Talli, he could never love you like I do.

I rolled my ball down that lane once more, the clicks of shutters not even registering in my brain.

Another strike.

See that, Paul? Are you taking notes?

A collective gasp rippled through the small crowd that had gathered, and I glanced over to my left where a ball was traveling down the gutter. Dr. Paul Coffman stood next to me, a sheepish grin on his face, shrugging.

"Oops," was all he said.

"You threw the game?" Talia asked incredulously. "You threw the game?"

"He just couldn't handle seeing us Adonis boys in our boxer briefs," Pete said with a laugh over Elizabeth and Michael, who were both cheering that we had won.

Regardless of how it was done, we had won.

Talia's expression was unreadable as she looked at me, biting her bottom lip, almost looking as if she regretted accepting my end of the dare.

Congratulations, babe. You just broke my heart a little more.

"Don't mean to burst your bubble," Paul said, reaching down and pulling his bowling shoes off, "but we've got company. And it looks like a lot of it."

Oh you have *got* to be kidding me... paparazzi at my son's birthday party? I rolled my eyes, pulling my bowling shoes off at the table, reaching for my Converse. "Need some help?" I asked Talli, who was putting on her... her... Doc Martens.

Wow.

Talk about a blast from the past.

"Elizabeth can change her own... Em! Get back here!" Emily had taken off with my hat again, running towards a table that was full of people attempting to look innocent as they snapped pictures.

"Okay, that's enough," I said, running up behind Em and scooping her up into my arms. I wasn't aiming my words towards her; they were all aimed at those assholes who just didn't know when to quit.

"I got her," Jaden said, taking Emily from me so that I could finish with my last shoe. One glance over at Talia showed that she was visibly shaken, and I suddenly realized why.

The both of us were about to get in a shitload of trouble.

"I... I can tell them that I just..."

"No," she disagreed, shaking her head as she finished tying her last shoe. "No, I asked you to be here, I'm not going to let you take the fall."

"Talli, I..."

She pulled her hand back when I reached for her, and I felt my heart sink to my feet. Gone was the playful girl who had challenged me just a short while ago, gone was the sassy girl who had teased me incessantly, leaving the girl who could care less in her place.

"Let's just go," she said, picking up her purse, reaching out her hand for one of the children to grab, which Michael quickly did.

"Just keep your eyes straight forward and don't engage in any conversation with them," Paul said softly.

"I think she knows the drill," I reminded him, my words clipped.

"Jase, not now, please."

My anger faded as I looked into her eyes, the sheer panic in there setting off alarms in my head. Without another thought, I took her hand in mine, pulling her up with me. Elizabeth grabbed Michael's free hand, and I took Emily from Jaden without even breaking stride, the five of us quickly making our way out the door. There were even more photographers outside, shouting names, not giving a damn when Emily began to cry.

"Fuck," I muttered under my breath.

There were two cars pulled in haphazardly, blocking Talia's van.

I felt her hand began to tremble in mine, and I said as low as I could, "I still have the car seats in, just stick close to me."

I heard her inhale sharply as we kept walking, Michael asking if we were there yet, and Elizabeth yelling at someone to get out of her way. What the hell was wrong with these people?

I briefly released Talia's hand as I reached in my pocket for my keys, thankful that I'd stuck to my gut instinct and driven myself, otherwise we would have been screwed. Elizabeth climbed to the back, buckling her belts expertly without a problem. Talia's hands were still shaking as she attempted to help Michael, and I reached over, gently placing my hand over hers.

"I've got this, Talli. Just get in."

I saw the hesitation in her actions, in her face, I knew she was questioning whether or not she should. But I was the only one parked in this area, the rest of the party guests were over by the door, the paparazzi hounding them as they exited the bowling alley.

"Talli…"

She turned her face away, moving past to get into the front passenger seat, the nostalgia over seeing her sitting there nearly overwhelming me.

But there was no time for nostalgia.

Not with…

"Jase! Jase! Are the two of you reconciling?"

"Talia, have you forgiven him for his affair?"

"Jase, what does Bree think of you being here today with Talli?"

I rolled my eyes, scowling as I slid into the driver's seat, slamming the door to the noise. The engine roared to life, and of all the damn songs to be on that stupid fucking radio, they just had to be playing *Hard to Believe*. I reached over, hitting the button to turn the radio off.

"Sorry 'bout that," I said with a grin, trying to break the tension before putting the car in drive, thankful once more that I'd parked where I did. We had a clear shot, right out of that lot, and I was able to turn right rather quickly, heading straight towards her building.

"My present!" Michael exclaimed from the back seat.

"Yeah, it's down on the floorboard," I said, glancing in the rearview mirror, his face barely visible. "I'll get it to you when I get you…" I hesitated, not wanted to say the word 'home'.

"We didn't get to play, Daddy," Elizabeth pouted.

"We will, Baby Girl," I said to her as convincingly as I could. "I promise."

"I have a bowling game, 'member Daddy?" Michael said quickly, excitedly.

Little Man… I can't push it… not today… no matter how much I wish…

"And Mommy owes you five minutes," Elizabeth added, and I felt my heart skip a tiny beat. "She told Aunt Jaden. And I heard."

I took a chance, glancing briefly over at Talli, who was staring at my… hands?

Whoa. Way to make me feel self-conscious there.

Oh...

Crap.

The ring. I'm still wearing it.

I can't take it off... I just can't...

Not yet.

I moved my left hand slightly, where it wouldn't be seen so easily, chancing another look at Talli, not liking what I saw.

"Are you feeling okay?" I asked.

"Hmm?" She looked up at me, her skin noticeably paler. "Yeah, I'm fine... I'm fine."

I scowled slightly, concentrating on the drive back to her building, knowing that she was lying.

"Are they following?"

I looked in the review mirror, not seeing anything out of the ordinary. "I don't think so."

"Good." She settled down in her seat, taking a deep breath and closing her eyes.

Ah. A panic attack. I knew she wouldn't want to say anything about it in front of the children, so I dropped the subject, instead asking, "Do you have a way to get your v...car?" I grinned as she shot me her 'the word van is not in my vocabulary' look, seeing her facial features relax slightly through my peripheral vision.

"Yeah, I'll be able to get it."

Paul will probably be more than happy to drive you, won't he?

"Good," was all I could think of to say that wouldn't start an argument.

"I'm hungry," Elizabeth announced, and I had to laugh.

"After all those cheese fries you inhaled?" I asked.

"What can I say? I'm a growing girl."

"I hungry, too," Michael agreed. "I want pizza."

"We'll have pizza, I promise," Talli said, her eyes closed tightly as she seemed to be willing herself to calm down.

"What about you?" I asked, looking over my shoulder at Emily, who was happily still chewing on the brim of my hat. Man, that thing was nasty. She merely grinned at me.

"Dase."

"Dase, that's right," I muttered softly.

"It's *Daddy*," Michael corrected her.

"Dase," Emily said, just as cheerful as she had before.

"They'll keep this up for hours," Talli said softly, and I couldn't help but smile. It wasn't so much what she said, but the fact that she'd just... told me something, given me just a tiny glimpse into their world that I'd been missing out on.

"Is that so?"

"Yeah," she replied, needing to speak up just a little over the kids' voices.

"What about you?" I asked, wincing inwardly after I'd said it. I wasn't so sure I wanted her answer.

"No, I gave up a while ago," she said.

No shit.

"I think she's just doing it on purpose now," she added, her arms folded securely, defensively in front of her.

"Really?" I asked, intrigued.

"Just listen."

And listen I did, the rest of the way to that building, stifling my laughter at Michael and Elizabeth's frustration, and Emily's giggles. And the more I listened, the more convinced I was that Talia was right.

And the more I glanced over at Talia, the more I remembered Keith's words.

"There's something wrong..."

And I knew it... I could sense it. The more I was around her, the more I saw, even in spite of her spunky mood earlier, I knew that Keith was right.

"It's right up there, Daddy!" Elizabeth called, and I felt my heart drop.

I didn't have enough time with them.

I never did.

I pulled into the parking lot, up into a spot by the doors. I was fighting back the emotions, not wanting to beg, not even wanting to push the fact that technically, I had won that bet and had yet to have that five minutes.

I couldn't push it.

I couldn't push her.

"Let me help you," I offered, opening up my door, but leaving the engine running.

"You're not coming up?"

Have you ever had one of those moments where your entire world stops, where everything just ceases and then suddenly takes off again? Because right then, when she said those words to me, I swear that's what happened.

She... she just invited me in? Into her condo? I mean, I know other people are going to be there, and that it's Michael's birthday party stuff... I'd actually read that part, where pizza and cake would be afterwards. I didn't think for one second, though, that she would want me there, just... the bowling party... and...

"Jase?" Her eyebrows were drawn together, her eyes searching mine for an answer.

I recovered as quickly as I could, grinning at her as I shut off the engine.

"Yeah, sure. Of course."

CHAPTER 25

TALLI

Let's go back in time, shall we?

See, once upon a time there was a girl. And this girl was flawed beyond belief. She was equal parts cocky and insecure, and she believed that love, while out there, was for her unattainable. The perfect guy couldn't exist, he didn't exist. Or if he did, he'd never look twice at her.

Because she wasn't perfect.

And it didn't matter that she wanted passion and security, because with all the guys she met it was one or the other. Either they were looking for someone to play house with, or they were looking for someone to screw.

And then...

Then there was this boy...

"You're cheating!" Jase exclaimed with mock surprise as our two oldest children tackled him in the middle of my living room. I smiled wistfully from my spot at the kitchen table, where I sat with Jaden, lost in the moment, lost in the memories.

And this boy called this girl... and...

"Stop tickling me!" Elizabeth squealed through her giggles.

"Aww, Baby Girl can't take it?" Jase teased, his laughter filling the tiny cracks in my heart.

... the girl fell for him.

Hard.

"Do you believe?"

"Oh," I said, blinking a few times, not expecting that question from the boy on the other line. *"Um, I've... I'm not much of a religious person, but..."*

"Not religion."

"In what, then?"

"Love."

Yes... in spite of it all, I do.

Those were the simpler times, weren't they? Just a boy and a girl on the phone... no expectations, no pretenses, no pretending...

"Pizza!" Michael exclaimed, running for the buzzer when the delivery boy announced his arrival.

"Want me to get that?" Jase asked, gesturing towards the button, and I smiled as best I could.

"Of course."

...no putting on a show.

"I want to believe, you know? I really want to believe that what I'm searching for is... out there. The kind of relationship that's not poisonous, or tumultuous, or... or co-dependent... I'll throw that one in for you."

"Thank you," I said with a half-laugh.

"I want... well, I want security."

"Of course," I agreed.

"No, I mean real security, the kind that comes from having complete faith that the person you're with has, you know, complete faith in you. And the kind that comes from knowing they're going to be there when you come home. And... and the kind that comes from knowing that it doesn't matter who's around, they... they are with you, one hundred percent. No matter what."

I felt my lower lip tremble as those words he'd spoken through that phone line so long ago flooded back, washing over me. I crossed my arms in front of me once more, hiding the rings from him as he picked up the tip I'd left on the table before answering the door.

As if it were the most natural thing in the world.

As if he belonged here.

Just like the first time he'd come to Ohio, after my mom died, when he'd just waltzed in and taken over, smoothed some of my frayed nerves, making others worse.

Only this time, we had grown apart instead of together.

This time the furniture was transplanted in Los Angeles, several miles away from him.

This time I was mourning us, and a love lost.

And this time, when children were running around, they were ours.

"Sit next to me, Daddy!" Michael said, jumping up and down excitedly. "For my birthday!"

"Consider it done, Little Man."

"But that's Mommy's spot, Daddy," Elizabeth corrected him, taking him by his hand to the head of the table. "This is your spot. Always."

I saw him falter for a moment, and I turned my head away, smiling slightly at Jaden before I walked back to the bedrooms, where Emily was playing quietly in solitude, just as she preferred most of the time. There was something so serene about her, and I wished for one brief moment that I could be that way—oblivious to the chaos, going about my business, the drama around me unable to penetrate that bubble.

And then it hit me.

I had been that way.

Behold the mess it had helped create.

But it wasn't always this way.

"We're having another baby?"

He looked at me with so much love, so much joy, my heart melted just a fraction more. It just couldn't stop that moment of panic.

"But... but this wasn't planned, Jase!"

"It doesn't have to be planned." He picked me up, swinging me around as he laughed in between kisses he placed on my face, in my hair. "Oh... oh, wow, I'm sorry... are you okay?" He set me down, pushing my hair back, his smile so bright it lit up the entire room. Slowly, almost as if he was afraid, he placed his hand over my lower abdomen.

"But Michael's still a baby."

"They're both still babies, Talli. It's okay."

"What if I can't do this?"

"Are you kidding me?" His arms wrapped around me as he leaned

down, placing his forehead against mine. "You can do this with your eyes closed, Woman."

"But what if something goes wrong this time? What if... what if my last pregnancy was a fluke, and this one is..."

"You worry too much," he whispered against my lips before gently kissing me, so much love in that one sweet gesture. "Just be happy, Talli."

Just be happy...

"Wow, she's certainly oblivious to the world."

I jumped, glancing over my right shoulder to where Jase stood, so close I could feel the heat radiating off of his body.

Or was that coming from me?

"Sorry," he said, that famous smirk crossing his lips briefly.

"It's okay, I'm..." I licked my lips nervously, looking back at our daughter while I dropped my left hand to my side, hoping he didn't catch a glimpse of it. "I'm okay."

"Panic attack over then?"

Panic attack? What... oh.

In the car.

When my heart had started racing again.

Why would he think it would be anything else, when I hadn't told him? Hell, I hadn't talked to him at all in...

Oh God.

The talk. The five... minute... talk...

"Come on, Princess," he called out to her. She glanced up from her stuffed puppy at him, eyeballing him curiously as if she couldn't figure out why he was still here. "Time to eat."

"I'll go..."

"It got it, Talli, it's okay." He grinned at me and shrugged. "The least I could do is tear the pizza into Emmy-sized bites."

I stood, momentarily stunned.

He called her Emmy.

He hadn't called her Emmy since... since... fuck, since before he went on tour.

"Are you sure you're okay?" he asked, his hand burning straight through me when he touched my arm.

But I couldn't pull away.

"I'm… fine," I lied.

Don't look at his lips, don't look at his lips, don't…

Damn it.

Too late.

I glanced back up as quickly as I could, my heart racing at a breathtaking pace at the look in his eyes. His gaze swept over my face, his eyebrows coming together slightly for one brief moment before his expression softened again.

I know that look…

I know that look so very well…

His hand closed around my arm, just enough pressure so send a jolt of electricity through my body, my entire body reacting as his eyes flittered to my lips before holding me captive once more. He closed the gap between us slowly, watching my expression, watching my pulse raging in that spot on my neck, and…

"Daddy, come on!" Michael was running between our legs, grabbing onto Jase's jeans and tugging. "Come sit by me."

And just like that, the spell was broken.

Or was it?

I felt his fingertips lifting my chin slightly until our eyes met. I didn't know what to expect—heat, friction, anger, lust, sadness…

But I wasn't expecting *this*.

This softness, this almost sweet, shy look on his face.

I wasn't expecting him to blush.

I mean… why is he blushing? That's so… odd. So random.

"This doesn't count, Talli," he said, his voice low, causing the hair on my arms to stand straight up.

"What are you…"

"We're not alone," he continued, stepping just a little closer, the mint gum in his mouth wreaking havoc on my senses. "This… is not our five minutes."

Fuck.

Me.

He grinned, the sly fucker that he is, hoisting Michael up on his hip and headed out to the kitchen leaving me clinging to that doorframe, waiting until he was out of sight before sliding down, holding my head in my hands.

He was going to be the death of me.

"Dase," Emily called out, her diaper crinkling as she toddled past me.

"Yeah, yeah," I said, my voice muffled behind my hands.

"Are you okay?" Jaden asked quickly as she came into the hall. I looked up at her, grinning and shaking my head.

"I'll be fine." I slowly stood, knowing my face was still flushed from the heat coursing through my body.

"Oh lord. I know you two. Just pounce on him and get it over with."

"What? No... no, it's not..."

"Whatever," she mumbled, making her way into the washroom.

"Jaden, it's not like..."

"You are not invited in to watch me pee," she cut me off, shutting the door in my face.

"This conversation isn't over," I said loud enough for her to hear.

"Just fuck him senseless," she called out to me. "You'll feel better."

I stood there with my mouth dropped open, and incredulous look on my face as I stared at that closed door, probably for a good two minutes, even as I heard the toilet flush and the sink turn on. "You... and your pregnancy hormones..."

"This isn't about *my* hormones, sweetheart," she said with a grin as she opened the door.

"I don't... I'm *fine*," I hissed as we walked closer to the kitchen. "And besides that, he's with..."

"There's your spot, Mommy," Elizabeth announced, pointing to the empty spot at the table just to Jase's right.

Where I'd always sat before.

"I'm... not hungry, baby, but thank you," I said, and it was the truth. My stomach was in absolute knots at the time.

And it didn't help that Jase's eyes dropped to the floor when I'd said it.

No... no, please don't think that...

"Mommy, you has to eat," Michael scolded.

"It's *have*," Elizabeth corrected him, as she always did.

"Das what I said."

"Nuh uh."

"This is not pick on Michael day," Jase said softly to Elizabeth, who rolled her eyes but remained quiet.

"Please, Mommy?" Michael continued.

"I'm okay; I'll eat when I'm hungry," I said, trying to smile as I passed them on my way to the living room. I heard Jase's breath hitch in his throat, and only then did I realize I'd briefly touched his shoulder as I walked by.

Absentmindedly.

As if it were something I did all the time.

Once upon a time, I had.

As I sunk into my papasan chair, I chanced a glance over at Jase. He was grinning at something that Michael was saying, then as if he could sense it, his eyes drifted over towards me.

"Why are you so good to me?" he asked over the sound of Chris blowing the car horn.

"Because I love you, Dork," I replied. "Now go... quick, before he hates me more than he already does."

"I love you," he murmured up against my lips before kissing me one last time. I watched him walk towards that car, that unbelievable sense of panic I'd been fighting taking hold of my heart.

Things weren't going to be this way.

Ever again.

"Jase," I called out to him, hesitating briefly when he turned around. "I..." I want you to stay, tell them that you can't go right now. Please don't leave me... I don't think I can do this alone.. "...wish we could come too."

He smiled back at me. "It's okay, baby" he said, covering his heart, "I carry you right here."

I was right.

Things did change.

We were never that close again.

"Paul said he'd be back up later," Jaden said as she sat on the couch, propping her feet up on the coffee table and placing the plate of pizza on her belly. "His sister was having some crisis."

"Doesn't she always?" I asked with a light laugh, anything to keep the nostalgia at bay. "So... did you two decide on a name?"

"Oh... oh, that's... hey! Boy!" Jaden called out.

"Speak to me, baby," Pete replied, and I stifled another giggle.

"She wants to know if we've decided on a name."

"That would be a firm no," he said, and Jaden threw up her hands as she looked at me.

"At this rate, I'm just gonna name him Mydadsadouchebag andcantdecide."

"So what part of that would be his middle name?" I asked, one eyebrow raised.

"His middle name?" Jaden asked, pointing to her baby bump, and I nodded. "Lee."

"And you'll call him?"

"Bubba, duh," she answered, then laughed at her own joke. "No, I think we're just gonna wait and see."

"Wait and see what?" I asked, murmuring my thanks to Elizabeth, who brought me a can of Diet Pepsi.

"Him," she said, taking a bite of her pizza. "I want to see what he looks like before I assign a name to him."

"Oh lord... here's to hoping you're not all doped up then," I said with a giggle. "What would you name him then? Morphine?"

"Nah, I'll just leave it up to Pete then. Maybe he'll do as good a job as Jase did with Elizabeth."

I don't know why, but I glanced over again at Jase when she said that, the touch of sadness in his face a sudden reminder... not of when she was born, but a few short months ago, when she turned five.

"Jeezus, Jase, I'm just sleeping. Would you quit waking me up?"

"You weren't moving."

"Because I'm trying to sleep! Something I haven't had much of lately, not that you would know."

"What do you want me to do, Talli? Cancel the tour? Fuck!"

"All you've done is mope around all day, and you leave again...when? Tomorrow? Oh, look... actually today."

"What was yesterday, Talli?"

"Our daughter's birthday, Jase. She's five. It's time to let it go."

If I expected some smart-ass reply, I would be sorely disappointed as he turned and walked silently out of Emily's room.

Had I really been that fucking heartless?

There was no question about it, I obviously had. And the guilt was sudden, overwhelming. I knew... I suppose I'd always known... that Jase wasn't the only one at fault.

And I needed desperately to apologize.

I don't know where the time had gone. Suddenly, here it was past dinner time, the last of the pizza was polished off, and Emily was holding onto her stuffed puppy's ear, toddling up to me and rubbing her eyes.

"Oh... come here Princess," I said, holding my arms out to her. She curled up on my lap, resting her head on my shoulder and yawning loudly.

"Now that's precious," Jaden commented. "And believe me, I'm about to do the same."

"I really appreciate you coming out here for this," I said to her, smiling warmly. "I've missed this."

"So have I." She pointed back to the kitchen table where Pete and Jase sat with Elizabeth and Michael playing a board game. "I've missed all of it."

I smiled wistfully, wishing that the carriage wasn't going to turn into a pumpkin, but knowing that the day was coming to an end. Paul and his kids had already come and gone yet again, Jaden was going to want to go to her hotel and sleep, Pete and Jase would want to get caught up.

And I would be here, with the kids.

Alone.

I wondered briefly, for the first time that day, what kind of excuse he'd given to Bree to get away. Just as quickly, I tried to push that thought from my mind, not let it taint what had been a good day.

A very good day.

Just not long enough.

"Oh... I think Princess is about to bite it," Pete commented as I stood to walk back to the hallway.

Jase turned his head to look, and for one brief, fleeting moment it seemed he was thinking the same thing I was... the day was ending, whether or not we wanted it to. I wasn't expecting him to stand and follow us back to the bedroom, his presence equal parts exhilarating and unnerving.

The room was relatively small, or extremely so if you compared it to our...his bedroom, so the space between the bed and the crib was limited. She'd already been changed, so it was just a matter of giving her a kiss and placing her in her crib, where she'd either settle in or cry incessantly until I picked her up again.

I placed a kiss on her temple, my heart catching in my throat as Jase leaned over and did the same.

Just like he used to.

I laid her in her crib, only then noticing that her other hand was clutched around that...oh...oh, no...

That picture. The one of us.

"Hey, I was looking for..."

Emily squeaked her disapproval as Jase attempted to remove the picture from her hand. She clutched it closer, turning on her side as she glared up at him.

"Taking that might be harder than taking her puppy," I said softly, afraid to look at his face. I could feel the heat from his hand that he stopped just short of placing on my shoulder, as if he was afraid to touch me.

Don't be afraid...

I turned to face him then, watching that muscle in his jaw twitch as he avoided looking over at me, the bed we once shared directly behind us.

Just kiss him, Talli... just one kiss and you'll know... just pull him on this bed with you, cover his body with yours... show him what he walked away from...

Wait...

He was looking for that?

"Thank you," he said softly, his eyes still on our daughter. "Thank you for inviting me. I know you didn't have to, but..." He licked his lips slightly, taking a deep breath while I was stunned silent, underneath that spell he weaves so easily. "But today's been... amazing, Talli. It's been amazing."

I felt a tear fall from my lashes before I could stop it.

"It's been... the way it should have, or..." His voice trailed off as he finally glanced over at me. "You haven't eaten all day."

I blinked a couple times in surprise, then reminded myself that's what our relationship had deteriorated to. Constant criticism.

"I'm not hungry," I said, my tone a bit harsh.

"I'm not saying... Talli, you're... just take care of yourself, okay?"

"I..." I swallowed, unable to speak for one brief moment. "You too. You look exhausted."

He nodded, his eyes dropping to the floor before he lifted them. "I... I have to go."

Why? Is your girlfriend expecting you? Some hot date going on that we're cramping your style for?

"I understand."

"This doesn't count either."

I rolled my eyes, unable to stop the smile. "You have to quit cheating..."

My voice trailed off at that word, the silence immediate and uneasy. Without another word, he turned and walked out of the bedroom, leaving me a quivering mess fighting off the tears that were sure to come the moment he left.

Why?

Just...

Why?

Emily was already asleep as I silently left that room, watching from afar as Elizabeth and Michael said their goodbyes to everyone. Jaden walked over to me...or waddled, actually... giving me a hug, telling me that she'd call before they went back to Missouri. Pete scooped me up in his arms, calling me his dearest, sweetest sister-in-law, cutting off my oxygen briefly before letting go.

And Jase...

Jase stood at that doorway, his eyes pained as he held my gaze, his hand on the knob. He mouthed the words 'Thank you' to me once more, and I smiled.

'Thank you,' I mouthed back, completely sincere. It had meant so much to the children… and they were what mattered now.

'See you Wednesday,' he mouthed, and for one moment I didn't know what he said at first, but once it sunk in I nodded.

'Them too,' I added, and his eyes closed briefly, as if he were saying a silent prayer. When his eyes opened again, Pete was announcing that they were all going, and the kids were saying their goodbyes, giving hugs and kisses. Jase's free hand was in Elizabeth's hair as she hugged him, but his eyes stayed on me.

'Five minutes,' he added, then pointed at me and back at himself. I felt the blush creep up in my face, and the moment he noticed he smiled.

I smiled in return and mouthed back the first, and only, thing that popped into my mind.

'Bring it.'

JASE

"Fuck you."

I said those two little words to Chris as he went about his Monday morning tirade in the middle of my office.

"Jase, do you have any idea how much trouble you will be in for going there?"

"Yup." I tossed Michael's little ball up in the air, catching it on its way back down as I kicked back in my chair.

"And you still don't think she's setting you up?"

"Fuck you," I said again. Perhaps if I didn't have some stupid cheese eating grin on my face it would come across more effectively.

"Jase, you could lose them altogether."

"Why, because she invited me to our son's birthday party?" I caught the ball once more and glanced over at him. "Fat chance."

"No, big chance."

"Chris…"

"What, 'fuck you'?"

One last throw and catch before I sat up, my grin even wider. "Exactly."

"Jase..."

"You're a family man, right?" I cut him off as I walked past him, down the hall, pausing to toss Michael's ball into his room.

He's gonna want that when he comes back.

"That goes without saying," he replied with a sigh as he followed me. "If I wasn't, I wouldn't have reamed your ass over Bree."

"I deserved that," I said suddenly, stopping to look over my shoulder at him. He stopped in his tracks, his face troubled momentarily before he nodded, and we continued down the stairs.

"Look... if it was legitimate, and she was sincere and not trying to get you into trouble, then it's..."

"Fantastic. Wonderful. One of the best days I've had in forever. Want a..." I paused as I glared at the contents in my refrigerator.

That's right.

No beer.

"Um... a Dr. Pepper?" I offered, and he shook his head 'no'. I shrugged and popped the top of the can, taking a long drink as Chris's tone suddenly changed.

"Jase, be careful."

"Dude, she's not setting me up."

"Perhaps she isn't, but... just... don't set *yourself* up."

"What are you talking about?" I asked with a short laugh.

"You. I know how you feel about her. It's never been a secret, Jase, not from day one. You were just starting to function again and..."

"I'm functioning just fine."

"I'd..." He paused and took a deep breath before continuing. "I know you miss her. Believe it or not, we all do. Just... don't... set yourself up, Jase. Because if what you're wanting and what she's wanting isn't the same thing..."

"I just want my kids back, Chris," I said quickly, then flashed my grin. "That's all."

"Okay then." He nodded his agreement although his expression didn't quite match. "Best of luck to you."

"You know," I said, trying to keep the tone light, trying to ignore what he'd implied, what my heart knew was true, "I can always hold that shit over your head, threaten to tell her."

"She'd never believe you."

"Stranger things have happened."

"Right… and I hate to bring this up, but… Bree."

"No."

"Jase, she's going around implying that you were with her last night."

"Which I obviously wasn't."

"After the party, Jase. After. Since the paparazzi noted what time you left Talli's home."

I almost… just almost… said that it wasn't Talli's home, but I stopped myself.

"Well… I wasn't. And that's that."

"You went to a hotel, Jase."

"I went to Pete and Jaden's hotel, Chris. Jeez, seriously? That's the best those assholes can do?"

"Well, when Bree checked in last night…"

"Holy fucking hell, you're kidding me." I groaned, running my hand through my hair. "I went in to spend time with Pete. That's it. Call him, ask him."

"You weren't spotted leaving until almost 4 this morning."

"Does it look like I've been to sle… aw, fuck. No, Chris. No. You don't believe it, do you?"

He looked at me through narrowed eyes and I almost felt like knocking the shit out of him for a brief moment in time… but he had a point.

Just a few weeks ago, I would have.

Like a complete fool… a complete *dumb ass* I would have.

"Yeah," he finally said as his expression softened. "Yeah, I believe you. You need to call…"

"I'm not talking to that bitch, Chris."

"I was going to say Talli."

"Oh." I grinned sheepishly. "Yeah…" My grin became a frown as it truly dawned on me the kind of damage this could inflict on our fragile truce. "Yeah, you're right. I need to."

"As soon as I leave, which I'm doing right now." He checked his watch and sighed. "Are you sure you still want…"

"No more shows, no more recording, no more anything until this is settled," I said, swallowing before I continued. "I know this may put me in breach of contract, but I hope they understand."

Chris put his hand on my shoulder, giving it a light squeeze. "We'll make them understand."

I held the receiver to my home phone in my hand, staring at it as if it would magically dial the numbers itself.

No such luck.

I was a nervous fucking wreck at the thought of bringing it up, but I had to. Talli had to hear the truth from me. Hell, at least this time I had Pete to back me up, right?

Please… please believe me…

I quickly dialed her cellphone number, my heart hammering as I held that receiver to my ear, biting my thumbnail, praying that she would just listen…

"Hello?"

She sounds like an angel…

"Um… hi."

Um hi? Jeez, Warner, how pathetic.

"Hi… I … well, I didn't expect to hear from you. Until Wednesday, I mean," she added quickly.

She doesn't sound mad. Maybe she hasn't seen. How do I handle this?

"I… just…"

"Your brother did a preemptive strike for you. I know you were with them last night."

"Oh… um… that's good, and… damn it, Talli, I'm just…"

"Don't sweat it, right?"

But I am sweating it, because I love you and I know you think the worst of me… you know the worst of me, but it's not… I'm not…

"I also kinda…realized I forgot to leave the home number with you. The new one," I said, my foot tapping nervously.

"Oh…"

My heart took a nosedive at the upturn in her voice.

Tell me it's a good sign… please…

"Okay, when you're ready I…"

I heard commotion in the background, a familiar voice telling her she had five minutes.

Fuck… it's Paul. I know it is. It was bad enough to watch him hug her, bad enough to see the knowing smiles he was giving her. Do I need reminded that he gets to see her nearly every damn day?

"I'll be there," I heard Talli say. "Give me a minute. This is important, okay?"

Important…me?

I'm… important to her?

Or the number is, but it's… it's my number, and…

"Sorry about that, I have an appointment that I have to get to, but I'm ready."

That damn stupid shit eating grin was back on my face as I rattled off the new number to her, mentally reminding myself to call Pete and tell him thank you.

But…

Oh, fuck.

I'm important.

"Listen, Jase," Kate said as she arrived in the early afternoon hours, stepping out of her heels, "you know I love you and all, but if you continue to give Rebecca extra work, she's bound to charge you double. And as for my frayed nerves?"

I stood there grinning at her, chewing on my thumbnail as she sat her bag down and sighed. One of her perfectly sculpted eyebrows shot up as she took in my appearance, then she frowned her disapproval.

"You look like you didn't sleep."

"Didn't sleep much, nope."

"Jase, I swear to you if you tell me you were with that godawful tramp in that hotel, I will…"

"Nope."

"The divorce is off!" she exclaimed, and my grin faded.

"No."

"Oh… but…"

I threw my arms around my best friend, holding her so tight she squeaked. "Kate, I had the most phenomenal day yesterday!" I said, unable to contain it any longer. I set her back down laughing at the look she was giving me.

"Who the hell are you and what did you do with the moping prick that was here the last time?"

"Whatever," I replied, slinging my arm across her shoulder and leading her to the great room… or the front room… or whatever the hell it was being called.

"Okay, spill," she said, "How much trouble are you in?"

"As of right now, none. Lucky for *me* the judge was in a forgiving mood, and Talli actually had Sherise Adler admit that she asked me to be there. From what I hear, it damn near *killed* her to say it, so I'm sorry I missed it."

"Ha!" she said, her grin matching mine. "I wish I could have seen it too. What a bitch."

"Yeah, to say the least."

We sat in the matching overstuffed chairs by the picture window, the sunlight filtering in the curtains as she pushed her hair back out of her eyes. "And I see that you are in this fantastic mood, so… spill."

"I spent all damn day with the kids, Kate. All day. I got to play with them… and eat with them… and just be me, you know? Just be me."

"That's wonderful," she said sincerely, her ankles crossing demurely. "It was Michael's birthday, right?"

"His party, yeah. His birthday isn't until Thursday."

"I know that, dork," she said with a giggle, but I continued on.

"But I was *there*. I was there when he opened his presents, I was there when they all started playing with them, and…" I stopped for a moment, the emotions consuming me. I covered my mouth to keep from shouting out to the world that Talli wanted me there, Talli said I was important, and she... she was...

God, she was so beautiful.

"Did you get a chance to talk with her?" Kate asked, and I felt the heat creep up in my face. "Oh dear lord you didn't."

"No... no, damn. Don't think that of me."

"How could I not think that of you, Jase?" she asked, and I could tell from her expression she was completely serious.

"Touché, touché," I said, grinning at her.

"So you would have."

"Oh, in a heartbeat," I admitted with a laugh, and Kate smiled, rolling her eyes. "Only..." I paused, contemplating the words as they flowed from me, "only if I thought it wouldn't make things worse."

"What do you mean, worse?"

"Well, it's... it's not a *fix*, Kate. Sex isn't... well, it doesn't solve anything."

"That's true, that's very true." She smiled at me, winking as she added, "I'm glad I taught you something."

"Oh, you taught me many things. Many things."

"As I recall, we learned together," she said, aiming a swift kick at my shins.

"Ow! Bitch!"

"Queen of them. Now." She held her hands wide. "Did you kiss her?"

"No."

But God, I wanted to...

"Hug her?"

"No."

I never would have let her go.

"Hold her hand?"

"No."

"You just beat Dr. Paul Coffman at bowling."

I threw my head back in laughter. "It's a good thing too, or I might have been brought up on public indecency charges or something."

"Oh, something tells me I don't want to know," she groaned, then perked up. "Oh, who am I kidding? Of course I want to."

"Okay, so... it wasn't really that dude I was playing, but it kinda was 'cause if it was just me and Talli it would have been no contest, right?" I said really quickly. "But, me and Talli... we always have these bets. And she bet that if I lost, I'd have to strip down to my boxer briefs and sing '*Itsy Bitsy Spider*'."

"Excuse me?" Kate asked with a laugh. "Shit, she and I are more alike than I thought."

"Yeah, it is something you would do."

"Of course. So, you won instead. I see no pictures of her stripped down, though. Or him, for that matter."

"Yeah, I bet something different."

"What was that?"

I felt the heat creep up in my face again as I recalled my body's reaction to her, her expression as I laid out my intentions.

"Five minutes. Alone. OW!"

"And you did *nothing*?" Kate asked, sitting back from where she knocked me upside the head.

"Damn, you two are alike," I muttered, rubbing my head. "I didn't collect. Yet."

"Oooohhhhh." She drew the word out, sitting back and wiggling her eyebrows. "And when you do?"

"I'm..."

Going to kiss her like there's no tomorrow, run my hands up and down those curves that I miss so very badly, make love to her until she forgets her name, and considering how long it's been for me that will probably take all of five damn minutes...

"...just gonna talk to her."

"Right."

"Right," I said. "Like I should have. Before, I mean."

Kate reached over and took my hand in hers, giving it a tight squeeze. "She's the reason, you know?"

"What are you talking about?" I asked with a laugh.

"The reason we never would have worked."

"Oh, good one Kate. She wasn't a part of my life then."

"No... no, listen. It was meant to be. Even if you can't work this out, you still have three wonderful children that you never would have had if it would have been John's number that you dialed."

I grinned at her, squeezing her hand back. "Yeah, you're right. And they're worth it… no offense, but…"

"Oh, none taken. And you… you are a *wonderful* father, just like I always knew you would be."

"Thank you." I pondered for a moment, combing over the memories of the past. "So what about you? Is your life looking… up?"

She blushed, shaking her head. "I'll never tell."

"Why the hell not?" I asked, sitting up a little straighter. "I just poured my heart out to you, and you won't tell me what's up in your world? What happened with the whole best friend thing?"

"In due time, Warner. In due time. But for now, I have to get going."

"Why? You just got here."

"Oh, I'm going to a show tonight," she said with a wave of her hand that she took from mine. "I'll be in L.A. through the end of this week, but I have a couple weddings out East that are coming up. I'll try to be back in time, though."

"For?"

"November," she replied. "Your divorce?"

"Oh."

Talk about taking the wind out of my sails. I felt myself sink just a little further into that chair as reality began to set in.

God, was Chris right?

"You know," Kate continued, grabbing her bag and throwing it on her shoulder, "you could always just… stop it."

"Stop it," I repeated, looking at her as if she'd lost her mind.

"The divorce. Just tell her you don't want it, tell her you want to give your marriage another shot."

"I couldn't do that," I said, my voice small.

"Why the hell not? Chicken?"

"No," I protested, pouting like a child. "I… well, I didn't want it to begin with, Kate. She asked for it. She did."

"So?"

"So… I just…"

"Oh, just do it in some big dramatic fashion, make it impossible for her to say no." She leaned over, placing a chaste kiss on my forehead. "You know you want to. In the meantime, though… would you do me a favor and stay out of trouble?"

"Sure," I mumbled. She caressed my cheek lightly before heading towards the front door. "Hey, Kate?"

"Yeah?" She turned back towards me, a soft smile on her face.

"Thanks."

"Any time, Warner," she said as she continued towards the door. "Any time."

CHAPTER 26

TALIA

"Dearest, sweetest sister in law of mine."

This was the opening line of Pete's phone call to me. This could not be good.

"What happened?"

"What do you mean, what happened? Like in *A Mighty Wind*, or like…"

"Pete, I love you to pieces but I'm trying to get myself plus three kids ready and out the door," I said with a laugh.

What was with my mood?

"Just… don't believe everything you hear today, okay?"

I groaned, pulling Michael's shirt over his head and handing it back to him right side out. "Okay, then, what did your brother do?"

"Nothing. I swear to you, he did nothing. He stayed here practically all night talking, and I walked with him out to the lobby. Then he left. That's it, and you know I wouldn't lie to you."

"Okay, so I believe you. Now tell me the bad news."

"Bree is implying that he was with her."

"Huh."

Just that. A simple statement.

Wow, I need my head examined.

"Did you hear me?"

"Yeah, I heard you," I replied as I brushed Michael's hair and motioned for him to get Elizabeth. "But I also heard what you said to begin with, and I believe you."

I don't know why, but right at that moment I did.

I only wish the feeling had stayed with me.

Because, see, once I was at work, once I was around the people who gossiped and pointed fingers and whispered behind my back, that stupid nagging voice crept up in my head.

Why should I believe Pete? He would lie for Jase in a heartbeat.

No, wait. Jase wouldn't go to her, not after our day yesterday.

Who am I kidding? Of course, he would go to her! He'd gone to her for months!

But he was so sweet, so kind yesterday. He was the man I fell in love with, the man I married, the man I had children with.

And he threw it all away for that tramp before, what was to stop him now?

If I had my head going back and forth between the angel and devil on opposite shoulders going at it all fucking morning, I would have had whiplash for sure. My heart just couldn't take it anymore, but no matter how much I threw myself into my work it didn't stop me from thinking about it, dwelling on it.

Hurting over it.

It was a damn good thing I had a therapy session coming up that day, one that Paul wasn't about to let me forget since he'd pulled a few strings to get me penciled in. I suppose he figured I'd need it after the day prior, and I wouldn't have, but...

Damn him.

He gets to me every time.

I was going over last-minute paperwork, my cell phone lying on my desk beside my hand, the office completely still and quiet. Out of the corner of my eye, I saw just a flash of color and I glanced at my bulletin board.

"Wow."

I remembered the last time I'd noticed that picture of Jase and me up there, the one taken the day of the storm, the day we'd...

I could have sworn I took it down, or had put it up there backwards or something. As I reached for it, my cell phone began to ring, causing me to jump slightly, and I frowned as I saw it was Private Name, Private Number.

I almost didn't answer it.

But, no… the paparazzi wouldn't dare.

"Hello?"

"Um… hi."

Oh fuck, it's him! It's… it's Jase!

"Hi… I … well, I didn't expect to hear from you. Until Wednesday, I mean," I said, then covered my face with my hands as if he could see me blush.

He's calling me!

Oh, wait.

Of course he's calling me.

Be nice, Talli. Be. Nice.

"I… just…"

I can't hear the excuses, not right now. Please.

Cut him off, Talli.

"Your brother did a preemptive strike for you. I know you were with them last night."

And I want to believe him. I really do. I mean, I actually did this morning, and then… then I got around all these people who just whisper behind my back. If I could hear it from him…

"Oh… um… that's good, and… damn it, Talli, I'm just…"

Every bit as frustrated as I am right now.

I can hear it in your voice.

"Don't sweat it, right?" I said with a shrug that he couldn't see.

Please can we not talk about her? Not right now, not when I still feel so vulnerable.

"I also kinda…realized I forgot to leave the home number with you. The new one."

His number! Oh… oh wow… um… well, of course I need his number. This is a necessity…

Right?

"Oh," I said, then winced at how high my voice sounded.

Not so cheerful, dumb ass!

After doing the obligatory face palm, I scrambled to get my pen and paper together, cursing silently when I dropped said pen, thankful he couldn't see me scramble for it and brush my hair out that had fallen into my eyes when I sat back up.

"Okay, when you're ready I…"

Paul took that time to stick his head in the door and announce that my appointment was in five minutes.

Seriously, you think?

"I'll be there," I said, pointing to the phone, mouthing to him that it was Jase. "Give me a minute. This is important, okay?"

Paul winked and smiled, closing the door as he walked out.

"Sorry about that, I have an appointment that I have to get to, but I'm ready," I said.

"Oh, I can let you go if…"

"Jase," I cut him off with a laugh. "The number."

I couldn't stop the smile as I wrote it down, double and triple checking that I had it right.

Funny, all I could think of while he was giving it to me were the numbers 2:35.

Six o'clock. That's what time the clock on the microwave said when the palpitations started. Holy fucking hell, they hurt.

"Mommy, what are we having for dinner?" Elizabeth asked excitedly.

"I'm heating up… some… chicken tenders," I said, smiling at her.

"Okay, I'll go tell them." She ran back to the bedrooms, and I attempted to stand for a brief moment before sinking back down in the chair.

Calm, cool, collected Talli. Talk yourself through this.

Wow… sweat on forehead. Gross, and… not good.

Calm, Talli. Calm.

The oven was heating, the water was on the stove for the macaroni and cheese, their veggies were already cut up. I could sit down for a moment and not have to worry about anything…

Except that phone.

I squinted at the number on the caller id, sighing at Lisa's name and number.

She's your sister. Just answer the phone.

"Hello?"

"What the hell is this nonsense about you being with Jase yesterday?"

"Well, hi, Lisa, I miss you, too," I said, a bit breathless.

"Seriously, Talli, he is just... he's going to walk all over you again."

"It was Michael's birthday party, Leesie, I'm not going to tell him his Dad can't come."

"You know what? Yes, you are."

"Excuse me?" I asked, then closed my eyes. *Deep breaths... deep breaths...*

"You are going to suck it up and grow a backbone and tell that asshole to stay away from you and those kids."

"Lisa... Jase is... is not Jack, okay? He's not going to hurt them, and I happen to have... one hell of a backbone, lest you forget."

"What the hell is wrong with you?" she asked.

"I'm ... I'm not feeling so good right now," I murmured, laying my head down.

"And you know what's probably causing it? Him."

"No... no he's... Lees, can... I need to let you go, okay?"

"Are you on something?"

I let out a short laugh. "I wouldn't take something when you were handing it to me, why would I take something on my own? I just don't feel well."

"You better not hang up this phone until you promise me that asshole is out of your life for good."

"Bye, Lisa," I muttered, hitting the end button.

Why do I feel so weak?

Suck it up, Talli. Get dinner done, then lie down for a little bit.

It wasn't as if the rest of my day had been stressful. The appointment had gone all right, minus the arguing over the mood stabilizing drugs. I wanted this to be done completely medication free; hell, I'd come so far already. Besides, I'd spent months not feeling anything, and even with as much as it hurt, feeling this was better than the being the zombie I had become.

I don't want to be a zombie anymore.

I want to feel it. All of it. I want to feel the love, the anger, the bone crushing sadness. If I can feel it, than I can move past it instead of playing the ignoring game, pretending as if it would all just go away.

It wasn't going anywhere.

Because every time I turned around there were reminders, if not of him, then of us. Sometimes, there were reminders of them still floating around, and while it was devastating, at least I could admit that now. I could feel that now.

But seeing Jase... yeah, it was absolute chaos on my soul.

What the hell do I want from him now?

I mean... I love him. I love him with everything in me. But love doesn't erase everything he's done. It doesn't change the fact that he had a relationship with someone else while he was still with me. It doesn't change the fact that I essentially let him, that I pushed him away, pushed him straight to her.

And I don't know if he'll ever forgive me, just as I don't know if I could ever... ever forgive him. And...

"Mommy?"

I opened my eyes, lifting my head to Elizabeth's concerned gaze.

"Mommy, are you okay?"

I fell asleep at the table? Fuck!

What the hell is that sound in the hallway?

"Mommy, wake up!"

"Don't... don't shake me, Baby Girl..." I pushed myself to a more upright position, the room absolutely spinning.

"Is... is dat an alarm?" Michael was asking.

Alarm? What...

Oh, wait...

Yeah, I think... I think it is...

I stood up, holding on to the table, making my way to the stove. I turned off the oven and the burner, even though the alarm wasn't coming from our apartment.

"What if... what if it's a..."

"I'm gonna check, okay?" I asked as I slowly made my way to that front door. "Where's... where's your sister?"

369

"Playing," Elizabeth answered as she followed on my heels.

"Go get her," I said, then questioned my own words in my head as I got closer to the door.

Go get her? Why would she need to go get her?

Why am I not making any sense?

Focus, Talli. Focus.

Now there's pounding on the door... who the hell...

I opened the door slightly, immediately beginning to cough at the white smoke filling the hall.

"Do you need some help?"

"Who the hell are you?" I asked before my brain registered that it was my neighbor.

"Honey...here, let me in, let me help get the kids..."

I stared at the back of this woman's head as she entered, reaching for her as she picked up Emily who immediately began to scream.

Oh, the smoke... Em... she won't be able to breathe...

"Mommy?" Michael said, his voice full of fright.

"Mommy's... okay..."

But that's a lie... I'm not okay...

"Mrs. Warner?"

Mrs. Warner... can I laugh now? She called me... Mrs...

Wait.

I am.

Where's Jase?

"Mommy!"

I didn't know if that was Elizabeth, or Michael... or my imagination as I clutched at my chest before sinking to the floor.

JASE

Just say no.

Kinda like that anti-drug campaign.

No divorce. Just... refuse to divorce her. Retract...

Should I retract my papers?

Tell her that I...forbid it? Right. She'd shove her foot so far up my ass I could open my mouth and see her toes wiggle.

Just... no divorce.

That should be easy, right?

"Okay, Mr. Warner, you're all set," the clerk at the cell phone counter said, smiling as she handed the bag over.

"It's just Jase," I replied, smiling also. "Is there a..."

"New car charger also," she finished for me, pointing at the bag.

"That's awesome on so many levels... Sarah," I said, adding her name after glancing at her nametag. "Thank you." As I turned to leave, she called out to me.

"I saw the pictures from the bowling alley."

I knew exactly what pictures she was referring to... the ones that the tabloids had all poured over. The main ones were of Talli and me holding hands, our two oldest trailing behind her, and Emily on my other arm.

Our family.

I glanced over my shoulder, eyebrows raised as she continued.

"I hope everything works out."

I smiled warmly at her, covering my heart with my hand. "Thank you, Sarah," I said. "So do I."

And I meant it, with everything in me. No matter the outcome, if everything would just be... okay, I could handle it so much better than the hell we'd been through.

I glanced down at my watch as I slid into the driver's seat, noting it was nearly quarter after six. Damn, no wonder I was hungry. I'd been running all day, and on hardly any sleep at all. I was fine with the lack of sleep, though, since I'd been able to talk with Pete. And I mean really talk with him.

I told him the truth.

I told him everything.

Aside from Kate, I hadn't told a soul that I hadn't slept with Bree, either because they didn't need to know, or I figured they wouldn't listen anyhow. I wish I could wear it as a slogan on a t-shirt sometimes, scream it from the top of a mountain, but I didn't figure it would do me much good. Don't get me wrong, it was wonderful to talk with Kate, to have that connection with someone who could understand everything, but this was different.

This was family.

"Jase, you have got to talk with Talli."

"I know... fuck, I know it. I just..."

"You 'just' nothing. She needs to know the truth, whether or not it makes a difference. At least then you'll know, and it won't eat you alive like this."

"It's going to eat me alive regardless, Pete," I said, rubbing my face roughly. *"I know I fucked up. I know it."*

"But you're right," he interjected, leaning forward slightly. *"The pulling away from you... that's... something's happened, something that has ripped you two apart. And it wasn't just Bree."*

"Thank you," I said, feeling at least a little vindicated.

"No, don't thank me, because you're still a fuckhead for that whole mess."

I smirked slightly, nodding, knowing what he was saying to me was the truth.

"I'm just saying," he continued, *"ask her what happened."*

"Pete," I said suddenly, my fears getting the best of me, *"you don't think it was... that... guy, do you?"*

"Who, Paul?" he asked, and I nodded. Pete paused, contemplating his answer before he said, *"No."*

I can only hope that he's right.

As I sat in that parking lot plugging my cell phone into the car charger, double checking that the numbers from the SIM card had transferred, I contemplated exactly how I was going to ask her. Do I use the direct approach? Do I try to be stealthy about it?

Who am I kidding?

I need to just... ask.

I was chewing on my thumbnail, my heart and head waging a war on whether or not to call her before I lost my nerve, or the nerve I was attempting to build up anyhow. See, that was the draw back to yesterday—just that short time near her, and I was craving more. I'd had to call her earlier, but then hearing her voice on the phone made me miss her, made me want to reach out to her. It had taken every bit of my self-restraint to keep from driving to the hospital earlier, waltzing back to her office and pulling her into my arms. I couldn't do that... not yet.

But right at that moment, I was craving her—her voice, her presence, the smell of the jasmine, and...

Well, I'll be damned.

I smiled down at the name and number on my display, my heart hammering in my chest knowing that Talli was on the other line. My hands shook slightly as I hit that button, answering the call. I wasn't even going to pretend like I didn't know who it was.

"Hi," I said, my smile fading as I heard the commotion in the background.

Sirens?

What the hell is going on?

"Talli?" I asked, sitting up straighter, nervous now for an entirely different reason. "Talli, what's..."

"Daddy!"

My heart nearly stopped at the sheer panic in Elizabeth's voice.

"Daddy, help... Mommy... Mommy needs help..."

Talli...

Oh...God...

"Where are you?" I asked, trying to keep my breathing under control. "What happened?"

"There's smoke... and...and there's..."

A fire... oh fuck, a fire...

"Where's Mommy?" I asked loudly, feeling myself break out into a cold sweat.

"Inside."

"Inside *where*?"

"They made us come outside," she said, and I heard her start to sob.

"Listen... listen to me, baby..."

"She fell and didn't wake up."

I felt a tear escape as I fumbled with my keys, cursing as I repeatedly missed sticking them in the ignition. She was hurt... and she'd been left behind? What the hell was going on, and where the hell was she? "She's inside where?" I asked, trying to pry information from my already distraught five-year-old.

"Don't yell, Daddy."

"Sssshhh," I said, finally firing up the SUV, my heart shattering into a million pieces. "Baby girl, where are your brother and sister?"

"The am…ambalance," she sniffled.

"Listen to me, okay? I need to speak with an adult. I need you to put an adult on the phone, Elizabeth."

"Noooooo, no don't go Daddy!" she cried, and I felt myself begin to weep along with her.

"Are you at… at…" *It's not her home, it's not…* "Are you at home?"

"No, the building," she said, and I stifled a sob.

"The condo," I said, putting the SUV in drive, not bothering to find my Bluetooth and just continuing on, that phone up to my ear. It wasn't even ten minutes from where I was… I looked over to my right as I turned down a side street, my heart plummeting as I saw smoke rising up into the sky. "I'm on my way, okay Baby Girl?"

"Hurry… they…"

"Elizabeth?" I asked, panicking even more as the line went dead. "Fuck… fuck, fuck, fuck, people get the hell out of my way!"

I drove like a bat out of hell to get to my family, the dread overwhelming me, a silent prayer to the heavens that everything would be okay, memories of a call from years ago coming back to haunt me.

I had stepped away from the others, joy in my heart at the name and number on my display.

She was calling me. During the middle of the day.

Wow, I love this woman. I… I don't want to tell her, not until we're face to face, but it's getting so hard to stop myself now.

"Hello, beautiful," I said, smiling warmly as I leaned up against the wall.

"Oh god, Jase…"

That wasn't Talli. I know that voice… but…

"Who… is this?" I asked slowly, frowning at the sheer chaos that seemed to be erupting on the other end of the line.

"Talli, wake up! Wake…up!"

Jaden. Holy fuck, it was Jaden, on Talli's phone, and… something's wrong. Terribly wrong, I can feel it.

"Jase, are you there?"

She was crying... oh... oh, fuck...

"I... I'm here. Jaden?"

"Yeah. Yeah... it's... oh, God, Jase, I'm so sorry."

No....no, no, no... "What happened?" I asked, panic and dread sweeping over me.

"There... there's an accident. There's been an accident, and Talli, she..."

Fuck, she's hurt... I have...I have to get to her. "She won't wake up?" I asked, feeling the tears fill my eyes. "What's..."

"There's... there's so much blood."

I covered my mouth with my hand, feeling that cold sweat take hold. Jackie was walking past and he stopped dead in his tracks, putting his hand on my shoulder, asking if everything was okay. I felt the first tear fall as I shook my head no.

"And... but... I'm sorry, I'm so sorry."

"Tell her I'm on my way, okay?" I asked, brushing Jackie's hand off before wiping my face. "Tell her to just hold on, and I'll be there. And tell her... Jaden, tell her..."

"Pete."

"I'll call him for you, I prom..."

"He was driving."

Oh...fuck...no...

"What do you mean he was driving, Jaden? Where is he?"

Please tell me he's gone to get help, tell me he's okay...

"I'm so sorry."

I sunk to my knees, the grief...the pain too much to bear. Not my brother... not my baby brother... we lost Michael, I can't lose him too...

That had been one of the worst days in my entire existence, the woman I was in love with and my little brother both hurt, and me... miles away, helpless, unable to do anything...

But not today.

Not today.

"I'm sorry, sir, but you cannot go over there."

I shot a glare to the young man in uniform, refraining from telling him to go fuck himself, trying to remain as calm as possible. I'd already heard from bystanders as I ran up that there were no known fatalities, but that wasn't helping the situation.

I had to see them... all of them... for myself.

"I need to get to my family," I said, my voice thick with emotion. I could see fire coming from the upper floors on the opposite side of the building, away from the side that Talli's condo was on, but that didn't change the fact that she'd been left in there, with all of that smoke and...

"Are you a resident of this building?" he asked, and I swore silently.

"No... my...my family. My wife, my kids... they were here."

"Sir, you need to..."

"Where is my family?" I nearly shouted, my hands shaking nearly as much as my voice.

"Sir, if you can't..."

"I've got this," another officer said as he walked up, motioning for me to follow him over to the ambulances. "This is where the injured were taken, you can..."

I took off in a sprint towards the flashing lights as I saw Elizabeth's frightened face turn my way. I could tell right when she spotted me, those big blue eyes of hers reflecting the relief I felt in my heart at seeing her. I dropped to my knees as she ran into my arms, her small frame trembling as she sobbed uncontrollably.

"Ssssh." I dropped little kisses on her face, in her hair as I held her to me, trying to calm her down. "Baby Girl, ssshhh, listen okay?" I pulled back slightly, my heart breaking at the sight of her so distraught, so terrified. "Elizabeth, where are Michael and Em?"

She gasped a couple times, showing how long and hard she'd been crying, as she pointed to the ambulance that she'd been standing beside. I gathered her close, carrying her back to that ambulance, just a little more relief as I saw Michael asking his five million questions, completely calm or perhaps just faking it... sometimes it was hard to tell with him.

I wonder where he gets it from.

"Daddy!" he said, his face lighting up. Elizabeth was still attached to me as tightly as she could even as I leaned and gathered Michael into my arms as well. I looked a little further into the back of the ambulance, where Emily was screaming, fighting against an EMT who was trying to examine her.

"She's... she's really afraid of strangers," I said, my voice catching at the sight of her, knowing all three of my children were safe.

"Are you her father?"

"Yeah," I said, sniffling slightly. "Yeah, I am."

"She's wheezing a bit and we need to administer a breathing treatment before transporting her for further observation."

Observation? Em... to the hospital...

Okay, I can handle this. They know what they're doing, she looks fine.

"O...Okay," I stammered, shaking in spite of myself. "My... my wife. Their mother... she... knows her medical history, all of it."

"Can we speak with her?"

"I... I don't know where she is," I stammered, trying to control my panic, not wanting the children to see me come unglued.

"They left her," Elizabeth repeated, her voice muffled since her face was buried in my neck.

"She... was left?" I asked, praying Elizabeth was exaggerating.

"The heart patient," I heard someone mutter behind me, and the EMT working on Emily nodded.

Wait...

"Heart patient?" I asked, turning around.

"What are *you* doing here?" one of the tenants... I recognized her, I just didn't know her... said as she pointed at me.

"What does it *look* like?" I snapped back, refraining from adding 'stupid bitch' to the end of that statement, knowing this person must be every bit as distraught as my children. I turned back to the other EMT who had made some reference to a heart patient and asked, "Where's my wife?"

"Oh, your *wife*?" the crazy lady asked mockingly. "You mean the woman that has a court order to keep you away from those children?"

I felt my stomach drop as suddenly all eyes turned to me.

"Don't... don't do this, you don't know what you're saying," I said slowly. "She doesn't want that any more than I do."

"Where the hell are the police when you need them?" the lady screamed, apparently forgetting there were police all around us.

"Listen to me… please,"

"Sir," an EMT cut in.

"Where's my wife?" I asked quickly, my hold on Elizabeth and Michael tightening. "She'll tell you."

"Sir, is there a court order keeping you from the children?"

"You… you don't understand, we… we're going to a mediator in… in two days! In less than 48 hours, and that's…"

"Sir, you need to leave the children with me." A female officer was beside me, one hand softly placed on my arm that was holding Michael.

"Nooooooo!" Elizabeth wailed, her arms wrapped so tightly around my neck. Michael's lower lip began to tremble and I felt his hand tangle in my shirt collar as I held him to me, another tear escaping down my cheek.

"Please," I said softly. "Please don't do this."

"I'm sorry, sir, but…"

"I won't take them anywhere, okay?" I said, stifling a sob as she reached for Michael, who turned in, trembling in my arms. "I'll stay right here, I promise, don't…"

"I can't allow that sir," she said, her tone showing her sympathy. "I'm going to have to ask you to leave."

"No…no, where's my wife? She'll tell you."

"They already transported her," the crazy bitch announced.

Oh fuck…

Transported?

"Sir, if you do not hand over the children and leave the premises, I will have no choice but to arrest you," the officer said a little more forcefully, before adding softly, "They've been through enough. Contact your lawyer, okay?"

Slowly… every inch breaking my heart, I lowered to the ground, biting back a sob as they both began to scream and cry in protest.

Why… why was this happening? I just… I just need the strength to walk away right now, and I swear… I swear on… on everything that I will fight, and I will get them back… and never let them leave again.

An officer the size of Jackie pried Elizabeth from me, grimacing as she kicked and twisted in his arms.

"Stop... don't... don't hurt her..."

I knew he wouldn't, but it didn't stop my heart from calling out, the same way it did when another officer took Michael from me.

This isn't happening... this isn't happening...

"Sir, you..."

"I need to leave, I know," I snapped, standing and wiping my eyes, glaring at the bitch from Talli's building as I pushed past her, through that crowd that had gathered around, rushing to my SUV to get to the hospital as quickly as I could. I ignored the flashes of the various cameras, my head low as I dialed a familiar number, praying that it would be answered.

"Okay, Mr. Warner," I heard Rebecca's breathless voice on the other end. "This had better be good."

"Rebecca," I sobbed, my world collapsing around me, "I need your help."

Coming soon

My Happy Ending
Part 2

All of my love and gratitude

Rose for always having my back and loving me and the worlds I create in my fucked-up mind.

Kayla for being so awesome and keeping my head on straight.

Cody for letting me just BE, and for getting me back on track when I have lost my way.

Stephanie through thick and thin you've stood by me. I love you so much!

My Visions loves on all of the message boards for giving me hell and demanding I fix this, fix them. I love you all.

Zachary, Marcus, and Jacob without whom I would be lost.

The Authors' Table for giving me an outlet and a plethora of advice. I adore all of you!

Jon and Amy DeNapoli for loving me as I am. May we all be #AmyStrong

My Donor Center tribe for putting up with me while I got this written, even when you didn't believe that's what I was doing LOL

Kimolisa for your amazing formatting work.

Typos I know you're there, mocking me. But you made it this far. Kudos.

My readers because without you, I am just a girl with a MacBook shouting into the abyss. Your love and support means the world, and I'm forever grateful!

Authors (especially indie!) rely on your reviews. Please take a moment to review this novel on the platform that it was purchased from. It is appreciated more than you will ever know!

ABOUT THE AUTHOR

Carlie Yates (That One Writer Chick) has been writing stories since she was in the fifth grade, convinced that if she didn't get her thoughts and characters down on paper, her head would 'plode; it could be ex- or im-, but either way, it wouldn't be pretty. Inspired by S.E. Hinton, she always said when she grew up that she would be a published author. This Midwest mom of boys has addictions to reading, road trips, hair dye, and the Oxford comma, and is thoroughly convinced at any given time the theme track to *My Three Sons* will start playing in the background of her home. She is currently renouncing her pledge to grow up.

ALL NOVELS BY CARLIE YATES

<u>The Entangled Series</u>
Entitled
Entrapped
Enlightened

<u>Time Stands Still</u>
Wrong Number
Right Reasons
My Happy Ending Part 1
My Happy Ending Part 2 (December 2021)
My Happy Ending Part 3 (March 2022)

<u>Standalones</u>
Everly's Hope
Broken (July 2022)

<u>Anthologies</u>
"Perfect" in Shattered Illusions (The Authors' Table)

www.ingramcontent.com/pod-product-compliance
Lightning Source LLC
Chambersburg PA
CBHW021214260626
47172CB00002B/427